# The Third Generation Series

## Book 10

# Royal Favour

by

Margaret Gregory

Cover designed by msgdragon
Cover images: © Can Stock Photo / katalinks
© Can Stock Photo / CBoswell
© Can Stock Photo / jamesstar
© Can Stock Photo / smeagorl
© Can Stock Photo / jgroup

Also by Margaret Gregory
TYMOREAN TRUST SERIES:
Book 1 - Power Rising
Book 2 - Great Ones
Book 3 - The Return to Earth
Book 4 – Earth Mission
Book 5 – Alien Contact
Book 6 - Invasion
ATAPI SORCERESS SERIES:
Prequel – Korvu: The Beginning
Book 1- The Wild One
Book 2 – Atapi Sorceress
THE THIRD GENERATION SERIES:
Book 1 - Wanda: From Bad to Worse
Book 2 - Wanda: Choosing Crime
Wanda – Early Days (anthology) Book 1 and 2
Book 3 – Wanda: Risking Life to Live
Book 4 – Erin: The Forcing of Wisdom
Book 5 – Wanda: A New Life Part 1 – Hidden Secrets
Book 6 – Wanda: A New Life Part 2 – First Mission
Book 7 – Wanda: Full Circle
Book 8 and 9 – Erin: The Call

For permission requests, address the request to the author c/o
Permissions,
TAT Indie Publishing
PO Box 2728
Rowville, Victoria, 3178
www.tatindiepublishing.com.au

# Table of Contents

# Chapter 1

Frequent flickers of lightning illuminated the magnificently landscaped garden of Weisboden Castle, creating contrast between the dark hedges and the green lawns. The view of it from the window of the third level was obscured as fierce squalls of torrential rain pounded the window.

The man who stood staring out past the heavy red curtains into the eerie afternoon darkness had white hair, thinning at the crown, and a regally erect bearing that belied his eighty-three years. In his mind, he saw beyond the garden to the distant range of mountains that marked the northern border of the tiny European kingdom of Weisboden. The storm that had blown in several hours earlier, obscuring those mountains, showed no signs of abating.

Years of public scrutiny had formed a tight emotional mask on the old man's features, and even now in the privacy of his own suite, he did not let it slip. It was this semblance of always being in control that had helped him guide his country through many a crisis in the sixty years he had been the monarch. Yet the tightness of the gnarled hands on the knob of an ebony walking stick and the rigidity of his posture, betrayed his intense worry.

Prince Michael turned from the window and allowed his mind to hear the soft strains of Schubert's Symphony no. 8 playing through his computer. Letting the music ease his mind, he returned to his desk and sat behind it. He left the correspondence on the desk where it was. After a short time, he heard the door of his suite being fumbled open. He recognised the familiar sounds of a chair being wheeled through and he looked up.

The young man, who propelled the wheelchair around the edge of the room with the ease of years of practice, had black hair, kept short at the back and sides and stylishly trimmed elsewhere. His oval face, fair skin and blue-grey eyes were a match for those of the older man.

"What can you tell me, Stephen?" Prince Michael asked as the chair rolled to an abrupt squeaking stop.

"Father, Derek has reported that Karl's plane has been checked thoroughly and no suspicious objects or possible explosives were found. The flight will be allowed to take off when the weather clears."

"Has there been word about the charter flight?" Prince Michael queried.

"No, Sir. I asked Derek. All he said was that the flight took off at ten, as we knew, and was passed out of German airspace at ten fifteen. The airport here has no record of the charter and no radar contact but they have said that in these conditions, the radar over the mountains is unreliable. They started a search, but the weather closed in and they had to recall the search planes. They have not detected a beacon signal."

Stephen studied his father's rigid posture and dared a question. "Couldn't Werner have waited until the storm had passed to come here?"

Prince Michael merely said, "There was a break in the weather and this delay may simply be that the plane was diverted to a different airstrip from the one we arranged. Tell Truman to return and have the owners of the strip call if the plane lands or gets in contact with them."

"I will do that," Stephen agreed.

Prince Michael changed the subject. "Have the two American's arrived yet?"

"Yes, Sir. Johannes advised me that they are in the visitor's room."

"Good. I will see them shortly. Will you get Derek on the phone for me, please?"

Stephen wheeled himself around two chairs and a low table to the cordless phone that was on a small side table, and dialled his elder brother's personal mobile number. When Derek answered without his usual flippant, "Hi pup," Stephen began to have a bad feeling. He wheeled himself to where he could hand the phone to his father and then backed off.

"Derek," was all Prince Michael said, before listening intently. Finally he said, "Keep me informed, and keep the media out of it."

Prince Michael placed the phone down carefully. His complexion was a ghastly shade of grey, even though his face was a tight mask, betraying nothing and he had swivelled his chair and seemed to be staring at the huge oil painting of the Alps.

"Will you have Johannes escort the Americans here, by our private stairs, and return to monitor the radio?"

Stephen didn't turn to leave immediately. He, of all his siblings, could probably read his father best. He had spent a great deal of time in his father's company since becoming his personal assistant three years before. He wondered why his father was so worried. Certainly, it looked like the plane carrying Werner was missing, and the palace courier was a cousin through his father's first marriage, but was that all it was?

"Father what is so important about that plane?" From his side-on position, he saw his father frown – sign that his father was displeased at being asked the question.

Stephen ignored it, and considered a number of previously unconnected pieces of information. "Karl is on it," he blurted, alarmed now.

Prince Michael's expression altered subtly, as if he had mentally sighed. "Yes."

"How? Why? What is so important for Karl to risk himself to fly through this storm?"

Prince Michael, who had been King Michael until three years before, turned the chair to face his son and spoke softly.

"When Derek spoke to me earlier, he told me that Werner was still at the airport. When Karl's plane was grounded due to that bomb threat, Karl reclaimed the diplomatic mail satchel and had apparently gone off in the car with Brantner."

"You said that," Stephen agreed.

"Derek tried calling him, but he could not get through to the Holstein Estate. He tried again after he spoke to you, and Alicia told him that Karl had visited briefly. He told her that the talks concluded successfully, and he had decided to come back here as he had important matters to discuss with me."

"Couldn't he have waited?" Stephen asked again.

After a moment's hesitation, Prince Michael revealed, "Karl has received what Derek and I both consider a threat against his life."

"The bomb threat?" Stephen asked.

"Not just that. He received a letter several days ago that gave him quite a shock. And I believe there was a follow up letter. He told me yesterday that he intended to come back today."

"So he did not want anyone to know he was returning today?" Stephen guessed. "So after that bomb threat he decided to swap planes?"

His father nodded stiffly.

Prince Stephen understood what an outsider to the family would not. In the complex history of Weisboden, tradition demanded that when the monarch was threatened, he should make his stand in his own country. Only now, the plane he was returning on was missing.

"And Queen Alicia?" Stephen asked. "Does she know that Karl's plane is missing?"

"Not yet. There is no need to spread unnecessary concern. She is to remain with her family, as will Crown Prince Albert, Prince Robert and Princess Adrianna. As far as anyone knows Karl will be returning with them next week according to the published itinerary."

Stephen felt suddenly ill. Karl, the Monarch of Weisboden, might be dead.

Prince Michael sounded completely calm, but he saw his son's reaction. "Appearances, Stephen. Until we knew exactly what the situation is, we must proceed as if all is normal."

"Yes, Father," Stephen schooled his own face and obeyed his father's earlier request. He wheeled his chair out of the room along the uncarpeted edge and went in search of Johannes. He found the tall fair-haired senior servant hovering in the passage.

"Johannes, could you show the American visitors into my father. He will see them in his suite," Stephen instructed politely.

"Very good, Sir. Was there anything else?" Johannes acknowledged. He gave a cursory bow, and straightened.

"No," Stephen said bluntly. "I have things Father wants me to do, but I will be available if he needs me to take notes or anything. Just page me."

Stephen wheeled himself in the direction of the communications room, and ignored the obsequious attention of the senior servant. Johannes seemed to think that because Stephen was Prince Michael's secretary and assistant, that he was actually little more than a servant. And as such, should keep him informed of all he had to do.

When Johannes returned downstairs, he moved to an unobtrusive alcove and studied the visitors that the door attendant had directed there. They both wore the uniforms of Scout leaders, and looked damp from the dash through the rain from their car to the entrance hall. Both had removed their coats and hats and were standing near the ornamental electric fire. The woman kept glancing around the room, as if fascinated by its 18th century décor, and the famous murals that covered the four walls from waist high to the tall ceiling. The man was talking quietly to her and from their accents, it was obvious that they were the Americans that had been expected much earlier in the day. Since he knew that the international airport was closed, he wondered how they had got there at all.

The conversation between the man and woman did not enlighten him. They were quietly discussing things they needed to ask Prince Michael regarding the possibility of holding a scout jamboree. The former monarch was the patron of the scouting movement in Weisboden. Johannes tuned out the conversation and studied the body language of the Americans.

The couple were young, probably in their twenties and had open honest faces that looked to be used to being outdoors. Both the tall male with short-cropped blond hair and the shorter woman with her long brown hair tied back with a clip, betrayed subtle signs of nervousness in the way they held their berets and shuffled in place. He studied the faces so he could recognise them again if they returned in the future. The man was ordinary in his looks, but the woman had an exotic facial bone structure.

No doubt though, Johannes thought, they had never approached royalty before – the peasants. He emerged into the room through one of the gold embossed white doors and hid a smirk at the way they both quickly checked each other's appearance and replaced their berets. The uniforms were impeccable, even if damp.

"Good afternoon, I am Johannes. I am to take you to His Highness," Johannes announced. "I believe you have a letter?"

The man, who took an envelope from his pocket and passed it over, automatically studied the servant. Tall, fair haired, grey eyed, classic Aryan features and a trifle supercilious. The elegant dark coloured suit the servant wore, which had the Weisboden heraldic arms embroidered on the pocket, seemed to imply that this was a high-ranking servant. The faint smell of his aftershave was pleasant and not astringent.

The woman turned to Johannes and spoke in halting German, "Thank you. Perhaps you would be kind and advise us how we should address His Highness?"

It amused Johannes to give her a faint bow and the slightest click of his heels. "His Highness is known now as Prince Michael, the correct address is, Your Highness, or if you prefer, Sir."

He watched the woman mentally translate his words and then nod at him. He could have told her the information in English, since he spoke it fluently, but it amused him to make them speak German.

"This way, please," Johannes gestured to a door that led to the private stairs.

Since the old man had chosen to see these visitors in his private suite, not his office, the private stairs were the most direct route - if you discounted the lift that had been installed for Prince Stephen's use. Usually visitors were seen in the Prince's Office, and were taken up the majestically impressive public stairs, but the Prince was probably feeling the cold in his old bones and wanted to stay in his heated room.

"Herr and Frau Davis, Your Highness," Johannes spoke in German, which was the major language of the Royals. He walked to present the introductory letter to the Prince and then stepped aside to let the visitors approach. He bowed and withdrew.

The two Americans walked across the thick floral patterned floor carpet towards the chair occupied by Prince Michael. They had taken in the décor with a brief flick of their eyes during that time.

"It is very kind of you to see us at this later time, Your Highness,"

Frau Davis said slowly in stilted German. She bowed, imitating the action of the servant.

Prince Michael nodded acceptance of the thanks and gestured again for his guests to sit down. He had moved to a chair near the electric fire, and two chairs, matching his own, were within easy talking distance.

"I would not have been surprised if you had been held up further. Did you have much trouble getting here? I understand the airport is closed." Prince Michael spoke in English to put his guests at ease. He took a moment to glance at the letter Johannes had given him.

Herr Davis moved to a chair, and managed a smile. He glanced at his wife as if waiting for her to sit first. "Not too much trouble, Your Highness. We were fortunate that our Austrian friends were able to find transport for us. Our charter flight from Munich was diverted to Salzburg."

"And the road was open?" Prince Michael asked in English.

"A trifle flooded in places," Herr Davis answered, also in English, implying they had driven into Weisboden.

Frau Davis had stayed standing, and although she had her eyes on the Prince, she seemed to be listening for the door to close behind them. "We have heard many good things about the scouting movement in your country. We were excited by the prospect of holding the World Jamboree here," she spoke in turn.

The door closed the rest of the way, very quietly.

Herr Davis, who had been in the act of sitting down, reversed the movement.

Prince Michael was surprised at the change in the attitude of his guests. Instead of nervous and forgettable, they were now sharp eyed and alert.

"Sir, I have further identification, if I may present it?" Herr Davis requested in perfect German and at the Prince's nod, reached into his pocket and pulled out a leather wallet. He placed it on a small table in reach of the Prince and stepped back.

Prince Michael scrutinised the two diplomatic passports closely. "You won't mind waiting while I check these details?"

"No, Sir," Herr Davis, whose real name was David Martin, agreed readily. He lowered his voice and continued. "We were briefed as to the importance of hiding the real reason we were here. In fact, I have equipment with me to test this room for listening devices."

The Prince nodded, used his stick to help him rise from his chair and walked to the far side of the room. His guests settled into their chairs and watched as he used a telephone extension that was a direct outside line but they could not hear what he was saying. Both took the opportunity to study the large wall mural behind the Prince's chair. It was a rural scene that hinted of the European Alps.

Prince Michael returned to his chair and gestured for David to use his device. He sat and watched David moving around the room, aiming the antenna of the device in all directions. The room was less opulent that the visitors room downstairs, but with the paintings on the walls and the 18th century décor, the heavy curtains covering three of the four windows and the ornate carved furniture - there could be many places to disguise a listening device.

"The room is clear, Sir."

Prince Michael waited for David to sit again and studied the woman.

"What is the code word for this mission, Frau Davis?" he asked in perfect English.

Wanda Martin, alias Frau Davis, answered him immediately. "Masquerade."

David glanced briefly at his wife. There had been no code word, but obviously, Prince Michael's contact knew of Wanda's unusual talent for sensing thoughts and devised this means of confirming their identity. That talent was not something their superiors usually revealed.

Prince Michael nodded thoughtfully, but kept his thoughts to himself.

"I will accept that you are who you say you are," he said. "How can you help me?"


"Sir, as our official identification papers show, we are both US State Department Special Investigators. Our superiors believe we will be able to locate the source of the threats mentioned in your request for help. We already know a great deal about your country and your family — what is known publicly, but there are things that we will need to know more about. I will outline those things in a moment," David explained. "Once basic facts are ascertained, we will report to the team that will neutralise the threat."

"Neutralise?" Prince Michael mildly queried the term. He brought his left hand up to touch his chin.

"Bring to an appropriate conclusion," Wanda rephrased it more tactfully. She smiled faintly and relaxed back into the chair.

"And I will be advised of all progress," Prince Michael stated, glancing at both Americans in turn.

"Yes, Sir," David confirmed. "The only other people who will be told of our findings are the five people in the team I mentioned. You may be assured that we and they will not pass the information on."

"Very well. What else do you need, Herr Davis?"

David leant forward and explained what he needed and allowed the Prince to organise his thoughts before speaking.

Prince Michael began speaking very quietly, directing his attention to David. That was fine with Wanda, she was listening intently, and sensing that the prince was not used to discussing private family matters with outsiders.

"I expect that no ruler in these times is without enemies or detractors, yet I would invite any who felt we were not doing the best for our people to speak out. No one has spoken openly against us, but since Karl came to rule three years ago, there have been mutterings amongst the people of his unsuitability to rule. Such an attitude is not unexpected. Karl and I differ in our views on many subjects, and when things have been one way for a long time – people resist the change, and feel threatened by it. Even I am not immune to such thoughts, but I saw clearly that it was time for change. Karl has proved to me that he understands these times better than I do, and I cannot fault his dedication to our people."

"Has there been an increase in the level of dissatisfaction, Sir?" David asked.

"The grumbles of sedition began after the coronation, and have stayed at a low level, but there have been incidents – coincidences perhaps – when Karl might have been harmed. The vigilance of our security staff has so far prevented accidents," Prince Michael explained.

"May I ask, Sir, what kind of incidents?" David inserted into a pause.

"Once the royal car was tampered with – the perpetrator was seen and chased off. Another time, there was a gas leak in Karl's suite – the servants noticed it quickly. Recently, an explosive was detonated in a building that Karl due to visit. Suggestive, but no direct death threats," Prince Michael explained. Wanda knew that there had been many other such incidents.

"And the occurrence at Munich this morning," David murmured.

"You have been well informed. I did not believe that matter was announced."

"If I may suggest," Wanda Martin spoke quietly. "The incidents so far seem designed to prove to His Majesty that he can be reached, but whoever is behind them does not yet want him dead. I suspect the mastermind wishes to manipulate him. What caused you to ask for help?"

"For the past two weeks Karl has been, as far as my country is concerned, visiting his wife's relatives. In fact, he has been attending talks, and negotiating matters of great economic importance to this country. Quite naturally, during that time, there has been a great deal of correspondence between here and there. Somehow, amongst the letters sent from here, under the royal seal, was a beautifully hand written invitation. On first glance, it seemed innocuous. It was simply an invitation to Karl to a reunion of a club known as 'The Cavalier'. There was no address for a reply and the police here have been unable to find out anything about such a club, as it probably no longer exists. I am told that the effect of the invitation when Karl received it was quite dramatic. His security escort reported that His Majesty went deathly pale and was trembling."

"Sir, do you believe this is a direct threat against his majesty's life?" David prompted when Prince Michael paused for a time.

"Karl is on his way back now, to discuss it. I believe that at the very least it might be leading to an attempt at blackmail."

Wanda, listening carefully to the conversation, detected a slight hesitation before Prince Michael mentioned Karl's name.

David didn't ask what Karl might have to hide, instead he prompted, "At the very least?"

Prince Michael sighed softly. "There are people in this country who would like to see the end of the monarchy. They have no wish to have us continuing to play a role in the governing of this country. Sources of my own, have told me that some would be willing to kill Karl, and in the ensuing confusion – make their move."

"Particularly if they are first able to discredit the monarchy," Wanda said softly, voicing what Prince Michael had not said. "Have any other of your children received similarly veiled threats?"

"You are very astute, Frau Davis," the prince noted to Wanda. "None of the others have mentioned anything to me, but there have been some rehashes of old incidents in the media. Once I have spoken to Karl, I will talk to each of the others."

Again that slight hesitation, Wanda noted, and she flicked a thought at David, causing him to glance at her.

Prince Michael sighed again. "I am an old man. It was with great relief that I abdicated in favour of my son. Yet I am still the head of the family - a family that has survived for generations with an unblemished name. It is my duty to preserve that name."

"Then that will be a prime concern for those who follow us," Wanda assured the former king.

"How will I know those people?" The prince did not verbalise his desire for complete secrecy - the need that no outsider learn he had called in help. He was looking at Wanda, meeting her gaze.

"Trust your instincts, Your Highness," David suggested.

The Prince was wondering why the face of a fair-haired stranger came into his mind.

David allowed Wanda more time to concentrate on the face of Jim Phillips, their director, before he spoke again, this time asking a series of questions that Jim wanted answers to. Finally, he made a request, "We will also need a complete list of the palace staff and to become familiar with the layout of the palace, Sir."

Prince Michael considered this, but did not reply immediately. He was reluctant to accuse any of the palace staff, all of whom had been rigidly screened before being employed.

"Very well," Prince Michael agreed, as the door to the room opened and Prince Stephen wheeled himself in. The young man's agitation was clear from the jerky movements of the chair and the ashen greyness of his face.

David had a moment of revelation, realising that the cleared area around the edge of the room was to give the wheel chair a clear way. Then Wanda sent him mental alert. "Something is very wrong."

# Chapter 2

"Perhaps we should be leaving, Your Highness," David suggested. "If it might be permissible for us to call again?"

Prince Michael seemed not to hear him. He too had realised something was wrong. "Stephen, what is it?"

"Father…" Stephen glanced at the two Americans. He did not wish to speak in front of strangers.

"Karl?" Prince Michael asked, and Stephen nodded faintly.

"You may speak in front of Herr and Frau Davis," Prince Michael decided abruptly.

"Father, I have just heard from Derek. They have detected the signal from the charter plane's emergency beacon and triangulated it to be near the top of Mount Desperate. The weather has grounded all planes so they can't start an air search."

Prince Michael seemed to become rigid. Then years of experience of dealing with crises came back to him. To his visitors, he said, "I'm sorry; this is a matter I need to act on. The plane that was carrying the palace diplomatic bag is overdue…"

Wanda interrupted gently, and with no apology, "And your son, Sir?"

Stephen's white face confirmed it.

Prince Michael sat tensely in his chair. "I don't know how you guessed, but yes." The admission wasn't easy. "Therefore it is important that the plane is found quickly, but I do not want it known who was on board. Naturally Karl is my main concern, but the diplomatic correspondence must be recovered as well."

David exchanged a look with Wanda and received a nod. "Sir, it seems that the only way to search is by road, but I would not like to trust the roads in the mountains after all the rain of the past night, and in the current conditions."

The tightening of Prince Michael's face betrayed his unvoiced agreement.

"Sir, there is a US military helicopter at the airport, available for our use. That is how we arrived in Weisboden. I requested it to be refuelled.

I will call Flight Commander Mathias and see if he is willing to fly to the crash site. Assuming there is a place to land, my wife and I will assess the situation. There is a comprehensive first aid kit on board and both of us are trained paramedics."

"Fly in this?" Stephen blurted. "Are you mad?"

"We flew just ahead of the storm front to get here," Wanda remarked quietly. "Mathias is an excellent pilot and so is David. The storm front has passed, so the conditions should improve."

"What if you can't land?" Stephen asked bluntly.

"Then David can lower me down on a line with a stretcher and the aid kit," Wanda stated with complete composure. "It won't be the first time."

She almost seemed to be daring Prince Michael and Prince Stephen to object. She added quite soberly, "This is not bravado or showing off. In matters such as this, the speed of bringing medical attention can be critical."

"Contact your pilot, and if he agrees, I will accept your offer," Prince Michael decided quickly. "Would you be able to bring out four men? Karl, his secretary Brantner and two pilots?"

"Yes, Sir," David confirmed. "The helicopter is normally used to transport freight, but it has four fixed seats and two bench seats that can be folded down for extra passengers. One moment, I will make the call."

David withdrew his mobile phone and when he was connected to the pilot, all he asked was, "Would you be willing to undertake a search for a downed plane?"

After a moment of listening, "Thanks, I will get back in touch shortly." He ended the call, and advised the Prince of the affirmative decision.


"Good, then I will come with you," Prince Michael announced.

"Father! You are…" Prince Stephen began to protest, but when his father turned to face him, he stopped. His father was not going to be dissuaded.

"Get on to the authorities – whoever is in charge of the search – then let me talk to them. I want no hint of the passenger details to reach the media," Prince Michael directed his son.

"Will I notify the hospital?" Stephen asked.

"Yes, although that might already be done. We can send details to the search coordinator when we have them, but I want Karl brought here."

Stephen wheeled himself over to the phone as David Martin exchanged a glance with his wife. Wanda shrugged slightly. He did not think that bringing the King to the palace was a good idea. The hospital had all the necessary equipment if the King was critically injured. Yet, they were not in charge. In this foreign country, they had to obey its rulers. Moreover, they both realised that Prince Michael was deliberately not considering that Karl might be dead.

"Sir, with due respect," David spoke up. "Once we have evaluated the scene, I will advise you if should take the survivors directly to experienced doctors."

Prince Michael studied the American, with a look that would have caused many men to back down. He didn't respond to the implied criticism, and simply asked, "Is there anything you need, Herr Davis?"

"Only the coordinates for the location of the crash beacon. We have charts and a GPS on board. Then once I am at the airport, I will need to notify air control of our intentions."

"I will talk to the air control," Prince Michael stated. He rose from his chair and strode to the phone.

Stephen wheeled himself out of his father's way and neared the guests. He beckoned Wanda and murmured to her, "I do not think it a good idea for my father to go in the helicopter. He is not a young man, and if Karl is dead, he will be needed to hold the country together."

Wanda spoke in a similarly low voice. "As I said, Mathias and David are excellent pilots, Prince Stephen. The Flight Commander has a great deal of combat and SAR experience. He will not take unnecessary risks. However, we can only advise His Highness of the risks, not tie him to the ground. Do you have the crash coordinates?"

Stephen dug into a pouch slung down the right side of the wheeled chair. He drew out a slightly creased piece of paper and handed to Wanda, she glanced at it and passed it on to David.

Prince Michael finished talking on the phone and called quietly, "Stephen, we are ready to go."

He strode from the room, expecting his guests to follow.

In the passage, he proved that he was still in excellent form, when he bellowed for Johannes.

"He doesn't sound frail," Wanda remarked. Stephen made a sound like a muted snort.

"Don't underestimate him; his mind is still as sharp as ever. He likes keeping Johannes on his toes, but he will not admit that he is no longer in his prime. It's only his hands that he will admit to being painful," Stephen murmured.

The senior servant was slightly out of breath when he appeared at the end of the passage.

Prince Michael wasted no time giving orders. "Johannes, have my coat ready and tell Truman to bring the car around to the front. I am going with Herr and Frau Davis to speak to some officials. I can be reached by pager if I am required."

Johannes hurried off.


"Our car is outside, Sir," David remarked to the Prince as they walked briskly along a passage, decorated with mirrors and more paintings, to a lift.

"You should head for the airport and get things ready. I will join you after speaking to the airport authorities."

"Your Highness," Wanda spoke up. "Is it wise for you to come with us? The winds will still be gusting unpredictably."

"Frau Davis, as you are both willing to risk flying in this weather, and neither of you seem suicidal, and I do not believe I am senile, I am willing to trust your skills."

Wanda ignored the tone of polite reproof. "Then, Sir, I trust you will not try to do anything foolish. I do not need for you to become an additional patient."

"I appreciate your concern, Frau Davis, but I do not need cosseting. I am not a feeble old man," Prince Michael rebuked politely.

"You are a precious resource," Wanda told him directly, and a daring him to refute it. "And if the King is badly injured, your knowledge and experience will be needed."

Prince Michael inclined his head slightly, admitting the truth of what Wanda had said. "I will rejoin you at the airport."

# Chapter 3

As David drove the small hire car as fast as he dared in the heavy rain on the slippery roads, Wanda was calling ahead to the airport and speaking to Mathias to give him more details of the task they had volunteered him for. She was relieved when he told her brusquely, "I have already been requested to help in the search, and have received discretionary permission. My superiors stipulated that I needed permission from you and your husband. I have a flight plan ready, and I am waiting on the most up-to-date weather forecast. It is looking like the rain will ease."

The rain had eased when they reached the airport, although the wind was still strong enough to be noticeably swaying the trees. David parked the car close to the terminal entrance, in the taxi zone, and they both raced through the glass doors and into the relative warmth of the terminal. The wide-open area leading to the check-in desks was almost deserted. David asked one of few staff in sight for directions to the helipad.

Mathias met them just inside the door that led to the tarmac, and the three of them ran from there through the rain to the helicopter. After climbing into the cabin, David helped Mathias with the pre-flight checks and glanced at the flight plan. "What did the weather report indicate," David asked.

"Conditions should begin easing. The wind is going to be the main problem…"

Wanda heard David mentioning the extra passenger, and Mathias requesting a weight estimate so he could modify his flight calculations and listened to their discussion with only part of her attention. She had gone directly to check what equipment was on board and to familiarise herself with it. She had noted the rescue equipment when they had flown in it before.

Mathias came and showed her and David how to use the side winch and where the safety harnesses were stowed. She checked the winch cable in case she had to be lowered on it. That was Wanda's area of expertise, and she did not intend to be injured herself due to lack of caution. The weather was dangerous enough, despite the easing of the rain.

As she checked the contents of the aid kit, she noticed two warmly clad figures walking briskly from the terminal and warned David. He came back and helped the men on board, directing them to the extra seats. At least they both were prepared for cold. The stranger introduced himself as Truman, and David assumed he was the Prince's chauffer. Wanda hid her amusement, for she was certain that Truman would also be watching Prince Michael.

Mathias quickly redid his calculations for a third time.


Three quarters of an hour after receiving word of the crash, the helicopter was airborne. David was acting as co-pilot and was in contact with Weisboden Air Control. He had advised them of their course and that they had five people on board. Mathias had his full attention on controlling the helicopter. Wanda, like David and Mathias, had radio headphones on, so she was also listening to the conversation between the pilots and Air Control. The other two passengers only had noise muffling earmuffs on. She kept her eye on the Prince, but he maintained a calm, dignified composure, even when the flight became turbulent. Truman grimaced every time the helicopter dropped or rose suddenly.

When Mathias announced they were over the search area, Wanda stood and moved to the side door. She donned a safety harness, connected the attached safety line to the rail next to the door, and then pushed the door open.

A blast of frigid moist air came into the hold. She spared a moment of pity for the other passengers, but she needed to have as clear a view as possible of the tree-covered terrain below. Even though it was not night time, the heavy cloud made it seem that way. David switched on the brilliant spotlight and directed it downwards as Mathias began an expanding square search pattern. The light was helpful, except when a squall of rain blew past, causing the light to reflect off the water drops.

Wanda was soon soaked, but she ignored the cold and discomfort because in another way she welcomed it. It seemed to make her feel less tired – 8 am in Los Angeles, when they had left to come to Weisboden, was a long time ago. She didn't try to calculate what time her body thought it was now – time for that later when the work was done.

After half an hour of searching, Wanda thought she spotted something white down between the pine trees and directed Mathias back to the position.

"Looks like something," he agreed. "Now, is there somewhere we can set down? There are not many flat spots in this area."

They discussed options through the headsets. Wanda was still scanning the area below looking for a clearing. "There! David – on the left. Looks like a fire break."

Mathias followed the break between the trees and spotted a wider cleared area. He hovered over the spot, getting a feeling for the wind. "We can do it. Close the door and strap in."

Wanda obeyed immediately, unhooking her safety line once the door was shut and moving back to her seat. She stopped briefly to warn the Prince and Truman, "We are going to land. Hang on tight; this is going to be rough."

Wanda had absolute faith in Mathias's flying, and David calmly helped Mathias with the controls as they fought the craft down. Once below tree top height, most of the wind was blocked, and Wanda took off the headset and replaced it with a smaller wi-fi unit. David had a second unit and she knew he would have that on when he came after her. Then she went to release the aid kit and unrack a torch. She grabbed a coil of rope and was ready to go as soon as the landing skids touched the ground. Once she opened the door, she set off into the rain without waiting for anyone to accompany her. David let her go; he needed to help secure the helicopter before going after her and she was for now, following the firebreak along a level contour of the mountain.

Truman helped Prince Michael out of the helicopter, before taking a torch he had brought with him. The Prince was using a metal hiking stick as they followed Wanda's path. They followed her progress by the torchlight flicking on the reflective tape on her harness.

Wanda had spotted a wing, not the fuselage, though her followers did not realise that. They only saw her moving quickly, as if she knew where to go.

For her part, Wanda was using senses other than the five common ones. Now she was away from the other searchers, she sensed that there was at least one injured survivor, and his pain was pulling her in the right direction.

The others caught up to her at a point along the road, where a narrower trail led up the hill and through thickly growing pines. David and Mathias were carrying the litter with blankets and extra rope.

David queried her. "I thought what you saw was down the hill."

"I think that was part of the wing. I am sure the rest is up there," Wanda insisted. There was no chance of seeing the wreckage from the road, since the view was obscured by the rain.

"I'll trust your instinct," David decided. "If the plane lost a wing, and kept going, it is in roughly the direction it would have been headed."

"The only thing is - this track is rocky, and steep. I am not sure if the two locals should try it," Wanda suggested.

"We can go ahead. Truman can help the Prince if he insists. We can only advise," David answered her concern.

Mathias was the one to suggest that the elderly Prince remain at the road. He did not know who the man was, but he agreed the fellow shouldn't try the climb in the wet and slippery conditions. As David expected, Prince Michael insisted, quoting past experience climbing many famous mountains. Mathias seemed to still disagree, but David compromised by saying he and Truman would take the litter, and escort him. Mathias nodded reluctantly and set off at a trot after Wanda.

He spoke as they followed the trail. "You seem sure we are going the right way. Did you spot the fuselage?"

She repeated David's reasoning, rather than try to explain her unscientific approach. After going what was probably half a mile up a reasonably steep slope, she was proved right.

"Good call," Mathias stated, as he looked up to where the fuselage had come to rest. "It looks like they were trying to pull up."

The plane had impacted the tops of the tall pine trees and the wings had been wrenched off. The fuselage had slipped tail first into a gap between trees and the whole of it was precariously balanced about twenty metres above the ground. At least, it hadn't slammed into the mountain and exploded.

Wanda carefully examined what she could see of the plane and trees from the ground, thankful that the rain decided to stop. Using the torch gave little more detail as there was still a lot of water and the light reflected off it. She lowered the torch to the ground next to the aid kit and coil of rope. She was going to have to climb and was already preparing. First, she removed the harness she still wore and her coat. The latter would catch on the branches and hinder movement, but the harness would go back on. Then she uncoiled the rope and tied one end to the harness.

"What are you intending," Mathias asked sharply. "I can't let you go up."

"I know you think you should do this because you have experience and don't know what I can do, but I am an experienced climber," Wanda said tersely, putting the rest of the coiled rope onto her shoulder. "I am also a paramedic and the lightest of all of us."

"Still, we need to plan this…" Mathias tried.

"I have. I will climb up level with the tail, drop this rope down and when David gets here with more ropes I will have him tie one on and I will pull it up and secure it. He can tie off the other end so that it provides some support for the tail. I will then climb up and drop the rope over a higher branch and drop the rest down, you or David can belay it for me, so if I slip, it won't be far," Wanda explained.

"I doubt the rope will hold the tail if it slips," Mathias disagreed.

"There is that chance, and there is also the chance it will at least slow it down if it does," Wanda countered. She continued her explanation, "When I am in the plane, I will pull in the rope and drop it for you or David to tie onto the aid box, or whatever else I need. And please keep the others back."

Mathias nodded stiffly, and watched as Wanda went to the pine tree she had chosen and began to climb. He likened her to a monkey and realised she probably did know what she could do. Even if he didn't know how she was getting up with no obvious foot holds for the first ten feet.

David, with another torch and two coils of double braided rope taken from the helicopter, spotted his wife already half way up to the level of the plane. He had heard what Wanda needed him to do, but he let Mathias tell him before he went to the base of the tree where Wanda's rope was trailing down. He quickly tied on the second rope and waited until Wanda finished ascending, and spoke into his wi-fi headpiece.

"How does it look?"

He heard Wanda's reply, though there was a lot of wind noise coming through the microphone with her voice. "Getting up here was easy. Getting people down will be a nightmare. This thing is resting on branches, but the trees are moving quite a bit and it is likely to slip when I try to get in."

She was already pulling the second rope up, and soon vocalised. "It's tied."

David did not waste effort telling his wife to be careful. She had been climbing on ropes strung between city buildings from before they had met and knew more about climbing and ropes than he did. In this case, his own assessment of the situation agreed with hers, and he went to the tree on the other side of the wrecked plane, tied the line to his harness and began to climb. Wanda was waiting for him to attach the rope before risking the next step. He hoped the plane didn't slip. "Ready," he sent to Wanda as he began to descend again.

"I'm going to go higher," Wanda told him. "And come down with the line over the bough. Can you be ready to belay it so if I slip, I won't drop far? Then you can lower me if I need you to."

"Right – I will tell you when I am ready."


Wanda eased herself away from the tree trunk, feet edging along one of the branches while holding on to a higher one and easing the rope along it. She was getting wet from brushing against the pine needles and had their resinous scent in her nose. The wind was blowing water from the boughs onto her as well. The tree itself was swaying but she didn't let that worry her. Her balance was instinctive.

Once she was over the plane, she tested the security of her safety line before lowering herself to land lightly on the swaying fuselage.

After touching lightly, she gradually increased the proportion of her weight on it. The plane settled a short distance and she had to repeat her manoeuvre. The fuselage was sloping steeply, and Wanda slid more than walked along the top of the plane until she was at the passenger door. Then she slowly slid over the side.

Those on the ground could not see how she opened the door, but could just make out her darker silhouette against the light coloured plane. Then she had it slid open enough to climb inside.

"I'm in, Dav. Release the line." Wanda carefully pulled the line into the plane so she could drop it down for the aid kit. One end was still tied to her harness; she undid it and retied it to the support of a seat. The rest of the rope she coiled ready for dropping.

That done, Wanda moved with extreme care as a sudden sharp movement might be enough to unbalance the plane.

Using a tiny torch she took from a pocket, Wanda looked around in the darkness. She saw that the nearest passenger was a dark haired man in the seat nearest the door. In the light of the narrow beam, she could see that the left side of his face was a mess of blood and the cause was easy to determine. When the wing had wrenched off, the fuselage had been weakened and a piece of the metal had been forced inwards, probably by a branch. The man must have been thrown against it. She didn't need to feel a lack of pulse to know he was dead. Moving further inward, she put the gory sight out of her mind. The man was beyond pity, and she had seen worse sights in her life.

Wanda sensed there was still someone alive, and shone her torch around and saw the second man further forward, on the opposite side of the plane. She drew herself up the steeply sloped aisle, by holding onto the seats.

This man was also dark haired, and he had been in the prescribed crash position, and so was leaning forward. His seat was just forward of where the wing had been, and Wanda could feel draughts from the cracks in the fuselage.

Again, Wanda checked for a pulse, and this time found one that was weak but regular. She played her little torch over what she could see of him, and decided he had been very lucky. However, she wasn't sure if this was the King or the secretary. The light wasn't good enough to be sure, but he was well enough for the moment, and she needed to check the pilots.

She pulled herself up, using the seats again, but she was already sure of what she would find in the cockpit. It didn't take long to confirm it. The two pilots were dead. The cockpit window had been shattered when a branch had been thrust into the plane. If the men had not died instantly, then it had been quick. The branch had caught both in the face.

"David?" she spoke into her headpiece.

"Here."

"Both pilots are dead, killed on impact I'd say. One of the two passengers is still alive."

"Do you know which?" David asked, knowing that Prince Michael was stoically waiting for the knowledge.

"Starboard side. They both have dark hair, and I haven't tried to move them. I'm going back to the door to drop the line down for the aid kit."

Before Wanda reached the door, she felt the movement. Either the effect of her moving inside or that of the wind had disrupted the delicate balance.

"Hang on!" Wanda heard David yell through the headpiece.

"Damn right," she muttered, instinctively grabbing onto the nearest support, as the sound of screeching metal and snapping branches became louder than the wind.

David watched with every nerve shrieking at him to help his wife. Logic didn't come into it – yet even though the radio was silent – he knew she was still okay and he stayed where he was. Most people would not believe that he could possibly be sure. He played the torch on the plane when it stopped moving. The rope had snagged the tail, but the nose had continued to fall until enough branches stopped it. At least it was at a more level angle. He estimated that it was now only five metres from the ground.

Mathias came nearer the plane, David told him to stay back while he shone his torch over the plane's new position.

"She is still fine," David told him.

Mathias spotted the headpiece David wore and was reassured.

"Wanda?" David spoke into the microphone.

In his headpiece was a noise like static and then he heard, "Sorry, the damn headpiece was knocked off. I'll toss the rope out for the aid kit."

Wanda still on the floor, and ignoring the bumps she had collected when the fuselage had slipped, crawled to the door. Before pushing the rope out, she checked the end that she had tied to a seat support, and then held the rope gently until she felt the three tugs that told her the kit was tied on. With infinite care, she pulled on the rope until she felt the weight come on it, and she braced herself to bring it up.

As careful as she was, the change in the balance point of the plane due to the weight of the kit dangling below, and her own weight on the same side, caused the fuselage to slip sideways and once again begin to fall.

Wanda fell against the half-opened door, and held on. Her mind was calmly saying, "Easy does it. Easy does it."

The plane settled with a jerk and more tearing of metal. Wanda had released the rope, but once the plane settled again, she went first to the injured man. He was still alive. She felt the floor move and a loud thump and turned to see David climbing in through the door after the first aid kit. The view out the door gave her an indication that they were much nearer the ground. He turned and took a torch from someone.

Wanda assumed it was Mathias and turned to begin a more thorough examination of the injured man using the light from the bigger torch. When she saw the ring on his right index finger with the arms of Weisboden etched on it, she knew this was King Karl. Part of her was relieved, but the rest of her was cataloguing his injuries and knew he was in a bad way.

"Is he alive," Prince Michael asked through the doorway. His head and shoulders were showing above the cabin floor level.

Wanda answered without turning from her patient. "Yes." She felt a surge of relief from Prince Michael. "All the others are dead."

The former monarch did not ask for a prognosis, but watched the two Americans working like a practiced team.

David murmured through the headpiece, "It is as well that he can't see Karl's other side." He was holding the torch so Wanda could see where she needed to place pressure bandage on a freely bleeding scalp wound.

"That happened when we dropped," Wanda said. "A branch came through where the metal was already cracked. Other than that, he probably has a concussion. The facial cuts are superficial. The neck felt okay, but I will put on a cervical collar before we move him."

Wanda finished bandaging the scalp wound and continued her examination. "The right shoulder is swollen, probably dislocated…ditto right elbow…can't tell about the ribs. Can you shine the torch down at the leg here – it feels trapped."

David handed Wanda the torch and lay down on the floor to investigate.

"Feels like a lot of blood here," David warned. "I can get him free… hand me a pressure bandage."

David eased out once he had applied the bandage and rose to his knees. "We need to get him out of there to fix that leg properly. If I lift from the shoulders, can you ease the legs out from the seat?"

Without fuss, they lifted the patient away from the seat. Wanda realised that the King had a case chained to his wrist, and the case was jammed. While David supported the King's full weight, Wanda reached into her pocket for a small tool that she always carried. In seconds, the chain was unlocked, and she took half the weight again.

"Damn," Wanda suddenly swore. "Another bandage, Dav."

Now that the king was in an easier position to treat, Wanda tightened the pressure on the leg gash.

"How bad?" David asked. "Does he need hospital?"

Wanda considered as she finished tying off the pressure bandage.

"Find out from Prince Michael what facilities he has at the palace," Wanda suggested. "That leg gash is bad, but I don't think the main artery is compromised. I would prefer he went to a hospital, but in this matter, we must allow for other considerations. I don't think we can overrule Prince Michael."

They felt the floor rock, and heard the end of the litter come through the door. David cursed, but crawled over to pull it in further.

They lifted Karl into the litter after Wanda had bound the right arm to Karl's body to reduce the chance of further injury. Then they covered him with blankets and clipped on the restraints to keep him secure.

David nodded to Mathias to take the end of the litter just protruding from the plane. He lifted the nearer end to ease it out. Truman came and supported David's end once it was clear of the door. When he dropped from the plane, David had the locked case and the torch, and waited to help Wanda out once she had repacked the loose equipment into the aid kit and collected the rubbish. He handed her the case and took the aid kit, then waited as Prince Michael approached.

"May I have a word, Sir," David asked.

"What do you need?" Prince Michael asked with no trace of imperiousness. He was impressed by these Americans.

Using terse words, David reported the King's injuries. "The leg is bad. It will need a skilled doctor to look at it." David hoped the Prince would take his advice, but he was not going to try to force a decision on him.

Prince Michael snapped a number of questions at him, but Wanda answered most of them.

"We will bring him to the palace," the Prince decided. "Our doctor is already on the way there. I have alerted the hospital, but it does not have a helipad, so the patient would have to go by ambulance from the airport. If Doctor Mueller decides a hospital is needed, we will take Karl there."

David accepted his decision, but had a question of his own.

"Sir, have you considered that our arrival at the palace will be heard?"

"Yes. Helicopter arrivals are frequent enough to be only a minor novelty but I have taken steps to keep interest in our arrival to a minimum."

That had to satisfy David.

"Are you planning to bring out the bodies as well?" Prince Michael asked politely.

Wanda didn't look at him as she answered. "It is more important to get your son to medical attention. We can do nothing for the others. David has a GPS fix on the wreck and will return to the airport and help the recovery team, if they want to come immediately."

"I will need to notify the relatives of the pilots and Karl's secretary of the accident," he said neutrally. He seemed to be encouraging an opinion from Wanda. She turned back to face him.

"Sir, the decision must ultimately be yours, but in regard to Karl's secretary –perhaps it might be wise to delay making his death public knowledge. I am thinking that you would want things to seem normal at the moment."

"I would like to talk of this later," Prince Michael said. "Is that Karl's case you have there?"

"Yes sir, but I will carry it for you until we are in the helicopter." She sensed that the Prince's hands were currently giving him a great deal of pain, due to the cold.

"How did you release the chain?" Wanda was asked.

"Should it have been locked?" she asked, neutrally. "It was fortunate that it wasn't."

Wanda did not wish to advertise her skill at opening locks. The Prince might be wondering if Special Investigators were taught such things. If so, that was better than his knowing that she was a highly experienced thief who had been taught to be an investigator. She was relieved when he accepted her answer.

"Your coat?" he asked instead, handing it to her.

"Ah, thanks, Sir," Wanda said immediately taking it. She didn't try to put it on over the harness but gestured for the Prince to precede her going down the hill. She sensed his amusement at her intent to assist him if he needed help. He had needed no help climbing up the trail.

On their arrival, they found that Mathias had already secured the litter and was preparing to warm up the helicopter's engine. David went to remove the tie downs. Wanda waited for Truman to escort Prince Michael back into his seat, and when she followed, she checked they were both strapped in securely and glanced at the Prince to indicate she wanted him to stay safe. A mild clash of wills.

Once they were settled, she handed the locked case to Truman. She then stripped off the harness and put her coat back on before strapping herself in.

David called back to his passengers and asked, "Where is the helipad at the palace?"

Truman answered. "Out the back in the middle of the Terrace Lawn."

"What overlooks that area?" David asked next.

"The kitchens," Truman considered. "The servant's wing is on the west end of the palace."

"Is the helipad lit?"

"Yes, and we can floodlight the lawn if you wish," Truman advised.

"Just the pad, will be enough," David told him. "Can that be arranged?"

"Yes," Truman agreed, having seen Prince Michael nod.

Wanda put the communications headset on again in time to hear Mathias asking "…the palace?" and David saying quietly, "This is a highly classified matter. Need to know only." He went on to begin speaking to air control, reporting they were lifting from the crash scene, en-route to the airport and cancelling the ambulance that had been standing by. He gave an ETA that would allow them to detour via the palace first.

The ascent was not as turbulent as the descent had been, due to the reduction in the force of the wind. Once they were above the trees and in level flight, Wanda went back to check on her patient.

# Chapter 4

The helicopter landed gently on the pad at the palace. Wanda unstrapped first and went to open the side door hatch. She used a special sense in addition to sight and hearing, when she emerged. She knew there were two presences watching, but they were concerned, not hostile or avidly curious. Other than those watchers, the area was deserted and she could see the outline of some nearby hedges and the traces of light from the windows of the palace. The dull light of the afternoon did not give her much chance to appreciate the palace's graceful architecture.

David heard Wanda say, "All clear," before he helped Truman lift the litter out, but once he had eased it to the ground, he returned to the helicopter.

Wanda took over David's end using two hands to hold the lifting rail. She saw two tall figures walk into view.

Prince Michael greeted them as Joseph and William. Wanda heard one of them mention that the servants were told to stay out of area of the guest quarters on the ground floor, and that Johannes had gone to speak to the wives of the two pilots. She pretended not to have heard them, but was relieved that the senior servant would be unaware of their return. She did not want to be recognised and have questions asked about why she was still around.

One of the tall men spoke quietly in Wanda's ear, offering to take over the carrying of the litter. She was happy to let him. The other took over from Truman, who immediately trotted back to the helicopter. He needed to return to the airport to get the royal car. Mathias lifted as soon as Truman was strapped in.

Wanda walked next to the litter, feeling her feet sinking into wet springy turf until they reached a paved area. Ahead was an open doorway with light shining out. She had a glimpse of Prince Stephen waiting within.

She was glad to get out of the wind and into the warmth of the palace, and gladder still that the wet footprints she was making were on vinyl tiles and not carpet. The two tall men did not worry about such trifles, they kept going past where Prince Stephen waited, deeper into the palace. Prince Michael had gone on ahead.

Wanda hesitated, feeling like an intruder, but needing to remain near her patient. She heard Stephen roll up beside her.

"How is he?" Stephen asked.

"His Majesty is pretty banged up," Wanda summarised, as she tried to watch where the king was being taken. "And in spite of trying to appear otherwise, I think your father is in a fair degree of pain. It might ease now he is back out of the cold."

"And you?" Stephen asked. He began to wheel himself along after his brothers but his gaze rested on the damp and begrimed state of Wanda's uniform that was showing through the opening of her coat.

"I am a little less than fit to be seen in the current company," she admitted as she tacitly followed along beside the wheelchair.

Stephen gave her a fleeting grin. "I think father will overlook that at the moment."

They had passed from the open hallway near the kitchens, to a new looking section. New, because the passage smelt faintly of paint and lacked the ornate decoration of the rest of the palace.

"This is a new wing," Stephen explained as he escorted Wanda along a passage and past small alcoves, some with doors set into them, and others with paintings on the wall. "It was built to accommodate extra guests."

They caught up to the litter bearers after walking around a left hand bend. "Excuse me," Wanda said as they reached the door that the litter was disappearing into. She followed closely, and immediately took in the details of the room.

This room was of modern design, or redesign, since it too smelt faintly of paint. The walls and furniture were blending shades of green. The public area of the suite was a large area with two chairs, a couch and a coffee table – in an expensive modern style. Standing beside one of the chairs and in front of a modernistic painting, an aging, but still obviously aristocratic man was speaking to Prince Michael. The latter nodded to Wanda, and she approached him.

"Doctor Mueller, this is Frau Davis, she is one of the paramedics that attended the crash site."

Wanda felt the gaze the doctor gave her begrimed appearance, and felt him dismiss her as little more than a first-aider. She spoke quickly, "I am willing to help you in any way possible."

"That won't be necessary," the doctor assured her. He glanced at Prince Michael and spoke to the two tall men taking the litter into an inner room.

"I will need assistance getting His Majesty onto the bed if you would be so kind."

He gestured Wanda away and moved off after the litter and closing the door after him. She kept her expression inscrutable and ignored the glance Prince Michael gave her before he followed the doctor. To hide her annoyance, she removed her coat, and held it folded before her.

Prince Stephen wheeled himself over to Wanda, but said nothing. A short time later, the two tall men emerged from the inner room and went to sit in the two armchairs. Wanda decided that the doctor was not going to ask her about the injuries she had treated and decided he was an old fool.

After a short time, Prince Michael re-emerged. He was no longer as tense as he had been, and seemed less formal as he came over to speak to Wanda. "Herr Doctor Mueller expressed his commendation for your effective first aid. You have my utmost respect and gratitude, Frau Davis and certainly proved the Scout motto of being prepared."

"My husband and I are pleased to have been available to help, Sir," Wanda responded politely. She was beginning to feel the effects of a very long day, but was as stubborn as Prince Michael was in not betraying the fact.

"May I offer you a place to rest and clean up?" Prince Michael offered. "And a late supper while you wait for Herr Davis to return."

"I will see to it, Father," Prince Stephen quickly volunteered.

"Thank you, Stephen. And would you also notify the hospital that they may stand down and make arrangements to have Herr Mueller's nurse brought here?"

"Yes, father," Stephen agreed. He began to wheel himself out, asking Wanda, "Have you arranged accommodation yet, Frau Davis."

"Yes, thank you. We have a room in the city," Wanda said, casting a glance back at the closed door of the inner room. She followed Stephen and tried to convince herself that the injured man was in good hands.

"I'll take you to one of the other guest rooms," Stephen suggested. "You can clean up in there, and I will go and get something to fix up your arm."

Wanda glanced at the sleeve or the scout uniform, where she hadn't even realised it was torn and bloodstained. "It's nothing serious," she dismissed the matter.

"I could find you a change of clothes. Yours are wet and torn," Stephen tried, but Wanda shook her head.

"I suppose I should at least, wash my hands," Wanda decided to admit.

Stephen said, "I'll show you where you can do that."

When they were out of the suite, and from the watchful eyes of the two men, who were so like Stephen in looks that they had to be his older brothers, Wanda decided to ask a question that was troubling her.

"Are you confident that Doctor Mueller is competent to deal with this? I am serious when I say that His Majesty's leg wound is very bad. I had hoped to be able to explain what I observed."

Stephen didn't answer immediately and Wanda wondered if she had made a complete breach of protocol. She was really feeling too tired to be diplomatic.

Her doubts were allayed once they were within a suite, identical to the one they had left, except the walls were painted pale lemon and the furnishings were beige.

"I have to admit that I do share your doubts," Stephen admitted candidly. "Mueller has been the palace doctor for many years, and while I find him adequate for tending my problems, I doubt that he has had to deal with such grave injuries as Karl's for a very long time. And his nurse is older than he is. Though Father seems satisfied, since he wants me to have the hospital stand down but...perhaps...could I ask you to do me a favour?"

Wanda sighed inwardly, but switched her attention to him.

"I think we need a doctor experienced in emergency medicine," Stephen began. "I know of an extremely good one, but I don't think I should be the one to approach her. If I was recognised, questions would be asked."

As much as she simply wanted to lie down and sleep for as long as she could, her mission came first and getting to understand the royal family was part of it. "Of course. Just let me wash up a bit first."

"Of course," Stephen echoed unconsciously. "Through that door. The en-suite is the door to the right. Soap and towels should be there."

Wanda didn't take more time than necessary to scrub her face clean, as well as her grimy hands and finish off by combing her tangled hair. She was out within ten minutes.

"Let's go," she urged trying to sound more energetic than she was. "How do we get to this woman? Can we call her?"

"I will try to warn her to expect you," Stephen promised. "Though I won't say why on the phone. And as to how, I have a van I can use. Follow me."

Wanda put her coat back on as she followed Stephen's wheelchair back out the way they had come in. She was glad of it once they were back outside in the gusting wind. He led the way to a large metal building, which she guessed was the garage.

They arrived just as Truman was backing the Royal Car into its position. He finished quickly and trotted to meet them. "What do you need, Prince Stephen?"

Stephen explained that he needed to drive into the city, unobtrusively. Truman merely bowed and volunteered to drive them in one of the palace vans.

Within minutes, Truman had an unmarked white van beside them, and hopped out to go to the back where an electrical lift system was installed.

Stephen backed his chair onto the platform, locked the wheels and let Truman activate the lift so he could roll into the van. When Stephen was inside, Truman folded up the lift and invited Wanda to share the front seat.

They left the palace quietly, going out via a back gate. Stephen directed Truman to drive into the city and then spoke softly to Wanda over the back of the seat. "I will need you to convince the doctor to come. I did try to call her but it went to her voice mail and I do not intend to leave a message." His attention went to the route Truman was taking.

"We need to go to the free hospital, Truman. Take us to the emergency entrance."

The chauffer made no comment on the destination, and obediently turned to go in a new direction.

"The doctor works in the casualty section most nights. Her name is Renée de Salle," Stephen explained to Wanda. "You need to talk to her, no one else. She is the only doctor I would trust to help us."

A trickle of excitement went through Wanda, banishing tiredness. She waited for Stephen to continue.

"She won't appreciate being dragged from her work, but she will come."

Wanda sensed there was more, and waited in silence.

"I shouldn't really be talking to you about family matters, but for some reason, Father trusts you. I hope I can too. Renée is my sister, but she hasn't told anyone else in the family that she is a doctor. She hasn't done more than send Father an occasional postcard in the last six years. And she has not let on to her colleagues who she is."

Wanda interrupted his waffling. "Princess Renée? I thought she was meant to be in Switzerland."

Stephen chuckled. "That's the rumour. Whenever one of her friends goes there, she gets them to send a postcard here."

"Well," Wanda said thoughtfully. "After this…she won't be able to keep it secret from your father. Does she hate the rest of your family for some reason?"

"No," Stephen hastened to assure her. "It's just…" He hesitated.

"Never mind," Wanda said quickly. "I think I understand. I have seen an old picture of her. Has she changed much?"

"These days, her hair is back to her normal black, but she keeps it shorter than mine, and she would be a bit taller than you. Otherwise, she is much the same."

"I'll find her," Wanda assured him.

"Here, take this." Stephen fiddled with something Wanda couldn't see, and then passed over a ring. "Show her that. Then she will know I sent you. Meanwhile, I will keep trying to call her."

# Chapter 5

When Truman pulled up near the door of the emergency department, Wanda removed her coat before slipping from the car. She entered the emergency waiting area through the automatic doors; looking dishevelled enough to need a doctor with her clothes damp and grimy and with the ragged tear in the sleeve with blood around it. She glanced around, seeing lots of plastic chairs and three other people waiting for attention and no sign of the medical personnel.

Trusting her instincts, Wanda went looking for Doctor de Salle. She walked into a passage that led off from one side of the waiting area and glanced into each of the open doors, and through the glass panel in those that were shut. It seemed that most of the staff were busy. Then she heard the vague ring of a mobile phone. The door of an examination room just ahead opened and a dark haired, white coated figure emerged, speaking into a mobile phone.

"Doctor de Salle?" Wanda spoke quietly when the woman had ended her call. The doctor looked up and turned around, admitting to the name. She instantly took in the state of the woman accosting her and was about to insist that the woman return to the reception area, when Wanda forestalled her.

"Doctor, I have a message from your brother, Stephen. He needs your help."

Wanda was carefully scrutinised. "Does he? Has he got his arm out of plaster yet?" the doctor asked, watching for a reaction.

Wanda grinned briefly, "His arm didn't have any plaster five minutes ago, but he told me to show you this. Can we talk?"

Renée de Salle, took the ring, examined it and gestured to a vacant examination room. There she made a show of examining Wanda's arm. "What the hell is going on? Stephen just said I had to talk to you. I gather you are Frau Davis?"

"Yes, and the arm will be fine, Princess Renée. Stephen is outside; he needs you to go to the palace. The King was badly injured in a plane crash and Prince Michael had him taken to the palace. He says, it is imperative that no one, not even the servants know that he was hurt or that he is here and not with the queen. I don't think Stephen feels the palace doctor is up to tending the King, and wants you to come."

Wanda sensed a series of conflicting emotions in the other woman. She sensed that the woman might refuse, so she summarised the King's injuries.

The doctor swore under her breath. "I'll come, more for Stephen's sake than Karl's, but I will have to get a replacement here first. Moreover, I will need supplies. Wait here."

Wanda was amazed at how quickly Renée organised everything. Her replacement found her just after she had finished putting a second box of supplies and extra equipment onto a trolley. Wanda eavesdropped without making it obvious.

"Anne, thanks for taking over. I have a family emergency and I am needed there. Karl is badly hurt and they can't bring him to a hospital."

Wanda sensed that this Anne was Renée's close friend and privy to her real identity and so refrained from asking questions.

Renée went to a small office, put on a dark brown hooded cloak, and collected her handbag and medical bag before returning to the examination room. She added her things to the trolley and asked Wanda to carry some metal stands. Rather than leave through the waiting area, she directed Wanda along a short passage that came out at the ambulance zone close to the van.

Though not marked as a royal vehicle, Renée recognised it. Truman saw them coming and lowered the platform at the back of the van for Renée to wheel the trolley in. Wanda did notice Truman's surprise when he saw who the new passenger was, but he kept silent as he took and stowed the metal stands. Renée stepped up into the rear of the van and took a seat next to her brother. Wanda went back to the front seat so brother and sister could talk privately.

Back at the palace, Wanda again carried the stands as she followed Renée and Stephen inside via the rear door. Truman insisted on pushing the trolley.

Just inside the door, Renée stopped and turned to Wanda. "Stephen says he doesn't know exactly why you are here, but that father knows of you and trusts you and he has let you have an idea of some of our private affairs. He said that you helped Karl earlier. I am going to need an assistant. Will you help me?"

"Of course, doctor," Wanda said immediately. She sensed that Renée preferred that title to the royal one. "Though I would need to clean up a lot more than I have."

Renée took the trolley from Truman, and began to wheel it down the passage. "Stephen will find you something clean to wear, and the suite has a bathroom. I have some clean gowns so you can use one of those for now. Can you bring the stands?"

Wanda nodded and followed Renée to the suite being used by Karl. Stephen must have told her which one it was. Outside the door, Renée straightened her posture and Wanda wondered what sort of reception she expected.

The outer room was empty. Renée put trolley to one side of the door and glanced around as she removed her coat. Wanda placed the stands next to the door as Renée took her stethoscope out of her medical bag and draped it around her neck.

Following Renée into the inner room, Wanda felt like an intruder, but only Doctor Mueller was with the King. To Wanda's eyes, he had not done very much in the time she had been away. She stayed back near the door and kept quiet.

Mueller challenged Renée as soon as he looked up and saw her. "Who are you?"

"I have come to assist you, Herr Mueller," Renée said formally. The doctor's belligerent expression changed when he finally recognised Renée, and she anticipated his challenge.

"I am a doctor too, Herr Mueller," Renée said quickly. "I trained in Switzerland and have worked in the emergency department at the Free Hospital for the past year." She gave a brief resume of her training and experience. "I have come to help. I have brought enough supplies to supplement what is here."

Mueller stepped back and let Renée close to his patient.

Wanda sensed his initial resentment fade into respect, and he finally admitted his gratitude at having competent help. She didn't try to understand the conversation which was full of complex medical terminology.

Mueller only noticed Wanda's presence when Renée gestured her to the door of the en-suite.

"My nurse could have assisted," Mueller protested. "We don't need a first-aider."

"Frau Davis is here, and is already aware of the situation. Father wishes as little interest in Karl's condition as possible."

Wanda didn't wait to listen further; she obeyed the tacit command to scrub up. She was determined to do so - thoroughly and quickly. First though, she removed the torn and filthy scout shirt and just left on the dark tee shirt she had worn under it. She used the soap provided to scrub arms and hands. She used her own fold up brush and comb to make herself more fit to be seen by royalty.

She emerged to find that Stephen had returned with a pair of men's trousers and a plain white shirt. He grinned apologetically, but Wanda thanked him and returned to the bathroom to change.

When she emerged again, she took note of the changes in the bedroom. It now looked more like an emergency ward at a hospital. There was a portable bio-monitor on the bedside table as well as a drip stand beside the bed with two clear liquid filled bags hanging down ready to use. A trolley had several bundles of wrapped instruments and a gown and some gloves ready for use. A portable light on a stand was positioned to shine on the patient.

Renée, already gowned, handed Wanda a gown and some gloves, and succinctly explained what she needed her assistant to do. Thanks to her paramedic training, Wanda obeyed the instruction to insert an intravenous drip into the patient with practiced ease, and at the same time assured Renée of her skill.

With Wanda helping, Renée helped Mueller manipulate Karl's dislocated elbow and shoulder back into place. While Mueller supported

Karl, Renée strapped them to keep them from moving. The ribs were bruising already, but Renée was not about to bind them. The royal doctor moved to cleaning up the facial contusions and stitching the head wound, so Renée turned her attention to most serious wound, the gash in the leg. In spite of Wanda's excellent first aid, it had begun to seep blood.

Renée untied a bundle of sterile instruments, ready to do any necessary stitching. She named each instrument to Wanda.

"I will need to examine this wound, so be ready to apply pressure with a clean pad," Renée told Wanda, as she began to loosen the pressure bandage to examine the wound underneath. "From what you described, I might have to repair some of the arteries. I will need you to pass me instruments."

Wanda nodded, and watched as Renée swabbed the bleeding wound and studied it. Then she held pressure on the wound while Renée injected a local anaesthetic into the patient's leg.

With the patient still unconscious, Renée began to work on the wound right away. Wanda followed Renée's instructions and as an observer, she was impressed by the doctor's skill. After that, treating the ankle was a minor matter.

Wanda stepped back as Renée checked the king's vital signs. He had not yet begun to regain consciousness.

When Renée stripped off her bloodstained gloves, Wanda copied her action, but something made her turn back to the patient. The old doctor had left the room, so Wanda wondered what had impinged on her awareness. Crossing back to the King, she placed a hand on his forehead. She wasn't facing Renée, so the young doctor did not see the unfocussed look on her face.

"He is regaining consciousness," Wanda announced. "And he is feeling a lot of pain."

Renée looked at Wanda in surprise. She rechecked the king's pulse as Karl groaned. "His vital signs are strong, so I will give him something for the pain."

Wanda moved to the head of the bed, which had been pulled away from the wall. She was interested in observing the reactions when King

Karl woke. Though she would have like to observe from where she could see both Renée and Karl, but it was not the right time for the king to see her and of the two, Wanda was more interested in Renée, the only member of Prince Michael's family that little was known about.

Renée stood close to her patient, filling a syringe from an ampoule. Suddenly her wrist was grabbed in a surprisingly firm grip.

"What are you doing, and why are you here?" Karl's voice was a harsh whisper.

"Karl," Renée rebuked him sharply. "Do you know what happened to you? And where you are?"

She saw him try to recall, but his grip was still strong. She enlightened him. "You have survived a plane crash, in which three others died. You had a dislocated shoulder and elbow, you still have bruised ribs, a serious leg and ankle injury, a deep gash on your left temple and probably concussion. I am giving you an injection for the pain, which, when you get over the shock of seeing me, will be considerable. And, I can assure you that I am a fully qualified doctor and Father knows I am here."

"You? Since when? How long have I been out?" Karl asked with difficulty, but he released his grip.

"Only a few hours," Renée assured him, understating the truth. If he couldn't recall details, explanations could wait. She shook her arm free of her brother's grasp and finished filling the syringe.

"Where's father?" Karl insisted on asking.

"Around, I expect," Renée said unhelpfully. She deftly injected the dose of analgesic into the drip. "You need to rest and sleep for at least a day, and for now, don't try to concentrate on anything. Without an x-ray, I can't tell if you fractured your skull. And you must put no pressure on your leg for several days."

Wanda was not deliberately prying, but she sensed the chaotic swirl of thoughts in Renée's mind, and one strong touch of amusement that Karl was at her mercy for once. But all that showed on Renée's face was a tight mask of professional neutrality.

Then Wanda touched the fringes of Karl's mind, and felt a sense of embarrassment there, and anger that his sister was in a position of superiority to him, and he should be in such a position of weakness.

"Brother, everything is in good hands. Father has been looking after the family for sixty years and is far from senile. He can look after things for one night. I am aware that I am not your choice of doctor, but I am a member of the family. Right now, it is important that no one knows your condition. That is why I came to assist Doctor Mueller."

Renée moved away from her patient, who should fall asleep very soon. She saw Wanda, and seemed almost surprised. She gestured for Wanda to leave with her.

In the outer room of the suite, Wanda saw David, Prince Michael, Stephen, Joseph and William deep in conversation. Only David was aware of the two women who looked out of the room and retreated back into the bathroom.

"Who are you exactly?" Renée asked in a very quiet voice. She did not want to be heard in the other room, and began running water to wash her hands.

"I expected you to ask that question," Wanda admitted soberly and studying the pale green tiles around the washbasin. "I don't know how much I should tell you, but there are things I think you need to know. Your father made a request of a friend of his – an American in high places. He needed skilled help to solve a problem and did not want to use anyone from this country. It involves threats made against Karl specifically and the monarchy here in general. My husband and I are go-betweens. We were discussing the situation when news came of the crashed plane. David, my husband, flew with me in a helicopter to the crash site, and he is also a trained paramedic."

Renée gave a wry chuckle. "Father – speaking to outsiders about our business. That's a first." She did not verbalise all her thoughts. Wanda clearly sensed Renée's mental comment, "I wonder if Karl's past is coming back to haunt him?" Then, the serious ramifications of that occurred to Renée, and she became very thoughtful.

It occurred to Wanda that Renée was almost an outsider in her own family and as such was probably a very good source of information on the royals. However, getting her to talk about it was probably not going to be easy.

"I was impressed by how well you helped in there. Karl was lucky you were available," Renée admitted. She took off the blood-spattered gown, and rolled it into a ball.

"I am glad we were," Wanda admitted in turn, going to wash her hands. She had already removed her gown.

"How did you know Karl was waking?" Renée asked suddenly.

Wanda sensed she was being tested, and knew she had to give a truthful answer. She didn't look at Renée as she answered. "I felt his awareness of his pain."

Wanda turned when she had dried her hands and saw Renée waiting for more of an explanation.

"I have always had a sense for knowing when other people were around - which has been handy at times. In there, I began to feel an awareness of someone else; it could only have been Karl."

Renée accepted that and went to wash her face. It almost seemed that she was reluctant to face her father and brothers. She carefully brushed her short clipped hair, drew herself up and led the way to the outer room.

"....this doctor must not be allowed to talk about this," Prince Michael was emphasising a point.

"Father!" Prince Stephen sounded shocked, as if he had sensed some unspoken threat.

Renée went to her medical bag was as if she had not heard the comment and acted as if she were checking the contents. She had the attention of all the people in the room when she turned around. In that moment, she noticed that Wanda had slipped over next to a man she did not recognise and thought to herself that Wanda had a knack for being inconspicuous. She then smiled faintly as she saw identical expressions of non-recognition on her father's face as on her two elder brothers.

"His majesty is resting comfortably. His vital signs are strong. He should be allowed to remain undisturbed until tomorrow morning. I will have to arrange for a portable x-ray unit, so if I am required before this evening, you can have me paged at the hospital."

Suppressing a grin, Renée picked up her handbag and medical bag and walked purposefully towards the door. The two elder Princes moved smoothly to intercept her. They were both six inches taller than she was and a great deal stronger.

"I am afraid we cannot allow you to leave yet, Doctor," Prince Michael spoke softly.

Renée drew herself up straight and turned around, looking regal and scornful.

"And I am afraid, Father, that if you truly want what is best for Karl, you will let me return to make arrangements at the hospital."

"Renée?" Prince Michael asked, almost in disbelief.

Renée inclined her head sideways in acknowledgement, and had a very faint smile curving her mouth. It seemed that Mueller had not mentioned who she was, possibly assuming that her father already knew.

"Perhaps then, before you leave – you might spare me a few minutes?"

It was phrased as what Renée privately called the Royal Order. "As you wish, Father," she agreed amicably.

"Herr Davis, Frau Davis," Prince Michael spoke to the American couple. "I would like a further word with you before you go. Perhaps in the interim, you would like a guided tour of the palace?"

"I would like that, thank you, Sir," David Martin, alias Herr Davis agreed.

"I wonder if I could perhaps wait here," Wanda asked. "I am feeling a little tired. Reaction, I think."

Prince Michael, the gracious host, agreed readily and Wanda sat in one of the comfortable chairs, leant back and pretended to doze. Renée and Prince Michael disappeared into the fourth room of the suite, which could be a second bedroom or an office.

Only David guessed that Wanda wanted to try to eavesdrop if she could. Renée only wondered why Frau Davis suddenly had 'a reaction'.

A 'few moments' with her father, now that she was twenty-six, began to feel like 'a few moments' with him when she was a teenager. She shut away the memory and remembered that she was a fully qualified and competent doctor, and no longer the least important member of a large family.

"How bad is Karl?" Prince Michael began on the most important topic. Renée took it as a good sign.

"He is in no danger now, Father," Renée assured him. "If he had been any longer getting attention, it might have been touch and go. Frau Davis did an excellent job of first aid. He has lost a lot of blood, but his blood pressure has stabilised and his vital signs have improved. It is important that he rest for at least twenty-four hours. I would like to x-ray him to check there is no skull fracture or internal damage that hasn't shown up. And it is important that he does not put pressure on his leg."

Prince Michael studied his youngest daughter. "How long have you been qualified?"

"Over a year, Father, and I have been working in casualty since then." Renée studied her father in return and added, "You meet a wide cross section of the population there."

"You look well enough," Prince Michael's comment was polite enough, but Renée expected a stronger, more reproachful one.

"I am quite content with my life as I have made it," Renée told him.

"It is not the life for a royal princess!"

"No? Then what is?" Renée challenged him unrepentantly. "Gallivanting around the world's pleasure places? Wasting taxpayer's money? Driving fast cars? Getting high on whatever is fashionable?"

Each question hit a nerve, though Renée didn't really enjoy watching her father flinch as he recalled the carefully hushed scandals of his family.

"I did not want to waste my life that way!" Renée continued. "My fancy schooling didn't train me for anything useful. I could have been a good ambassador – I can speak five other languages, but with ten older siblings, I wasn't needed for that. At least my language skills are useful in my work. I wasn't allowed to do the subjects I wanted at that fancy school. I had to repeat the last two years of high school before I could begin to do what I wanted to do. It has taken hard work, and I adopted mother's maiden name, de Salle. Believe me; the biggest handicap in this job would be making it known who I really was. So you needed worry, even if you do consider my actions scandalous."

"Always the rebel," Prince Michael spoke, watching Renée's face going red with controlled anger. "I was never sure what mischief you would discover next, that might bring disgrace to the family. Is that why you cut your hair so short?"

"What of it? I am not a child and I have never...done anything dishonourable."

"You are working in the slums!" her father kept his voice low, but his anger was apparent.

Renée knew exactly what to say to stop that argument. "People live there, father - subjects of the crown. Are they any less important than those who are rich?"

Renée saw her father's anger drain away. It touched on the honour of the family. He had always emphasised that 'a king's loyalty is to his subjects'. Her own reaction eased and she touched her father's hand gently. They hadn't even stopped to sit down. She gestured to the chairs with her other hand.

"I thought you were still in Switzerland," Prince Michael admitted, settling himself into a chair.

"I did my medical training there," Renée told him, choosing the chair nearest her father. "But I kept in touch with Stephen, so yes, I know about Fred, Sophie, Julian and Edward."

"You rarely let me know how you were," Prince Michael reminded her. "I thought you did not like us."

"There may be only one person I am close to, but I do care about my family. But I had had enough of being told what to do and how to behave. And now, I hear a lot from the varied people that come to the hospital. No matter how carefully things are hushed up. I listen to people, I read the papers and I watch the news. I can put things together, because I know my family and I know human nature. In Julian's case, I am godmother to one of his illegitimate daughters. I had to deal with the aftermath of that liaison. The woman and I are friends, but she does not know who I am."

"I suppose you are Stephen's source of information about the poor?"

Renée nodded. "Some of it. I do what I can but I can't solve the problem of poverty by myself. Now, Father, can you tell me who these Davis people are?"

Prince Michael decided quickly and explained all he knew about the threat against Karl. He then admitted that he had asked for help, breaking one of his own strongest tenets.

"I will listen out for anything my patients might know," Renée promised.

"It is important not to mention anything to people not in the family," Prince Michael stressed.

Renée sighed, with a hint of exasperation. "Father, at a very young age, I learnt two things or rather two very rigid rules. First that I don't talk of family things outside the family. Karl took it upon himself to impress that upon me. Secondly, I learnt that you don't need me to tell you your business or how to run the family. You never listened to me, but thank God, you do listen to Stephen. Perhaps you never saw past Karl's cruel teasing that I was born after the family ran out of good looks. You certainly never realised that after ten unsuccessful attempts, you finally produced two children with brains?" she saw her father begin to react to her slur against her elder siblings. She quickly continued. "Stephen doesn't miss much, he listens to what I learn from listening and can pick out the significant details. Now – I really do need to get back to the hospital."

Prince Michael didn't stop her leaving, but he remained seated as she went out into the main area of the suite. William and Joseph now ignored her as she went over to Wanda who seemed to be dozing.

Wanda woke, instantly alert, as she felt a light touch on her hand. Her muscles tensed as if for instant action, but only briefly until she saw who had woken her. The reaction surprised Renée, but Wanda smiled disarmingly.

"How are you?" Renée asked.

"Fine now. It is a bit of a shock having to help someone so important."

"I don't think that is the truth," Renée told her directly, and very quietly.

"No," Wanda admitted very softly. "But I was tired."

"I would like you to come with me to the hospital."

Wanda could not discern the reason for her request, but it suited her purpose to agree. She wanted to discover more about Renée, so she stood up without replying.

Renée turned back to her older brothers who were just standing relaxed against the wall near the door. They were still watching her as if she was a stranger.

"Please inform father and Herr Davis that Frau Davis is with me. I will be returning later this evening."

There was nothing of sisterly affection in her tone, but the two Princes did not stop them leaving.

Outside the suite, Renée simply said, "Keep up with me."

<h1 style="text-align:center">Chapter 6</h1>

It sounded like a command, but Wanda guessed it was an unconscious mannerism, a sign of her upbringing in the Royal house, and her training as a doctor. Her mind was occupied with some problem. Wanda didn't try to sense it. Her own mind was alert for dangers and other presences, a habit of her own. It was obvious that Prince Michael didn't want the servants knowing anything, and she had pegged the manservant Johannes as a busy body.

Renée led the way through quiet passages in the palace to yet another rear door. Also out of habit, Wanda was memorising the route and the unobtrusive security monitors. They emerged near the palace garage, and rang a bell near a small door. Truman came down from his quarters above the garage his livery seemed hastily donned. He was surprised to see them, but he covered it well, betraying no hint that such a visitation was unusual.

"I need to borrow Stephen's van," Renée told Truman, wasting no time getting down to business.

The chauffer walked across to a cupboard just inside the door and opened up a panel of keys. He reached for one and handed it to Renée.

Renée thanked him and told Wanda to, "Come on."

The relevant door was opening upwards as they arrived at the front of the garage. Renée went directly to the driver's seat of a grey vehicle.

The van was set up with only hand controls, and Wanda deduced that it had been converted for Prince Stephen to use. Renée handled the controls deftly, implying she was familiar with it. They left via a side entrance, one probably used by tradesmen and servants. It wasn't the one Truman had gone out of to get to the hospital. That was probably a private family only entrance.

Nor was it the entrance Wanda had come in by on her first arrival. That was probably a guest entrance.

After five minutes of driving, Wanda began to sense a delicate shiver of warning. Glancing around, and checking the rear-vision side mirror, she located a car that might be following them. She continued to watch it. Renée watched her furtive actions.

"Frau Davis, what is wrong?"

"Call me Wanda," she said absently. "I think we are being followed, but I cannot be sure yet. Can you drive to a drug store?"

"Yes, there is one near the hospital. That is, I gather you mean a dispensary?" Renée asked for clarification.

"Sort of," Wanda realised that it was only partly what she meant.

Renée changed their direction and headed for the shopping centre.

"I know you were going to arrange an x-ray machine, Renée, but if we are being watched that might be hard to hide," Wanda remarked. "Let me arrange the machine. When we get to the dispensary, go in and buy something, either for yourself or for a sick servant back at the palace. I will be making a phone call."

Renée felt that Wanda was being melodramatic, but a car did follow them to the shops and pull up close by. She went to the dispensary, and once inside glanced through the window and saw Wanda taking an indirect route to the nearby phone box. She went past the car that had stopped near their van. A man got out of the car and followed her. Another man emerged and began walking towards the dispensary.

Wanda dialled the American Embassy on a number that put her through to their pre-arranged contact. Before she spoke, she glanced around and spotted the man approaching. The call was answered without names, in fact, nothing was said at all, but Wanda had expected that.

"Hey! That's gratitude!" Wanda spoke clearly in German. She casually scanned her line of vision, and then just as casually turned around to increase it. The man seemed to be waiting for her to finish. She studied him without making it obvious, and then turned around as if her call had been answered.

"Hello, it's me," Wanda said again in perfect German. She had to be careful, for the man outside might be able to hear her. "Did you look at the car? Oh? He won't be back until when? 2110 – Use proper time!" The last three words were in English. The car registration had been 2110UPT. "Don't forget to check when the rego is due. I don't want to have to pay that right away."

The voice on the other end repeated the data. "You want me to check on a car registered 2110UPT, right away? I'll have it in a few minutes. Anything else?"

"I don't have to tell you to use your x-ray vision on the mechanical bits – do I? No...I have to go back to the palace soon. Two of us just came out to visit the dispensary."

Wanda waited for her contact to understand her next request.

"You want to x-ray someone back at the palace?"

"Yes, look, I have to be back there pretty soon. We borrowed Prince Stephen's van, and still have a few errands to do."

"A portable x-ray unit, deliver to Prince Stephen, urgent?"

"Uh-huh," Wanda confirmed.

"I have those details you wanted. Car is registered to a V. Toch, 123 Rhine Strasse, Capitol."

"Thanks," Wanda finished. "Talk to you later."

Wanda hung up the phone. She pranced back to the van as if she had exciting news.

She ignored the man she had seen, but when she glanced back, the man was gone and the booth was empty. If he had gone in, it had not been for very long.

Renée was in the van waiting for her. "Is it okay to go to the hospital?"

"Probably safe enough," Wanda decided, and as they drove away, the other car was not following them.

"I think we were being followed, but I am sure we are not now," Wanda said. "I know who owns the car, and I can check it further. There was a man listening to my phone call, but I think he decided we were not important. I got a good look at him. Unfortunately, he also got a good look at me. Good thing I won't be here much longer."

Renée was silent for the rest of the trip. Her driving seemed to be instinctive and her mind busy with some problem. At the hospital, she was again abrupt in her, "Follow me."

They parked in the doctor's car park this time, and the attendant had recognised her and waved her through.

Renée led the way through casualty, ignoring the waiting patients, and along several other corridors that according to the directory signs would eventually bring them to the main entrance. They only went as far as a tearoom. It was a quiet place with comfortable chairs, a small kitchenette for making hot drinks, a fridge for milk and food and a dozen armchairs.

"Wait here. I will be back in about ten minutes. Help yourself to a drink."

Wanda, still had no idea what Renée was up to, but she made herself a strong coffee and sat back to run over in her mind all the information she had. It was almost enough for Jim to have a start. And somehow, she felt that Renée was a key piece.

When Wanda had almost finished her coffee, Renée came back with an armful of medical records. The folders were tagged with various colours. "Just let me skim through these for a minute."

She glanced at each folder until she reached one in the middle of the pile. This one she read in more detail. When she finished, she sat back and looked at Wanda for a while. She had something on her mind, and Wanda sensed she wanted to bring it up but did not know where to start.

"Doctor, let us have details of the first case," Wanda said briskly, and then she grinned faintly. Renée smiled, surprised, but then knew how to start.

"The patient was Pierre Roderick. He seemed French. He came into the emergency room, unconscious and badly cut around face, hands, chest and legs. As I tended to his wounds, he became conscious. He claimed to have been jumped by knife wielding youths. I have seen many knife wounds, but these were decidedly odd. I chided him about coming off second best, but he said he was still alive, wasn't he and then he boasted that he had once bested the king in a sword duel. I acted properly sceptical, but he swore it was true. Some of what he said, I did know to be true. During the conversation, he mentioned a name, Duvall, and a club that Karl used to frequent, the Cavalier. I recall that it used to have a bad reputation. I kept the information to myself, as Karl would not like to know that I knew things about him. Anyway, the patient died a few days later."

"Did the police investigate?" Wanda asked.

Renée nodded, and wordlessly handed the file to Wanda. Wanda scan read the contents and memorised the photographs of the wounds. She had an eidetic memory. One detail caught her eye. Roderick had given his address and it was the same as where the car she checked out had been registered.

"Bingo," Wanda thought to herself.

"I will have to talk to Karl. All this may be irrelevant, but once I do, this becomes family business and I am so used to not discussing that with strangers."

"I think we might be onto something here," Wanda said softly. "I will have the police records checked later, but can I be present when you talk to Karl? He will not be aware of me."

"Yes. But why?"

"To study his body language," Wanda told her.

"What will you be doing with the information you are finding out?"

Renée wanted honesty, Wanda sensed. "Others will be coming after David and myself – with no link to us. They will need to know all they can to find out the source of the threats and neutralise them."

"When do you have to leave?"

"We intended to be gone tomorrow, but we still have things to find out," Wanda admitted. "At the latest, we will leave early the following day. It will be dangerous for us to stay longer."

"I want to meet the person who will take over from you."

Wanda was thoughtful. "Why?"

"I want to help."

"You have helped a lot already."

"I am willing to do more. This may sound strange, but I don't care what happens to Karl, some ways, but I would do a lot to preserve the good name of the family."

"I will tell my superior, Renée, but he must decide and he'll approach you if he chooses."

"That will do," Renée agreed. "I wish you didn't have to go."

"I must. I have been spotted as it is," Wanda reminded her. "Have you finished here? The x-ray unit will be going to the palace tonight. I'd like to get back."

"I just have to return these. Most were only for camouflage. The extra supplies won't take long to collect."

They returned to the car park by a different route, sharing the bundles of extra supplies. It was getting dark now, and they splashed through several large puddles left after the rain. They returned to the palace without incident.

When they were back the suite, coming in again via the back entrance, only Prince Michael and Prince William were in the outer room. Renée was informed that an x-ray machine had arrived. David, Stephen and Joseph had gone to bring it. She glanced at Wanda in surprise. There had scarcely been time. Wanda shrugged faintly.

Wanda turned to Prince Michael and bowed briefly. "Sir, would I be allowed to use the phone for an international call?"

Prince Michael nodded curtly and showed her to the phone in the suite. He told her how to dial out, and then politely retreated.

When her call was answered, she spoke softly. "Jim? Wanda. Rendezvous tomorrow. Important development. Activate."

She was going to mention the people who were showing interest in her, but changed her mind. It wasn't a strong enough concern to warrant instant evacuation, and she and David had a few more pieces of information to obtain. Even so, if they had to leave, they had enough data for Jim to start with. Wanda hung up after Jim's brief acknowledgement.

Renée had gone in to check on Karl, she reappeared when she heard the sound of heavy equipment being moved. David and Prince Joseph were manhandling the bulky equipment, which was on a wheeled trolley. She directed it into the room where Karl lay awake.

When it was placed to her satisfaction, she shooed the men out, but let Wanda sidle into the room, to keep out of sight near the door.

Renée handled the equipment proficiently, and soon obtained scans of all parts of her brother that had been injured. He had been awake, but not enough to object to the procedure.

Collecting the undeveloped x-rays, she then pushed the unit back near the door, providing Wanda with cover to hide behind. Renée returned to Karl's bedside, checked the drip, and asked. "How are you feeling?"

He should still be feeling the effects of the painkillers and hopefully not awake enough to rant at her.

"You've done a good job, sister," Karl admitted. "But I will want my own doctor from now."

"You should talk to father before you bring in an outsider," Renée told him. "There are things going on that he hasn't discussed with me, but he has stressed that he wants no one to know of your injuries or that you returned here. I am willing to treat you but it certainly isn't from filial love!"

"I am the monarch now – that will be my choice!"

"Argue with Father – I don't care."

Karl stared at Renée, but she didn't look away. She meant what she said.

"How did I get here then?" Karl demanded. "Someone knows I am here."

"True," Renée agreed. "You actually owe your life to a couple of American scout leaders. I believe they were talking to Father when he got word of the crash. If they had not flown in and got you, I wouldn't be having you try to rile me. Only a helicopter could have got in. The woman was, fortunately for you, a trained paramedic."

"My case!" Karl suddenly remembered. "How did you get that off me?"

"I didn't, but I believe father has it."

"You talk about bringing in outsiders..." Karl began to accuse her.

"Father invited them, brother, not I," Renée calmly informed him. "And before you start to talk again, I have a question for you, and a story to tell."

Karl waited for her to go on.

"Where did you get the scar on your side?"

"None of your damn business," Karl said, trying to glare at her, but his voice seemed tired.

Renée went on, "Was it in a sword duel with Pierre Roderick?"

"How did you know? That was twenty years ago, when you were an infant! And Roderick is dead!"

Karl reached out with his good arm and gripped Renée's wrist, in an attempt to dominate her. "Pierre died twenty years ago, and I never told anyone about that duel."

"Karl, I treated Roderick a year ago for knife wounds," Renée went on to tell her brother what she had earlier told Wanda, and she could see the fear in his eyes.

Wanda, quiet by the door, with her eyes unfocussed in concentration, sensed the deep-rooted fear in this man who had never been afraid before.

"So, Pierre has been alive all these years and Duvall is in the picture again?" Karl mused aloud.

"I didn't say Roderick was alive," Renée interrupted. "His wounds were infected and he did not respond to antibiotics. He ...died. He was an evil man, but I dislike losing patients."

The last statement came out almost emotionlessly, but Wanda sensed more – some kind of hidden shame. The man had died – fortuitously.

"If I had known he was still alive," Karl said softly. "His life would have been forfeit. I wish I had known ... You should have told me!"

Renée shook her hand free. "You were well out of his sordid duel, and he's dead!"

She began to check his bandages.

"You should have told me!" Karl insisted.

Only Wanda sensed her reasons for keeping it to herself. Her brother would have learnt of the career she had worked hard to build – and made sure she gave it up.

"For all I knew, it was bravado. He was delirious at the time," Renée told her brother, but it wasn't the truth. "Besides, the last time I tried to give you advice, you packed me off to Switzerland."

Wanda sensed the pain in that memory, but Karl did not.

Renée turned back to the efficient doctor. "I have made you talk too much. I will be staying nearby tonight. I will check you every so often. Try to sleep. You will be safe enough. Father, William, Joseph and Stephen are taking turns hovering in the outer room."

"Who else have you told about Roderick?" Karl demanded.

"The police did not hear of his delirious ravings, and I have said nothing of it until today. I mentioned it to you now, because I thought you ought to know. Now, go to sleep or I will give you something stronger to knock you out."

Renée turned and walked to the door. Wanda opened it and helped her push the x-ray machine out.

David caught Wanda's eye, he held a neatly washed, ironed and mended scout uniform. His own looked freshly washed and ironed too. She understood his silent signal. They had to go.

Wanda took advantage of the questions being asked of Renée to slip into the bathroom to change. When she emerged, Stephen and David were waiting near the door. They all moved out of the room, with Stephen carrying the undeveloped x-rays on his lap. He guided them through the unlit and deserted kitchen and then through a storeroom to a delivery entrance.

The van that was parked there was not one of the palace trucks, but the one that had delivered the x-ray machine. David had already confirmed that the driver was their contact at the US Embassy.

"Prince Stephen, please accept our thanks for your help, and pass on our thanks to your father. Someone will be in touch within the next few days."

"How will we know who he is?" Stephen asked.

"Your father will know," Wanda assured him softly. "Oh, and would you tell Renée, that after this is concluded, I will be in touch."

Stephen nodded; the movement was just visible in the darkness. When David and Wanda had climbed into the back of the truck, he passed up the x-rays and helped push the rear doors shut. He turned and wheeled himself back into the palace.

The van started up as David slid aside a sliding panel and spoke to the driver. He double-checked the man's identity with a few casual sounding remarks that contained code words and required specific answers. When David was sure the driver was the same man, he opened the sliding panel further and passed through the x-ray plates and a large envelope containing information given to him by Prince Stephen. The driver placed them immediately into a safe under the front passenger seat and locked them in.

He promised to get the x-rays developed and delivered to the doctor at the hospital and the envelope to Jim.

"We'll be off then," David told the man. "Drive slowly to the gate and stop before you get there for a moment."

In the brief time that the van was in motion, Wanda and David made some subtle changes to their scout uniform. By turning both the slacks and shirt inside out, they had outfits that would not reflect light. The scout cap, when pulled out of shape and inverted, became a black beret. Wanda pulled her hair up under it.

David tapped on the dividing panel, and the van slowed to a crawl. Wanda nodded to David, and alert for possible watchers, slipped out of the truck and into the dark of the palace gardens. It was now fully dark.

They moved like wraiths, using the details of the palace security David had learnt from Prince Michael to leave the grounds unobserved. They went over the fence in a narrow security blind spot. Before they had dropped to the ground, they observed the van driving off down the road, with the car that had observed Stephen's van earlier, following it. The driver of the embassy van was warned to be alert for followers. He would take the needed steps to confuse them.

Wanda followed her husband the two blocks to where their hire car was parked. David had left it two streets away from the palace on his return. They went back to their central city hotel unobserved.

# Chapter 7

Their small second floor hotel room contained only the most basic of amenities. The bed was the one thing they were most interested in, though both needed a shower and a drink. As they were undressing, Wanda related to David everything she had learnt. As they prepared the bed and shared a warm shower in the small en-suite, he told her of the information Prince Michael had given him when she was away.

"We need to check out that address," David said, but he suddenly yawned.

"Tomorrow," Wanda decided. "I'm running on fumes and I am about to crash. I gave Jim the go ahead, but I need to try to ring him on our secure phone."

She tried unsuccessfully as David made hot chocolate for them from the guest supplies near the kettle. They should have been hungry, but both were too tired to eat.

"It has been a while since I had to do it, but do you realise that counting the 13 hour flight from LA, we've been on the go for over 24 hours," David remarked. "No wonder I'm bushed."

"Now you add it up, Dav, it makes sense. I can't reach Jim; he must be on the way."

Wanda crawled into the bed and as soon as David joined her she cuddled up to him under the thick quilt.

After eight hours of solid sleep in their room, and a huge breakfast down in the hotel's private dining room, Wanda and David were ready to continue their mission. They tried again to reach their director, Jim Phillips, but his phone was still off.

There were some things that needed checking, like the police records on the death of Roderick, but that could be done through Interpol by someone else. Then, the Cavalier Club, or whatever it was known as now, needed to be researched. The Capitol police had not been able to locate such a place and Prince Michael felt that the place no longer existed. David and Wanda agreed it had probably gone 'underground', or existed now as an ultra-private club; with its location only known to members.

Before they departed Weisboden, David and Wanda intended to check the address Wanda had found for Roderick and for the car that had been interested in them. They could not infiltrate the place until that night, but the preliminary scouting could be done during the day.

They prepared carefully for this foray, particularly as Wanda had already been noticed. In a manner reminiscent of her nefarious past, Wanda proceeded to make up her face with great care. No one, not even the man who had studied her while she had used the phone, should be able to recognise her. David helped to darken her hair to black and braid it to the back of her head. She then worked similar 'magic' on him. They both added eye lenses to change their eye colour from blue to brown.

On leaving the hotel, they first they drove to the centre of the main business district of Weisboden's capital and found an internet cafe - a tiny shop front in the middle of classy glass fronted boutiques and gift shops. Here they acted like tourists, looking up cafes, nightclubs and theatres, and bringing up a street plan of the capital.

They soon located the street they wanted, and after studying the map, were sure they would not lose their way.

Since they wanted to blend into the local scene, they were dressed as a young couple on holiday and carried bags from some of Weisboden's most expensive shops.

David was in jeans and casual long sleeve polo and Wanda was in a stylish skirt and jacket, both wore comfortable walking shoes. When they spoke, it was in French since they deliberately wanted to seem anything but American.

On returning to their car, David drove past the address they wanted and then around the block. The building was a magnificent four-storey edifice, dating from the time when money really got value. Once there had been buildings around it, but now it stood in an extensive park. David completed the circuit and drove two streets away before parking.

"Well?" David quizzed his wife. "What do you think?"

"Hmm? If it isn't the most impressive building after the palace, it is not for lack of trying," Wanda commented. "I reckon, that's it!"

David nodded. "You noticed all the security lights, and the lack of bushes?"

"Of course. But the green area around it is noted as a public park, so it could be for public safety as well as making it hard for people to sneak up unseen," Wanda commented. "Did you bring your little detector thing, to check if they have detectors through the park?"

David merely grinned at her. "Leave the security to me; you look for the way in."

After seeming to wander idly for half an hour, an anonymous couple amongst many other pairs and groups, they sat for a time on a bench feeding pigeons, with the remains of a bread roll purchased from a street vendor.

Wanda said, "I think this side, don't you?"

"I'll follow your lead," David agreed. "I have the locations of the sensors. I'll plot them when we get back. Ready to go?"


While they were enjoying a leisurely lunch in the hotel restaurant, Wanda's phone beeped the message sound. She gave David a glance, and they both decided to finish their meal and leave.

Once back in their room, David checked the room for listening or surveillance devices before Wanda replied to the message.

"Jim," she greeted, and she heard in response, "What have you got?"

She wasted no words, giving their director all the essential details of what she or David had learnt, and what she had sensed. Then she told him of the matters that needed investigating that were better done by other people. Their actions in rescuing the king were both commended and censured. He hoped no one in particular had noticed them. Wanda did not mention the man near the phone.

"That address, have you checked it out?" Jim got directly to the point.

"No, we were running on fumes by then – we had to crash. We have scouted the outside and will infiltrate tonight and report in the morning."

They didn't need to be reminded to leave as soon as they had reported.

During the afternoon, they used David's computer to research aspects of life in Weisboden, as well as hacking into supposedly secure databases. They found mention of the Cavalier club, but nothing recent. It had supposedly burnt down fifteen years ago. Then they went to Google Earth and found a picture of their target, and zoomed in to see what they could learn from the aerial view. Coming on evening, they prepared for their night's work.

They had not removed their earlier makeup. However, they now dressed in close fitting, stretchy black body suits, with a loose fitting black shirt over the top and a glittering vest held close by a wide matt black belt. The shirt hid the small but highly efficient tool kit they each carried. As they left the hotel, they looked to be headed for a nightclub, and had light coloured coats over their arms as they went out to their car. Before their morning excursion, the hotel had recommended several places to them. And for the first part of the evening, they would enjoy themselves. The glittery vests would be removed later when they were away from the nightclub again and the coats would go on once they were ready to slip away to their target, and would be removed once they were ready to go to work.

Therefore, when it was nearly midnight, a young couple strolled through the park, looking to be interested in only each other. In time, they came to the service road that led to the building, and strolled along that. They went out of range of the security cameras and removed their coats, rolled them up into a very small bundle and hid them in an unobtrusive place in a group of young trees. They each put on an almost invisible wi-fi headset, so they could communicate. Even so, they kept speaking, even sub-vocalising, to a minimum.

David knew where the cameras were and where there were gaps in the coverage. He led the way to the seven-foot high brick wall that protected the privacy of the house from the service road at the rear. Wanda edged along to the west. The other way led to where the drive came from the main street to a car park at the rear. That side of the house only had a chain link fence and was more open. The side Wanda wanted was where the brick fence continued around to meet the house behind the large six-car garage. She knew there was an enclosed yard at the rear of the garage and for a distance of half way along the rear wall.

Wanda had indicated to David that she would climb the brick wall at the point where it met the garage. The camera that overlooked the yard had a blind spot there. She scaled the wall like a spider, paused at the top to sense what was below, and then reached the ground using a stack of empty kegs as a ladder. David followed quickly, and immediately scanned the area with his detector device to check for further security. He shook his head, saying there was only the one camera.

Several windows overlooked the area, but only one was lighted. Light also came from a door partway along the yard.

Wanda was aiming for the window below the lighted one - which betrayed its occupancy only by a faint glow around the frame. David let her begin her climb, and stealthily scouted the yard. He found the ground level lighted room was a scullery. When he returned, Wanda was already perched in the first floor window frame, forcing the window.

He knew she would have first run her fingers around the frame, to sense if there were live alarms on it. He still found this skill hard to believe, but whenever he had checked, he had never found her to be wrong. Moments later, she had the window open a fraction and after listening for sounds from within, opened it just far enough for her to slip in.

David waited while his wife checked the room to ensure it was empty and then she was back at the window, letting down a strong thin line to help him climb up.


"This must be the master bedroom," Wanda said in a barely audible whisper, as she silently closed the window again. David activated an electronic jammer that would freeze the picture on any security camera.

Without further word, they worked as a team to search the room. They examined the room thoroughly, using it as a guide to the rooms on that level. The narrow beam torches revealed it was a well-appointed bedroom with its own en-suite and a well-stocked mini fridge. The furniture was all of high quality, and the wardrobe and drawers contained patently expensive clothing.

When they were done, Wanda moved to the door, opened it a fraction, listened, opened it further to glance out, and went into the open area beyond. To their left was a staircase for going down. Opposite was an open area in front of two lifts and a second staircase going up. Ignoring those directions, Wanda went left along a short passage that led along the back of the house.

Two doors were ajar in the left wall. These were entrances to small suites. In each case, the cupboard and drawers had no personal belongings in them so the rooms were currently unoccupied. Neither room would shame a high-class hotel.

The first had a window overlooking the yard where they had entered, and the second room overlooked the yard at the back that had two delivery trucks parked in it. David used his small electronic detector and found no alarms or cameras in either room. Both Wanda and David marked these rooms as possible escape routes.

A longer passage led from there, past the stairs going up, along the length of the house. Two more doors led off to the left, both were closed and Wanda whispered, "Occupied." There was subdued lighting along this passage, and it allowed them to see what was ahead.

David followed the longer passage to three sitting rooms, whilst Wanda followed a side passage off to the right and found another unoccupied bedroom that had clothes hanging in the cupboard, but an air of disuse.

As they moved, David activated the mini jammer, to freeze the screen picture of any camera within its range. Therefore, when they had climbed up to the next level, the cameras on the lower floor began working again.

A tingling sensation ran up Wanda's spine.

"This won't be easy," Wanda said in a quiet whisper. David nodded, understanding the warning to be careful.

The third level had a different layout. The stairs went up and wound around to near the lift well. Opposite were two powder rooms – male and female. Wanda glanced in to check that they were unoccupied. The door opposite the lifts, and above the master bedroom on the floor below, was where they had seen the lighted window. That the room was still lit was betrayed by the thin line of light under the door. Wanda gestured for them to go right, past the stair rail. Here she found a door, on her left and immediately set to work, whilst David watched.

Wanda ran her fingers around the frame of the first door.

"Wired," she whispered to David, even though there were no visible signs.

David used his detector and copied her action. "No current," he said after interpreting the display.

Wanda did not wait any longer to enter. She had the door unlocked and opened it slowly.

"Ok," she breathed to David as she went in. He entered and closed the door after them.

The room was an office but it was dusty, as if it had not been used for some time. On the desk were diary, appointments book and other good quality desk paraphernalia. The paper in the file, and the books were calligraphed with the name Pierre Roderick. Wanda gave a slight grin of triumph, the sobered quickly. Carefully, so as not to disturb the dust, she examined the books. The last diary entry was nearly a year old. She took out a mini camera and photographed the books, some of the pages and the notepaper. Then she took several pictures about the room, and of the furniture. She checked for a safe, but did not find one. There was little else to hold their attention.

Returning to the door, David was about to open it when Wanda gripped his arm. He unlocked it and moved the door no more than a quarter of an inch. From the passage came the voices of men speaking French. David put his eye to the crack, and counted as the men walked past. "Ten," he muttered. "Going to the left."

He opened the door a bit further, and edged his head out intending to get a glimpse in that direction. Wanda suddenly pulled him back, and David eased the door nearly shut. He could still glimpse the passage, and a single man passed by. He edged the door open again and saw where that man went. The watchers heard a door shut.

"Hurry," Wanda urged.

They left and locked the disused office, and ran lightly to the room which had been lighted. The door was not locked, and David quickly checked for alarms. None.

This was another office, with a similar layout to the one they had left. The main difference was that this one had a display wall, and on it was a collection of swords. Wanda photographed it in detail, and then moved to the desk and photographed it and some of the diary pages. David quickly found two safes and checked them for alarms, but they did not try to open either. This room was being used by Claude Duvall, and Wanda was getting a strong sense of needing to leave. They left Duvall's office and ran quietly to the door beyond Roderick's empty office. This door was opposite the stairway.

This gave them less information than the first. The name on the stationary was, Michael DuPont. There was no dust on the desk, and nothing of a personal nature anywhere in the room.

They did not linger. David gestured that he was going to scout the fourth floor. Wanda had already told him she would do the lower floors. She gave David the mini camera before he left the office.

Wanda knew she had the more dangerous job, but her instinct for illegal skulking was much more sensitive than David's. Downstairs, she was more likely to encounter people. And as if the thought had caused it, she heard voices just as she was about to descend from the second floor. A flare of alarm surged through her and she retraced her steps but did not go back up the stairs. In an instant decision, she did not go to the rooms overlooking the yard. They now had lights on. Instead, she went to the first room along the longer passage. The door was slightly ajar, and the light was still on; it was one that had been occupied earlier. Her senses said it was unoccupied now and the first part of the room was indeed empty. There was not even a place to duck out of sight. One door led further in to a bathroom and the other to a bedroom. Wanda, hearing the voices getting closer, went into the bedroom and was relieved that she could fit under the bed. She had a quick glimpse of the mess in the room, the unmade bed, the empty bottles of wine and the glasses, and noticed a musky smell, before she pulled the valance back into position, to hide her. From there, she saw the owners of the voices, and guessed they were servants who had come to repair the room.

Another voice began to give orders to the servants, and then a whiff of expensive perfume wafted under the bed. She glanced under the valance and saw the hem of a very expensive gold silk gown. This twitched out of view and moments later, Wanda heard the sound of water running in the en-suite and then an expletive spoken in French.

"I have lost one of my earrings. I will pay you well if you find it."

"Yes, Madame," a less aristocratic voice answered.

The nearby sounds seemed to be of the bed being stripped, and Wanda hoped her curtain-valance would not be touched. The servants did not speak until after the sound of the outer door closing. Then one of them exploded in a torrent of German. Wanda mentally translated it.

"Vixen! How she gloats over us having to clean up her messes. Ten dollars for finding what she is always losing. It is nothing when she earns a hundred times that much for this night's work. I should keep it if I find it, because someone will give her a new one tomorrow."

The second spoke in a calmer tone, until she went into the en-suite and exclaimed in disgust. The first went to join her. Wanda used the distraction to crawl out from under the bed, collecting the lost earring, which had been a mere six inches from her nose. She dropped it where the servant would soon see it, and left the room, to return to the stairwell.

Wanda crept down the stairs, and stopped just before the stairs turned. She pressed herself next to the wall and glanced around the corner. The stairs ended in the well-lighted entrance hall, and although she could not see anyone, her senses told her there were people nearby.

Therefore, instead of following the stairs down, she climbed over the rail and dropped down into an area of subdued light, quickly sprinting to use the lift shaft as cover. From there, she glanced across the lighted foyer. She was in time to see a well-dressed couple ascending the stairs from a lower level. They were met by a uniformed man, who had emerged from a small room, and escorted to the front door.

Wanda turned to go in another direction. Where she had dropped had three doors – two were powder rooms and the third was marked private. She guessed fleetingly that it might lead to the garage. She kept moving towards floor to ceiling glass doors. The area beyond was dark, except for subdued security lighting, and in this she could see tables with upended chairs.

Some light came from a room to one side, and this she guessed to be the scullery that David had seen from the yard and another possible way out if she needed one.

She slipped unnoticed into the dark restaurant through the wood framed glass doors, and like a mouse, skirted the edge of the room. She glanced in the lighted scullery and saw two men obliviously scouring pots and plates. The next opening was a deserted kitchen. Around the corner were glass windows and doors leading to an enclosed terrace, but these were now covered by vertical blinds. Wanda edged past these to where the rear wall began again. On her right was the bar, and a passageway led further on.

She was hearing odd whirring and tinkling noises, and her guess was proved right as she edged into a room with gaming machines. She drew back when she heard a soft curse in French and the sound of someone thumping one of the machines.

Her danger sense rose a notch and she backed away and ducked down under the wooden bar servery. She sensed more than saw, two guards walk past the other end of the bar and around to where she had been a minute before.

She listened as someone spoke in French. "Mr Daintree, this area is closed. If you wish to gamble, the casino is still open downstairs."

The reply was garbled, but by the change in tone of the guard's voice, it had not been polite.

"Sir, I think you should go home now. Do you have a car here or should I obtain a taxi?"

Another garbled comment led to the guards escorting the slightly reeling figure back past the bar. She assumed he was to be taken outside and put that man out of her mind. The guards though were her immediate concern.

She wanted a glimpse of the casino, but at the moment it would be a very bad move. She considered where she might find another way down. The lift was her first thought, but that was too dangerous. Then she considered all she had seen or subconsciously noted. There were extra doors at the rear of the building that she had not accounted for. One was on the corner of the house where that gaming parlour was, and she should check there was not an emergency exit behind one of the machines. If there wasn't, it might be an access to the casino. Yet to get to that she would need to get out into the car park.

Then she considered where she was and wondered how they would get supplies to the bar. She couldn't see deliverers wheeling a trolley through the scullery and over the expensive plush carpet.

Did they wheel them in through the entrance hall? Instinct told her no. This looked to be a high-class restaurant, and so the service would need to be unobtrusive. She let her mind consider things she had noticed years back when she was frequenting nightclubs and such in preparation for her illegal jaunts. Then, she risked using her torch, keeping it well shielded, and finally found what she was expecting - a crack suggesting a hidden door. Turning off the torch, she felt the crack and followed it to where the opening mechanism was – behind an empty but not deodorised dregs bucket. The door was the width of a normal door but only half the height. It was not locked, only secured by a sliding bolt on the bar side. Wanda slit the bolt aside and silently opened the door.

She saw only darkness beyond it, and sensed no one was there. She crawled through and pushed the door shut after checking the opening mechanism on the other side. Then she felt around her and encountered a trolley parked next to the door – confirming her guess that supplies came in there. So these cellar tunnels should lead outside, probably to a rear delivery area – like where the kegs were stacked.

Wanda moved carefully, keeping one hand on the wall, and found herself descending via a ramp. When the floor became level, she went two more paces and found a wall. She felt to her right and found a door handle. Before she tried to open it, she listened, but could hear nothing. She turned the handle and pushed a fraction and began to hear sound, and to see a thin trace of light. This door led to the casino, but she doubted it would be obvious from the other side. If it was, she would expect it to be locked.

The darkness of the passage was suddenly removed as overhead lights came on. Wanda ducked back to the ramp, only now aware of a door next to her. She quickly picked the lock and went into the darkness. Before the door closed, she heard the sound of trolley wheels and voices – both were getting louder. She risked a flash of her torch. She was in a storage room and there were plenty of boxes piled in discrete heaps for her to hide behind. Moments later, the storeroom lights went on. She heard boxes being moved and crates of bottles being stacked. Another door was opened, at the far end of the room. The casino sounds were clear now. Someone spoke sharply to the deliverymen about the rough handling of the wine. They grunted and went off. The voice muttered curses, before dousing the light and locking the doors.

Wanda moved from her hiding place and went out the door she had entered. She heard the trolley noise moving away and she began to follow the sounds to the exit. Into the otherwise silence, she suddenly heard a sharp 'thunk'. She stopped as her warning sense kicked her mind into high alert.

Some distance away she heard a loud curse, and realised that all doors must have just been locked by some remote means. As if confirming that an alert had just been issued, the passage lights came on again, still subdued, but bright enough to reveal her. Wanda retreated quickly to the ramp leading up to the ground floor bar.

She was now above the door that had opened from the casino, and it was open again.

"He cannot have gone too far," a French speaking voice stated. It had an odd accent. "Search everywhere!"

Wanda heard the tramp of trotting feet and drew herself against the wall.

"Who, Sir?" that voice was the man who had spoken to the deliverymen.

"Daintree," the first snapped. "The guards said he came down here. Did you see him?"

"No, Sir. Not this evening."

Wanda sensed anger, but did not try to probe the man's thoughts. He went on to ask if the back door had been opened, and was told a delivery had just come in. The storeroom was opened again and searched. Then Wanda froze.

"If he knew the storage area was here, he might know the ramp up to the ground floor."

"Check it!" the odd accent voice ordered.

Wanda felt for the door handle and tried to open it. It didn't budge. She had nowhere to go, unless she ran for the exit the trolley had come from. That was not an option she preferred. If she had to, she could take on one man...

Her thoughts were diverted by a commotion. The noise came from the way she had thought to run. Instinct made her edge back to glance down that passage. A dark clad man was being dragged, resisting every step, back from the way out. For one terrible moment, she thought it was David, but as they neared, she saw the prisoner was too stocky. He was cursing in gutter French and exuding terror. Wanda drew back, thinking they were going to come past her position, but they turned off at a side passage that went, Wanda guessed, down the other side of the storeroom.

She glanced out again and saw the long passage was clear, but something held her back. Her danger sense had not diminished. That only left the way up to the bar on the ground floor – and that was doubly locked. Still, it would not stop her; just take longer to get through. She returned there and set to work. The dim light was a help. She took out a slender file and began to work it around the doorframe to locate the dead bolt. Two obstructions top and bottom. The question in her mind was whether every door lock in the building had been electronically locked and would they reverse the locking now the man they sought had been caught. She could not wait to see. She had the feeling of time getting short. She took a tiny tube of oil, squirted it onto the bolt, and began to work with the thin file, to cut the bolt. All the while that she worked, she was thinking, "Don't let anyone look here."

She jumped when she heard the second "thunk" but wasted no time opening the half height door.

At that moment, she sensed the increase in light and soft voices. She edged back to peer around the edge of the short passage, and looked down towards the long passage. She saw, to her amazement, men walking past, all dressed in cavalier costume, complete with wigs and swords. They had to be coming from the casino. She had definitely seen enough. She wasted no more time, returning up to the ground floor. The restaurant was still dimly lit, and the voices she heard were coming from the entrance foyer, where her glance showed her that people were leaving.

"David!" she called mentally. "Coming out now! Ground floor. Scullery." She sensed his reception of her thought.

Wanda crouched and ran between the tables to the scullery door; it was now dark and deserted. The inner door was not locked. She ran the length of the washing room to the outer door leading to the yard. It was deadlocked, but that was no problem. She used her tools and heard it click open very quickly – in spite of working in the dark. She had just put her hand on the handle when she felt it begin to turn.

Wanda's danger sense kicked into high alert again, as David sent a warning thought to her. She pulled herself close to the wall as the door was pulled open. Wanda smelt the night air.

A big man entered cautiously. Had he realised the door was not locked? He had. He was sub-vocalising into a microphone and had a gun in one hand. Wanda didn't wait for him to see her, only for him to start taking one more step inside, and then she dived for the gap behind him. Her sudden move startled him and her sideways kick unbalanced him. She ran, nimbly scaling the stacked kegs and reaching the fence before the man was back on his feet.

She was dropping over the far side, as the man bellowed an alarm and ran for the gate. She was a fast runner; that was one of her assets. She sent a warning to David, and knew he had seen her escape and that she was being pursued. His mind told her the man was fast, and had the advantage of longer legs.

Wanda's mind went into high gear. She wasted no time looking behind her, but scanned the way ahead for a means to trip or slow or lose her pursuer. She saw several couples walking ahead of her and headed for them. The man behind her called something, and before Wanda realised his meaning, the man of the nearest couple spun around and came at her. She had to change direction abruptly and as a result, tripped over the edge of the path. Instinctively, she twisted and turned the uncontrolled fall into a springing up movement. Still, it had cut down her lead and now she had two men after her.

The third came at her unexpectedly, grabbing her as she ran past a tree. She fought free, but the other men were on her, catching her from behind.

The fist that came at her was so quick, so unexpected that she sensed it only at the last second and barely had time to move her head in front of the blow.

# Chapter 8

David went up to the uppermost level. It was dark and deserted. He soon realised it was a gymnasium, equipped with the very best of fitness equipment. Except for two offices at one end, the gym and changing rooms occupied the entire floor. There were no changing rooms for women indicating that the gym was strictly male only.

The only place where there might be useful information was the office and this is where David went. He found the locked filing cupboard and made short work of opening it and beginning to flick through files and memorising names. He only pulled one out and that was marked Duvall. He photographed some of the pages in case they might be useful, and refiled it. He relocked the file cupboard and decided it was time to return to the second floor bedroom and wait for Wanda.

Once he was there, he had time to worry. He knew that she had been doing illegal sneak and peak raids long before he had met her, and she had never been caught. But now, she was his wife and the mother of his son, and he worried. He seemed to have been waiting for a long time, even with needing to hide while maids dusted the room. His nerves were at a high pitch. He had the window open a fraction of an inch, ready for their getaway. To pass the time, he was watching the outside, whilst listening for the slightest of warning noises from within the house. He felt the sudden sense of Wanda's fear, and then the sensation eased to determination. After another seemingly endless wait, he heard in his mind, "Coming out now! Ground floor. Scullery."

David began to open the window, but he caught movement below him. A man was at the scullery door. He felt Wanda's knowing of that fact and held his breath. Then he saw her dart out of the door and scramble up the kegs and drop over the wall, he breathed easier and then saw the man going after her, through the gate.

From his vantage, he saw Wanda racing off through the park, felt her determination of purpose to get away from the man. He began to make his own way out via the window when he felt her spurt of terror. He had to stop as images came into his mind, one after the other. Then, "David, go! Report! Get help! Basement!"

She wasn't dead, or unconscious, but he knew she was thoroughly caught. He wanted to go and free her, but she was right. One of them had to get out and report. He retreated into the bedroom and watched the men carrying her inside, he thought through the kitchen entrance. He decided to wait before he climbing out the window and it proved wise. He saw more men emerge from the same door; this time carrying what looked like a body which they put into one of the vans. His heart lurched, but it wasn't Wanda. He would know if she were dead. He dared not leave yet, but his mind was alert for trouble. Would they be looking for other intruders?

Yes, they were, David soon realised. From the window, he saw men and their escorts seeming to be wandering aimlessly through the park. All might be thought to be going home from their club, but after a time, the men all began to drift back. He waited until he had seen no movement for half an hour before working his way out of the house, down to the yard, up the stack of kegs and over the wall. He blended unchallenged into the night, and went directly to his car and drove to the American Embassy.

His phone call woke their contact and the man met him at the gate and led him inside and into a vacant office. There David made out his report for Jim Phillips, added the film from the camera, and the fact that Wanda had been caught. The contact promised safe delivery of the report to Jim, and David left, unobtrusively, to return to the hotel.

In the early hours of the morning, as Renée dozed in a chair where she could monitor her brother's condition, her pager beeped. She grabbed it and silenced it, even as she read the message. She was relieved that Karl had not woken. She walked out of the bedroom to the outer room of the suite and used the phone.

Stephen smiled at her as she emerged and shrugged his right shoulder in the direction of William and Joseph who were snoring faintly in two armchairs. The former woke up when she began to dial.

When the hospital answered, she asked to be put through to the emergency clinic, and then for her friend.

"What is it, Anne?" she asked, and then seemed to be listening for a long time. "I will come now."

"Where are you going?" William demanded in a fierce whisper. He looked far from indolent now, even if he was still in the chair.

"Hospital," Renée said tersely.

"You are needed here!" William stated.

"Karl is out of danger, and won't wake for a while yet. Herr Mueller is due to relieve me soon anyway. I will come back as soon as I can," Renée's voice was equally firm.

"Since you are awake, Will," Stephen prevented further comment, "I will drive her to the hospital."

William glared at his youngest sister, but made no move to stop her.

"My pager number is by the phone," Renée announced as she gathered her coat and bag.

They disturbed Truman again for the keys to Stephen's van and drove out into the early morning hours. Renée's mind was full of her colleague's cryptic message, and so she did not notice the car following them at a distance back. Stephen did, however, but said nothing. It was likely to be some paparazzi. He guessed they had decided something was in the wind.

At the hospital, Stephen decided to wait for her, even though she said she could drive her own car back. He dropped her off at the entrance to the emergency clinic and told her where he would be parked.

Renée went directly to the duty desk, where Anne Stanley was sitting. For once, the area was quiet, though there were some people sitting in the chairs. She greeted Anne casually, noticed the look in her friend's eyes. It warned her not to ask questions. Instead, Anne gave Renée a gesture indicating for her to follow, and walked down a passage past half a dozen doors to the farthest examination room. There was a police officer sitting on a chair outside the door, but Renée did not find that surprising. He did not stop them from entering. There was a second police officer inside.

From the cryptic comments Anne had made when she had called, Renée knew what to expect. She went directly to the shrouded figure on the examination table and carefully folded the sheet back.

The man had been alive when he was brought in, but had died soon after. His clothing was cut away, exposing the multitude of wounds that he had suffered. She studied the wounds without touching the body. When she had seen all she wanted to see she asked, "Has the pathologist been notified?"

The police officer nodded, and then asked, "Have you seen wounds like this before?"

"Yes," Renée admitted, turning to face him. "About a year ago. That other man had fewer wounds, and claimed to have been attacked by youths with knives. I believe that one of the 'knives' had been poisoned. I saw a trace of a greenish substance on some of the wounds of that other." She pointed to several of the wounds of the current body. "That other man died three days after he came in. The wound pattern was very like this one and the poison could not be identified."

"What is your opinion of the type of weapon used to make these wounds?" the police officer asked.

"Sir, your records should have the pathology report on the previous case, and I am not a pathologist. However, the wounds on this man do not look like the normal knife wounds that we occasionally have to deal with in here. Some of them look to be too deep. Do you know who this man is?"

Anne answered. "He carried no identification."

"Sir, that is all I can recall. The records of the case should be on file in the archives. So, if you do not need me further, I need to return to another serious case." Renée glanced at the police officer.

"I appreciate you coming, Dr De Salle. Can you be reached if we have further questions?"

"Certainly. I have a pager," Renée assured him, and quickly withdrew.

Anne followed her back to the duty desk, but made no comment.

"Thanks," Renée murmured to her friend.

"You knew him, didn't you?" Anne asked equally quietly.

Renée nodded. "He used to work at the palace, and I expect that the police will find that out eventually. However, it seems to support my feeling that there is something nasty going on, and it might be aimed at my brother. That and the fact I seem to be being followed everywhere."

Anne looked concerned, but Renée waved that off. "I've had to dodge the media ever since I can remember. Can I borrow the office? I need to make a confidential call."

David paused in the doorway of his hotel room, alert to someone inside. Then he heard, "Close the door." He recognised the voice and obeyed.

"Jim!" David identified the unexpected visitor. His voice was taut with worry and he had intended this visit to his room to be brief. Then he wondered why his director was there. Those Jim sent in to scout for a mission were never allowed direct contact with the team who would act on the findings.

"Why are you here?" David asked, anxious to return to the mansion to help his wife.

Jim was studying him, and David knew his director was aware of trouble.

"Jim, they have Wanda. I'm going back – my report is with the contact."

"No, David," Jim said quietly. "It will be too dangerous. I have a tap on the phone lines there and Grant is monitoring radio frequencies too. They summoned the police half an hour ago and they are searching the park and the yard of the mansion. They found Wanda's headset and are looking for her accomplice. The owner has his own men searching inside the building."

"Jim…" David tried to protest.

"Tell me what happened," Jim insisted. His face betrayed concern but he wasn't letting emotion interfere with the mission.

David pulled himself together and reported the main points of what they had discovered, up to when he knew Wanda had been captured and taken back into the mansion.

"But, Jim, however they re-entered the building and bought that odd bundle out from- isn't a door that is marked on the floor plan we sent you," David concluded, hoping for a reason to go back.

Instead of commenting, Jim went and fetched his laptop computer and brought up the email file David had sent after finding the plan of the mansion on the city planning website.

"Show me where you think it is," Jim directed and David moved the mouse arrow to the area under the window that Wanda had opened for them to enter.

"Tell me about the bundle – describe it," Jim asked then.

David did, his first thought had been that it was a body, but he said it could have been a roll of carpet.

"At that hour? Unlikely they were mere tradesmen. What can you add about the man Wanda saw? The one they were looking for?" Jim went on, still focussing on the mission.

"The man they were after was called Daintree," David told Jim. "And after the man was caught, she saw the Cavaliers."

"That mansion is definitely important, David. I don't want you trying to get back in," Jim warned. "Bad enough that Wanda was caught, but I can make that seem like coincidence. I don't believe they will think a woman to be a real threat."

"Jim…I just can't…" David said helplessly.

"David, they don't know Wanda, and you said you were sure she was conscious. Don't sell her short. You know she would not want both of you to be caught…"

"Sorry, Jim. You're right," David admitted. "She was pretending to be unconscious."

"Right. If they were intending to kill her, they would not have taken her back inside. They will want to try to find out why she was there. I think she will delay them for long enough that they will have to keep her there until tomorrow night. Meanwhile, if Grant hears anything, I will tell you. Can you try finding out what you can about the man Daintree?"

David nodded, a trifle stiffly, but he would rather keep his mind busy.

"Stay available. I may need you," Jim told him. "I will be visiting Prince Michael this morning as the Austrian Trade Ambassador. The others will be meeting up at my hotel."

Jim relaxed a little as David took over the laptop and began inserting his presence into the local government websites and working his way to the tax department site. David was an excellent agent, but having him working with his wife had both advantages and drawbacks. They worked seamlessly together, knew how each other thought and would react, but if one was in trouble, the other knew it. Only lately, since they had become parents, David had become particularly protective of Wanda.

As far as missions went, Jim did not have them both working together anymore. However, for the current matter, he had needed both of them to find the information he needed. Moreover, they had produced the goods, and should have been away from here within hours. They were booked on a flight leaving Weisboden late morning - though they would actually be leaving on the marine helicopter.

Jim stayed in David's room and went about his planning, working from what Wanda and David had discovered. He arranged for the photos David had left with the embassy contact to be delivered to him and already a plan was forming to attack the problem of the threat to the monarch.

"I think I have him," David announced less than half an hour later. "Herman Daintree, is an executive assistant in the Weisboden Department of Trade. I cross checked him with driver registrations and have a photo of him."

"Suggestive," Jim remarked as he looked at the picture and read the few details. "See what else you can find."

David turned back to the computer, but a tinkling music box tune began to play. He glanced around the room. It was Wanda's phone; she used the tinkling sound as her ringtone. He homed in on the place Wanda had left it and checked the number before answering. It was unfamiliar.

He answered the call, feigning sleepiness. A woman's voice asked for Frau Davis and at first, he didn't recognise it.

"Frau Davis isn't available," David said neutrally. "This is Herr Davis." He gave a moment of consideration as to who might be calling

Wanda. The only places he had used that name had been at the palace, and here at the hotel. He didn't rule out the possibility that the people who had followed Wanda earlier, or who had taken her not long ago, had found out her name and were trying to find him.

"Where is she? This is important," the voice sounded urgent. Then David heard in the background the voice of someone paging a doctor. David knew then who was calling.

"Is that you, Doctor?" he said, dropping the sleepy act. "Can I speak to you at the hospital?"

"Yes," came the instant agreement. "Doctor's lounge, second floor."

"Fifteen minutes," he promised.

Jim ended the call he was on and waited for David to finish.

"That was Princess Renée. She wanted to speak to Wanda – something important. I'm off to meet her at the hospital."

Renée was pacing the small room, sipping coffee from a foam cup. When David entered, slipping quietly through the door, she put the cup down on the table and gestured to two chairs in the corner. She studied the man and recognised the stranger that Frau Davis had gone to after helping her with her brother.

"Why couldn't your wife – if that is what she is – come here?" Renée asked. She hadn't spoken to the man before, and was cautious.

"She's…checking something out," David said, knowing it sounded lame. "She couldn't leave what she was doing."

Renée sensed, from the man's body language that he wasn't telling her the truth, but she guessed he had to be cautious. "What is your name?"

"David."

Renée relaxed. "Did your wife mention a chat we had here?"

"Sword duel," David said, picking two words that summarised the information.

"I have just seen another case – identical," Renée told him. Very briefly, she gave the little she knew. "He was alive when he came in, but died soon after. I knew him. His name was Herman Daintree and he used to work at the palace seven or eight years ago. However, I didn't mention that to the police. He had no identification on him."

"Where was he found?" David asked.

Renée mentioned a place, and seeing David did not recognise the name, added, "Down by the river. Is that important?"

"It might be," David told her, but without giving a reason.

"This means something to you," Renée challenged.

David considered the wisdom of speaking frankly, and decided he might need Renée's help. "Wanda and I were…investigating a big house in a park…we saw…Wanda saw…a man named Daintree being… caught. I saw…what might have been a body…carried out."

Renée realised suddenly that David was admitting to being illegally in 'the big house'.

"Did you see faces?" Renée asked, and she noted David tensing.

"No…and I can't speak of this."

"I guess not. Is that where Wanda is?" Renée saw David's face turn pale.

"Yes."

Renée shared his dread. If her guess was right, the dead man she had been called in to look at had come from that 'big house'.

"You must get help for her," she urged.

"She's …okay…I can sense that. She should be able to get herself out. I dare not go back."

Renée reached over and touched David's arm gently. "Let me make some calls. I have many friends in the poorer districts. I will put the word out to look for her. Some of them work at Duvall's place."

David didn't volunteer the information that the place where they had taken Wanda was probably a secret part, privy to very few.

When Renée returned to sit, David asked, "Why did you mention Duvall?"

"Big house in the park? That belongs to Claude Duvall, the great philanthropist," her tone was sardonic. "It would not surprise me that he is involved in the business you are looking at. He was a friend of Roderick…and my brother."

"I see…" David mused. He knew from what they had seen in the house that Duvall and Roderick had worked together. "What else do you know about Duvall?"

"Bits and pieces, but now isn't the time to go into it. You need to help Wanda, and I have to get back to the palace. I told your wife, I want to help. Not just because of the threat to Karl, and my family, but because Duvall is not what everyone thinks he is. Too many of the poorest people have no love for him."

"I think I understand," David told her. "I could take you to my friend now, if you wished."

"No, I do have to get back, and I am being followed everywhere as it is."

"Do you think they know who you are?" David asked with concern.

"I have no idea," Renée admitted. "I haven't been home for six years, so …maybe not."

"When did you notice being followed?"

"When we left to get the x-ray machine. Wanda spotted them. I think we convinced them we were servants on an errand. They stopped following us at the shops."

"Be careful," David warned. "I hope they don't think someone at the palace is ill."

"It is more likely that one of the servants was rushed here or is ill. If one of the family was that sick we would go to City General, not come here to the Free Hospital."

"I'll give you my mobile number," David decided. "Will you call me if your people find my wife?" He drew out a small notebook and wrote his number.

"Of course, and I will give you mine, and my pager number. You'll do the same?" Renée took a page from David's book and used her own pen to write two numbers.

David said, "I will do that," but a shiver suddenly shook him. He took the slip of paper with the two numbers from Renée and gave her the paper with his own.

"Are you all right?" Renée asked.

"Yes," David forced himself to sound positive. "I'll leave after you."

Renée wasted no time heading off. David followed her unobtrusively, and was in a position to watch as she drove the van out of the car park. He saw the car that moved off after it. It was the same car Wanda had identified before as being registered at the address of the big house. He went to his own car to return to the hotel. His mind was on the brief sense he had felt of Wanda. A surge of alarm followed by…nothing.

# Chapter 9

Wanda made her body go completely limp, surprising the two men who had hold of her. She heard them exclaim quietly in alarm, but they felt her neck for a pulse and muttered words of relief. To get her back to the house, they lifted her to a standing position and the two men supported her with her arms across their shoulders so that each could grip one of her wrists. Their other arms were under her shoulders and around her waist. An onlooker would probably think she was too drunk to walk.

Neither man noticed that their captive's eyes were partly open and watching the ground. Nor did they suspect that the woman was able to learn things about them.

Firstly, Wanda learnt that these men had been alerted to watch for her – probably by the man she had encountered in the scullery. But they had already been patrolling the park for some reason. And, they hadn't expected her to be a woman. Then one of them had spoken into a headpiece microphone, reporting they had caught the intruder, and she was out cold. Wanda had the sense they did not expect trouble from her.

Well, they probably had cause to think her out cold – the fist that had been used to subdue her had been unexpected, she had been barely able to move her head and the blow had connected, though not with the full force. Still, her head was aching and her vision on the edge on blacking out. She needed time to get over it, and to get her breath back. For a while she was helpless, so it suited her purpose to be thought unconscious.

Wanda thought strongly at David, forcing into his mind the most important details of what she had seen and found. She sensed he had received her images and the terse order to go and report. She couldn't do much more than that, since she had managed to drop the wi-fi headpiece in the initial struggle. If her captors had seen that, they would be looking for her accomplice.

As they got near the house, Wanda felt her strength returning, and she tested the grip of her captors. Too strong. This method of moving a prisoner was highly efficient. More so since she was shorter than the men were, and had nothing to brace her feet against to try to escape. Then her chance was past. They were back inside the gate and heading for the door inside. Only, they didn't take her in through the scullery or kitchen. Now her mind was back in high gear. They were going towards a solid brick wall – above her head was the window she had entered through two hours before. Still with her eyes mostly closed, she watched the arm of one of her captors push on a particular brick, and a section of the wall moved in and aside.

A whiff of air, with the faint odour of car exhaust and car polish, confirmed her guess that this was a way into the garage. Once inside, with the door shut, a dull light came on. Wanda was hustled past four ultra-expensive sports cars and a more sedate Mercedes to a set of concrete steps going down. At the bottom, they went through into a passage – unadorned concrete floor and walls and ceiling. Wanda placed this passage as being under the entrance hall, and not in the section of the lower level that she had explored.

The passage led to a small room, also lined with concrete. She wasn't able to get a good look around, but did see two wooden armchairs and a table. This was her last chance to get free and she acted when one of the guards released his grip to drag one of the chairs closer.

Wanda suddenly twisted and ducked, taking the remaining captor by surprise, but he didn't fully release his grip. He reacted swiftly, and kicked her feet from under her. She fell, but his grip meant she didn't slam into the floor, but was pushed down and her arm twisted up behind her back.

The second man took hold of her again and both dragged her up and into the chair. Wanda resisted, still trying to get free. Her struggles were ended when one casually punched her in the diaphragm, forcing the air from her lungs. Then, whilst she was unable to do more than try to suck in air, one guard used the headpiece mike to report. He spoke in French, saying they had the prisoner in 'the room' and needed something to restrain her with. The other drew out a gun and held it into her neck, almost daring her to move a muscle.

Two more men entered the room through a door opposite the one to the garage. These had black suits and black shirts, with some kind of logo or emblem on the collar points. Both had pieces of leather in their hands and went immediately to tie the prisoner to the chair. Wanda considered trying to escape, but the passage door had clanged shut. Instead, she used Houdini's trick and tensed her muscles as they tied the straps on wrists and ankles to hold her to the chair. The men did not realise that they did not have the bindings as tight as they intended.

It was only when she was no longer a threat that a fifth man entered the room. The four men in suits seemed to hold themselves straighter and stiffer. One reported what they knew of her, and warned that she had played unconscious and made an attempt to get free.

Wanda couldn't get a good view of the man, and expected he had come to question her. She didn't intend to let him succeed, so before that fifth man could get started, she relaxed her body as she had before, and it slumped in the seat. Only the bindings were stopping her from slipping out of it. Then she willed her consciousness into a deep dark place of silence, where she could not feel her body, and could see it as if she were apart from it. This was a trick that these men would never expect. They would simply think she had fainted.

In this way, she was able to watch the newcomer who was wearing an emerald green quilted silk lounging robe, as he moved over to her body and slapped her face. His expression was of disbelief.

"You are sure this one was in the house," he turned to say to one of the suited guards.

"Yes, Sir, the bitch ran right past me."

"Have you looked for identification?"

"Not yet, Sir."

"Do it." He stepped back to give the man room.

Wanda saw one of the men feeling all over her body, and finding several of her tools but nothing to identify her, or indicate her intentions.

Then the man in green gripped her face, and studied it. "Do any of you recognise this woman?"

All four of the other men shook their heads.

"I want to know how she got in and where she went. Check the security cameras and find out who was meant to be monitoring them."

"At once, Lord Duvall," one of the men answered promptly and left as quickly.

Duvall then asked, "Did Daintree have a woman with him?"

"No, Sir, he came in by himself."

"But he was wondering around by himself. He might have let her in," Duvall proposed.

None of the men protested the idea.

"Bring her around," Duvall directed.

Wanda, in her distant watching place, felt none of the slapping and shaking; her body remained limp. Even the drenching with icy water did nothing.

Duvall controlled a snarl. "Two of you remain here. Tell me the instant she wakes up."

Wanda watched as her body was left alone with only two guards. And at first they were alert, standing ready for trouble, but the hands hanging loose, feet apart stance grew wearisome, and first one and then the other relaxed their stance and began to stroll around the confines of the room, muttering to each other.

It would not have surprised Wanda if the men had tried to force her to wake. That they didn't touch her implied Duvall had firm control over them. One of the men stopped in front of her and stared. In that moment, Wanda drew her awareness back nearer her body and opened her eyes. She forced a thought into his mind and stared back into his now blank looking eyes.

The man was drugged, Wanda realised. She couldn't say what type of drug, but she guessed the initial effect was wearing off. That combined with the man beginning to feel very tired might put him in a very suggestive state…

Wanda had studied hypnosis, but it was something she had never tried in the 'out of body' state. But then, when she had last been in that state the circumstances had been very different. She pushed away the terrifying memories of that past time and concentrated on the man in front of her.

At first, she tried to send the idea of untying her, but that showed no sign of working even when she sent the image along with mind words in French and German. The man was not very receptive to her telepathic thoughts, but she hoped he'd be susceptible in that drugged state. So she considered something simpler – like the need to sleep, that nothing would change, that he would notice nothing…

The second guard moved into her view, attracted by the odd stance of his companion. He glanced at the prisoner, saw the eyes were open, but that was the last conscious thought he had before his mind felt the force of the command to sleep.

For over an hour, it had been quiet in the basement room of the Cavalier Club.

Wanda brought her full awareness back to her body very slowly, and was careful to make no movement. All she did at first was to ease her stiff and aching muscles with minute flexing and relaxing movements to bring about a return of circulation. As she did this, she scanned the walls in her limited view and saw nothing indicating a monitoring camera. One of the men still had a wi-fi headpiece, but if she was quiet, no one would hear anything.

She tested bindings on her hands and, with infinitely slow movements, she slipped her wrists free. With her mind, Wanda emphasised a hypnotic suggestion for each guard to sleep. Neither moved nor opened their eyes as she leant forward and freed her ankles. They stayed unmoving as she stood and slowly looked around, scanning the room for alarms and cameras. Yes, there it was – a tiny little fish eye lens. The question was whether it was being closely monitored. She had to assume it was, and that others would come very soon. She wasted no more time in going to the door. The one to the garage was solid and felt like metal and the lock mechanism was hidden within the door. Even though she had been searched by the men, they had not found all of her tool kit. She quickly rolled up the clinging black fabric covering her right shin and withdrew a slender sliver of metal from under a layer of false skin. With this she tested around the door, and found where the wide metal bar was securing the door. That would take hours to cut through if she could cut it at all.

She crossed to the other door, the one leading to the house, and which she guessed came out somewhere near the lift shaft. This door was not as obvious, but Wanda knew it was there and was an expert in opening doors illegally. However, she did not have time – she sensed that people were assembling on the other side of the door.

She continued to examine the room – not ready to give up. Hiding was not an option. Apart from two chairs, the only other furniture was the table.

As she contemplated her situation, Wanda heard scraping sounds beyond the hidden door. Too many people were there for her to attempt to flee past them. She refused to panic. She had been in worse situations before – and as she thought that, an idea occurred to her.

When the door opened, she was sitting regally, on the table, facing the door. She was concentrating on sending an aura of confidence towards the men. Fortunately, they would not sense her terror behind it.

The men entered and she did not have to force herself to act. The eight men were clad in perfect reproductions of Cavalier costume complete with swords and wigs. Wanda laughed, a loud hearty laugh, and Duvall's eyes blazed with anger. She sensed his deep dedication to his fantasy. The other seven men were less intent, and if Wanda had stopped to consider them she would have realised they were also being influenced by Duvall through the agency of some drug. But it was Duvall she must concentrate on. And now there was knowledge in her mind that she could twist to her purpose.

Her laugh had thrown him off balance, but he did not betray it. He looked around for the two guards he had left there and saw them seemingly asleep on their feet and unaware that he and the others had entered. He glanced at one of the cavaliers and shrugged his shoulder slightly in the direction of the guards. Then he began to walk purposefully towards the prisoner who should not have been free.

She saw the cavalier shaking the guards and them waking up, but she dared not take her attention off the leader. Duvall must not be allowed to regain the initiative or Wanda knew she would end up like the unlamented Pierre Roderick.

"Ah! The Great Cavalier Duvall!" Wanda spoke in perfect French and Duvall was convinced she had the accent common to the period in which Duvall believed he belonged. "How pleasant of you to return with your ...friends."

Wanda made sure Duvall had no doubt of her meaning. That he was not manly enough to deal with one woman by himself and that he required others to be with him. Her implication was that the other seven men were his paramours. Duvall's face flushed with anger.

"No, you are not the Great Claude Duvall," Wanda persisted before Duvall could get in a word. "Not like the Great Claude Louis Duvall that I knew. He would turn in his grave if he saw the weakness that fills his descendants!"

"Who are you?" Duvall demanded and he levelled his sword at her heart and came so that it was within inches of her.

"Me?" Wanda asked the question incredulously. "The Great Duvall never asked that."

Again, Wanda laughed a rich laugh that filled the room and echoed in the minds of all.

"Why did you come here?" Duvall changed the direction of his questioning.

"Why? To see if the Duvall bloodline was still strong," Wanda said with a trace of mockery. "You should ask how I came here."

Wanda brushed the sword aside, and stood up off the table. She showed no sign of fear, and that was confusing Duvall. She ignored him and seemed to examine the other seven men. They were uncertain about her, and waiting for Duvall to give orders. Only one of the seven started to make a move at her.

"Touch me at your own risk, Cavalier!" she said sharply. "The Great Duvall does not like others touching his property." The man moved back as if stung. Wanda stored that reaction in her memory.

Duvall held his ground, and was not afraid of her. He was confident of his skill with a sword, especially against an unarmed woman.

Wanda had only seemed to be ignoring him. She knew he was the one to watch, but her indifference was to anger him, and she was succeeding. Any moment he would make his move, and Wanda could see that his sword was brilliantly shiny and sharp. He began to make a sweep at her and Wanda timed a collapse so it passed harmlessly above her.

Now was the most dangerous part of her plan. It was something only she could do, and Duvall would never believe that she was conning him.

Duvall prodded her with the tip of his sword. Wanda noticed in part of her mind that the cuts were minor. She inserted a picture in Duvall's mind and spread it to the so far silent others.

That she succeeded was proved by the gasp of fear. Her image was of a woman, fabulously dressed in a gown of the cavalier period, who stood up from where her body lay and walked away and upwards as if she was ascending stairs. Then she made the image vanish, at the wall.

She heard muttered oaths from the men, and before Duvall thought to prod her again, she withdrew her mind from her body once more, retreating to the dark silent place in her mind and reducing her body functions to the barest minimum. The men would think her body was dead. The bleeding from the sword cuts had stopped.

Here was the time of greatest risk. Duvall could still inflict nasty wounds that would bleed when she chose to wake up.

At a gesture from Duvall, one of the cavaliers leant over the body and felt for a pulse. He tried the wrist, and then the carotid artery. He thought he felt one throb, and then nothing. Then he studied the face and rubbed a finger over one cheek.

"This woman is dead, Lord Duvall," he stated. "But I think I have seen this woman before, without the face disguise. The face structure is most unusual."

"Tell me!" Duvall demanded.

"A woman and a man came to visit His Highness. An American scout couple. They were discussing a Jamboree. His Highness went off with them later."

The Cavalier that was standing next to the confused guards, ventured to ask, "Do you think they might be American agents? I mean, we know she was in the house but none of the security films showed her."

"No," Duvall said immediately. "The old man's strictest rule is – no outsiders in his business. I can't see him changing now. Glockner, when did the old man get back that day?" Duvall asked sharply.

"I don't know, Lord Duvall. I was sent to talk to the wives of the two pilots of the courier plane."

"What about the courier, Werner Mont Pelier?"

"I don't know, Lord Duvall. But he has not been to the palace for a few days."

Duvall stared down at the woman, and poked her arm with his sword again. Not a twitch, and no blood. His mind was full of French curses and he leant down and felt for himself the lack of a pulse. He was half-convinced, in spite of evidence to the contrary, that the woman was faking. He stood abruptly, and ignored the looks of his cavaliers, as he scanned the concrete walls. What he had seen had to have been a projection, but he could see no place it could have come from. Except for the furniture, the room was empty. The light globe and the monitoring lens were the only other things, but neither was in the right position to have been corrupted to project something.

"Get rid of the body!" Duvall ordered. He was more than a little jittery right then. He did not believe in ghosts, but he could not explain what he had just seen.

"I saw it walk through the wall," one of the cavaliers said in awe.

Duvall glared at the man, but the others were all nodding. Some were still staring at the place where the apparition had disappeared. He turned his full attention on the two guards.

"You two," Duvall pointed. "Wait here. The rest of you had better sleep upstairs tonight. Michael, see they all have rooms. No one is to talk of this! Not even between yourselves!"

The seven other Cavaliers left through the door leading into the mansion's lower level. When they were gone and the door was shut, Duvall rounded on the guards. They were pale, and one was wiping sweat from his face.

"How did that woman get free?"

"Sir...I ..." one guard tried to work up the words to explain the inexplicable. He really didn't know. He had woken up and Duvall was in the room.

"You morons. You let the woman trick you and hypnotise you," Duvall told them venomously.

"But she was unconscious," the other protested, but Duvall slapped him hard.

"She tricked you – again – and convinced you to free her and forget you had. Fortunately, no one can get out of this room without my say so. I should keep you both in here for a week, but I need to get rid of the body. Go and get what you need and come back. Hurry. It will be getting light in a little over half an hour."

The men bowed stiffly, and retreated into the garage through the door that was now unlocked.

Duvall returned his attention to the woman, trying to forget the ghostly apparition and figure out what she had been doing. He had intended this woman to die, but he had wanted information first. His anger at being thwarted translated into action. He took his sword and slashed at the body. Not in an undisciplined fit of pique, but with deliberate intent. He placed his foot on one wrist and slashed. He did the same to the other wrist. Now the body would look like a suicide, but the slashed wrists did not bleed! To hide his shaking hands, he took out a cloth and cleaned his blade.

The two guards returned. They had removed their suit jackets and donned nondescript grey coveralls that were not completely clean, but not grease covered either. They carried a folded sheet of tough black plastic and some plaited rope. They wasted no time trussing the body in the plastic.

Duvall watched as his men lifted the body, and began to carry it out to the garage. He did not need to tell them what to do. He stalked off to the lift to go up to his bedroom. Once there, Duvall poured himself a large drink of brandy. He felt it steady his nerves as he slowly prowled around his room.

He wanted to know who the woman was, and what the old king knew about her. Then he dismissed the idea. As he had told his assistant, Prince Michael would not bring in outsiders. Whatever she was up to had to be coincidental to his plans – but he wanted to be sure.

Why had the woman come there – and died? It made no sense. Had his men seriously injured her? Surely not, she had been well enough to try to escape. Was she a fanatic? Was she a ghost? He did not believe in ghosts...but suppose it had been? The woman might have been dead already and the ghost animated it. Therefore, the woman was not important. If it was a ghost, why had it appeared to him? Because he was a Duvall – like it had said? Did ghosts hang around people? He thought they only hung around places.

Then an idea occurred to him. It appealed to him ... didn't that prove he really was related to the Great Duvall – as he had always believed. That thought consoled him and he sipped the rest of his brandy. He was calm when there was a tentative knock on his door.

"Come in," Duvall called, and he turned to see his assistant walk in, no longer attired in the Cavalier costume. "Are they all settled, Michael?"

"Yes...Claude...did you require me for anything else?"

Michael DuPont was looking pale, Duvall noticed. "Help me out of this costume, and go and get some sleep. First thing in the morning, get onto Hessler and ask him to find out about those scout people. Have him watch the roads, the trains and the airport and contrive a reason to bring in the man."

"Maybe he won't try to leave until the woman is found," DuPont suggested.

"Then we will find him, Michael, and he will tell us what the woman didn't."

Duvall saw his assistant shiver, and it amused him.

# Chapter 10

Duvall's guards, the two assigned to remove the woman's body, had already decided to head towards the produce market, for if the van were seen there it would be assumed they were buying fresh foods for the restaurant. The real reason was that there were several old, dilapidated buildings in that section of the lower city. Supposedly, these were due for demolition, but it was known that tramps sometimes slept in them. It would not be surprising if a fire started in one.

When the driver stopped, the guard in the passenger seat went to investigate the first building. He went to a side door, shoved it open and flashed a torch around; he saw nothing. He had to hold his nose for the smell from within was appalling. He doubted that even a tramp would want to sleep with that stench but it would do for their purpose. He gestured for the driver to back up to the little lane beside the building.

That was when their plan began to unravel. When they lifted the body, it began to moan. Dead bodies were not meant to do that. Then they recalled how they had seen a ghost leave this body...and then all the legends of vampires and other un-dead creatures that were part of their national heritage came into their mind. They dumped the body just inside the building and fled - all thought of setting the place on fire vanished. They drove off as fast as they could.

Only when they were almost back at the house did they start to think that Duvall would be angry if he knew that body might be alive.

In their urgency to flee, the men did not realise that they had been seen. But then, the witness did not venture into view until the van was well out of sight. This man was on his way to work at a bakery, and in the neighbourhood where he worked, one did not get too nosey about the business of others. The van was not familiar, and should have had no reason to be near the condemned buildings. There was a wire fence around the buildings to keep people out, but that had only ever deterred obedient children. He would have shrugged and ignored the matter except he had received a very early morning call to look out for a woman needing help. In the faint light of pre-dawn, he had seen what might have been a body, being dumped.

Therefore, once the van was out of sight, he ventured into the old building and looked around in the dark, almost tripping on the plastic wrapped bundle. He leant down to feel what he had kicked, and heard faint moaning and drew a knife to cut the plastic open. He could not be sure that this was the woman the doctor had wanted looked for, but it was someone who was hurt. He might only be a lowly baker, but he knew first aid.

Wanda felt herself being dragged out of the foul smelling place and into fresher air. Gentle hands untied the ropes and gave her room to move. She could not see her Samaritan, but sensed genuine concern. Her head had been knocked as she had been put in the truck and again as Duvall's men had dropped her in the building. She was losing the concentration she needed to 'play dead'.

She opened her eyes. There was only a trace of light but it was enough for her to realise that her eyes would not focus. Undoubtedly, she had a concussion. Things might have been worse. She lay still.

"Awake, lady?" the man spoke in German.

"Yes," Wanda managed. "Need doctor."

"I will call an ambulance," the man assured her.

"No!" Wanda tried to insist. "Not hospital. Call…" She couldn't remember the name she wanted – just the face. Then the name came to her. "Call De Salle…"

"Yes, yes," the man agreed. "She is a good doctor. She asked us to look for you."

Wanda didn't have the strength to wonder how Renée had known.

"Can you walk?" the man asked.

"No," Wanda told him without moving her head. "Concussion. Move flat."

"You should not stay here. Those men may return, and the police patrol these empty places now."

That motivated Wanda to try to sit up, very carefully, but as soon as she was upright she had the need to be sick.

"Lady, wait here I will bring help."

Wanda collapsed back onto the ground, and passed out.

The baker took a long look at her then took off at a run. He found one of the women from the fruit stalls and her husband. Both were friends of his and of the doctor.

It was still early and very few people were around. The two men carried Wanda to the fruit stall, and sent the woman off to call the doctor. Only when they put her down did they realise that she was bleeding badly. Without a word, they began to bind the wounds, fearing the woman would bleed to death.


Renée's pager chimed as she was changing the dressings on the leg of the now awake King Karl. She checked the message, which was not informative, but could not reply immediately.

"It looks a lot better," she told her brother. "I will give you a smaller dose of pain killers so that you can stay awake if you choose."

One she finished sticking the new dressing in place, she removed the waterproof sheet from under his leg and recovered it with the blankets. She knew her brother was only barely tolerating her ministrations, and preferred to think of her as a nurse rather than a doctor. He tried to push himself up.

"No, you are not well enough to get up yet," she insisted. "You need rest for at least a week. And it is imperative that no one knows you are back here."

He snarled at her. "I don't need your services anymore! Why don't you go back to wherever you hang out these days?"

Renée merely shrugged. "Suits me brother, I have better things to do than treat insensitive boors." She knew that telling him to rest would do no good. He had never listened to her anyway.

At that moment, Prince Michael entered the room through the opened door, and the whole atmosphere changed.

"Your Majesty," Prince Michael spoke with only a trace of a bow, but very correctly. "You would be wise to continue to have Princess Renée as your physician. As she told you, it is imperative that no one outside of the family know you have returned. No one but one of the family can be relied on to have that absolute discretion. I have not even let the servants come here. The more you rest now, the sooner you can get up, and for appearances, you will need to address the media after your official return early next week."

Prince Michael did not dismiss his daughter, and as he spoke to the King, his tone had all the authority that fatherhood and sixty years of kingship had given him.

Even then, it seemed that Karl would ignore the advice. As king, he had in theory, the right of final decision. He did not want to be indebted to his sister. Yet he had been taught to listen to his advisors, and his father was his chief advisor.

"Very well, sister, you may continue to treat us," Karl acknowledged. Renée did not miss his use of the royal plural. She knew he intended it as a subtle insult to her — as if she was an inferior.

"How is your patient, Doctor?" Prince Michael asked. Unlike with Karl, there was approval in his voice.

Renée told him succinctly and repeated the instructions she had given Karl. At least her father had a chance of getting Karl to comply.

Prince Michael returned his attention to his son. "When you have eaten, you and I must talk."

Karl nodded, knowing the matters that his father referred to. He did not realise that Renée also knew.

"Renée, when you are finished here I require a word with you also," Prince Michael told her.

"Yes, Father," she agreed, as she continued to repack her medical bag, and ignore her brother's glare. He hated feeling helpless.

When her father had gone back to the outer room, she spoke as she turned off the bright overhead light and just left the bedside lamp glowing.

"Don't worry, Karl. You can be sure of my discretion," Renée told him. "Professionally, you can be sure of my skill — I won't be anything but the best. Privately, you can go to hell."

Karl laughed at her comment. It surprised Renée into looking at him. "I won't permit anything but the best," he told her. "Or anything less than absolute loyalty to me."

Renée spoke in quick retort. "My loyalty is to the crown."

The chuckle disappeared from Karl's tone. His face hardened into anger. The slight had not gone unnoticed - loyal to the office of King, not to the holder of the title.

Renée walked quickly from the room before Karl thought of a cutting reply. She saw only her father in the outer room. However, before she answered his request to talk, she went to the phone and made a call. What she heard caused her to hang up quickly and make another call. She gave her name, listened, and then issued a series of instructions. She followed that call with a third, but that one was not answered, and that worried her.

"Father, I must go. That call was about a patient."

Prince Michael forestalled further apologies or explanations. "I simply wanted to say several things. I am proud of what you have achieved. I am grateful for your part in saving Karl's life. Moreover, I want to emphasise that that the events going on here must not be disclosed to outsiders. No, I know you do not need to be told. I want to clarify my definition. I am only letting those who already know about Karl, in on the larger issues. So in addition to myself, only William, Joseph, Stephen, and you will know about the threats. As you know, I called in outsiders to help. The same people are to be the only other ones to know about them. You, Stephen and I will be of most use to them."

"I understand, Father. But I really must go. You can probably let Karl sit up later. I don't expect him to want to stay that way for long. Mueller can watch him when he comes and if you have any necessary but dull administrative matters – get Karl thinking on them."

Price Michael nodded, understanding that it would keep Karl occupied.


Renée quickly sent a text message to the number Herr Davis had given her, and then she grabbed her bag and headed towards the kitchens and the back entrance to the palace. As soon as she left the guest wing, she was virtually pounced on by Johannes. He was about to object to her presence when he belatedly recognised her.

"Your Highness," he said, quickly changing what he had intended to say. He was less quick in controlling his face. Her short-cropped hair had his attention.

Renée hoped that he hadn't taken in the fact that her grey suit looked like it had been slept in. "What is it, Johannes?" she asked impatiently.

From Stephen's comments, Johannes Glockner hadn't changed in the years she had lived away. She wouldn't get rid of him until she let him talk.

"There is a young man in the visitor's room who insists he has an early appointment with you. His name is Herr Davis; he is the American scout person."

Now Johannes did notice the creased suit but only betrayed it by the faint twitch of his left cheek. At least her bag didn't look like the traditional idea of a doctor's medical bag. It was more of an oversized brief case.

"Yes, thank you. I was on my way to see him. Father thinks it is a good idea for me to be involved in the jamboree thing, though I wish he had made this appointment for later in the day. I didn't get here until late last night and I had to spend the night in a guest room."

"Will you need your old suite prepared?" Johannes offered.

"No need. I have organised a place in the city." Renée walked off, dismissing Johannes without saying so.

She sighed; it didn't rid her of the busy body, who chose to follow her on the pretext of turning up the lighting in the areas she chose to walk. When she came to the main hall, Johannes slipped into a side room. He was probably going to listen in to her conversation. Not that it was anything more than being available if he was needed, and she should be used to it, but since living away from the palace, she had come to appreciate her privacy.

Renée entered the visitor's room and saw Herr Davis spin around. She immediately noticed the tenseness in his face and posture as he bowed politely.

"Good Morning, Herr Davis," Renée said as if greeting a stranger. "I understand that my father explained that I will be deputising for him?"

"Yes, your Highness," David said with a straight face at the lie. He followed her lead and went on, "Thank you for seeing me this early. My wife and I are due to fly out later today, but the Committee has some last minute questions."

"So I believe," Renée agreed. "I am looking forward to meeting your wife as well. However, let us get going. Do you have a car here, or should I get Truman to drive us?"

"My car is out the front. I would be honoured to drive you," David confirmed.

Renée, beckoned for David to follow her, and both emerged back in the magnificent gold and white painted, high ceilinged entrance hall.

David caught sight of the edge of Johannes suit, and shoulder shrugged slightly to warn Renée, when she glanced back at him.

"Damn nuisance," Renée muttered. "A moment."

Renée summoned Johannes, who approached promptly.

"Would you please tell my father, when he deigns to be awake today, that I have gone with Herr Davis to speak with the dignitaries and I don't know when I will be back. Oh, and assure him I will be appropriately dressed."

Johannes bowed respectfully, but the faint smile on his face was more of a smirk. He thought, judging from her hurry, that Renée was keen to put distance between herself and her father.

Renée spoke again when Johannes was just in earshot still. "Herr Davis, would you be kind enough to drive me to my apartment? I will need to change."

David acknowledged politely, and as soon as they had a door between them and Johannes, they took off at a trot.

The car David now drove was a station wagon with the back seat folded down to extend the cargo space. It was waiting at the front steps. He opened the passenger door for Renée and ran to the driver's seat. He drove along the curved road inside the palace grounds at a pace just above dignified, and sped up after turning onto the main road.

"You got here quickly," Renée commented as the palace gates closed behind them.

"I was already on my way. I was driving when your call came through. You know where Wanda is?" David said, his question intense.

"Yes. But from what I was told, she is in a bad way and refuses an ambulance," Renée told him.

"She's right," David said flatly. "We dare not be officially noticed. Just tell me where to go. I should have everything you need."

"Head towards the hospital for now," Renée told him, but she noticed that David had a GPS on the dashboard.

They hadn't gone far when David became aware of a car following them. It was not the same one that had followed Renée back to the palace the previous night. He skilfully lost the tail.

"Stay on this road," Renée directed when David was free of observers. "Turn at the newspaper building, it's the one with the big yellow globe on its roof."

She continued to direct him along unfamiliar roads, and he drove as fast as he dared, not wishing to attract undue attention. He betrayed no surprise when their destination seemed to be a fruit and vegetable market, nor questioned her when she had him drive up to the back of a fruit stall.

Renée was out of the car with her bag as soon as it stopped, but David took a few moments to remove his hat, scout shirt and tie. He took a second medical bag into the stall with him.

David quickly sensed that Renée was alarmed at Wanda's vital signs. He joined her and did his own examination. He was not as alarmed as Renée, but he was exceedingly worried. His wife normally sensed his presence, but she had not even reacted.

Wanda was lying on a low mattress, the sort found on sun lounges, and was covered in blankets. They were in an open but roofed area, with fruit boxes pushed out of the way, but behind the stacked display boxes of the fruit stall. It wasn't a very big area, and although it was swept, it wasn't the cleanest spot for doing emergency first aid.

"She should go to a hospital," Renée said as she checked the places where the baker had applied bandages. Those at the wrists were blood soaked.

"Something is being arranged," David told her. "I will need to know what is required."

Renée removed the blood soaked bindings on one wrist and couldn't smother an exclamation. The cut was deep, and the blood was flowing sluggishly. She looked at David with concern, but he told her to go on. He would help. He had a fresh pad ready to replace on Wanda's left wrist.

"The blood vessels need repairing," Renée said, looking around and considering the surroundings.

"I have what you need?" David told her. He reached for his bag with his free hand, not removing pressure on the bandage with the other. "Sterile sheets, gloves, gowns, face masks – all in sealed bags."

Renée checked his bag and it seemed to her that David had indeed come prepared. From that preparedness, she guessed that objecting to working there would be useless. It was unstated, but evident, that the American, David, trusted her skill. She asked the stall owner for a bowl of hot soapy water and when it came, she scrubbed quickly and donned sterile gown and gloves. She took over holding the pad in place while David copied her example.

David proved to be as able an assistant as the one who was now a patient. Renée repaired as much of the worst of the damage as she could under the primitive conditions. She could not fault David's medical kit for that. It was almost as if he had seen what was needed.

The owners of the fruit stall had left them alone with the patient. David was grateful for that as he helped Renée remove Wanda's dusty clothes. It was then that they found the other cuts that were oozing blood. Renée set to work using butterfly dressings to close these wounds.

When they were finished, David produced a lightweight coverall and helped ease his wife into it.

"What were you doing at the big house?" Renée asked.

David didn't answer.

"Was it worth it?" Renée insisted.

"We were doing our job," David said quietly. "And you would agree that the people who do things like this must be stopped."

"Yes. That is why I want to help."

"You are," David assured her. "How is she?"

"Alive, though the Braun's thought they had let her die. She has lost a lot of blood, and I am surprised she is not worse. I could not get here as fast as I would have wished. It is fortunate that they did not have poison on the blade they used on her. She needs a hospital and I do not like her vital signs."

"You were in time, and Wanda is a stubborn bitch," David told her. "But no to the public hospital. What else needs to be done?"

"The wrist wounds need to be repaired properly. I cannot do that here. She will need observation to be sure there is no infection or other complications," Renée told him.

"Can you do the repairs?" David asked urgently.

"Yes, but a micro-surgeon could do it better," Renée told him, impressed by how well David was dealing with the injuries his wife had suffered.

"A private hospital is being arranged. Who is the best surgeon?" David asked, flipping open his mobile phone. He pressed a button and waited.

"Jim, its David. We have found her. She is alive, but needs more attention. What is the status with the hospital?"

"Arranged," the voice coming through the phone confirmed. An address was given.

"Lanzecki is the best micro surgeon," Renée supplied.

"Jim, get Lanzecki, he's a micro surgeon. We will bring her in," David went on.

If Renée was surprised, she hid it well. Her first thought was, "You don't just 'get' Lanzecki." She then realised that she would have the opportunity to assist the world-renowned surgeon.

"I will get her ready to travel," David said. "Talk to the people here. I will be borrowing these blankets. Ask if they wish to be reimbursed and caution them to silence."

Renée did not object to the abrupt commands, but went off to comply. She returned quickly with the shop owner who helped David carry Wanda to the car. He already had a thin mattress in the back of the wagon and the windows were tinted.

David did not tell Renée where they were headed until they were in the car. Nor did he need her to give him directions. He pushed buttons on the GPS and a route came up.

"How did you know?" Renée repeated her earlier question.

"A good scout is always prepared," David countered as he concentrated on driving according to the route shown on the GPS.

"That is not good enough," Renée insisted.

"Your Highness, there are things I cannot tell you," David apologised, not looking at her.

Renée accepted that in general, but, "You knew exactly what to expect."

David kept silent for a while. "There are some things I can't tell you about Wanda. Medically though, there are some things you ought to be prepared for. I must trust to the ethics of your profession to keep quiet about them."

"You have that promise," Renée assured him.

"Well, firstly, I know you are worried about Wanda's vital signs. I can bring her out of that."

"Do you mean that they are self-induced?" Renée wasn't quite shocked.

"Yes," David admitted. "She scared the hell out of me the first time she tried it. She can slow her breathing and heart rate to almost nothing and I think the only reason she is still alive is that she was able to do that to stop the blood loss."

"So when you bring her out of it, we can expect the bleeding to get worse?"

David nodded. "What is worrying me is that she hasn't reacted to my presence. That is why I think there is still a problem. All her concentration is focussed on maintaining this state. I think she escaped from...them... by pretending to be dead, and then when she felt it safe enough to wake up, she realised what they had done and continued it. I felt her call me, briefly, then nothing."

"Felt her call you?" Renée prompted.

David took one hand off the steering wheel and touched his head. "Up here."

Renée began to ask another question, but David shook his head, reminding her that he was not able to tell her.

"Don't start thinking I am a telepath or something. I...am not," David said, placing emphasis on the pronoun. He glanced at Renée and saw she had picked up his innuendo. He went on, "I will have to wake her before you try using any drugs. That way you will be able to gauge her true condition. I will need to be there to assist you."

"That should be possible," Renée agreed.

Renée recognised the private hospital when they arrived. It was part of an exclusive clinic for the ultra-rich. David seemed to know where to go for he went directly to the ambulance entrance, and backed the car up to a door where a man in a doctor's white coat waited with a patient trolley. David betrayed no sign of recognition as the man assisted him to lift Wanda, nor as the man directed them to a room that was fully equipped and adjacent to an operating room.

When they had settled Wanda in the room, and the doors were fully closed, Jim Phillips simply said, "We have the use of this room for as long as necessary and Lanzecki is on his way."

Renée nodded at the comment and glanced from David back to the speaker. She did wonder who he was if he had been able to command a doctor as eminent as Lanzecki. David got the hint.

"Jim, this is Princess Renée. She is using the name Renée De Salle." David would let Jim introduce himself as he chose.

"Thank you for your help, doctor. It is greatly appreciated," Jim said.

"Thank you," Renée responded automatically. "I know you are helping my father, and your friend needs help. But I am willing to do more."

David answered that. "I have mentioned that already, Doctor. However, if the surgeon is coming, we should discuss that later and prepare my wife for him first."

"You are correct," Renée agreed, and she went to examine the equipment and supplies available in the room.

Jim stood quietly near Wanda and simply observing and evaluating Princess Renée. He moved back when Renée directed David to rouse Wanda. She had gloves on and a tray of supplies ready to be used.

Those looking on saw David place his hands on either side of Wanda's face. He was standing on one side of the trolley bed, leaning over and whispering something no one else could hear.

Renée glanced from the patient, to the white haired man. He did not seem surprised by what David was doing. That eased some of her concern. Then she glanced back to Wanda, just as her eyes opened. The expression she saw there caused her to look away. There was no doubting the joy of togetherness, relief and love in that look. Then it was gone and the two seemed like strangers by comparison.

David moved away, and Renée examined Wanda again. She was relieved that the breathing and heart rate were nearly normal, but now she was seeing the cuts beginning to seep blood. However, she had fixed the worst of them. The wrists were oozing again, but she left them alone. Her primitive repairs were holding enough for the time being.

Wanda spoke fuzzily. "My head was banged. It feels like concussion."

"Oh, are you a doctor as well?" Renée asked with a trace of humour. She was relieved to see Wanda smile faintly.

"I have the advantage of feeling the inside of my head!" Wanda told her.

"Indeed," Renée agreed. "Was your night jaunt worth it?"

"Yes. I came out alive. I got what we needed."

"You could have died!"

"Didn't."

"You are not out of danger yet! So I shouldn't make you talk. But at least, you can follow a conversation. I don't want you to try to do anything."

David murmured a comment, more aimed at his wife. "Then you had better make sure she stays in bed. She has an unacceptable idea of what functional means."

Renée gave him a sharp look, but he was in turn looking at Wanda. So while she worked at patching the wounds that needed more bandages, she wondered why someone would risk their life for a king and country that was not their own. "There. I have done all I can for now. Lie still, Wanda."

"Thank you again, doctor," Jim said. "Why don't you rest for a while? There is a small tea room – two doors away."

David recognised a tacit dismissal and promptly agreed he could use a coffee. It gave Renée no excuse to refuse the suggestion.

Wanda smiled faintly at Jim. She didn't waste energy apologising for the state she was in. He had moved a chair close to the bed and sat where he could take the fingers of her right hand in his. "What can you add to what David has told me?"

Speaking very softly and slowly, Wanda described all her movements and observations from the time she had run from the mansion. David would have told him all she had seen and done up to then.

Jim realised that Wanda was forcing herself to recall all the details and to find the strength to keep talking. He held her hand a little more firmly and willed his own strength into her. Wanda sensed the offer and drew on his energy, but even so, the effort of concentrating was obvious. After a while, Jim began to get images in his mind to supplement the brief descriptions. Her photographic memory recalled exactly the costumes of the 'cavaliers' and commented on minor variations. She explained the nuances of the men's body language, and her belief that the men were drugged. Then she finished by explaining the effects of her mind tricks on Duvall.

Jim nodded, "Excellent work. I can work with all that. How are you really feeling?"

"Honestly? Like hell. I hope you don't need me for anything else."

"No, and I have an excellent surgeon coming to finish fixing you up. Tomorrow, at the latest I want you and David on the helicopter and out of the country."

"Suits me," Wanda agreed. She knew she was in no state for a more active role in Jim's mission. "But there was one more thing that just occurred to me. I said that I thought Duvall had a really strong hold on his cavaliers, and that I thought they were his private army...but I had a fleeting sense of how he saw his fantasy. He doesn't see himself as dying for king and country, but as king and country bowing to him."

"That is an interesting idea," Jim murmured, considering it. "Anything else?"

"No, that's everything."

"Good. Now, I want you to do everything the doctor tells you, and let them fix you up. You will be perfectly safe now."

Wanda couldn't understand why she had a sudden doubt about that assurance, but she didn't mention it. The way her head was pounding... her mind might be addled.


Jim had gone before Lanzecki arrived, so Renée met the noted micro-surgeon when he presented himself at the hospital reception desk. David had received a message giving warning of when he was due to arrive. Renée recognized the unobtrusive brown haired man from when she had sat in on several seminars. He was of medium height and slender in build, but his blue eyes were the true indication of his intelligence. He was neatly and casually dressed and carried a small overnight bag, in one of his graceful long fingered hands.

"Thank you for coming, Dr Lanzecki," Renée greeted him. She introduced herself and forestalled questions by adding, "I'll take you to your patient."

The surgeon waited until they were away from the reception desk and in a deserted passage to ask, "Who is so important that I had to cancel two clinics to come here?"

Renée sensed that Lanzecki resented powerful people demanding his service as if he were some lowly servant. She didn't disagree with that sentiment.

"Your patient isn't rich, or powerful," Renée explained. "She was injured while investigating a matter involving rich and unscrupulous people."

"Someone must be paying to have this person treated here," Lanzecki pointed out. He didn't mention his fee, but Renée thought he might be reserving judgement on that until he learnt about his patient. It seemed he did realise he needed to keep this patient confidential.

"It was necessary to be discreet," Renée murmured. "Something that wouldn't be possible at the Free Hospital where I work, or at City General."

Lanzecki gave Renée a sideways glance as if reassessing the situation. "Tell me about the patient."

"She was dumped in a derelict building and left for dead. Fortunately, one of my friends saw the incident and called me. Those who attacked this woman wanted it to appear as a suicide attempt. Her wrists were slashed. I have made a rough repair, but those who summoned you want her to have the best care to ensure maximum hand and wrist movement in the future. The other injuries, including a mild concussion, are under control."

Renée quickly summarised the other damage, and she heard Lanzecki give a faint hiss of condemnation of those responsible.

"I see," Lanzecki acknowledged, feeling more sympathy for the patient he was to treat.

They reached the private room. It was not one of the wards, but a pre-op preparation area.

"Through here, Doctor," Renée directed.

Lanzecki recognised the room for what it was and gave it a thorough survey before placing his bag in an out of the way position near the door. He took in the tall blond haired man in nurse's scrubs standing next to the trolley with the patient.

He had many questions, but he went first to the bottle of hand sanitiser by the door and washed his hands. Then he went to the patient and automatically moved to check the woman's pulse. He saw the bandages, with signs of oozing blood, and moved to feel for the carotid pulse instead. When he looked at his patient, he saw the blue-green eyes calmly returning his scrutiny.

"What is your name?" Lanzecki asked as he began his evaluation.

"Wanda."

"I hear that you encountered some nasty people," he commented, as he worked to build a rapport with her.

"Yes," his patient admitted with a faint wry smile. "So it seems."

Lanzecki directed questions to Renée, and she was able to answer his questions until, "Where are the theatre staff?"

David spoke up. "No theatre staff. Dr de Salle and I will assist you. I am a qualified paramedic."

He saw Lanzecki about to object and added, "Sir, I expect this is not what you are used to, and I appreciate your willingness to take on a strange patient at short notice but this patient must be kept safe.

Powerful people will try to have her killed if they learn she is alive."

"A matter of national importance," Lanzecki commented. He seemed to shrug slightly – possibly recalling how he had not been allowed to refuse the summons that brought him there.

"Very well, we will begin." Lanzecki began issuing directions, and found that the young Dr de Salle had anticipated his requirements and most of the preparation was already done. He had little to do except get dressed in the gown and hat provided and scrub up, and supervise his two assistants doing the same.

Lanzecki had another shock when he expressed his concern about the lack of an anaesthetist.

"You will have to do this using a local," David stated.

"No! Delicate repairs such as I am needed to do, take time. The patient must remain still." Lanzecki was finding the situation intolerable.

Wanda spoke up. "Doctor, a local will be fine. I react unpredictably to some kinds of drugs. In my current condition, unfamiliar medication might be dangerous. I will stay still, and you can prop my wrists to keep them from moving."

Wanda ignored the ensuing disagreement, and simply wished the doctor would hurry up and start.

Lanzecki agreed to the stipulations, with stated reservations. He reserved the right to overrule his assistants if the matter warranted it. Then nodded for Renée to administer the local anaesthetic at the positions he indicated. He studied his patient while he waited for the drug to work, and was impressed by her calmness at the idea of being awake during a potentially long and difficult operation. When he started, he had no time to worry about anything but the delicate work he needed to do and only later realised that the patient had not moved during the whole time.

# Chapter 11

When he left the hospital in the early hours of the day, Jim Phillips returned to his modest hotel room to await his team.

Grant Collier had arrived with him the previous day and already knew the basic situation. He was settled into a watching position – monitoring calls into and out of the mansion that Jim believed was the Cavalier Club. He was using an anonymous utilities van to keep the building under observation and had a secure radio link with Jim. He intended to leave his equipment on record and attend as he had some specialised equipment to show the rest of the team.

Max Hart had obeyed Jim's instructions to meet and deliver a certain man to a certain address before coming on to the hotel. Nicholas Black came after collecting a series of tapes and films of King Karl's public appearances. He had met up with Shannon Fletcher and they arrived together. There were some moments of greeting until something of Jim's manner affected them.

As soon as Nicholas arrived, he began to brief the rest of his team. He closed the curtains and turned on the data projector.

"This is King Karl IV, the Monarch of Weisboden. He has been king for three years, since the abdication of his father, who is now addressed as Prince Michael. The image of the former King appeared on the screen beside the image of his son.

"The King has been involved in successful talks with neighbouring countries, and several major European countries. The agreements made, are of vital importance to the long term goals of the King to turn the government of this country into a full democracy. Any major scandal at this time could ruin that plan, and part of our mission is to ensure that nothing prevents the signing of those agreements in seven days' time.

"There have been many hushed scandals in the Royal Family over the years. Prince Michael has twelve children from two marriages. Karl has a particularly wild past and it seems to be catching up with him.

There have been threats made against the monarchy in general and Karl in particular and rumblings of civil discord."

"So, where do we start, Jim?" Max Hart asked from his position by the window.

"We have only one clue," Jim told his team. "During the talks, there was a great deal of correspondence going back and forth from the palace to the Presidential house in Paris and the Holstein Estate in Bavaria where King Karl, his wife Alicia and three children were staying. In one of the diplomatic pouches from here, was an envelope containing an invitation, beautifully handwritten and correctly addressed to his Majesty."

Jim produced the original and handed it around. "It has been tested, but without results."

"How did the letter get into the pouch?" Nicholas queried. "Surely the only correspondence in it would be from the palace?"

"True," Jim agreed, "Someone in the palace must have placed it in the pouch. However, as you can see, the letter is an invitation to a reunion of the Cavalier Club. This was an ultra-private men's club some twenty years ago. The younger Karl was a member there, and the place had a wild reputation. It was eventually forced to close, and the building was later destroyed in a fire. What is significant is that it was reported that the King went very pale and shaky when he opened the letter."

"What has the King said of this?" Shannon asked.

"That we don't know, but Prince Michael suspects that it is a precursor to blackmail. However, his majesty was on his way back yesterday by plane. What is not generally known is that the plane he was on crashed due to bad weather. The King was the only survivor. We know of it because our agents were talking to Prince Michael when the news came and were in a position to offer to fly a rescue mission. The king was badly injured, and he was taken back to the palace in secrecy. I will be going there later today to talk to him, as our instructions are to work closely with the royal family."

"Have we any clue about the location of this Cavalier Club? There was no address on this invitation." Max pointed out.

"Nothing is known of it in official circles," Jim said. "However, the agents that did the preliminary investigation believe that this is the building."

As Grant Collier entered the room, Jim displayed the imposing building on the screen and gave them the address. "It dates back to the beginning of the 18th century, but the interior has been completely renovated. The top floor is a private gymnasium – for men only – and more than half of the current Government attend that fitness centre. As do many very influential members of the community. The third floor is offices and meeting rooms. The second floor is bedrooms and private lounges. The ground floor is a restaurant, bar and gaming rooms. There is a casino in the basement as well as storage rooms."

Jim flashed the photos Wanda and David had taken of the upper rooms, and described the others. He showed the floor plans for the house, and made amendments based on what Wanda had told him.

"The owner and manager of the building is Claude Duvall. He is a millionaire philanthropist, outwardly respectable, very influential. He has many highly placed acquaintances, and he is expanding into politics. He almost certainly knows King Karl and it is likely that he is the prime mover behind the current intrigue. His father was the owner of the original Cavalier Club."

"You seem very sure that he is our man, Jim," Nicholas challenged.

"If he is not, then this club is the most likely source of information. Whoever is out to discredit the monarchy has to have powerful friends, and it can only be an attempt to take control of the country. Duvall is the key to getting into the club, and no one is allowed in without his agreement. So that is our first aim."

"Shannon, Duvall will be attending a fundraising tea tomorrow afternoon. You will be attending as the Countess Felice D'Alembert, a French Heiress of an old family."

"A good cavalier sounding name?" Shannon suggested.

Jim nodded. "Getting close to him will not be easy. He isn't known to be interested in women at all, but you struck the right note. He does fancy himself as a cavalier."

"So I should emphasise rich, noble, ancient lineage," Shannon summarised.

"With links to European Royalty several generations back," Jim suggested. "You will also be a hard headed and shrewd business woman – who likes men with muscles and watching fights."

Shannon smiled in anticipation.

"Max, you will be Shannon's chauffer and body guard," Jim outlined. "Scornful of wimps like Duvall who don't fight but needs to use a sword. You are out to impress him with your physical ability. You work for the countess because she pays well."

Jim put a subtle emphasis on the last two words.

"Not just with money," Max deduced. "Money, women, fighting partners?"

"Right," Jim confirmed. "Duvall also has a passion for swords." He showed the picture of his display wall. "Grant has reproduced a sword of the cavalier era."

The sword was held up so that the gems on the hilt sparkled.

"I recognise that!" Nicholas said. "Isn't it the sword of Oliver Cromwell? Historians have been searching for it for centuries."

"Precisely why Duvall will do almost anything to get his hands on it," Jim explained. "We won't make getting it easy for him."

Grant took over the description. "This sword contains a miniature camera, recorder and transmitter, along with a projector," he said with a faint smile. "Sensitive enough to pick up voices through two thicknesses of wall."

"Shannon, you will casually let slip information about the existence of the sword," Jim continued. He switched his attention to Grant.

"What have you got from the phone tap?"

"Duvall has left a message with an international detective agency. I intercepted it. They are to call him back at ten o'clock. He has asked for their top operative."

"Nicholas, you will make that call and arrange to meet him. Grant will cover you. I will be a visiting diplomat from Austria," Jim told his team.

He went on to outline what he intended to achieve, and said finally, "Don't underestimate Duvall. Our agents know of at least three people who came out of Duvall's club with what appeared to be knife wounds. Two died. Fortunately, our agent was lucky. She is recovering in hospital."

The team took in Jim's warning, and understood the tightness in his tone.

"Let's go," Jim finished.

In the privacy of the hired room, Nicholas began to dial the number Grant had given him. The call was being monitored by a computer set up.

Grant spoke first, and passed the phone to Nicholas who spoke in French.

"Mr Duvall? This is Malcolm Monet, World Inc. Detective Agency. How may I assist you?"

"I require the services of a top class detective. You were recommended," Duvall said flatly. "Can you meet me at Capitol Park at 10.30? Carry an umbrella, I will find you."

"Certainly Monsieur," Nicholas agreed. "I was recalled so that I might serve you."

"The matter I want to discuss is highly confidential," Duvall cautioned him. "Be sure you are alone!"

The phone connection was ended.

Nicholas nodded at Grant who grinned back.

In the brief time period that Duvall had given him to reach the meeting place, Nicholas had been able to find a picture of Claude Duvall. So, he was aware of the man's approach from the moment Duvall had seen him.

Nicholas had chosen a very public spot to stand – a grassy mound well away from trees and bushes and the nearest seats. It would be easy for Duvall to see he was alone.

"Monsieur Monet?" Duvall greeted as he approached within talking distance.

Nicholas nodded agreement.

"May I inspect your credentials, Monsieur?" Duvall requested, coming right up to Nicholas who took a laminated identification and a folder from his pocket and passed it to Duvall.

"Thank you," Duvall said as he handed the documents back. "Shall we walk as we talk?"

"As you wish, Herr Duvall," Nicholas agreed. "I am at your service."

Nicholas gave no sign of being aware of a certain jogger, who was keeping just out of sight and monitoring their conversation. Grant would not be far away if he needed back up.

"I have a need for the strictest secrecy about my request," Duvall began, and the detective nodded gravely. They walked across the grass, rather than follow the paths.

"Of course," Nicholas assured him. "Please, proceed."

"One of my business premises was entered by a woman, after it had closed for the evening," Duvall related. He gave a very detailed description, which Nicholas noted in shorthand in a small notebook as he walked along.

"We checked the security films, and a woman like this was watching the place for several days or nights. This is a photo taken from one of the cameras."

Nicholas took and studied the picture. He gave no sign that he recognised Wanda Martin.

"Last night, the woman had makeup on and did look slightly different to this. However, the age, build, facial bone structure and hair length are consistent. I want this woman identified and found so that I can question her. I have given a confidential report to the police and I do not want this matter made public. At my place, a good many sensitive government discussions take place and I dare not risk a breach in my security. I am afraid this woman might be part of a plot to discredit me."

Grant, hearing this through his receiver, grinned briefly.

"I had a good look at her last night before she escaped. She pretended to be unconscious and my men did not hold her carefully enough," Duvall said finally.

Nicholas seemed to consider all that Duvall had said. He had a hunch that Duvall already had some ideas about the woman, and decided to be blunt.

"Have you any idea as to who this woman might be? Someone related to business rivals or who might be jealous of your position?"

Duvall did not answer right away. He seemed to be thinking.

"I considered such possibilities and could think of no one. However, I have a vague feeling that I have seen an older woman, who has a strong resemblance to this one, at some time in the past."

Duvall was not about to admit that he thought he had seen a ghost, and his thought that the ghost had been a projected image – could not be substantiated. He had made his men examine that room thoroughly. Then again, the woman who had seemed to die had not tripped any of his security sensors either.

Nicholas was a bit confused as to what Duvall wanted. He had thought at first he wanted the woman thief caught, but now he seemed to want something else.

"I made a sketch of the older woman that I just mentioned. I have an eidetic memory for faces, and I have drawn this from memory."

"Impressive," Nicholas praised. The sketch was quite detailed, a head and shoulders view. He glanced from the sketch to the photograph – there was a muted resemblance – allowing for differences in hairstyle, age and expression.

Nicholas summarised the information Duvall required – firstly to identify and then locate the intruder, and secondly to find out if she had a relationship to a woman such as in the sketch.

When Duvall confirmed that, Nicholas terminated the conversation, after promising that he would work as swiftly as possible. He bowed slightly to Duvall and walked quickly back to the path.

Nicholas was aware, from Grant's viewpoint, that two men were following him. He gave these watchers no reason for suspicion when he returned directly to the building that housed the detective agency.

In the guise of a visiting diplomat, and slightly disguised, Jim Phillips was admitted to the palace visitor's room. He waited while Johannes took his name and credentials to Prince Michael. During that time, he took in the details of the room and correlated it with the description supplied by David.

It was Prince Stephen who came back with Johannes.

"Herr Fischer, my father is currently occupied by matters of state in my brother, the King's, absence. However, he has agreed to see you. If you do not mind waiting, I can escort you to my father's office."

"Thank you," Jim bowed slightly.

Johannes, preceded them, opening up a door. He would have continued, but Stephen dismissed him. All the same, Jim made no attempt at conversation as they walked through several corridors. Instead, he was studying the youngest Prince, and comparing him to Renée. There was little resemblance.

They did not go to Prince Michael's office, but to his private suite. The former monarch rose from his seat when Stephen and his guest entered. He studied the white haired man closely.

"I have been expecting you," Prince Michael greeted, and Jim bowed respectfully. "Please come into my private sitting room. Stephen, I do not want to be disturbed."

Stephen heard, "I was most impressed by your two agents..." before the door closed.


Jim followed Prince Michael into the inner room. Once inside, Jim presented his identification, and a letter from the man Prince Michael had first contacted. He waited for the prince to seat himself, before accepting the invitation to do likewise.

While he waited for Prince Michael to peruse the letter, Jim looked around. This private room was furnished in a simpler, but no less elegant fashion. It had comfortable armchairs, a low table, a place for books and papers close to one of the chairs, and modern conveniences of television, and music system – both able to be controlled remotely. The books on the polished wood bookshelf were an eclectic mixture of classics and modern literary works.

"As I indicated, I was very impressed by your two agents. They promised that I would be kept informed of all they discovered," Prince Michael commented.

"I have their preliminary report, your Highness," Jim informed him. "They have completed their part and will be leaving Weisboden tomorrow."

Jim began to outline the progress of the investigation, and Prince Michael was impressed, but he questioned the findings not from disbelief, but because he wanted to be absolutely sure of the facts before accusing any one of treason.

"I am aware that we must, in no way, discredit the monarchy," Jim assured him. "However, I will require a clear field to work in. It is our intention to prove conclusively who is behind the threats and thoroughly discredit them. I will need to talk to his Majesty, if he is sufficiently recovered."

"Of course you would have been informed," Prince Michael said thoughtfully. "He seems better today, although the doctor was to have returned this morning to examine him."

"I met your daughter earlier, Your Highness," Jim told the Prince. "She is helping to...one of the agents you met yesterday was injured. She is being tended now. May I speak to his majesty?"

Nicholas spoke to Jim when he returned to the hotel from the palace.

"He wants to identify and find the woman who was in his club – just as you predicted," Nicholas told Jim. "He had a photo he said was from security cameras outside. But then, he seemed to want to know if she had any relation to a woman that looks like this." He took out the sketch that Duvall had given him as well as the photo.

Jim studied both. He spoke thoughtfully to Nicholas. "You know who that first picture is of, don't you?"

Nicholas nodded.

"Wanda was disguised when she and David scouted and infiltrated the club, so that photo was taken after she left the palace, but before she went to check his mansion. David told me that Wanda had been followed and observed when she was out with Princess Renée. So somehow, Duvall has connected a woman from the palace with the female intruder. We might assume that he has also linked the woman with the visiting American Scout Leader, Frau Davis and assumed she is an American agent since he slashed Wanda's wrists after he thought she was dead."

Jim heard Nicholas's hiss of anger.

"She is alive, if only because she has an odd ability to slow her vital functions right down, to seem as if she is dead. She did this trick on Duvall, and it meant that when Duvall slashed her, she didn't bleed. He must be trying to distance himself from the woman intruder, lest he be implicated when her body is found."

Jim went on, "However, that sketch is interesting. Wanda told me that she had been playing mind games on Duvall. When she dropped, supposedly dead, she projected a mind image to him of a ghostly, cavalier era woman." He tapped the sketch. "I believe that this is a very good likeness. I think that Wanda didn't give all this detail, but rather stimulated his memory to recall someone."

Jim kept thinking.

"We can use this to our advantage. Wanda was trying to give the impression that she was the ghost of his ancestor's mistress. Her story will be that she was mugged, and does not remember anything for a period of time. We can work on the idea that she was possessed by the spirit of this dead woman."

"But Wanda will be all right?" Nicholas asked.

"Yes, I had Max collect an excellent surgeon to repair the damage. She and David are at a private clinic and will be leaving early tomorrow. They will be evacuated by a US marine helicopter and Wanda will receive any further needed treatment at the base in Germany. Though I have arranged for a booking in their name on the ten am flight to Munich."

"What if our target has people watching the airport – he hasn't mentioned David – but if he knows of the scout connection he will know about him."

"The helicopter will be gone well before ten am, but just in case, I have arranged for several men from our embassy to watch the airport. I will be called if anyone shows interest in Frau and Herr Davis."

Nicholas relaxed. Jim had things under control as usual. "I will start studying King Karl's tapes. I shouldn't expect a call from Duvall until tomorrow. My investigations will take time."

"Good, Nicholas," Jim told him. "I will be going with Shannon to see Herr Brun. He has agreed to help us. I will take the sword to him to keep in his safe."

"Max has established his presence at the Regent Hotel, as Countess De Alembert's man. By evening, he will have arranged for the countess to attend Duvall's afternoon tea tomorrow," Jim commented aloud. "Grant will call if he hears anything important from the mansion."

Jim mentally ran through his plans and confirmed he had all arrangements underway. They would be ready to spring their plan into action the next day.

Then his mind returned to the matter of his two agents, and he thought of the need to get their bags and belongings from their hotel room. Not that he was worried anyone would find clues amongst their belongings, he knew David had the few sensitive items with him, but simply for neatness and so there would not be an investigation if things were left behind. He would contact the embassy and have an agent deliver the luggage to the hospital.

# Chapter 12

Renée visited the clinic again late in the evening to check Wanda's progress, and to bring a supply of analgesic medication for her. She was pleased to find Wanda sleeping, with her wrists elevated on pillows. David was able to assure her that there had been no problems since she had left earlier in the day.

Lanzecki had left instructions with Renée for follow up care. David quickly memorised the instructions and promised, "I will make sure Wanda is aware of what she should and shouldn't do."

"I really think Wanda should stay here for a few more days," Renée expressed her concern. "She needs rest to get over the concussion."

"I understand, Doctor, and in theory I agree. However, we must leave at first light. The US Marine pilot will fly us by helicopter to a marine base in Germany. I will ensure the doctors there take over the care."

"I guess that will have to do," Renée reluctantly agreed. "All the best then…"

"And thank you, Doctor, for all you have done too," David said, sincerely.

"Renée," she invited. "Perhaps later, you might get back in touch?"

"We'd like that," David agreed.

Renée closed her bag and gave him a smile before leaving.

In the morning, Wanda was awake early, and David helped her dress in clothes taken from her case.

"I'm glad Jim thought to have our stuff brought here. I did not fancy the idea of travelling to a marine base in one of these hospital gowns." Wanda was trying to sound like her normal self, but as yet, the painkillers Renée had given her were not working.

"Yes, and the hotel bill has been attended to," David assured her. "How are you feeling? Better?"

"Some," she claimed. "Functional."

David gave her a disbelieving look.

"Do you have our official passports?" she asked, trying to prove she was thinking straight.

"Our embassy contact is to meet us at the airport," David assured her. "I left our passports and laptop at the embassy while I was waiting for you to turn up again."

Wanda grimaced. "Wise move. Does he know we are going to be leaving at first light?"

"Yes, he was the one who told me that Mathias has his recall orders. He is just waiting for us. Our orders are to book our luggage through to Munich as if we are going on the morning flight, and then slip out to the helipad as soon as we have met our contact."

Wanda felt like all was under control and subsided into silence as she walked with David to their hire car. He had already taken their luggage out, and on this last trip was carrying her bag so that she didn't try to use her wrists for anything.

The last thing David did before driving off was to send Jim a brief SMS, so that their director knew he could tell the hospital they were finished there. Jim responded immediately with a blank message, but David had not expected anything else.

The roads to the airport had very little traffic at that hour, and he made the comment, "At least we can enjoy the scenery this time."

"I guess," Wanda responded. "Not that we have much time for that."

To David, his wife sounded unusually subdued. He went on to say, "I'm glad to be leaving."

"I am too. But I would have liked to get to know Renée better."

"And she, you, I think."


They drove into the airport car park, and into the section where the hire cars were returned. David saw a trolley bay nearby and went to fetch one to take their luggage. Before they began to move to the terminal, he took Wanda's coat from her case and urged her to put it on.

"It will hide those bandages better. Anyone seeing them will be looking at us to wonder what happened to you."

Since she was already feeling unusually vulnerable, Wanda didn't argue. She was busy trying to convince herself not to look for trouble that wasn't there, and by the time they reached the glass doors, thought she had succeeded. However, the instant she passed through the door, she felt eyes on her, and mentioned the feeling to David.

"Jim asked for some Embassy observers," David whispered in her ear. "That group near the coffee lounge I would say."

Wanda glanced around and noted the group – all were dressed in suits, and it did seem the men were watching her and David, even if they stayed where they were. She tried to shrug off the awareness of watchers, but couldn't quite rid herself of an uncomfortable feeling.

Normally she trusted such feelings, but she knew she hadn't recovered from the shock of Duvall's treatment of her, and thought she was being paranoid. Certainly, having the severe headache wasn't helping, neither was the fact that the last traces of the local anaesthetic was wearing off and her wrists were throbbing too.

So, ignoring the watchers, and keeping her eyes away from the milling around or sitting early passengers, and the airport staff who were moving about purposefully, Wanda walked beside David to the luggage check in, and saw their bags loaded on the conveyor to go to the plane. Then she followed as he returned the car keys to the rental desk.

"Do you want a drink? Or Breakfast?" David asked her. They had not had a chance for any at the hospital.

Wanda shook her head. "To be honest – I want to get gone. Any sign of the Embassy contact?"

David glanced around. He knew the man by sight. "No, but he shouldn't be long. Let's go and watch the planes getting ready."

Wanda agreed, not admitting to misgivings.

They walked past two patrolling airport police officers, who seemed to pay them no attention. One carried a walkie-talkie set, with the microphone in ready reach on a tab on his shoulder.

"Mathias is expecting us," Wanda asked.

"He will be ready to go just as soon as we get there. We should be able to see the helipad from the observation window."

"I'd rather wait out there," Wanda said abruptly. She couldn't get interested in the planes outside, or the colour in the sky from the imminent sunrise. Every instinct was telling her to get away, but there was nothing to indicate trouble. The two police officers were not looking their way, even if one was talking into the radio. No one was taking any notice of them.

"Couldn't we get the embassy contact to send out stuff to the marine base in a diplomatic pouch or something?"

"He'll be here soon," David told her again, but then sensed her edginess. "What is wrong?"

"Dav, I want out of here – now."

"We're safe…" David began to assure her.

"David, please!"

"Ok, give me a moment to call the contact and tell him," David urged. He too was glancing around now, catching her fear. He quickly dialled the number and waited. "No answer. Like I said, he's on his way."

"Call him back as we go, and leave a message," Wanda urged. She pulled on David's sleeve, to get him moving, as she watched three suited men strolling towards them. There was nothing about them to cause her danger sense to kick in, but beyond them, she saw police officers shepherding a group of people out of the terminal building. She instinctively glanced back towards the coffee lounge and saw two more police officers herding people from there too.

"David," she whispered a warning. "We need to move. Three men, at your six o'clock. Heading this way. And police are moving people out of the building."

David glanced around and suddenly knew Wanda's apparent paranoia had good cause. He grabbed his small 'carry-on' bag and Wanda's arm and began to walk purposefully towards the door leading to the tarmac and the helipad.

None of the three approaching men were the Embassy contact, and to his experienced eye, the men were all armed. They might not be intending to stop two supposed scout leaders, since they were not hurrying to reach them…but if he assumed that his wife's edginess was not due to the crack on the head…

A fourth man stepped out of a side passage just ahead of them. "Herr and Frau Davis?"

David nodded cautiously.

"This way," the man invited, indicating the passage, and glancing beyond them to the approaching men.

Thinking that this fourth man was an ally, David drew Wanda into a small room, after the man, who stepped aside and locked the door behind them.

"What is going on?" Wanda asked quietly in German. Her danger sense was in high gear.

The man didn't explain. Instead he said, "You need to stay here for a while. I had instructions to bring you here. Please make yourselves comfortable."

David caught Wanda giving the man an appraising look and shrugged a shoulder towards a two-seater leather couch. She didn't take the hint, but moved towards one of the four single chairs. She chose one next to a small table containing magazines and one of the three potted plastic plants. She sat after a careful look around the windowless room.

There was nothing to indicate what this room was normally used for, except that it seemed to be a private waiting room. A second door led off from the room, but again, there was no indication of the nature of that inner room. The only other items of interest were the security camera in on corner near the ceiling and a water fountain.

Wanda chose one of the single chairs as a tactical move. She would not be able to rise from the couch without help, but could from the chair.

"Is there a problem here?" Wanda asked the man as David went to the water fountain to fill a cup.

"No problem. You are to wait here."

Wanda studied the man and tried to read his body language. She was sensing nothing of is thoughts, but he was keeping both of them in sight as if he didn't trust them.

"I saw police evicting people from the terminal," Wanda noted casually. "Has there been a threat of some kind? Will it delay our flight?"

"Someone will be here shortly to talk to you. Please sit down."

"I'd rather stand," David declined, politely. "And perhaps you might be so kind as to tell us who you are and who sent you?"

Both saw the man stiffen as if considering the question a threat, but that was all he did. David deliberately took out his mobile phone and flipped it open, as if intending to make a call. That brought an immediate reaction from their escort.

"Herr Davis, you will please sit down next to your wife. There are questions you need to answer."

The man approached and held his hand out for the mobile phone, when David ignored the gesture, a small handgun appeared in the man's other hand, and the man gestured with it.

"Hand the phone over, please, Herr Davis."

Prudence directed him and the man took the phone and closed it, ending the surreptitious call David had tried to make.

"What is it that you think we have done if you feel a need to aim a gun at us," Wanda said with mild anger. "We are scout leaders, not criminals!"

"I have my orders," the man countered.

"And this detention is unlawful, since you have not explained why you have done it," David stated. "We are United States citizens and if we are to be questioned, we have the right to call the US Embassy."

Without redirecting the direction of the gun, the man took out an ID wallet and flipped it open.

"State Police. You will please wait quietly. I am sure the matter will be cleared up quickly."

With a feigned sigh, Wanda said, "I hope this will not take much longer. We have a flight to catch and a very important meeting with the World Scout Jamboree Committee this afternoon."

"There is still three hours to your flight, Frau Davis," the man told her. "If you co-operate, you will be in plenty of time to catch it."

David walked closer to his wife and held up the cup of water as if offering her a drink. With his back to the man, he soundlessly formed the word, "Anything?"

Wanda shrugged slightly, and lifted one hand as if to take the water. She really couldn't tell if this man was a threat. They dared not try to disable him and flee the room. There were still those other men outside. This man may distrust them, but his action might be a simple precaution, or a misunderstanding.

With the cup held to her mouth, because she couldn't have held it, Wanda took a sip and let David place it on the small table beside her. Then, with the distraction of his jiggling a second chair close to hers, Wanda whispered, "I don't get anything from him. All he knows is that there was a threat made against the airport and he had to get us out of sight. He knows nothing."

They both felt disquiet, but with no evidence that they were being detained for a nefarious reason, any attempt to overcome the man would blow their cover.

A threat against the airport would explain the evacuation of all patrons and staff, but not why they were put into a small, enclosed room.

David kept quiet, but Wanda was aware of what he was thinking. Mainly, it was that Mathias was waiting for them, and the Embassy contact was due anytime. He hoped that if either of them called his phone and found it off, they would not investigate.

Mathias knew not to approach them, but if they were delayed much longer, he would be agitating because he had orders to leave. He might ring the Embassy, and they might know of the trouble already and reassure him. The Embassy contact, was an unknown quantity. If he ran into the lockout situation, he would surely try to ring. Would he try Wanda's number? She had her phone on silent, but would be unable to answer it.


Just then, a phone did begin to ring, and David jumped. The gun wielding man pulled his phone out and answered it. His half of the conversation was uninformative, but when he ended the call, his manner became friendlier. "Herr Hessler will see you now."

The door furthest from the passage opened and another man gestured them inside another room.

A huge man sat behind a table that only had a telephone on it. Through an open archway to his right, a bank of security monitor screens showed scenes around the airport terminal and outside service areas.

"Be seated," the huge man directed.

As they obeyed, Wanda saw the three men that had begun to follow them earlier emerge from the monitoring room. Two moved to the outer door, and the third lingered next to a filing cabinet by the door they had entered.

The name Hessler was common enough in Weisboden, and David had not connected it to their recent investigations. However, seeing the severe looking man behind the desk, caused him to identify the man. He was the minister in charge of law enforcement.

"Well, well," he thought in his mind, hoping Wanda would sense his thoughts. "What is Dietrich Hessler, a member of the Government doing here?"

His unspoken question was answered.


"Stick to our cover story," David said very quietly. His lips hardly moved. Aloud, he spoke in halting German, "What is the trouble, Sir?"

"I have received information that the two of you are spies and a threat to his Majesty, King Karl," Hessler said bluntly. "You will be kept in custody until your identification is checked."

Wanda knew the best defence was to attack. "I am sure you will have no trouble verifying our identity, Sir, but really, this is the last straw. We came to talk to Prince Michael about holding the world jamboree here. We should have left yesterday except some friendly local separated me from my husband and I woke up in hospital with no idea of what happened. Now this ridiculous accusation!"

The comment from the parliamentarian astounded them, revealing as it did that their cover was broken.

"A woman of your description was identified as being illegally on private premises the night before last. You were injured trying to escape."

Wanda acted astounded. "I wouldn't do any such thing! And, what would that have to do with a threat to your King?"

"We have been given certain evidence and you will understand that we must investigate the matter," Hessler stated reasonably.

David spoke up. "I expect you must, but are we allowed to be given some form of legal assistance here?"

"If you know of someone, you may call him," Hessler invited.

"We are visitors in this country," David pointed out, reasonably. "How will we find someone?"

Wanda spoke to David's mind. "He thinks there is proof against us! Someone else is directing him. He personally can't have recognised me. No one should have."

David's mind pictured her hands, and she sensed his question. She shrugged slightly.

Having little choice but to comply, they allowed themselves to be led via deserted passageways to an official looking car that was parked at the rear of the terminal. Two of the suited men sat with them in the car, and the driver ignored them. Hessler went into a second car that followed theirs to a building in the Capitol.

David knew that Wanda still had hidden tools, as he did himself - though he had doubts that Wanda would be able to use hers to free herself. He would have to free them both.

During the ride, Wanda wondered if she had slipped up somewhere. When she had been in the club, she had been disguised. No one should have recognised that woman as herself. David had removed the last traces of that make up after he had found her. Or had they realised she was disguised? No. She had been conscious the whole time. Unless her makeup was smudged after she began to play dead?

Had she left any clues? Not fingerprints. The lacquer spray they sprayed on their hands would prevent fingerprints, until washed in detergent. What?

Wanda thought as clearly as she could, but her mind was not fully recovered from that bang on the head. She tried to concentrate.

Maybe David was right – it was the bandages on her hands. But those who had dumped her had thought she was dead!

Wanda reached out to sense David's mind. She sensed his frustration and the feeling of having been tricked. He was also concerned for her. She sent him reassurance, but he was afraid they would need to try to escape and she would further damage her wrists. Again, she sent reassurance, and with it a picture of two scouts. She sensed his agreement - they would stick to their cover story and see how things proceeded.

At the judicial building in the city, Wanda and David were placed in separate interview rooms. Wanda prowled the room at first, examining the walls and door for opportunities to escape. If her hands were not bandaged so heavily, she would have no trouble freeing herself. However, she would not do that without trying to free David too. For now, there was still the chance that Hessler would question them, realise they were innocent and let them both go, even though a voice in her mind said, "Fat chance."

Finally, she felt the need to sit down and did so, resting her aching head on her folded arms and trying to wish the ache away. Then she used the time for silent meditation, glad of a chance to prepare her mind for whatever these people planned for her. She did doze for a short time, enough to relax her head and allow her to think more clearly. She was able to reach out and touch David's mind – and realised she was only just in time.

It seemed that his interrogators had tired of questioning him and receiving answers they did not believe. They had offered him water, and he had seen them fill it from a tap in the room. He only realised later that they had still managed to add something to it. His mind was becoming fuzzy.

David was used to sensing Wanda in his mind. He was relieved now to have her there. At least he knew she would be aware of everything he said, and hoped she would help him answer the questions. He quickly summarised what they had asked him already.

Wanda listened to the questions through his mind, and inserted answers before the drug made him speak the first thing he thought. It seemed to her they were repeating earlier questions, to try to trip him up.

Obviously, he had already told them why they had come – their jamboree cover story. They did not believe this was the only reason. Wanda slipped in a comment and David repeated it. If they did not believe this, have someone ask Prince Michael. They changed the thrust of the questions.

Where was he two nights before?

"At the hotel," David told them.

Where was his wife?

"With me, until we went out for some air and exercise and someone jumped us. My wife was knocked out. I ran to get help but when I came back she was gone."

The men asking questions did not know that David spoke the answers that Wanda put in his head, and not the truth that they believed the drug would produce.

Was he sure she was unconscious? Could she have run off to visit the big house in the park?"

"She was completely out," David insisted. "And she is not a thief. We are scout leaders – that's all."

How long was his wife missing?

"Hours! She was found early that morning, with slashed wrists."

Had she been raped?

"They didn't think so."

The men were not pleased. Their comments, heard by David and understood by Wanda, betrayed them. They were under orders from someone to find things out – and couldn't. They thought that David was involved with the raid on Duvall's club, and had been looking for him to question him, and hadn't expected to see her. However, they would start on her soon. Well, she would not be tricked.

These men were members of the secret police who had a mandate to guard against treason. That much was true, but Wanda was becoming convinced that they were also members of the organisation that she and David were looking for.

They would have no idea that King Karl had returned to the country, but they knew that David and a woman had been in touch with the royal family. They were fishing for information, in case the royals had heard of their plot and asked for outside help. They were paranoid, guessing. And yes, the woman they had dumped, believing her dead – was believed to be David's scout leader companion. Even though she did not look like the woman in the description they had been given– she did have two damaged hands.

If they were merely fishing for information with David – they would be earnest with her.

Wanda drew her mind back to herself as she became aware of two men in the room with her. When one of them spoke to her, she opened her eyes and blinked a couple of times and only then seemed to be aware of the people.

"Sorry! I must have dozed off. Lingering effects of the bang on the head," Wanda apologised. She did not recognise either man. They were not the ones that had picked them up.

"Do you feel you are well enough to answer questions?" one asked with outward concern.

"I think so."

"Come with us, then. We will go somewhere more comfortable."

This new room was a larger room, with four men sitting around a table, Hessler was in the head seat, and he had a folder opened in front of him. The man immediately beside him had a computer in front of him, and his function became obvious when the questions began and he began to type the answers.

Wanda was trying to act helpful, and had gone along without complaint. After answering a number of questions, however, she noticed the time clock and swore softly, and then asked, "We are not going to be able to make our meeting. I will need to ring the committee and let them know. Otherwise they will begin a search for us."

She sensed a moment of panic from the men, and it amused her.

"We don't have access to international lines from here," one of the men said quickly. "Is there someone local we could ring?"

Wanda hid a smile. "I have not the contact number for the Scouting Association here, but I believe that Prince Michael would know it."

To Wanda, it was obvious that they did not want to ask Prince Michael anything, because what they were doing was unsanctioned.

"We will contact the palace for you," they offered, but Wanda doubted it.

As with David, they asked her if she wanted some water. She did, but to be awkward, she asked if it would be possible to have orange juice, with a straw to drink it through. Either way, they would put their drug into it, but this way she was irritating them – in all innocence of course.

They agreed, and when the juice arrived, it came with cups of coffee for themselves. Wanda sipped her drink until she had taken in a quarter of it. In between sips, she answered their questions. All these were innocuous ones, identical to those they had asked David, and she gave them much the same answers that he had. The men drank their coffee faster, as a hint for her to copy their example. After a few more routine questions, they put some water beside her anyway, and asked if she was going to finish her juice.

Wanda took a few more sips and said, "If I drink it too fast, I am likely to bring it back up."

Again she had scored on the men, both hid feelings of revulsion. They were also inwardly fuming at the delay and the need to be pleasant and nice.

Wanda was beginning to feel the effect of the drug, and was prepared for it. These men would have no idea of her past and the training she had been given. She now had a strong resistance to hypnosis and to truth drugs and they would have no way of knowing that her system reacted very differently to many drugs.

In short – their drug would not affect her. Well, it did to the point of relaxing her body and detaching her mind from it - enough to reduce the discomfort from the operations on her wrists. Had she taken the full dose, her body would have gone rigid. Instead, she was still in control of her mind and her answers.

Her story, as they elicited it with their questions, and Wanda had to admire their skill at questioning, was identical to David's, only told from a different viewpoint. She claimed to have no memory of an eight-hour period – from when the supposed attack occurred to when she woke in a doctor's clinic with slashed wrists. They could not shake her story and they did not like it.

Then, thinking she was out to it, they used the phone in the room. They called Duvall, and reported tersely to him. Wanda could not hear the conversation at the other end, but when the man had hung up the phone, he produced a syringe and filled it from an ampoule containing a pale yellow solution. Wanda could only speculate as to what it contained, but she did not believe that they intended to kill her, for they had told Duvall that questions would be raised if any harm came to her and her husband.

Wanda was relieved when the part of her mind monitoring her physical self, felt the reduction in the drug's effect. She prepared herself to wake up, and when she opened her eyes, the men were seated as they had been and one of them started a question in mid-sentence.

Wanda shook her head as if to clear it.

"Sorry, I must have started to doze off. What did you just ask me?"

The man repeated the question, and Wanda answered it as best she could. After a few more questions, Hessler closed a folder and rose from his seat behind the table.

"Thank you for your cooperation, Frau Davis. I am sorry it was necessary to detain you. You bear an uncanny resemblance to the woman we are seeking. However, Prince Michael himself has confirmed what you and your husband have told us. You have been very helpful."

"You were, I suppose, only doing your job," Wanda conceded, with only a trace of annoyance. "However, there is no way we will be able to make our appointment. Would you please notify the airport and arrange for our tickets to be transferred to the next available flight to our destination?"

Hessler nodded to the secretary, who rose and left the room.

"We have a lounge where you can wait while we make arrangements. Your husband is there."

He took her to a different part of the building and David was indeed waiting for her. He had their luggage and her handbag. David was prepared to play the outraged and innocent victim. Wanda knew it was an act and played the conciliator and saying that. "They were only doing their job."

David quietened down after a while, and when the other man left the room, gave Wanda a quick embrace, never forgetting that they might be under observation. They paid no attention to their luggage, both guessing that it had been searched. Both privately decided that if these men had collected their luggage from the airport, it was to search it, and probably because they did not intend to let them leave the country yet. They knew that they had nothing suspicious in the bags. The only dangerous items were their official ID's and David's computer, and it was luck that they had not yet met their Embassy contact.

The man that had been sent to see to their departure details returned. He was almost obsequiously apologetic. It was an act, but Wanda and David pretended not to realise it.

"We apologise, but your morning flight had to leave without you. I was not able to get you on the last flight tonight. The next flight is tomorrow morning," he told them. He saw David about to get angry again and said hastily. "I have arranged for you to be accommodated tonight at the best hotel in the capital. All expenses paid. Prince Michael insisted."

The last was added hastily and Wanda made a mental bet with David that the Prince probably had no idea of what was going on with them.

"It is to make up for the inconvenience that we have caused you," the man went on. "A car will be coming to take you there. I will return when it comes. Please make yourselves comfortable."

The man departed, and Wanda gestured to the two-person sofa.

"Of all the nerve!" David said in English. "Don't they care that we have commitments? We need to ring the committee."

"It's been done!" Wanda told him. "I asked them to do that for us. I will ring them again from the hotel, and give them our new flight details."

"But they can't possibly think we would do what they were implying!" David went on.

"They don't know us," Wanda shrugged again. "Anyway, I might never have another chance to stay at a really posh hotel. It will be fun, especially if we are not paying for it."

"Hon, I wouldn't go and spend too much..." David began.

"I won't, really. Though it is probably just as well that we are staying over. I haven't been feeling really well and after that knock on the head…"

David changed his tone to one of husbandly concern. He put an arm around Wanda and let her rest her head on his shoulder.

"I really want to order food," Wanda said. "I am starting to feel like I can eat again without bringing it back up."

"Well, that's promising," David commented. "I think I will join you."

# Chapter 13

Jim's plans were proceeding smoothly, and he was with Nicholas and Grant in the van monitoring the big house in the park, when his phone rang. He instinctively glanced at his watch, before answering with a cautious, "Yes?" He was expecting to hear from Max and Shannon.

It wasn't his team members, but the contact from the Embassy. As he listened to the message, his face went tense with concern. He ended the call with a simple, "Thank you."

"What's wrong, Jim?" Nicholas asked.

"Wanda and David are missing. Our Embassy contact was to meet them at seven this morning. He had just entered the terminal when the police put the building into lockdown – a bomb scare or something. Everyone in the building was evacuated and kept incommunicado. They were allowed to return to their business half an hour ago, but the Embassy contact could not find Wanda or David. He did not know about the helicopter, but he was able to confirm that they were not on the ten o'clock Munich flight, and that their luggage was removed from the trolley for that flight."

Grant and Nicholas waited for Jim to continue, in case they needed to do something.

"Grant, call this number, I want to find out if Herr and Frau Davis went on the helicopter. Mathias was waiting for them."

Using the phone switchboard, Grant made the call. He did not identify himself, just asked for Mathias and handed the phone hand set to Jim.

Once again, Jim listened after asking the important question. Then he finished with, "You return to base. If you are required again, we will notify the flight HQ."

Jim was thoughtful and worried. "They were not on the helicopter. Mathias confirms that there was a flap on, lots of police cars."

"Would they have snuck out," Grant asked.

"If they had, they would have gone directly to the copter," Jim said. "No, I think the bomb threat was a false alarm to cover their removal.

I know this is a leap of logic, but the people we are up against probably have contacts in the police force."

"You mean Duvall?" Nicholas asked for confirmation.

"If he is the one behind this, as we believe, yes," Jim agreed.

"Surely he thinks the woman intruder is dead," Nicholas said. "I know he implied he wanted her found…but he can't know she was rescued."

"I am not assuming anything, but if he somehow linked her to the scout couple at the palace, he might have been after David – to try and get answers from him. He was probably having the airport watched. He may not be expecting Wanda to be with him, but if he sees a woman with bandaged hands…he'd have to conclude she was the intruder and she is obviously alive."

"It's nearly eleven o'clock now," Nicholas remarked. "Whoever has them has had four hours to try to get them to talk. How much do they know?"

"Too much," Jim admitted. "They don't know how we will be approaching the mission, or our cover identities but they provided most of the information we are working with and know that the King is back in Weisboden."

"What if they use drugs, or torture or hypnosis and make them talk?" Grant asked with concern. "They could endanger the mission."

"He dare not use torture," Jim said thoughtfully. "If they did, they would not dare let them go, for the same reason as if they were to die or disappear. Too many questions would be asked at a high level. Both David and Wanda are extremely resistant to hypnosis, and Wanda is resistant to most truth drugs. They do not have the expected effect on her. If they use them on David there is some risk, but not if Wanda is aware of what is going on."

"Can we be sure they will not be made to talk?" Grant insisted.

Hunches had always played an important part in Jim's success. He based his answer on one now.

"Yes. So we use this as a distraction and make Duvall think this is a personal matter – against him, but not that they are looking into the threats against Karl. He will not be expecting our sideways attack."

"How much should I tell Duvall?" Nicholas asked.

"Nothing that Wanda and David do from here on will be in the least suspicious," Jim assured him. "And if Duvall is distracted by them, it will help us. So, I think it is safe enough to tell him their cover story. That will be easy enough to check and it is solid. David gave the police an edited version of how Wanda was injured. They will both claim Wanda was assaulted, abducted and found later with no memory of events in between. I'll give you the details of the cover story in a moment. Nicholas, show that sketch to Shannon, if she can project a subtle hint of that woman, she may intrigue Duvall even more. Naturally, Monet will have found out nothing about that woman, but we can concoct a reason for the woman intruder to have a go at him."

Nicholas nodded. He pushed his concern for Wanda and David to the back of his mind. He had work to do.

"Grant, see if you can find out where Wanda and David were taken. I will be attending Duvall's afternoon tea with Prince Stephen. You can contact me there. In the meantime, let's get Shannon ready to be the star attraction."

The man returned as promised, but he was not alone. Wanda recognised his well-dressed companion, but in no way betrayed it.

"This is Claude Duvall," the newcomer was introduced. "He is the owner and manager of the Fleur-De-Lis hotel, where you will be staying tonight.

"Owner?" Wanda feigned surprise. "We're honoured. I really expected a minor flunkey to drive us. I am beginning to feel like royalty."

Wanda was out to charm the man, as if she didn't know what an evil creep he was. David stood and shook Duvall's proffered hand, and thanked him in German.

"It wasn't necessary for you to come yourself, Herr Duvall, though I am flattered."

"I did not wish to leave you with a bad opinion of my country," Duvall explained, and he turned his attention to Wanda and offered her his hand.

She could not grip his, so she simply rested her bandaged wrist on his and stood up by herself, with deliberate awkwardness. Duvall turned it into a graceful gesture whereby he kissed the bandages as if they weren't there – in a naturally courteous gesture. He spoke a few sentences in French, and although Wanda understood every word, she did not let on.

Shaking her head with a smile, she spoke to him. "I'm sorry. I may speak passable German, but my French is appalling. I understood about three words of what you just said."

Duvall repeated his words in German and Wanda managed a blush at his very flattering remarks – but only by remembering the most embarrassing thing she had ever experienced.

"You are very kind, Sir," Wanda replied. "But, if I am not being rude, I would really like to get away from here. I am feeling very tired."

Duvall became the solicitous host, and he helped them down to his car and ordered the police officers to bring their bags down. That the man obeyed without the faintest trace of resentment told Wanda a great deal.

Duvall had apparently been briefed on their purported reason for being in Weisboden. He conversed with them on the subject all the way to the hotel, with what sounded like sincere interest. The public side of Duvall was, after all, that of a great philanthropist.

Wanda was content to let David do the talking. She made little secret of examining the luxurious interior of the chauffeured limousine. She was pretending to be fantasising about being used to such luxury. She knew Duvall was surreptitiously watching her, and she hoped he thought her a naive, dumb female.

Duvall was leading up to something, but Wanda could not fathom what. This failure surprised her, but she could wait to hear it. He finally broached a suggestion, when they were outside the suite he had put at their disposal at the hotel. It came almost as an afterthought, except Wanda knew better.

"I have been wondering how I might help you turn this delay to your advantage," Duvall said thoughtfully. "I have many acquaintances in business circles. I am sure many of them would be interested in supporting a scout jamboree. Perhaps I could arrange for you to talk to some of them?"

He opened the door to the suite and gestured for them to precede him.

David appeared to consider the idea. He had the distinct feeling that Duvall was trying to manoeuvre him into some position.

Wanda sent him a thought. "He wants to split us up. Have each of us as a hostage for the behaviour of the other. It will be dangerous, but we might learn something more."

David nodded, as if agreeing to Duvall's suggestion. "Normally, at this early stage of proceedings, we don't start to seek support from local businesses. The Committee must still decide between several possible venues. They may have already decided, as that was on today's agenda. I really must call them to find out about that. I would like to see it held here – Prince Michael really impressed me. I guess though, that it would not hurt to talk to some of your acquaintances. It may save us a trip back later."

"I will see what I can arrange," Duvall promised. He turned and caught Wanda making a face. He did not pretend he had not seen the look, but waited for Wanda to comment. She fell for the tacit request for an explanation.

"Oh, yes, I agree it would make our delay worthwhile, but the way I am feeling, I think talking to dull, old fogey businessmen would give me a worse headache than I have already. I think I would prefer to stay here and rest."

"Perhaps, after you have rested, you might like to be my guest at a little garden tea I have arranged for this afternoon? There will be a number of important people there, possibly some of the royal family, ambassadors, actors and others. It is to raise money for charity. You might find people who would aid your cause."

Wanda pretended stage fright. "Me? Oh, no! I had stage fright for the week before we saw Prince Michael – ask my husband! I wouldn't know how to talk to such people!"

"Wear your uniform, talk about scouts," David said with a grin.

"You don't get tongue tied talking to ordinary people."

"I couldn't," Wanda insisted. She was busy trying to find out why Duvall wanted her to go to this party. "I have heard about these events. They're strictly black tie – or slinky dress! I would be totally out of place!"

Wanda did not want to sound eager, but she was hoping that Jim would be at the party. Duvall was going all out to persuade her, more so since he saw David grinning at her 'stage fright'.

Wanda finally agreed, after Duvall offered to find her something more suitable to wear. Though she really did need a rest, and said so. In the end, it was decided to let her rest for two hours, and then come down.

Once Duvall had left, Wanda gave David a grim smile as they continued their charade, assuming they were still being observed.

Duvall had decided to go and see for himself the woman his minions had questioned. Having done so, he was practically certain that she was the woman who had infiltrated his club. Her behaviour in his presence could be an act. The woman at the club had been supremely confident, and that confidence would make her a good actor. Moreover, he had slashed the wrists of that infiltrator, and this woman had bandaged wrists. Yet, he had seen no sign of recognition from the woman.

Before coming out, he had received a preliminary report from the detective, Monet. In summary, Monet had checked Interpol records and found no file on her. He had asked his office to request similar checks in all countries. Had checked immigration and visitors records, and from security footage at the airport, found the woman when she arrived. From there it was easy to identify her as Gwen Davis, a scout leader from the USA.

Duvall had learnt only what their cover story had been and was told that Monet had requested further information from the American office, and should have the results by morning.

Duvall was impressed by Monet's quick results, and his promise of further information by morning. He could not delay the people leaving for much longer.

Yet he really wanted to know why the woman had been in his club. Was she a pawn? Had someone drugged her and sent her into his club? He would not be satisfied until he knew.

When Jim arrived at the charity afternoon in the company of Prince Stephen, the event had been underway for an hour already. In his role as an ambassador from a neighbouring country, he was acting as one who felt quite out of place in the gathering. He was wearing a slightly outdated style of formal suit and glasses with thick-lenses that augmented his distance perception.

He wandered through the formal garden of the Fleur-De- Lis hotel, observing in passing the way the paths wound around precisely trimmed bushes, but noting in detail the face of every person he looked at. He kept an eye out towards the hotel but his first aim was to spot Shannon and Max. That was not hard. It was easy to see that the Countess was a great hit. He did not spot Claude Duvall, the host of the event, and that made him thoughtful.

He whispered to Prince Stephen to move gradually toward the hotel that dominated the gardens.

Stephen complied without comment. He knew this man was working for his father, and had taken over from Herr and Frau Davis. He had instructions to co-operate with the man in any way possible.

Therefore, his nervous companion, who was a direct contrast to the confident man that had spoken to his father, amused him. He was astute enough to realise the man was dissembling and made no comment.

"Nervous, Ambassador?" Stephen queried with a half grin. "You should be used to dealing with important people."

"Well, yes," Jim played along. "But I deal with leaders, on important matters. Not starlets and who knows what. I have never been good at small chatter."

"Well, it is not something that one learns as part of lessons in statecraft," Stephen admitted truthfully. "But father did insist that we all learnt to deal with the general population, so we all attended regular schools instead of being tutored. Hence, I am filling in for him today. The charity this event is raising money for, is one that father instigated. So as father said, your presence, as well as improving relations between our countries, will also help raise money."

"Well, I guess I will manage," Jim said in the querulous voice. He was aware of a hovering waiter, so well trained as to be inconspicuous until looked for. "Perhaps, your highness, I could fetch you some refreshments?"

Jim did not even glance at the waiter as he asked the question.

Stephen began to wheel his chair forward as he answered cheerfully. "That is one thing I do enjoy about these events."

Jim glanced around, seemed surprised to see the waiter there, and deferred to Prince Stephen before selecting a drink of his own.

"Well, well," Stephen murmured to himself after the waiter had moved off. Jim looked in the direction of Stephen's gaze. "Edward and Julian - I had not heard they were back."

Stephen began to wheel himself in the direction of his siblings using one hand to wheel and another to hold his drink. Jim followed without difficulty. It was, after all, his intention to meet as many people as possible and Stephen had assured him he could introduce him to just about anyone who would be there.

Jim held back as Stephen greeted his brothers with apparent friendliness.

"Edward, Julian - I didn't know you were here!"

"I just got in," Edward said with a charming smile. "Julian got in last night. We tried to see father, but he's too busy. What's up?"

"What – broke again?" Stephen teased, changing the subject as if to remind his brothers not to discuss family business around others.

Edward's expression hardened for a moment, and then he smiled again. "No, Brat, just to say hello. I thought he was going to be here."

"I'm filling in," Stephen managed to sound bored, and then turned to Julian. "I thought you would have attached yourself to the prettiest woman here by now?"

Julian scowled. Obviously, he was in a foul mood. Edward answered for him. "He tried for that wench in the lime green outfit. She simply ignored him."

Stephen searched the direction where Edward pointed.

Edward went on, "She looked at him like he was a puppy that wasn't house broken."

"Then I had better not go near her," Stephen chuckled. "She would probably treat me like a puppy that hadn't been born yet."

Suddenly Julian chuckled. "She's just a tramp. Rich – but still a tramp."

Jim saw a hint of the woman charmer coming out. Julian smiled at Stephen, cuffed Edward on the shoulder and walked off without good-byes.

Stephen turned to introduce Jim to Edward, and the nature of the eye lenses hid the fact that although talking to Prince Edward, Jim was actually watching Julian's purposeful striding across the gardens.

Stephen and Edward drew the Ambassador into some casual talk, before Stephen recalled his duty to introduce his father's guest to as many people as possible. He started to move off, but suddenly turned back to Edward. "Who is that woman in the green dress?"

"Some French countess, I heard," Edward chuckled. Stephen grinned and continued to move away.

After pausing for Stephen to introduce the Ambassador to various dignitaries, members of the government and business people, Stephen and Jim had come within earshot of the Countess and her bodyguard.

Jim heard Shannon's rich throaty laugh and turned in her direction. He was in time to see Wanda coming down the stairs from the hotel. His glasses enabled him to study her face, and he saw he signs of strain as tension around her eyes. She was hiding it well, even though it seemed that Duvall was steadying her. It was a relief to see she was fine. Grant had reported that she was here with David, as guests of the hotel, but – where was David?

"I need to speak to Frau Davis," Jim spoke so only Stephen could hear him.

Stephen nodded slightly, and after a long moment appeared to notice Wanda when she was only a few feet away. Jim had not glanced in her direction.

"Why, Frau Davis," Stephen said in surprise, and both Wanda and

Duvall turned to look at him. Wanda seemed relieved to see someone she knew, but Duvall seemed to be summing up the Prince and his companion. Wanda did not glance at Jim until Stephen introduced them, and then Wanda gave him only cursory attention. In that glance, Jim saw her fear.

Prince Stephen had not heard of her "accident" and exclaimed with concern when he saw her bandaged wrists.

"I had a rather unpleasant experience, your Highness. I would really prefer not to discuss it," Wanda told him.

"That is terrible! You must come and stay at the palace until you are well enough to travel." Stephen was genuinely appalled. "I can't have you thinking my family was as remiss in hospitality as to let such a thing happen."

Wanda forced a smile – genuine though – finding humour in her current situation.

"I don't think anything like that so you don't have to worry. Mr Duvall is being so kind. He has given us the use of his best room, and given David the chance to speak to some of the important businessmen in the Capitol. He let me come here to speak to others that would help support the jamboree if it were to be held here. It has worked out so fortuitously that I can't complain – even if I do feel like a grey duck in swans' clothing."

"I feel a little that way myself," Jim, the Ambassador admitted. "Though I feel you are a wonderful example of the ideals of the scouting movement. You are turning an unfortunate episode into a means of achieving more than you anticipated. Though, do forgive me, I think you really look like you should be resting."

"Really, I am okay," Wanda insisted. "I have not been doing a great deal today. I almost had a litter of kittens when Mr Duvall suggested I came here, but I am never going to get another chance to rub shoulders with so many rich and famous people. I am starting to get an un-scout-like kick out of it."

Wanda's dissembling seemed to amuse Duvall, so she went on, "Mr Duvall has promised to introduce me to Richard Naylor, the actor." Her expression was one of adulation. "Just as well my husband isn't here – that would take half the fun out of it."

Wanda had kept one arm through Duvall's, during this conversation, but had not missed Jim's subtle cues. He had a job for her and wanted her to stay in one place for a while. He obviously had a good reason, so she went off with Duvall, for about half a dozen steps before stopping and grabbing him as if for support.

"I think, perhaps I had better sit down, Mr Duvall," Wanda managed to sound fuzzy. "Just on the edge of the stairs, perhaps?"

Duvall was very solicitous and sent one of the hovering waiters for a chair and when it arrived, very promptly, he helped Wanda to sit and hovered as if uncertain what else to do.

Jim watched Duvall intently. He was amused by Wanda's dissembling and clever reporting of her situation, but having Duvall glued to her was not in his plans. He kept back as Prince Stephen took charge and offered to stay with Frau Davis until she felt better. Duvall did not like that at all.

"I am sorry, Mr Duvall, I am keeping you from your guests," Wanda reminded him apologetically. "I will be fine in a while."

"I will find the young lady a drink," Jim offered. He brushed past Max on his way to the nearest drink waiter.

"Get Shannon over to Wanda when Prince Stephen leaves," Jim told Max very quietly, and without looking at him.

Max nodded imperceptibly, still acting in his character of the Countess's body guard but obviously keeping one eye on the countess and the other on any other woman that came close.

So far, Shannon had not attracted Duvall's attention and probably wouldn't while Duvall's mind was on Frau Davis and trying to figure out what her game was. Well, that was an excellent distraction – if Duvall suspected a plot from that direction, he would be less likely to suspect a second plot.

Jim returned and found that Stephen had manoeuvred his chair so that he was right next to where Wanda sat with her head down. He passed the drink to Stephen, who in turn offered it to Wanda.

Duvall still hovered, but Prince Stephen emphasised that he would stay with Frau Davis so that Duvall could attend to his other guests.

There was no reason to stay, so Duvall stalked off, but within moments, there seemed to be more of his party attendants in the vicinity than there had been. Those attendants were good, able to approach so quietly that you barely knew they were close enough to overhear your conversation.

Wanda sipped her orange juice. She held the glass awkwardly in the fingers of one hand, and supported it on the bandages of the other. When she set the glass down, Stephen took her nearest hand in his and Wanda felt something small touch her fingers. She closed them as much as she could trapping the bead like object against the bandages. She glanced at Jim, who was looking away from her, and thought at him. "What?"

The Ambassador reached up and scratched an ear. Wanda understood at once. The thing in her fingers was a bead-like micro receiver. She needed to put it in her ear.

Making the motion seem like needing to put her head down again, Wanda slipped the device in her ear with just a little fumbling. A few feet away, Jim sub-vocalised into an equally tiny transmitter.

"Ok, Grant, transmit the data." The assurance came through to Jim through a tiny receiver such as he had given Wanda.

Wanda expected the voice when it began – no more than a quiet whisper.

"Supplementary character data," Grant began. "Same background as exists, except mother's name Esmeralda Truscott. English, but lived most of her life in France and several years in present country. Father believed to be Pierre Roderick. Mother died fifteen years ago, father believed to have died twenty years ago, actually died one year ago. You saw him once, two years ago..."

Wanda listened carefully, memorising it all. It was obvious that Jim had already built on her earlier findings, but some of this information was new to her. Grant went on to tell her what she had spoken to her 'father' about, where they had met, an approximate date, and how she had found him. It was enough to spin a convincing tale.

Wanda raised her head slightly when the voice stopped, mentally reviewing the data. She guessed correctly that she would hear it spoken once again. When it finished, Grant had several instructions for her.

"You may not need this," he told her. "Duvall will learn part of this data, and it may help you out of a tight situation. Use it only if necessary – and remember you did not visit his club."

Wanda sat up properly and reached for her drink again. Another voice spoke into her ear, this time Jim speaking directly. "Tell Stephen to go!"

Wanda chuckled suddenly and spoke to Prince Stephen. "Wait until I tell them that I had a Prince playing nursemaid to me," she said softly, implying no one would believe her.

"You sound better," Stephen remarked.

"I feel better. That old-fashioned remedy of putting your head down really works. I'll be fine now, and if you don't go and rescue that poor Ambassador, who looks like a fish out of water, people might decide to start a royal scandal about you cuddling up to a married woman!"

Wanda's comment made Stephen sit up straight. Then he grinned in mischief. "You are right. It would not look good to be named in a divorce suit. If you are sure you will be alright, I will check you later."

Prince Stephen merged into the crowd, with Jim beside him. Wanda stayed where she was, watching the people around her. When she finished her drink, she caught the eye of one of the attendants, who came at once to take her glass and was only too pleased to comply with her request for some food from the buffet. As soon as that attendant departed, another one took his place. She knew Duvall was having her watched. Even so, some of her earlier fear had dissipated, knowing that Jim was in control – but none of her wariness had gone.

The attendant returned with a plate full of delicacies, and placed it next to Wanda. She ate for a while and then decided to mingle. She could not manage to carry the plate, and needed to ask one of the attendants to help her up and left the plate on the chair.

She thanked the attendant and began to move into the fringes of the crowd, on a converging course with the group of admirers around Shannon.

Wanda winked at Max when he was close to her, and after that, no one could say exactly what happened. However, one of the young men around Shannon, a complete stranger to Wanda, somehow tripped, and pushed Wanda over. She fell, carefully protecting her wrists, but the young man's red wine, coated her exquisite gown.

Wanda listened, without making it obvious, to Shannon venting aristocratic anger on the hapless young man. Her followers were all too stunned to help the unfortunate female on the ground. Wanda, who was making a difficult attempt to get up, suddenly felt strong arms lifting her up and setting her on her feet.

"Get your hands off me you great lout!" Wanda said ungraciously. "I am not an invalid!"

Max had a smirk on his face as he obeyed. "Yes, my lady."

To everyone around her, his comment was a subtle reprimand for her countrified manners in the elegant company.

Wanda turned in as controlled a manner as she seemed able to manage, and walked off in the direction of the staircase and with every outward intention of returning to her room. She was aware of Shannon hurrying after her.

"You poor thing," Shannon said in French. "Let me help you clean up."

"Whatever you said – I can manage," Wanda parried, speaking in English.

Shannon spoke again, this time in English with a marked French accent. "Let me help you. You will have trouble with your poor hands."

Wanda spoke very quietly. "Duvall is coming - in the maroon tux."

Shannon turned and spoke to the first person she saw. It was Duvall, and she spoke to him as if he were a hotel flunkey, insisting on the use of a quiet room where Wanda could clean up.

"Lady," Wanda said urgently. "That is Mr Duvall, the host and owner of the hotel."

Then Wanda spoke to Duvall, apologising for fainting, for wrecking his party, and the dress she had borrowed and generally prattling on. However, as had been intended, Duvall now had eyes only for Shannon. His mind was registering not only the natural charm of Jim's agent, but Wanda's subtle mental reinforcing over image of his ghost from last night – the cavaliers lady – rich, French and regal.

The countess did not back down on her tone, but Duval was all gracious host, and intent on charming the countess, as well as reassuring Wanda that he would arrange for fresh garments so she could return to the party. He himself led them to a quiet parlour, so the three of them could talk.

The countess was going to great lengths to draw out the American woman, who was suddenly shy and embarrassed. As for Duvall, Shannon paid as much attention to him as scant courtesy allowed – keeping her conversation directed at Wanda, until she deigned enough to unwind enough to ask, "Are you really a countess?"

It changed the course of the conversation so that both women could talk about themselves, and to insert information for Duvall to overhear.

Duvall did not learn what he wanted to about Wanda's assumed character. He heard that her father had been French, but had lived a lot in Weisboden. He had met, but not married her mother here. Her mother had been English by birth, French by adoption, and had come here for a time. When she had become pregnant, she had gone to America, and when she had died, her child had been fostered by an American couple.

Felice de Alembert admitted that she was indeed a countess, as Duvall's attendants had reported of her. They had heard nothing to have sparked his interest. Now, her casual references to royal ancestry, and a family dating back to the cavaliers, her interest in history and historical items, not to leave out flourishing business interests – decided him to pay more attention to the charming woman. He unconsciously put the mystery of the American woman into abeyance.

Duvall could tell that Wanda was struggling to maintain polite conversation - and that required no acting on her part. While the women had been talking, he had made a phone call, and arranged for Herr Davis's business meeting to terminate, so the American's husband would return to end the conversation between the women.

Wanda, with her uncanny awareness of David's arrival, steered the conversation to hobbies, and enabled Shannon to mention swords, just as David entered. She knew Duvall was hooked.

After Herr Davis was introduced to the Countess, and the other courtesies were discharged, the Davis couple were escorted back to their sumptuous suite where a royal supper was prepared and nothing they could possibly want was neglected.

Wanda ate little, but David put away a decent amount of food. They spoke little, for Wanda was so obviously tired, and they turned in early – giving those monitoring their movements no cause for concern, or anything of note to report to Duvall.

He expected little else, as it had been his intention when he had given instructions for having a mild dose of sleeping medication to all dishes.


Duvall finally left his garden party in a disgruntled frame of mind. The lovely Countess had politely and charmingly declined his invitation to dinner, choosing instead to stay accompanied by her hired bodyguard.

The conversation between the countess and the American woman had interested him. Not only was the countess well off and intelligent, but she seemed to be a shrewd businesswoman. She was the sort of person he liked to be acquainted with - she had a noble lineage and liked swords.

When all of his attendants had come to his hotel office and reported to him, a picture emerged. In the opinion of these specially chosen observers, the countess liked men with muscles and her bodyguard liked beautiful women. He had been eyeing, not only the countess, but every other woman in sight.

Duvall directed a few of the attendants to follow the countess and report. He then left the hotel to go to his club where he went directly to his private business office.


On the way, he greeted club members with a smile, wave or a few words. Later he would be expected to make an appearance for the meeting of his elite members, but for a while, in the quiet of his office, he sat back and appeared to study his display of swords. His mind considered his plans and was satisfied that everything was under control.

Karl would come to him, if only to settle the outstanding matter between them. With Karl in his power, and he had enough evidence against him to control him – he could force him to do his will. He had enough evidence against more than half of Karl's siblings to completely ruin the monarchy if he did not comply.

He had worked for this for a very long time. The desire for power being the hunger that drove him on. As a youth, he had met Karl and preyed on his friendship – encouraging Karl's natural, wild recklessness. His cavalier fantasy had begun back then – Duvall, Roderick and the young Karl – the original cavaliers and inseparable. They had lured to them the bright young stars, destined to become big in finance, politics, business and the arts. Duvall had collected information about all of them. Then he had waited.

He had manufactured an argument between Pierre and Karl, encouraging the resultant duel between a half drunk Karl and an angry Pierre. The result had been better than he hoped. Karl thought he had killed Pierre.

Duvall had taken Pierre to Paris for treatment, and through mischance had fallen foul of the French police – who now wanted him for murder. Leaving Pierre, he had fled back to Weisboden, knowing it did not have an extradition treaty with France.

The Cavaliers had fallen apart, and Duvall had kept clear of Karl for many years, becoming in time an apparent pillar of society and philanthropist. He had joined the Loyal Democratic Party, and had the secret backing of many of its members – all of whom were members of his elite.

They thought he was loyal to the King and themselves like cavaliers ready to fight for the king. Most felt a little foolish in the exaggerated costume, until the effects of the carefully mixed 'toast' to the king took effect. Then they became Duvall's – body and soul – through low-level drug addiction and hypnosis.

Many had, without realising it, changed their views on certain subjects to that which Duvall directed. Already, Duvall had more power than the Prime Minister did, but he wanted more. The PM only had authority in internal affairs – the monarchy was still the absolute authority in international affairs.

It was going to change.

Duvall had heard about the secret talks that Karl was having, and the treaties he was discussing. Some of these were counter to his own plans. He had sent his subtle threat as a warning to Karl.

His informants had told him that Karl was to return in two days' time. The day after that, the media would break a story of a scandal in the highest circles of the Prime Minister's Department. The men so 'exposed' were not in his control. They would be forced to resign. The King would have no option but to have them step aside. The scandal would cast doubt on the information Karl had presented at the international talks.

With Karl in fear of having his own indiscretions exposed, he would be made to dismiss the present government, and put Duvall in as caretaker, to appoint a new cabinet.

Then, he would make Karl break any treaties with foreign powers – disallowing extradition treaties with any country, thus making Weisboden a sanctuary for international crooks, who would pay Duvall handsomely for that safe haven.

Then, Karl would be discredited and forced to abdicate, or have all the royal scandals published. If Karl would not, then Karl would apparently commit suicide, and a note would reveal all. The scandals would still be made public.

The country would be in turmoil, but he, Duvall would hold it together, and at the next election – he would gain absolute control and legislate to keep the monarchy out of power.

# Chapter 14

Michael DuPont, Duvall's aide, entered Duvall's office. He had knocked several times with no answer and had thought his employer was out - perhaps having an evening with that French Countess he had been monopolising for the latter half of the afternoon.

Instead, he found his employer in his chair, and changed his intention of leaving a note on Duvall's desk to a quiet greeting, but that made him the target of Duvall's fanatical gleam. He shuddered. Before he had become Duvall's aide, he had been his ward. For years, he had been completely dominated by Duvall who had done so much for him. Sometimes he felt he would never repay the debt.

That debt was a means by which Duvall had made him do many unpleasant things and some had sickened him. He did not have the courage to disobey, not anymore. Not after two thrashings when he had been younger – by Duvall's private army of cavaliers. He knew that Duvall would not hesitate to order the same punishment for him again, if he tried.

"Sir," Michael spoke quietly again, controlling his dread.

Duvall sat upright in his chair and demanded, "What is it?"

Michael flinched from the force of the demand. "Sir – Glockner wishes to report."

"Where is he?" Duvall modified his tone.

"Downstairs. Will I bring him up?"

"Yes," Duvall agreed. "Yes, bring him here, but make him wait ten minutes first – then give me a reminder call."

Du Pont departed with a sense of relief.


Duvall's thoughts had been drawn back to the past forty-eight hours. To the still unexplained intrusion of two nights ago and the failure of the interrogation of the American couple and finally the appearance of the fascinating countess De Alembert.

His next thought was to find a link between the scout woman and the Countess. Even though the Countess had ignored him, and befriended that apparently countrified American woman, he wasn't convinced the French woman was involved with her.

Making a sudden decision, he dialled the detective agency and asked for Monet.

The male voice that answered, apologised and said Monet was not available. Duvall convinced the voice to contact the detective and have him call on a matter of urgency. He was advised that he would have Monet return his call within half an hour. With that, Duvall had to be content.


Not far away, Grant looked at Jim and began the process of contacting Nicholas who was already en route to Castle Holstein where Queen Alicia was staying – so that he could return with her to Weisboden.


Duvall waited until Du Pont called him, before giving instructions for the man to come to his office.

Inwardly, Duvall was amused by the man's obvious disguise. He said nothing, except to dismiss DuPont. He waited for his agent to speak.

"Something is going on in the private wing of the palace," Glockner told Duvall. "Prince Michael, as well as Joseph, William and Stephen have been spending a great deal of time in one of the guest suites, and the servants have been kept busy elsewhere. Also, Princess Renée has been there. Prince Michael fobbed the American scout leaders onto her, so something important must be going on."

Duvall smiled, deducing that his letter to Karl had been read.

"And Karl has not returned?" Duvall asked idly.

"No. He is still expected tomorrow on the royal plane even though officially he is meant to return the day after."

"Have you seen that scout woman again?"

"No, only the man."

"Try and find out what is going on," Duvall directed. "I think, perhaps Karl has returned secretly and they are having a family discussion. Do you have anything more on those Americans?"

"No. They were only interested in the jamboree thing."

"Fine – keep in touch." Duvall handed the man an envelope and dismissed him.

Du Pont, summoned by Duvall, escorted the man back downstairs, and knew he was to return for further instructions.

"Go and tell Giselle to make herself look stunning. I will be taking her out. She has fifteen minutes to get ready. You might have to take the cavalier toast for me."

Before DuPont could answer, Duvall's private phone line rang in its subdued tone. Du Pont was dismissed with a glance.

"Yes," was all Duvall answered, once he was alone.

"This is Monet," the voice on the line told him.

"What have you to report?" Duvall asked bluntly, as he glanced at the clock. It had been almost exactly half an hour.

Nicholas Black assumed the voice and accent of his detective character. "I have no information on the woman in the sketch," he began. "But I have confirmed from other sources, that the other woman is actually what she claimed. She is a member of the scouting association, who arrived in Weisboden two days ago with her husband who is also a member. The woman is Gwen Davis, nee Truscott. She is American, but her mother, Esmeralda Truscott was English. The mother spent most of her life in France, and then moved to your country for a number of years. She arrived in America shortly before her child was born. I have someone checking the birth records for the name of the father. Just one moment ..."

Duvall could hear talking in the background at the other end of the line, but could not make out the words.

"Mr Duvall, I now have that information. The name of the father given was Pierre Roderick, nationality French."

"Excellent!" Duvall said, controlling his voice to hide his inner thoughts. "I have another request for you." He proceeded to describe the Countess De Alembert, her body guard, and asked for the names and addresses of any antique shops or dealers that she may be in contact with whilst she was in Weisboden, or those she regularly dealt with in France."

Monet surprised him, since he was able to give him some information right away. He claimed it was common knowledge and then he promised to investigate further.

Duvall replaced the phone on its receiver thoughtfully. His mind was on the American woman. He was more convinced than ever that she had been in his club, and must have powerful friends behind her. He decided on that instant to take her and her husband out of circulation until after his plan was completed. Putting decision into action, he dialled the number of his sub-manager at the hotel.

Before speaking, he placed a scrambler over the mouthpiece of the phone. The one at the hotel had the descrambler built in.

The night-duty manager at the hotel was able to report that the guests in the nominated suite were asleep. They had not stirred when the maids had come in to remove the supper trays and the pair had not made any calls or received any. Then, at Duvall's instruction, he agreed to increase the watch on the room.

Duvall, then called another number, still with the scrambler in place, and gave instructions. To all those concerned, he would have those two Americans regally escorted out of the country on the next day's flight to Munich. To his loyal followers he would declare them persona non grata, so his bought off police would arrest them if they tried to return. In the meantime, they would not sneeze without him knowing it. He did not need another of Pierre's bastards trying to get their hands on his supposed fortune. In fact, it would be better if the two Americans disappeared somewhere between Paris, where they were to stop over, and America.

Grant, monitoring the phone call, was not able to find the key to unscrambling the conversation, but he was able to identify the number dialled as being Duvall's hotel. He reported that tersely to Jim.

"Go and get them out," Jim instructed immediately.

Grant knew who was referring to and wasted no time departing – he suddenly shared Jim's anxiety.

Duvall gave Michael Dupont very specific instructions. He was to go to the hotel and remove the two Americans from the room he had assigned them, which was the Presidential Suite, and bring them back to the club and put them in his secure room downstairs. He was to make sure they could not get free. He gave a description of both of the Americans. He did not explain his order, nor did DuPont ask for one. He knew better. He knew to obey.


Wanda had not been able to sleep for long. She woke after an hour because her wrists were throbbing, and she would need help to take something for it. David was asleep next to her, and he was still in his clothes. She nudged him, but he didn't wake up.

Her danger sense flared. She shook David gently, and then harder – with the same lack of response. She then listened to his breathing, it was slow and regular. She felt for her torch on the bedside table. She needed two hands to hold it and turn it on. It had a very narrow and focussed beam, and with it, she checked David's pupils.

"Drugged!" Wanda murmured to herself. Then she thought, "It had to be the food." She also realised that it was lucky that she had not eaten very much. She had been too exhausted to eat then, but now she was no longer sleepy.

She got out of bed and went out into the room where they had been eating. The food remains had been cleared away. She had not even heard the servants, or sensed them and that proved that she had been affected for a short time. Then she went back to the bedroom and checked for the small serving of food she had kept aside in case she got hungry during the night. It was still hidden in the little cupboard. She found a small towel and wrapped it as best she could and put it in her small pack. Then she managed to get dressed in her dark tracksuit. Somehow, she was going to have to get David away from the suite and hidden. Something told her that Duvall had given orders to drug them to keep them where he could get to them.

Before she had considered where to take David, she heard the slightest of sounds coming from the door of the suite. She moved swiftly into the main room and moved around the wall to near the door. That way, if the door opened suddenly, there was no chance of her being seen as a silhouette against the light coming in the windows.

Injured she might be, but she was not completely helpless. Someone entered the suite. Wanda had the advantage. The faint illumination was not enough for proper identification – but enough to guide her hand to a vital point on the man's neck. The man froze, and this reaction told her he was a friend.

"Frau Davis?" the man asked softly. "Jim sent me."

Wanda removed her hand, and identified him. "Grant!"

"Jim said to get you out of here? Where is David?"

"Bedroom. I can't wake him. Can you carry him?"

"Yes. What else do you need?"

"Not much." In fact, there was very little of importance in the bags they had travelled with and what she needed was already in a small carry bag. She quickly checked David's things before she left.

Grant checked the corridor, and then went to fetch David. Carrying him easily, Grant led the way to the service corridors, deserted at that hour, and through them to his car parked at the rear. As they went along, he noticed Wanda eyeing the security cameras and told her he had fixed them so nothing would be noted. She relaxed, and was relieved to get into Grant's car. They both checked for followers, before they headed to Jim's temporary headquarters.

Wanda greeted Jim with relief. She apologised for the trouble they had got into and told him what she thought had happened to David.

Jim simply smiled at her. "All is well. However, I don't think you should leave the country just now."

"No, I suspect not," Wanda agreed. "So, do we stay here instead?"

"Depends. Are you up to working?" Jim asked her.

In answer, she held up her hands and put a look of, "What do you think?" on her face. Work, for her, often meant climbing and opening things.

"Strictly on one level. How do you feel?"

Wanda turned serious. "Exhausted. I wasn't been able to sleep much. Otherwise, you know I would jump at the chance to be useful."

"See how you are in the morning," Jim advised. He didn't mention what he had in mind and Wanda didn't ask. She wasn't meant to be any further involved in this mission.

"I will see if our friendly doctor can come and look at David."

Relieved to be safe, and knowing David was in good hands, Wanda agreed to try to sleep. Subconsciously, she realised she had still been alert for trouble at the hotel, and had probably only slept because David had intended to stay awake. Here she was with people she trusted.

Sleep didn't come, so Wanda began some breathing exercises to help her into a trance state where she could try to reduce the pain in her wrists.

An hour later, she became aware of another presence in the little room with her. Even though she sensed no threat, she was made aware that she was not at her best. She should have sensed the person arriving.

Without indicating she was awake, Wanda tested the sense of 'someone' and identified Renée.

"Highness?" Wanda asked softly.

"Please, just Renée. Your friend said you were asleep. I didn't want to disturb you."

"No, I wasn't sleeping. I am really tired, but I can't seem to sleep. I was sort of meditating. Have you seen David?"

"He's in no danger. He should wake around morning. I was told you brought some of the food with you?"

"Yes, in my bag. Probably a mess everywhere by now. I didn't eat much, and kept some for later. I guessed that something had been put in the food. Can you get it analysed?"

"Yes, that is no problem. How are your hands? Are you in much pain?"

"I'm well enough. Functional. There's a bit of pain, but I have learnt ways to dull it a bit."

"That is something I would like to learn – later. Do you want me to give you something to make you sleep?"

"No thanks. I didn't want the first offer of that either." Wanda sounded amused. "Truthfully, though, I would rather have nothing. Some medications have strange effects on me and I don't feel like dealing with that now."

"Do you mind if I put the light on in here?" Renée asked. Wanda told her to go ahead.

Renée stood and walked to the switch near the door. She returned, carrying her bag. She set about examining Wanda's wrists – unrolling the fabric bandaging until she could see the dressing underneath.

"You have been doing too much with these," Renée told her sternly.

Wanda looked steadily back and said, "Not really. I have been positively slothful."

Renée sighed, realising that Wanda had her own way of considering things. "I really don't understand you. You risk yourself for matters that...."

"Are none of my business?" Wanda suggested when Renée broke off mid-sentence.

"I am not trying to judge you," Renée said quickly, apologetically. She began to re-bandage Wanda's wrists.

"Maybe it isn't really my business," Wanda agreed. "But you cannot deny that those matters...are important to you and concern you deeply."

"But it is my family, my country..." Renée said, without looking at Wanda.

"And should I be indifferent because this isn't my country?" Wanda asked. "A lot of what I do is dangerous. But I weigh the value of the outcome."

"What is valuable to you?" Renée asked. She looked into the eyes of the American woman and saw depths of character that she could not read.

"Doing what has to be done, because I am the best one to do it," Wanda said, being deliberately misleading.

"Even if you get hurt? Or killed?" Renée insisted on trying to understand.

Wanda wasn't going to explain. "Renée, you can have no idea of what I am and what I once was, and I am not at liberty to explain. Let's just agree that I work for Jim, and I trust his instincts for what is important. And you are right in thinking that I get a kick out of living dangerously."

Renée felt a shock, as Wanda told her exactly what she had been thinking. She recalled David's comment about not being a telepath. Could Wanda be one?

She put that thought aside, and asked, "When are you leaving?"

"We were meant to be going today. Duvall had our flight rescheduled," Wanda told her.

"Meant to be?" Renée queried.

"Well, Duvall's private goons stopped us leaving and questioned us about things. When they didn't learn anything, Duvall comes on the scene and becomes our benefactor. He thinks we don't realise he's a creep. So he put us in his hotel where he could keep an eye on us and had our food drugged. Now that Jim got us out of there, I don't intend to be found again. We will leave with him and the others. Therefore, Jim will probably put me to work. He knows I would rather be doing something."

"He asked me to get you into the palace to nurse my brother," Renée told her. "I told your friend that Karl won't be a good patient and won't be willing to play a passive role." She shrugged. "However, he should stay asleep until morning, since I gave him something in his coffee."

"I can manage him," Wanda assured her.

"Your friend said you were an expert at manipulating people."

Wanda just grinned.

Renée went on, "Try to sleep. I am staying here a while to check on your husband."

Wanda watched Renée leave the room, and turn off the light as she went out.

The doctor's mind was unconsciously broadcasting many conflicting thoughts. Most centred on her eldest brother and the picture they formed was of an older brother, who as king, was meant to have her full devotion and respect, when she thought of him as an arrogant, self-centred bully. A man who was so sure of his own perfection, that he could not tolerate anyone or anything that wasn't. Wanda decided that the absent Queen Alicia must be a remarkable woman.

Renée sat in an armchair and watched as Herr Davis slept. She was absently aware of the comments passing between the dark skinned

Grant and the white haired Jim.

"Duvall has arrived at the restaurant," Grant was saying softly. "He is pretending that he can't see Shannon or Max."

Then later, Grant said, "They will be leaving for Duvall's club."

"Good," Jim sounded pleased. "Ok, Grant, you get there and wait outside, when the servants leave, pick one up. We will slip David in as a replacement tomorrow night."

The mention of Duvall brought Renée's full attention to the conversation.

"Isn't that risky? You might pick one that is loyal to Duvall," she challenged quietly.

Grant paused by the door, but Jim indicated for him to continue.

Jim came over to near Renée and asked, "What do you know of Duvall?" He was prepared to hear her out, but he did not expect what he got. Still, a major part of his success was the ability to change his plans quickly if new information came to him.

"That he walked over too many 'little people' to get where he is," Renée said quietly. She assumed this man knew of Duvall's public image. "I know several people who work at Duvall's club, who have no love for him. One is a cook; one is a cleaner, and the other a waiter. I can contact any of them tonight and all would do all they could to help you."

"Tell me about each of them." Jim requested. He received a comprehensive character description and profile."

Jim decided the waiter might be the most useful, and true to her word, Renée made contact with the man. Sooner than expected, the reply came back that Herr Fraenkel would help.

# Chapter 15

The Countess De Alembert and her escort, having dined and consumed a lot of wine, were making an impact on the dance floor of the expensive restaurant. Max wore a clinging gold lame shirt, designed to display his muscles. Shannon was a match for him in a strapless white and gold creation. The colour changing flashing lights glittered off them and drew all eyes their way so even as women were surreptitiously watching Max, their partners were eyeing the countess.

They were dancing flawlessly, with an almost bored indifference, and other dancers were instinctively moving out of their way.

A brief tightening of Max's grip, warned Shannon that Duvall had arrived. She watched Max's eyes following someone beyond her. He turned her around, so she could see for herself the stunning male bait Duvall had with him.

Finally, Duvall and his escort found them, as if by accident, on the dance floor. The countess expressed her surprise and betrayed none of the disinterest that she had implied earlier.

Duvall, oozing charm, invited them back to his table. He didn't quite hide his satisfaction, that her 'body guard' could not keep his eyes of the lovely Giselle.

Waiters arrived in moments to bring fresh drinks to the table. Max ordered ale, and seemed to toss it down on one long gulp. The countess watched with bored amusement, and Giselle was openly amazed. Max didn't quite smirk at the reaction.

Duvall, kept up a patter of small talk, directed at the Countess – all polite and non-committal, but at the same time, pointedly ignoring his own escort.

Giselle was trying to get her partner to dance again. Shannon passed a look to Max, and the 'body guard' seemed to take a hint, and got up to offer to partner Giselle.

Duvall's questions became more probing, but the Countess seemed to have her attention on the pair dancing on the floor. After a while, the she unwound and spoke a little of herself, seeming to be unconscious of giving Duvall the opening he wanted to take up the conversation she had been having with the American woman.

It suited Duvall that the countess was still intent on her bodyguard. He thought she was less likely to be paying attention to what she was saying. He wanted to know what this fascinating woman liked to do for excitement. She seemed to be breathing more rapidly as her 'body guard' flaunted his virility while dancing, but in answer to his question, she had said, "watching sporting events and closing tough business deals to her advantage."

He changed his line of questions to hobbies. To which she said she had none, but when he mentioned swords, her attention switched to him. Duvall saw then the hint of the hard businesswoman, and seemed to sense that the acquisition of swords was a passion of hers. She seemed to think that his claim of an extensive sword collection of his own was no more than a boast and a reason to invite her to his club. She waved the offer aside, and went on to regale him with her collections of old jewellery and art.

Then it was her turn to seem to be unaware of his abstraction. She had hinted at something that excited him as no woman ever did. She had come to Weisboden to look at a recently discovered collection of 17th century artefacts - artefacts that were believed to have belonged to Oliver Cromwell.

If there was one thing that Duvall lusted after, more than mere power, it was Cromwell's lost Sword. One of the most famous sword's in history.

Duvall repeated his invitation for her and her escort to come to his club for guaranteed top entertainment. The Countess didn't answer until the music finished and Max and Duvall's partner were returning.

"I would certainly hope it is more entertaining than here!" the countess sounded bored. "I was told this place was excellent. Yes, Milton and I will accept your offer. I can see he is besotted with your friend. Is she your wife?"

Duvall was taken aback but only for an instant.

"No, my Lady. She is merely an acquaintance." Duvall belittled Giselle to her correct proportion. "And if I may ask, without being rude...?"

Shannon anticipated his question before he finished. "Milton? I merely employ him."

"You will not need a body guard with me," Duvall assured her.

The Countess seemed to size him up, finally saying, "Milton won't be in the way."

Max and Giselle were coming into earshot, and Max spoke, knowing his voice would carry. "I don't know what you see in that wimp. I'm twice the man he is."

Giselle did not make a reply, for to her it was obvious as Duvall turned that he had heard the comment and was angry. He did not like to be belittled.

He was about to utter a cutting remark when he caught sight of the fierce excitement and anticipation on the face of the Countess at the prospect of a confrontation. He controlled himself and simply said, "Yes, Herr Milton must come with us."

He settled his account and that of the Countess, and escorted them to his limousine – a gleaming black Mercedes. His driver took them to the front door of his club. He was unaware of the unobtrusive van that followed him.

By the end of the drive, Duvall was satisfied with the progress he was making with the Countess. They had progressed to first names, and the odious Milton was still besotted with Giselle, and that little whore seemed equally interested in him.

Upon arrival at the club, Duvall took his guest to the casino, and no effort was spared to ensure the countess enjoyed herself.

After an hour, Duvall was hiding his amusement at how Milton, was showing off for Giselle, who was subtly egging him on. She had a talent for that.

When the countess seemed to be growing bored, Duvall invited her upstairs for private drinks in his office. He hoped that Milton was too engrossed in his gambling, but to Duvall's annoyance, the bodyguard followed his mistress. He could think of no good reason to stop him, and decided that he probably didn't matter.

He planned the entrance to his office to astound his guest. Her reaction to his sword display was everything he could have hoped, and the discussion proceeded as he wanted it to.

Duvall almost resented the interruption from his aide, Michael Dupont.

"Sir, I was to remind you of your appointment," the younger man said in a subdued tone.

For a moment, Duvall considered sending his aide to do the Cavaliers' 'toast', but he preferred not to miss two nights in a row.

"This won't take long, my dear countess," Duvall said. "My assistant, Michael will keep you company. Please let him know if there is something you would like to drink."

Back at his headquarters, Jim monitored a very interesting event through the tiny 'bug' that Shannon had slipped into Duvall's pocket. First his Cavalier's toast, and the session of mind conditioning that followed after the drink had been consumed and later, when the Cavalier's watched the Sword duel between Duvall and Max Hart.

The audience was cheering unrestrainedly for their leader – and not quite yelling for blood.

Shannon hid her concern for Max under an intent look. Duvall was an expert swordsman, whilst Max Hart was simply a well-rounded sportsman. Max did not betray his fear that Duvall would defeat him and kept his half smirk on his face all the time as if this bout was a joke.

Duvall had hoped to impress the countess further, but he saw that she was watching Milton's movements.

He chose to halt the bout, but belittled Max with, "I should like to challenge you again, Herr Milton, when you have had lessons. You might then be a worthy opponent."

Max had only smirked his smug, vaguely superior smirk, and with seeming recklessness challenged him, or any of his friends to a bout of wrestling.

Neither Shannon, nor Max had failed to notice the brightness in the eyes of Duvall's elite - that and their readiness to obey Duvall's slightest command. However, every one of those who took on the challenge, ended up thrown to the floor.

In spite of himself, Duvall was impressed by Milton's strength and skill. He was also annoyed that his elite cavaliers had not performed better. He himself prided himself on his physique and expertise, and wanted his cavaliers to reflect the same. So he ignored the nauseating smirk, and offered Milton a position at his club to teach his the members his skills. His Cavaliers would be improved by the training, and when he was busy, he would have Felice to himself.

Without a word being spoken, a look passed between Felice and her bodyguard, Milton. It was as if each read the other's expression.

"Milton may, if he wishes, do as you ask," Felice agreed. "When I have no need of his services, of course."

Milton responded, "It'll be fun, Countess!"

Shannon merely smiled, as if she understood exactly what he meant.

"While he is busy, perhaps you will tell me more of your collection."

Duvall smiled a genuinely satisfied smile and offered to have her and Herr Milton, picked up from their hotel the next morning.

Duvall strode into Michael Dupont's office as soon as he had escorted the countess out to his limousine. He did not bother to announce himself, and he caught his aide pacing the room in some degree of agitation. Dupont turned and looked like a startled animal. Duvall went and sat behind his aide's desk.

"The Americans. Where are they?" Duvall demanded without preamble.

Dupont took a deep breath and faced his employer. "Gone! I checked with security before going up, and they were there – asleep. The room service people had already cleaned up the left over supper. When I went into the room, their luggage was there, but they were not. I lit a fuse under the guards, and finally found the two who were supposed to be watching the corridor. They were bound and gagged in a janitor's closet. Neither saw who nor what hit them, but they said they had not been in there very long. I found no one who saw them leave.

The fury in the gaze directed at Dupont lost intensity, but was still present.

"We are being made fools of," Duvall stated after a prolonged silence.

"Sir?" Dupont dared to query.

"That woman has to be an agent. She is, supposedly, the daughter of an expatriate English woman who was living in France, but moved here for a time. Her father...."Duvall paused for effect, and was watching his aide, "...is believed to be Pierre Roderick. The mother, it is said, moved to America after Pierre died. I wonder how many other women Pierre was stringing along back then."

"There were many, if my mother was telling the truth. It makes me wonder how many other bastards he had who think they are entitled to a share of his supposedly vast estate."

Dupont spoke impassively. He had come to Duvall's attention back when he had thought his father, Roderick, had been fabulously wealthy.

Duvall smiled, but it was not a pleasant smile. Dupont knew it to be because, somehow, Duvall had taken control of all that had been Roderick's – including himself.

"That maybe is all it is," Duvall thought aloud. "But that woman is not just some bitch with dreams of wealth. No one has ever penetrated my security before, and resisted questioning. The man – he may know nothing of her activities and may believe her lies. Perhaps I should have let them leave but..."

Duvall didn't finish his thought, giving Dupont a chance to raise another possibility.

"Could Karl have asked the Americans for help? He may have met some during his vacation."

"Karl would never ask for help," Duvall stated flatly.

"What about Prince Michael?" Dupont persisted. "Didn't you say they went to see him?"

"The old man?" Duvall spoke contemptuously. "No. Karl always told me that it was his father's strictest rule – not to discuss family business outside of the family."

Dupont fell silent, waiting for instructions, and trying not to fidget and betray his anxiety.

"See if you can find out where they have gone. The airport is being watched, set someone onto the bus and train terminus though I doubt if they will be caught again. Check Pierre's room for signs the woman checked there and have Glockner deliver the next letter. Is everything ready for tomorrow?"

"Yes, Sir," Dupont confirmed.

Duvall rose and went to the door. "Check again to be sure," he instructed as he left.

Dupont let out a breath of relief and eased his tie. He felt as if he had just narrowly escaped with his life. He spared a moment of pity for the guards at the hotel, but did not allow himself to think further. Duvall was unforgiving of those who failed to meet his expectations.

Jim was thoughtful as he listened to the voices of Duvall and Dupont. He was no closer to knowing Duvall's exact plans, but it was now obvious that Duvall was behind the letter that Karl had received.

The little bug was continuing to transmit, but nothing of importance was being sent. The bug itself had limited value. If Duvall changed his suit, it would be of no further use, and as soon as the suit was unattended, the bug would short itself out.

Grant returned with Renée later that night, after speaking to Herr Fraenkel. All had been arranged for David to infiltrate the club the following afternoon when the evening staff arrived. Grant had reports from Shannon and Max, but they had little they could add to what Jim had already over heard.

The radio had been silent for a while, so Jim decided to have a few hours nap. Grant said he would keep a listening watch, but Wanda volunteered.

"I have slept a little," Wanda told Jim. "But I can't really sleep well. If I stay by the radio, and doze off, the slightest noise will wake me."

Jim agreed, and went to suggest that Renée went for a sleep.

Renée had seen the sense in Jim's suggestion, and made use of the bed Wanda had deserted. She thought, later in the early morning that Wanda had indeed dropped into sleep in the chair by the radio. She walked quietly past her, on her way out of the suite.

Wanda woke with abrupt suddenness, and startled Renée.

"I will be back in half an hour," Renée whispered. "Jim asked me to get some information for him. I am going to check on progress. When I get back, I am to take you to the palace. Oh, David woke a short time ago. He is still woozy but he is fine."

Wanda nodded in the faint light from the window. "Thanks. Take care."

Renée smiled. "I have been studying you, and how you manage to be inconspicuous. I will be fine. I am more at home in the poor quarter than in the palace."

Jim listened to Renée's report as soon as she returned. Wanda was preparing breakfast for them all, by boiling water and adding it to instant oats. Grant was monitoring Duvall's movements – the bug was still working. David was drinking coffee and beginning to look more awake.

The small television set was tuned in on the news on the local television channel. The imminent return of King Karl was in the headlines.

Grant alerted Jim when his monitoring revealed that Duvall was moving to visit a certain antique shop.

"Right," Jim said quickly. "David, leave as soon as you've eaten. The Prime Minister is expecting you. You will be relieved in time to go to work. Wanda, you will have to keep Karl quiet until we move into the palace."

"Consider it done!" she told him.

Grant tested the transmitter/receiver that Jim wore. "That's perfect, Grant. We will go as soon as Brun calls."

Renée watched with fascination as the white haired man took a mask out of a case and applied it to his face. With that in place, he rubbed grey hair dye through his hair, and inserted contact lenses that changed his eye colour. He retreated to one of the bedrooms and emerged looking and acting like a testy old pensioner.

Wanda said, quietly, that it was so Duvall would not recognise him.

Renée just shook her head in wonder.

# Chapter 16

The Brun antiques Gallery was situated in the old part of the Capitol, where the old Viennese style of architecture was not overshadowed by the modern glass and concrete business towers.

In its original location, between an exclusive men's outfitter and the Capitol Library, it blended with the other traditional stone architecture, and it was identified by the gold lettering on the oiled mahogany signboard.

Georges Brun, the patriarch of the family business, was a white haired man of seventy-five, tall and elegant. He belonged to a dynasty of experts that went back twelve generations.

The gallery itself was known worldwide for the quality of its displays of restored antique furniture of many styles and makers. The gallery also dealt in paintings from Old Masters, and some silver, porcelain and crystal, but not precious stones or small items.

Brun and his assistants, two of whom were his grandsons, made it a service to greet the people who came into browse or buy, and offer information on any of the items on display.

Claude Duvall brushed off the attentive greeter by demanding to speak to Georges Brun in person.

Henri Brun kept his expression neutral and politely offered to escort the visitor to his grandfather's office at the rear of the gallery. Then, after making the introduction and discretely withdrawing, he remained within hearing of the ensuing conversation – a precaution in case of attempted theft or coercion.

"I understand that you hire out strongrooms to collectors," Duvall stated bluntly, without even introducing himself.

"That is true," Brun agreed, bowing slightly. "We have two that are not currently in use, Herr…"

"My name is Claude Duvall, but I am not wishing to hire a strong room, but to see a sword owned by Herr Franz."

"M'sieu, I regret I cannot open the private strong room hired by

Herr Franz without his permission."

A faint growl preceded Duvall's next comment. "I believe he has several swords dating from the early 17th century that he is interested in selling."

"Herr Franz does have several swords amongst his collection. However, if he is selling them, it is a private matter," Brun apologised. "I could call Herr Franz's message service and pass on your interest. If you leave a contact number – he will call you back if he is interested in your offer."

"Do you have his address?" Duvall demanded.

"I do not. Herr Franz is something of a recluse," Brun explained.

Forcing himself to be civil, Duvall accepted the offer of the call being made. Then he stalked from the gallery and back to a café he had seen when he arrived.

When Jim arrived, an hour after Brun had called; he in no way resembled the shy Ambassador of the previous day. He was rude, suspicious, and a difficult man to try to talk to. He was a stark contrast to Duvall's suave demeanour.

"What is it you want you young lout!" Jim returned Duvall's polite greeting.

Duvall cut to the heart of his business. "I want to purchase Cromwell's sword."

"It's not for sale," was the prompt answer.

"I know otherwise, Sir," Duvall forced out the polite title. He told the old man, bluntly, what he had learnt from the countess the previous evening. "I will offer you twice as much."

The old man seemed to consider it, but said, "That is very generous of you, but I have promised Felice the first option. I do not go back on my word."

"No, of course not," Duvall didn't snarl, but he wanted to. "Felice said you were an honourable man. The fact of the matter is that I know how much she wants it. That is why I wish to present it to her as a gift, this evening."

Duvall saw the old man's expression changing as he considered that statement.

"Felice was to return on Friday," he thought aloud. "Such a lovely young woman. She has to talk to her trustees, I think."

"If we could make an arrangement, she would have it before then," Duvall cajoled. "You see, I want it to be my betrothal gift to her. You may check with her tomorrow, to see that she has it."

The old man visibly wavered, and after little more coaxing, capitulated.

Duvall was anxious to see the sword. "Felice was most vocal about its beauty," he remarked. "It must be a remarkable piece of work."

He did not have to act when he saw the sword. He wanted it with visceral desire. His reaction won the old man over, enough to admit that such a blade belonged on a man, not in the hands of a woman, no matter how beautiful she was.

When the subject of the price came up, he wrote a cheque for twice what Felice had offered, without a qualm. He would have willingly paid thrice that much.

It was with extreme impatience that he waited for the owner of the antique shop to wrap it, and the scabbard, for transporting. As soon as it was done, Duvall left with his prize.


Back at the palace, Renée had more surprises as she watched Wanda prepare herself for her role as nurse. She had noticed first that the American woman had reduced the thickness of her bandages and covered the dressings with a tube of thick flesh coloured elastic bandage. Then she had rummaged through the makeup case and selected a number of items. After that, she set to work to change the whole look of her face and hair. When she had finished, she had a slightly Asian look, and hair that was black and not brown.

"Jim said you thought to bring some clothes for me," Wanda remarked.

Renée nodded and went to fetch a neat bundle from near the door.

"He said you left the hotel without your bags," Renée remarked in turn.

"Yeah," Wanda agreed. "In any case, I didn't have anything suitable for a nurse."

"And I assume from your new look that you don't want to be connected with Frau Davis?"

"You assume correctly," Wanda told her. "I am not actively suicidal, and there is every chance that someone at the palace is feeding information to Duvall."

"Have you any idea who?" Renée asked.

Wanda shrugged. "I may be able to find out, but that is not what I will be there for. Hmm, not exactly what I expected for a nurse...."

"These are some of my less formal clothes. More fitting for a well-dressed servant than a princess, but having you looking like a nurse will attract questions. In these, you could be my secretary or an assistant of some kind." Renée had thought things through carefully. "You will look nothing like the scout leader that came two days ago."

In fact, the outfit was a business suit with slacks and jacket, over a loose fitting blouse. Renée helped Wanda into the suit and provided elbow length beige gloves, for Wanda to wear over the bandages.

"So, apart from convincing my brother you are there to keep a medical eye on him for me, can you tell me why Jim wants you there?" Renée asked.

"Mainly to be extra protection," Wanda admitted. "Looking out for dangers."

"Like David is doing for Heinz Rasmussen?" Renée proposed. "Will you be armed too?"

Wanda shook her head. "I won't be taking any guns with me – I couldn't use one right now, but don't be tricked into thinking I am helpless."

"No," Renée agreed thoughtfully. "I hope you are not intending to use your hands for much."

"I do realise the mends are still delicate, and I will be careful," Wanda promised.

"You should be in hospital. Lanzecki won't like to have to come and fix you again."

When Wanda made no further comment, Renée sighed and asked, "Are you ready?"

Wanda nodded and they left together.

Renée walked into the palace without bothering to announce

herself. She hoped that Johannes would not notice her, but the man was always where he could see what was going on. He did not appear until they were almost at the entrance to the closed off wing where Karl was hidden.

With faultless civility, and impeccable manners, Johannes greeted Renée, and asked if her companion needed anything. He was obviously intent on finding out who Renée had brought with her and why.

"No, Johannes, Fraulein Wong is here to help me with the little jobs father wants me to do. I will let you know if we need anything. She is a whiz at writing PR stuff and can type faster than I can."

Wanda gave Johannes a slight bow, and felt him relegate her to 'secretary' and 'not important'.

Johannes backed off, and Renée took Wanda through to the kitchen and introduced her to the staff, and requested them to help her if she needed refreshments or food.

Renée did not go back the way she had come, both she and Wanda knew Johannes was still hovering. "We will go a different way," Renée told Wanda. "I hope I don't get you lost, but Johannes is the biggest busy body in Weisboden and I do not feel like indulging his rampant curiosity."

Wanda agreed, but made no comment. Instead, she memorised the devious route Renée showed her. "I know more ways to get around the palace than he does," Renée muttered to Wanda.

Prince Michael was with Karl when Renée entered the suite and they stopped talking abruptly.

"Who is this," Karl demanded, sharing his glare between Renée and the strange woman.

"Consider her a nurse," Renée said bluntly.

"I do not need a nurse!" Karl told her.

Renée maintained a professional attitude. "Your Majesty, you are the King! I cannot expect you to change your own dressings."

Wanda sensed her amusement and spoke for herself. "Your Majesty, I am not here as a nursemaid, as you seem to be implying. But I am a trained paramedic, and I do have other skills that you may find useful."

Karl studied her. "Are you the woman who was here two days ago?" He glanced to his father for confirmation. Then he accused, "You are an American covert agent!"

Wanda bowed slightly.

"Very well, we will let you stay!" Karl decided for his own reasons. He refused, however, to allow her to be present when Renée checked him over.

While Wanda waited, Prince Michael advised her of the precautions being taken to minimise interest in the suite of rooms and the security arrangements. Her superior, when he had visited, had set up some sensors that would cause a buzz when someone was approaching. She did not say that Jim had already told her of these, and their individual locations.

Renée gave her instructions for her brother's care, before she left with her father.


Karl emerged and sat in one of the chairs in the suite. He watched Wanda as she worked unobtrusively about the suite.

"Why are you really here?" Karl demanded. He did not invite her to sit, and tried to hide how much his injuries were still hurting him.

Wanda turned from her careful scrutiny of the suite, disguised as dusting, and answered him. "Your majesty, I am sure you were told why we are here," she challenged softly. "But I am, as you guessed, an American agent. I am actually also a paramedic and can take over some of the medical concerns from your sister. My other task is to be extra protection for you. I work with the gentleman you spoke to yesterday – and no, the name I am using is not my own."

Karl looked even less friendly. "I don't like strangers. I prefer to fight my own battles and I do not intend to sit like a mouse in a hole."

Wanda did not flinch. "Your majesty, in your present condition, I could throw you, hog tie you and brand you single handed – to use an American analogy. I am also sure, that you do not need reminding of your importance to this country. My associates and I, at your father's insistence, are not to put you in danger. Now, if you were to watch the television at present, you will see yourself arriving at the airport.

Later today, I am to do you up to resemble your late secretary. It is not our intention to exclude you completely, but you do need time for the worst of your injuries to heal. It is our intention to confuse those who sabotaged your plane."

"How did you know that?" Karl demanded.

"Never mind," Wanda suggested, and before Karl could challenge her further, a soft bell tinkled. She knew at once that someone was coming.

"Please return to your room, Majesty."

Karl went, not happy at being ordered about by the young woman.

Wanda sensed the person's arrival and the thoughts of stealth. She knew from that, that it was not one of the allowed visitors. She walked to the table and seemed to be studying several pages of paper.

No one knocked at the door, it just opened quietly. The man that entered was surprised to see a stranger.

Wanda looked up. "I left orders that I was not to be disturbed," she said sharply and the man stuttered an apology and turned to leave, but spun around as he drew a weapon from his pocket. He did not manage to aim it, for the woman was not where he had last seen her.

Karl observed the incident from the slit opening of the bedroom door. Wanda had moved rapidly to be behind the man when he turned, and as soon as he had produced the gun, proceeded to disarm him and incapacitate him in a matter of seconds, using her mainly her feet and arms. She only used her hands to tie his wrists together behind his back.

Without apology, she searched the man's pockets and found his ID. He was supposed to be a palace servant. Wanda dialled out and a few minutes later, Prince Joseph arrived, identified the man, and removed him, with an apology for her being disturbed.

Karl came out and tried to walk past Wanda to the door.

"Where are you going, your Majesty?" Wanda asked neutrally, moving smoothly to stand in his way. She had a very good idea as to the answer.

"Move aside! I intend to find out what is going on here," he told her forcefully, pushing her out of his way.

He never felt the pinch at his anaesthetised shoulder and neck joint.

He cursed as he fell to the floor, helpless William arrived and helped him back to bed. He swore at his 'nurse' and promised reprisals if his injuries were made worse.

William whispered fiercely in his ear and Karl subsided. His face was flushed with either anger or embarrassment.


The effects of Wanda's action wore off slowly, but Karl's foul mood persisted. She ignored his threats of punishment for attacking him and after ten minutes while checking his injuries, had tired of it.

"You are not thinking clearly, your majesty. Think of the way things would look, if that man had seen you here? When you are officially just arriving back at the palace? You were the one who decided to return here secretly. People would start to say you were hiding secrets."

Karl subsided instantly, but no less annoyed that this woman had out thought him. Instead, he glared, and watched as she exchanged the cloth gloves for surgical gloves, before checking his dressings. He did not seem to realise that her wrists had been injured for the flesh coloured bandage hid her own dressings. Wanda did not say any more as she continued to work.

Finally, Karl spoke again. "I don't like you! I won't let you catch me like that again."

Wanda had the impression of a rich spoilt brat. She shrugged, and finished her task, aware that Prince Michael had returned to the outer suite.

"I am going to insist you be deported and never allowed back here." Karl suddenly found he could move again and grabbed her wrist.

Wanda went still, to prevent Karl from wrenching her own injuries. In a moment of spite, he gripped harder. She bit her lip as pain shot up her arm.

A gnarled hand with a surprisingly strong grip landed on Karl's arm.

"Karl, that is a very ungracious way to treat someone who has saved your life, twice. She has already risked her life to help solve the mess we are in. Release her."

Karl scowled, but obeyed. Prince Michael wasn't finished. "Frau Davis, please remove the gloves you are wearing."

Wanda glanced at Prince Michael, but did as he requested, without comment. She found the tension between Karl and his father too complex to fathom.

Karl had looked away from Wanda, to deliberately ignore her, but his father's request startled him. He watched as she removed the gloves and unrolled the stretchy bandage to reveal the dressings on the recently treated wounds.

His expression betrayed nothing, but his mind revealed shock. Wanda wordlessly replaced the bandage and the gloves.

"In case you are not aware, Karl," Prince Michael began saying. "Frau Davis and her husband flew a helicopter in to rescue you from the crashed plane. The weather was dangerous, and the flying done by Herr Davis was remarkable. I know; I flew with them. If it were not for this young woman, and her quick actions at the crash site, you would not have survived the flight here. And if not for her quick reflexes a short time ago, you might now be in a million pieces. Max Horst, who has been a servant here for many years, had two small bombs on him. He will not talk and tell us why."

Karl spoke in a German dialect that Wanda did not know, but his meaning was clear in his mind. "Why ever did you bring outsiders in?"

Prince Michael did not answer that. "This young woman and her husband found Claude Duvall's new club in one evening, when our security forces failed utterly. I think that my decision has proved sound. We cannot trust those who are meant to be loyal to us. Frau Davis, would you be so kind as to tell his Majesty what you found in Duvall's club?"

Wanda, maintaining a modest demeanour, quietly recited the events of that night. She was watching both men as she spoke. Prince Michael was trying to get a point across to Karl, who was trying not to be impressed by her detailed observations. It was not until she described the costumes of Duvall's elite, that Karl's expression changed.

"Why did you say that about his cavaliers fighting for him, rather than for king and country?" Karl demanded.

"I sense these things, Majesty. It is a useful survival skill," Wanda said quietly.

Karl turned to his father and said, "All right father, I will consider that Claude could be behind this business."

"What secrets does he have against you?" Prince Michael demanded.

Karl looked away. "It is nothing compared to the enormous fraud you and your Americans are pulling on our citizens!"

"Karl...."

"Twenty years ago, Claude, Pierre and I had a falling out. I do not now recall the reason, but Pierre and I duelled. Until yesterday, I believed that I had killed Pierre. Yesterday, Renée told me she had treated a man for stab wounds, a year ago. His name was Pierre Roderick. Claude accused me of murder back then, but he swore to me that he would never mention it. What this woman has said, simply confirms what Renée said. Who were the men you recognised?"

Wanda recited a list of names. Almost all of them were members of the current parliament. Karl, slumped back in his chair, and considered the implications. He saw them clearly, and realised how he had played into Duvall's plans.

"What is happening now?" Karl asked, subdued.

"The king's cavalcade is on its way here," Prince Michael told him. "And another letter has arrived for you, and this woman's colleagues will be moving into another suite later today."


The phone in the outer suite rang twice, stopped, and then rang once. Prince Michael gestured for Wanda to pick up the extension in the bedroom, when it rang again.

"Yes?" was all Wanda said, but she listened intently for a time, and her face stayed impassive. She said, "Yes," again and hung up.

"Sir," she looked at Prince Michael. "It has started. An attempt was made on the life of the Prime Minister as he was welcoming the king at the airport. His guards pushed him aside, but a young girl was killed. Herr Rasmussen collapsed, a short time later. He had a heart attack and he has been taken to the hospital and placed in intensive care. He is reported to be critical. The king will be arriving here soon. I need to prepare his majesty for his role."

Prince Michael nodded. "I will let you explain his part to his majesty."

The older man left the room.

Wanda directed Karl to sit in a chair in beside the mirror. She explained to him what they planned to do to expose the people behind the threats, and why she was to make him look like the man who had served him as secretary for five years and why the crash and its victims had been kept secret.

Karl remained silent, and as Wanda requested, kept his head still. He heard how she was going to achieve the effect using a plasti-skin mask, and what to do and not do, so the disguise did not slip.

"You are a talented woman, Frau Davis. But I still do not like you!"

Karl did not compliment her work. Wanda did not expect it for the king was annoyed that he was being pushed around like a chess piece.

Wanda packed up her bottles and equipment, as she answered. "You are not the only ruling monarch to be irritated by my skills," she told him matter-of-factly. "Only this time, I do not care if I have your good opinion or not."

Prince Michael returned when she had finished and studied the result. He nodded at Wanda, confirming she had done a good job.

Karl rose, and walked slowly after his father. They were to go to his own suite, while the palace servants were all waiting near the entrance to greet the returning king. There he would meet Nicholas Black, the man who was impersonating him.

Wanda remained in the guest suite, packing everything up and removing all traces of the occupation. She packed everything into small cases and carried them to a storage room, well away from the guest room that Karl had been occupying. On each of the trips, she was highly alert for any indication that she was being observed. She was confident that she was not.

Jim had directed her go to the suite he was occupying as the Austrian Ambassador. He had not needed to stress that she remain unobserved. However, she felt that it might prove interesting if she were to keep a watch on the guest suite for a time.

She did not know what pretext had been used to keep the servants away from that suite, but the fact that one had come with a gun and explosive devices was an indication that interest was being shown in the unexplained actions of the royal family in that area.

Wanda was not convinced that the explosive devices were going to be detonated. She hadn't sensed that kind of threat from the man. The gun, yes, but that was all. So she slipped into a vacant suite further down the hallway from the one she had left and kept a watch through a crack in the doorway. When she saw Johannes appear, she wondered if Prince Michael had lifted the restriction on going there. When the manservant's manner turned furtive, and he glanced around before entering, she began to wonder.

After five minutes, Johannes reappeared looking perplexed. Wanda guessed he had done a quick search of the rooms and found nothing. She wondered what he would have done if he had found people within. As quickly as he had come, Johannes walked away.

Wanda guessed he had sent the other man, and had not heard back from him. She didn't follow the servant, but slipped along deserted corridors to the suite of the Austrian Ambassador. This was next to the Royal suite.

Grant greeted her with a grin. He had moved his equipment in, and was still monitoring Duvall. He told her, very quietly, that Jim and Nicholas were with Prince Michael and the King in the Royal Suite.

Wanda glanced at the case sized bank of smaller screens set up on a table. The nine screens were showing different places.

"Duvall's club," Grant said softly. He pointed to each screen as he said what each one showed.

"Max planted a bug in the gymnasium. David has planted one near the main bar and one in the passageway behind the door you found. There is also one in the area opposite Duvall's office. Shannon placed one in Duvall's office. The sword is in a box at the moment, so no visual, but we are picking up sound clearly. That last screen shows the king's suite."

Wanda picked up a second pair of headphones, and sat down on a second chair so she could help listen to the audio pick up, cycling through each channel in turn.

Even though she was concentrating on her job, Wanda wondered how David was doing. She had not betrayed the fact that he had been the one who reported the attack on the Prime Minister, or that the report of his heart attack was a ruse. David travelled with him to the hospital, making the opportunity to brief the man as to what they needed him to do. He was still profoundly shocked by the death of the child, who had taken a bullet meant for him.

Convincing King Karl to play a subordinate role had been difficult. Wanda, listening to bits and pieces of the discussion going on in the adjoining suite, was glad Jim had that part of the job. Karl finally agreed, but contested the belief that Nicholas had his mannerisms perfectly. She smiled when Prince Michael settled the point by stating, "That is because you do not pay heed to your actions."

She turned her attention from the monitor in the King's Suite to the one now showing David preparing the bar and tables for the afternoon and evening. Every now and then, she heard the friend of Renée, telling him how things had to be done.

Grant was paying more attention to the monitor in Duvall's office where Shannon was holding her own in a discussion with Duvall about his swords with every indication of fascination. Max was teaching five men basic moves in unarmed combat up in the gymnasium.

# Chapter 17

Prince Michael spoke to Karl, but looked at Nicholas. "Most of your brothers and sisters have received veiled threats – implying future blackmail. You, they have tried to kill - or perhaps it was meant to fail, but be a warning."

"Where is the letter," the real Karl demanded from his seat in his favourite chair.

Nicholas, sitting in an identical chair next to him, handed it over, never once slipping from his characterisation.

The beautifully written card simply conveyed greetings to the King – using the correct formal phrasing, and this was followed by "8pm, tonight."

"It assumes that I know where to go," Karl interpreted.

"Do you?" Prince Michael asked.

Karl was uncharacteristically thoughtful.

"The Cavalier Club," he said. "Was owned and operated by Françoise Duvall. That was thirty years ago. I know he died fifteen years ago, and his place was burnt down some years later. So I have to concede that the first invitation has to be an overture from Claude Duvall. However, I haven't spoken to him, except formally, for nearly twenty years. Nor to anyone else who was a member back then. They were all meant to be the future up and coming elite, but few reached their potential."

"You and he were close," Prince Michael pointed out.

"Until that incident with Pierre," Karl admitted. "If I look back to that incident, I think Claude orchestrated the fight. He must have. For twenty years, I believed that I had killed my friend. If Renée is correct, and he only died last year, then where was he for all those years?"

"I will put Derek onto it," Prince Michael decided. "He has access to Interpol files and can have people contact the foreign police agencies."

"But as to where...." Karl went on. "I have no idea. I know I kept track of Claude because he knew things about me that I was ashamed of. He promised not to tell...However, I thought, once he had taken over his father's businesses and begun to amass wealth of his own, that he too had put aside his youthful wildness."

Jim asked carefully, "Can you think of a reason why he would wish to contact you at this time?"

"Until that woman told me what she knew, I would not have considered that Claude could be connected to the threats," Karl admitted. "The early ones were general enough. They might have been tries from the anti-monarchy groups. Even the reference as given in the invitation is innocuous enough to an outsider. However, when I read the name, my mind immediately went back to the secret Claude was keeping. I thought then that someone else had found the secret out and planned to reveal it now to disgrace the monarchy. It fits with the other threats."

"Even as a very young man, Duvall struck me as ambitious," Prince Michael challenged. "He has certainly made his name in business, and now, haven't I heard, he is thinking of going into politics?"

Karl gave a strangled laugh. "Ambitious? He always claimed he would become Prime Minister when I was King. It occurs to me now that maybe it is not Prime Minister he wants but absolute rule. Therefore, if it was him, and he wants to talk to me...his hotel would be the best place. It is exclusive enough for the rich and famous to patronise and until today, I did not know that he had recreated his father's club. None of those patrons of his club have mentioned it to me. I always assumed their club was the parliamentary club, and Duvall cannot go there because he is not a member of the Government. So, I would go to one of his restaurants, and wait for him or some other to contact me."

Jim nodded, that suited him. Karl's arrogance would force him to want the upper hand. "Then that is how we will play it," he decided. "However, we will not be on time, or too obedient. The sender can't really expect you to be alone. Any way, you have had urgent matters of state to attend to and the indisposition of the Prime Minister to consider."

A quiet knock at the door, and the fumbling at the door handle, caused a hush in the discussion. Prince Michael walked to the door and held it open for Stephen to wheel himself in. He carried an envelope on his lap. When the door was closed, he wheeled himself over to Nicholas, who was disguised as King Karl, and handed it to him. Nicholas opened it, scanned it and handed it to his "secretary" to read. Karl handed it to Prince Michael, saying, "It is from the deputy Prime Minister, tendering his resignation."

"Stephen, have Herr Bock present himself here. I will have an explanation of this extraordinary dereliction of duty, before we consider it," Prince Michael directed.

"Yes, Father," Stephen agreed. "Also, Julian and Edward are down the hall, insisting on seeing you."

"Are they indeed," Prince Michael commented. "Tell them I will be along to see them shortly."

Stephen left the room.

Karl spoke up. "It was my intention to call a press conference this afternoon to announce the outcomes of the talks I attended. The ones with the most impact on the economy of this country. However, if the press know of this they will want to know if I intend to appoint a caretaker Prime Minister to take charge."

"I do not believe that Herr Bock would tell the press of his intention before speaking to us," Prince Michael said confidently.

Jim dared to contradict him. "Nor would you have thought anyone would try to kill your Prime Minister. I think you should be prepared for the media already knowing of this."

Prince Michael turned his attention to the American. "Do you think that these events are related to the threats against us?"

Jim nodded. "How would a caretaker be chosen? From the existing Parliament?"

Prince Michael saw where the question was heading – half or more of the current parliament were members of Duvall's club. He explained the situation.

"Our constitution permits the king the power to veto any decision made by the parliament, though it has happened only twice since the parliament was formed. Normally, if the Prime Minister is incapacitated, the deputy steps up. If the Prime Minister dies or resigns – there would be a ballot amongst the sitting members to elect a new leader. It is however, within the King's power to appoint a caretaker in the interim, and that person does not necessarily have to be a sitting member."

Karl also saw what he was being forced to do. "Though the Prime Minister is still alive, without the deputy to take over – I will have to declare a state of emergency and appoint someone."

"Could you perhaps appoint one of your brothers?" Jim asked.

Karl shook his head. "Our constitution was written with the intention of transitioning the monarchy to a democracy. A member of the royal family cannot be Prime Minister."

"So someone like Duvall, could be selected?" Jim asked and both Prince Michael and King Karl nodded.

"Your agent has shown the nature of Duvall, but we have not the time to prove it to the people at large," Prince Michael said.

"A lot of thought has gone into the plot," Jim said. "But having Duvall officially in a position of power will not be wise. May I suggest that you make no official announcements today? Delay your press conference until tomorrow. You will have a better idea of how the Prime Minister is responding to treatment, and it will give you time to find out what pressure was exerted on the deputy to resign."

"I agree," Prince Michael stated. "I will invite the media to a press conference tomorrow morning. We can organise it in the ballroom. Karl, you will need to instruct your doppelganger in his speech. I will leave that with you, while I see what Julian and Edward want."

Jim departed with the former king, but only went as far as the adjoining suite where Grant and Wanda were monitoring the rest of his team. He was beginning to see Duvall's overall plan, and he suspected they had only seen the tip of it.

"What is happening?" Jim asked Grant.

Wanda stood and handed her headphones to Jim so he could listen.

"David is playing waiter," Wanda told him. "And Max is teaching arrogant aristocrats unarmed combat."

Grant added, "Duvall seems besotted by Shannon. He was prancing around his office wearing the sword, until Shannon was announced. He has put it away in his safe. He and Shannon are discussing his collection."

Jim had carefully coached Shannon for this phase and she was performing brilliantly. She was not blatantly admiring Duvall, but was feeding his ego by her admiration and envy of his collection. He listened to the conversation and was soon sure that Duvall wanted to prove to the Countess how smart he was. He would soon show her the sword he had purchased from under her nose.

The view from the tiny bug Shannon had placed earlier, did not show much detail. However, from her tone of voice, the Countess was magnificently angry when she recognised the sword Duvall revealed last. She stopped short of accusing him of stealing from her, and of using rude language. She said her piece and waited for an explanation.

Duvall smiled, and the Countess seemed to grow angrier.

"My dear – I purchased it for you," Duvall claimed, his smile growing as the Countess seemed to be stunned. "Please, take it. It would give me great pleasure to see you wearing it."

Shannon took the sword and handled it carefully as she examined it with eyes that seemed to covet it. "Claude, I do not know what to say," Shannon spoke, infusing emotion into her voice. "But...ladies of my station do not wear swords." She sounded genuinely regretful, and then seemed to be looking at Duvall with new eyes. "Could...Could I see you wearing it....Claude?" she said, almost shyly.

Duvall met her eyes and did as she asked. He buckled it on and moved casually about his office, stopping to stand under a magnificent painting depicting his ancestor. He knew that the countess would have to be comparing him to the man in the picture.

"It looks...so right... on you," she said wistfully, and her anger had completely gone. She moved, as if drawn, to Duvall and put her arms around his neck and drew him into a passionate embrace.

Jim handed the headpiece back to Wanda. His next comment was not related to Shannon's performance. "Have you seen enough to be sure of getting into Duvall's safe?"

"I saw enough the first time I was there," Wanda told him, without boasting. "David said there are no nasty traps on either of them."

The door of the suite opened abruptly. Jim and Wanda both swung around, expecting Prince Michael, but tensed for trouble. Grant looked up but continued to monitor his screens.

The tall man that strode in, held up a badge, as he closed the door behind him.

"Interpol," was all he announced.

Wanda sensed Jim relaxing, as the man asked, "You would be Jim Phillips?"

"Yes," Jim admitted. "Derek Mount Pelier, I presume."

Prince Derek smiled. "Yes. Father said you were a consultant. I had you checked out. Your associates have impressive resumes."

The prince turned his attention to Wanda as he spoke. He studied her, and then moved on to look at the array of monitors.

"Quite an impressive array of illegal monitoring equipment," he commented neutrally. "Unfortunately, information obtained this way cannot be used."

"We have the permission of the monarch of Weisboden," Jim remarked.

"True, but I must obey international law," Derek fenced. "I must obtain my information in such a way that I can obtain a search warrant based on that law."

"Are you saying, Sir," Wanda asked deliberately. "That you wish to examine the premises in the pictures you see?"

Derek turned his attention back to Wanda. "I have no reason to do so."

"But if someone came to you with evidence of a crime, or sufficient information to deduce a crime had been committed – you could?" Wanda asked, to see if she was reading the Prince correctly.

"Do you have such evidence?" Derek asked casually.

"Yes," Wanda stated.

"You have been within those premises?" Derek asked her.

Wanda nodded.

Derek drew out a photograph from his pocket and handed it to Wanda. "Can you recognise the room where this photo was taken?"

Wanda studied the photograph and ignored the man and woman shown in a compromising and highly intimate position. She considered the few details of the decor that were visible.

"Yes," Wanda said, looking directly at Derek, and positive of her facts.

She sensed something akin to excitement from the man. "This is one of the bedrooms on the second floor of the house at 123 Rhine Strasse," Wanda told him.

"And under what circumstances were you on the premises?" Derek asked.

"I had the misfortune to find myself locked in that place one night," Wanda said, deliberately. "I had to look everywhere for a way out."

"Tell me what you saw," Derek directed.

Wanda glanced at Jim, who nodded. She quietly, factually described what she had observed while she was in the house. She did not state how she had gone in, only how she had got out, and subsequent events.

Derek listened intently, but part of his mind was on the array of screens. Grant waved at Jim to come to the monitors. He pointed to one, and Jim picked up a microphone and asked, "David?" He heard no reply, but the angle of the camera changed to show a group of three men.

Derek stopped Wanda's report with a hand gesture and went to study the new picture. She knew he had identified the men. He seemed to come to a decision.

"I think my father chose well when he asked you to help him," Derek said to Jim. "I will tell you some confidential information. Duvall is wanted in France for murder. We have enough evidence to convict him, but we cannot yet extradite him from Weisboden. Father never felt the need for extradition treaties. I finally convinced Karl and that was on the agenda at those meetings he was having. Those three men are all international crooks and are on our lists of wanted men. It seems obvious that they know Duvall. What have you learnt of Duvall's motivations?"

Jim summarised, "We believe he is behind the anti-monarchy movement, and certain threats being received by your family."

"Yes," Derek mused. "I had an interesting letter myself. Someone discovered I am not as clever as your young friend here at sneaking around places. What about this matter of Rasmussen and Bock?"

"The Prime Minister is not as ill as the media believe. Your father is going to talk to Herr Bock," Jim said.

"His indiscretion is on the front page of the afternoon's early edition of the Weisboden Herald," Derek said. He picked up the photo.

Wanda decided to speak up. "I would not put it past Duvall to have set him up."

"And why is that?"

Jim answered, mentioning the need for a caretaker Prime Minister.

Derek nodded. "I agree. I do not like the things I have been hearing. Tell me, Mr Phillips – what exactly are you planning?"

Jim drew Derek aside and outlined his plans. Derek nodded and said little.

"Excellent. I intend to be present when Father talks to Herr Bock, which will be after he finishes with those foolish brothers of mine. Have you need of your young friend for this evening?"

"No, she should have left the country already," Jim remarked.

Derek glanced at Wanda. "I am officially seconding you to Interpol. I will be applying for a search warrant for Duvall's club, and I want you with me. However, that won't be until this evening. If Duvall attends that dinner Karl is going to have, then that is when I will go there."

Jim made a comment. "David is going to replace the waiter that prepares Duvall's cavalier toast. He is going to try to get a sample of the wine used. We believe it might be drugged. We do not know what time that will be."

"Very well, I will give you a number to call if the toast has not been done before the dinner."

Jim accepted that.

"In what capacity do you require my help?" Wanda asked Derek.

"My reason for being in Weisboden right now parallels yours. I will be seeking evidence against Duvall. I understand that you are skilled at that."

Wanda smiled wryly. "Duvall has made it harder for me to be as good as I normally can be." She raised both wrists.

"Do you wish to prefer charges?" Derek asked.

"No, but he is likely to want to make me dead on sight - which is why I am hiding here right now. However, do not take that as wanting to refuse to help you. I am in, and David will be pleased to help as well."

"Excellent. I will be in touch."

"One other thing," Wanda said quickly, as Derek looked to be leaving. "You should have a word with Renée about Duvall."

"Renée? What does she know?"

Wanda merely stared at Prince Derek and added, "I suggest you stop thinking of her as your baby sister! You can have her paged by calling ...."

# Chapter 18

Michael Dupont cowered in the huge bed, as Claude Duvall dressed himself in his impeccable suit to be ready to go down and greet his guests of the evening.

As always, Michael felt sickened and dirty, even as he was relieved that his torment was over for a time. He wished he could refuse to obey his onetime guardian and now employer – but he knew that if he did, Duvall would punish him in an unpleasant way.

Today, Duvall had announced that he was pleased with him. He had brought in the new girl, Jessamine. The little whore had been high on something. She had enjoyed having Duvall fondle her while Dupont had...it might as well have been rape. She had no idea and he had had no choice. If he had refused the present, Duval would have been angry. If he looked less than pleased now, he would be angry.

Then, Dupont had had to pleasure Duvall. The bastard had been gay for so long that he knew all the tricks of rousing other men. He knew Michael's body intimately. He had been touching it in varying degrees since finding out whose child Michael was.

Duvall came over to the bed, and waited for Michael to come nearer. He unashamedly kissed Dupont on the lips and Michael knew he was expected to rise, naked and embrace him.

"I expect you to be at the toast this evening, Michael, and after that we will be speaking to his majesty – the man who killed your father."

"Yes, sir," Michael agreed.

"Take as much time as you want with Jessamine – I am paying her by the hour."

Michael glanced at the sleeping girl and Duvall chuckled. "We will celebrate again tomorrow."

"Surely you and the countess..." Michael tried to suggest. He hoped, fervently, since Duvall had been with her most of the day.

"Perhaps, once I am Prime Minister," Duvall countered. "I might even marry her. She would make a worthy escort. I might even let her keep her toy – for pleasure. I do not need her for that. I have you."

Duvall turned and departed. Jessamine continued to sleep. Did Duvall really expect him to rape her again? Want to? She had seemed to enjoy it, but he had seen her eyes. They were too bright – like the eyes of Duvall's elite. He had told her she would enjoy it – and she had.

Michael jumped off the bed and grabbed his clothes. He couldn't just dress and leave. He smelt of...

He'd have to use Duvall's shower. His boss was unlikely to return this time - though on other occasions he had.

The shower had clear glass around it - a fact that made him feel exposed. He tried to ignore it and kept his back to the rest of the room as he showered quickly. He turned and reached for the towel and a tiny red light caught his eye.

He froze, still naked and exposed. Shaking, he drew the towel around his hips, went to the mirror, and used Duvall's brush to groom his hair. He eyed the tiny globe, that was no longer red, but in the mirror, reflecting from behind he caught a second red blink.

The bastard was filming him, Michael realised with a shock. Had he been filming him in bed too? No, not then, unless Duvall's own features were obscured or his identity not apparent.

Michael forced himself to dress carefully. Duvall had a strict dress standard but Michael's movements were automatic; his mind was trying to understand why Duvall would film him.

The first reason was obvious - the man was gay, he liked naked men. Then there was the spectre of blackmail – or to ensure Dupont stayed loyal. That was Duvall's style. Or it could be Duvall was about to discard him? Or he didn't trust him. No, that wasn't likely. Michael had been trained as Duvall's top assistant and this afternoon had proved Duvall was pleased with him and still enjoyed using him. If he didn't want Michael anymore, he would find others. Half of his elite were his catamites when they were high and didn't know what they were doing. Or was Duvall planning on framing him and having him arrested?

Even the thought of being arrested was not frightening. Then he would be free of Duvall. That thought was quickly quashed. He'd be branded gay, and in a prison, other men, rougher and cruder, might target him.

Michael poured a stiff drink of Duvall's best brandy, before leaving Jessamine asleep in the bed in the master bedroom. A maid saw him leaving and gave him a knowing look. Michael felt his face flushing.

He started to feel odd, as he walked downstairs. He took deep breaths once he was outside and that helped. He walked out past the two door attendants, who merely mouthed a polite, "Sir," and reached his car.

He wanted, needed, to get well away from the club. To run, and keep running. He started his green Ferrari sports car and took off from the front of Duvall's house with his car revving fiercely.


Julian and Edward were pacing the corridor, stopping at the point where Prince Joseph stood casually guarding the more distant rooms.

"Let us through, Bro," Edward demanded. "We need to talk to father."

"Stephen has gone to tell him you are here," Joseph told them evenly.

"What's going on around here?" Julian demanded. "Why are we being treated like outcastes? Why does the infant know and we don't?"

"It might have something to do with your private lives," Joseph remarked. "You've both had your names in prominent places in the scandal rags. I wouldn't want to talk to father if I were you."

"He sent for us!" Edward stated. "Was it just us?"

Joseph knew it wasn't, but only shrugged. Both men went back to pacing.

Prince Michael emerged from the passage behind Joseph. With a silent head gesture, he directed his two younger sons to follow him.

Joseph, who knew Johannes was hovering, went in search of the senior servant who was about to become too busy to be interested in any of the goings on of the royal family.


Julian stopped in the doorway when he saw who was with his father.

"Derek?" he managed to say.

"None other, brother. Shut the door after you," Derek directed.

Edward had come in first, and was now collapsed into a chair, looking white. However, he was defiant. He asked, abruptly, "What did you want to see us for, Father?"

Prince Michael was not sitting down. He moved to face Edward, while Derek moved back near the door.

"Why don't you tell me, Edward?" Prince Michael suggested in a voice that his sons knew well.

Edward felt ill. He tried to say that he had done nothing, but his father's next words stopped him.

"Tell me what hold Duvall has over you?"

"I owe him 100,000 Euros," Edward forced himself to admit.

"And what must you do to repay him?" Prince Michael insisted.

Edward squirmed. "Give him information about the family."

"And?"

"Attend his business meetings to impress his clients," Edward said, trying to forget the details, but his father did not let him. There was worse, and he wanted to shrink into the chair when Derek moved to stand beside his father.

"I want to know every detail of your dealings with Duvall," Prince Michael insisted. "If you are completely forthcoming, you might not be arrested as an accomplice to treason."

Edward lost all traces of colour from his face. His father meant that literally. Derek being there made this discussion official. He tried one last line of defiance. "What do you mean?"

Derek answered. "Someone sabotaged the plane that Karl was returning in."

Edward blurted, "But I saw his plane land safely. I saw him arrive this morning."

"But you feared it wouldn't," Derek suggested. "You thought he was going to arrive earlier?"

"He said he was going to leave three days ago, but the weather closed the airport..." Edward said before realising that he had incriminated himself.

Prince Michael spoke the words that made Edward imagine a prison door slamming behind him.

"Karl returned three days ago, his plane flew through the storm. It crashed and Karl was the only survivor, and then only by extreme good fortune."

"But I didn't hear…" Edward stammered. "How…how is Karl? And who arrived today?"

Derek had not seen Karl since his accident, but knew he was recovering. "Karl is alive, and recovering, but we needed to keep up appearances. He will be able to appear at the press conference tomorrow."

It did not take much more pressure for Edward to start talking. When he finished, he listened to the "royal lecture" from his father. When it was over, he was white faced and trembling.

Derek offered advice to his severely chastened brother. "It is fortunate for you that Duvall had not yet compromised you completely. I advise you to liquidate however much of your personal assets you need to pay Duvall back, and have that amount as a cheque or bonds or something, on his desk by morning. I suggest that you do not ask or expect anyone in the family to help you. Your foolishness put you in this position, but you are an adult, a member of the ruling family and an example for the lesser people. Once Duvall is paid off, he has no hold over you and if he tries to further incriminate or dominate you we can charge him with extortion."

Edward nodded dumbly, able to breathe again only when Prince Michael turned his attention to Julian.

"How many women have you whelped bastards on, Julian?"

The younger of the brothers looked to be trying to disappear in the chair.

"I want an answer, Julian," Prince Michael insisted.

"I don't know," was the almost inaudible answer.

"How many of your women did you meet at Duvall's club?" Derek suggested.

"Five or six," Julian murmured.

"And what were they rewards for?" Prince Michael asked.

Julian knew he was not going to get off any lighter that his brother. "Bringing packages into the country. He knew we were exempt from customs searches."

"Drugs?" Derek suggested. When Julian nodded, Derek went on, "I advise you to be very detailed in your description of people and methods and places."

Julian knew he had as little choice as his brother, and yielded to the inevitable. He voluntarily added details of other things he had done for Duvall.

"Let us hope that Duval's whores are clean – with no nasty infections," Derek commented after Julian had stopped talking. He saw Julian go as pale as Edward.

"Why...do you say that?" Julian managed to ask.

"Because one of the women who claims to have bedded with you has decided to cite you as the cause of her own problem," Prince Michael told Julian. "A woman named Marguerite."

Julian sank lower. "She's a whore!"

"Julian..." Prince Michael warned him about his disrespectful language. "She may be, but you chose to fornicate with her."

"Father, all the women I take into my bed know I can't marry them. They like to boast that they had sex with a Prince. I give them an expensive gift and send them off. They know not to try for more," Julian tried to justify himself.

Derek cut him down to size. "So you are little more than a gigolo, except you pay them. What about Estelle De Angelo?"

"What....about her?" Julian asked trying not to look intent on the answer.

"Her father is talking of placing rape charges against you," Derek told him.

"It wasn't rape," Julian insisted. "It wasn't...but her old man broke us up. He told her that she had to stop seeing me. But I..."

"What?" Prince Michael insisted.

"She...and I...are married."

He managed to silence his father, but not for long. "You have the marriage certificate?"

Julian nodded. "We haven't told anyone. She didn't want the attention of the paparazzi. I haven't wanted another woman since and that is the absolute truth."

"How did you meet her?" Derek asked abruptly.

"At a party her old man threw," Julian said defiantly. "He introduced us."

"Was Duvall there?" Derek asked.

Julian paled and turned white. "Yes."

Prince Michael spoke to his son, bluntly. He told him the many ways in which his womanising and the things he had done for Duvall could be used against him and the family.

"I suggest that you make it your business to ensure you provide for any illegitimate children you have fathered," Prince Michael advised. "Does your wife know all of this?"

"No," Julian admitted. "She doesn't like Duvall, so I didn't let on I knew him. She knew I'd had other women..."

"Has Duvall asked you to do anything recently..." Derek asked.

Julian shook his head.

"I think, Julian, that you had best be prepared for him to have a job for you. He might produce evidence of infidelity, or some other matter to force your hand. We think he is trying to discredit all of us. If he has any inkling that you have married Estelle De Angelo, he may try to force you by trying to alienate her," Derek warned. "Do you think she will stand by you if you tell her all of it?"

"I...don't know," Julian said, his voice breaking slightly.

Prince Michael saw the genuine grief, but did not relent in his displeasure. "I want both of you to answer one question. Will you side with the family, or with Duvall?"

They both promised to stand by the family, no matter the cost.

"I will accept that promise," Prince Michael told them. "And I will hold you to it. If either of you mention anything more to Duvall, do anything more for him, I will consider your promise broken and you will receive no consideration from the law of this country."

"If we avoid him, he will be suspicious," Edward finally spoke up. "He expects us at his club this evening."

"Well then," Derek considered. "Go, but be aware of the stakes. Do not forget what you personally will lose."

Two very subdued men were more than grateful to be allowed to leave.

When they were gone, Prince Michael said to Derek, "I will call for you when Wilhelm Bock arrives." He sounded old.

"Father, we will get through this. Your consultant has a good plan to expose Duvall, and counter his strategy."

"I certainly hope so, Derek. But I think that Duvall has only just started," Prince Michael sighed. "Who knows what other nastiness he has planned?"

Derek understood his father's worry. "The young woman with your consultant suggested that he set up Herr Bock, to force him to resign. I agree. And I think you should expect more scandals to appear in the evening paper."

"That is what causes me concern. But there is a matter you could look into - the whereabouts of Karl's friend Pierre Roderick for the past twenty years."

"What are you meaning?" Derek asked.

"Karl believed he killed the man twenty years ago. Renée has proof that he died only one year ago," Prince Michael summarised.

Derek raised his eyebrows in surprise. His father related all he knew.

"Renée? Where does she come into this?"

Prince Michael smiled. "She is a doctor and has been treating Karl for his injuries - helped by that young woman calling herself Frau Davis."

"That young woman suggested I should talk to Renée," Derek said thoughtfully. "I think I should do that now."

# Chapter 19

David and Otto Fraenkel were in the conference room at the end of the third floor passage, setting up glasses on the bar for the evening's Cavalier Toast.

Duvall had already noticed the new face and challenged David's presence. David's terse and respectful attitude had satisfied him, after Fraenkel had explained that they had needed a last minute replacement for the man who had usually served Duvall. After hearing of the freakish accident, Duvall dismissed the problem and quizzed David.

"What were you told to do here?"

David repeated the gist of his briefing, finishing with, and "I was to ask for your preference for wine, Sir."

"I will bring that," Duvall said tersely. "Have everything ready by seven o'clock."

Duvall left as abruptly as he had arrived. David released a breath of relief. Fraenkel shared his relief. "He must have a lot on his mind. He's pretty fussy about who serves in here."

David had Fraenkel watch the passage, whilst he located a second tiny camera and voice receiver where it would cover the room. It was a precaution in case the sword's camera transmitter did not work.

David turned his attention back to the job. "Why the two glasses by themselves?"

"For him, and his assistant, Dupont," Fraenkel told David. "Only the most expensive wine for them. Oh, the stuff he gives the Cavaliers is above the ordinary, but nowhere near the best."

"His Cavaliers?" David queried, although Wanda had mentioned the men in costume.

"You will see what I mean," Fraenkel promised.

He did not have to wait long. Duvall returned, dressed exactly like a Cavalier, and wearing the famous sword of Cromwell. He led a group of twenty men, including Princes Edward and Julian into the room.

David glanced frequently at Duvall, waiting for his signal to start pouring the drinks. While waiting, and projecting a disinterested attitude, he studied the men. Some strutted arrogantly; others looked as if they felt silly in the elaborate costumes.

Once Duvall had given the signal, David began pouring the drinks. He seemed to be oblivious to the conversation in which Duvall was urgently requesting to know where his assistant was. While Duvall was intent on the answer, David contrived to spill some of the wine, and quickly wipe it up with a special cloth. Later he would put the cloth in a sealed bag.

Half way through the elaborate ritual, Dupont entered the room. He slipped past the bar, took his drink and joined in. If he had hoped his arrival was not noticed, David decided he had failed.

As soon as the Cavaliers finished their drinks, David and Fraenkel moved amongst them and collected the glasses. The men began to move into little groups to chat. David heard comments about the arrest of two members of the Parliament, and the resignation of the deputy PM. All were concerned at the condition of the Prime Minister.

David had listened to the words of the "Toast", and it seemed as if they were indeed working to support the King and their country. The talk of the men was naturally on the scandals and how it would affect them and the parliament.

He didn't know where the whisper began, but the word went around that if the king needed to appoint a caretaker Prime minister, Duvall would be the best choice.

David began to wash the glasses, whilst Fraenkel wiped them and put them away. The tiny sink was placed so the person washing could still watch the gathering, and David did so without making it obvious. He saw Duvall corner his assistant and begin a private conversation.

It looked as if Duvall was angry. David studied Dupont and decided the younger man was on the defensive. His observation was echoed by Fraenkel. "Wonder what Duvall's fair haired boy has done to upset him, besides being late? A change from earlier when he was right pleased with him."

The comment interested David. "How do you mean?"

"Duvall and Dupont were together with one of the girls for over an hour."

"What?" David actually thought he had heard wrong.

"Huh! No one dares mention it, but those two are a couple," Fraenkel stated.

David glanced at him to see if he understood the man.

"Duvall's a homo – he doesn't use women. However, he likes to watch and play with the whores while one of the other men has them. They got a new girl in, and the boss gave her to Dupont for a present..." Fraenkel stopped suddenly, seeing Duvall approaching. "Sir?"

"As soon as you finish cleaning up, you may return to your other duties." Duvall instructed.

"Right, Sir. We won't be more than five minutes."

He forgot the previous conversation and said, "Look at the eyes of those cavaliers. I reckon he has drugs in the wine. I think he brain washes them, and that is why we get kicked out."

David kept quiet as he finished his work and ensured everything was tidy. Only when the two of them were well away from the room did David ask, "Does Renée know about Duvall being gay and weird?"

Fraenkel shrugged. "It isn't something you mention to a high bred lady."

David didn't disagree. He could accept that Duvall was gay, with perverted desires, but Dupont's body language was all wrong for him to be gay too.

He thought on what he had seen and heard. He knew Jim would have heard all of the conversation through the sword, or the microphone he had concealed on himself.

Later he saw Duvall come down into the entrance foyer with Dupont in close attendance.


When Dupont had returned to the club, he was relieved that no one looked closely at him. He felt like a worthless cur, returning to his violent master, since he was the only master he had.

He'd left, intending to keep going, or to end his life, which had become intolerable. Instead, here he was back where Duvall owned him, and hoping his master would not be angry with him.

Foolish thought. He was late, and he wasn't perfectly presented. He would have to grovel, and promise to please Duvall – perhaps if he said he preferred Duvall to foolish little whores. He certainly did not like being forced to perform in front of Duvall, but then he didn't like performing for Duvall either.

He took the time to change his suit before going to the conference room. He used some of the perfume Duvall liked, and when he entered the room, he slipped to the bar and quickly joined in the ritual.

Duvall turned when he had finished, and head gestured to a corner. Michael saw his expression and his guts seemed to quiver.

"You are no longer a child, Michael," Duvall began. "I expect the utmost efficiency from you. Particularly now, when everything I worked for is in my grasp. Whatever did you think you were doing speeding though the Capitol? Fortunately, I was able to convince the officer who ticketed you to forget the affair, but I will not do it again. Is this the way you repay me for the gifts I give you? Didn't Jessamine please you?"

"She was an empty headed wench," Michael said. "It was like coupling with a doll. I am used to adult co-operation, like with you!"

Michael looked at his feet, but Duvall lifted his head and smiled. "Then you shall have it, later. And if the time is mutually enjoyable, I will not have you punished, this time."

Memories of the lessons and punishments flashed through Michael's mind as Duvall continued to vent his displeasure.

Duvall finally released him, but said, "You will stay with me. I wish you to accompany me to the Fleur-de-lis. I have had word that his majesty has chosen to dine there."

Michael nodded agreement, feeling totally humiliated, and only craving for Duvall to forgive him.


Duvall's Fleur-de-Lis Hotel was the most resplendent in the Capitol. It attracted the cream of the upper classes of Europe. Even so, since ascending the throne, King Karl did not make a habit of dining out. Therefore, the arrival of his party created a stir of excitement.

The staff, believing that Nicholas was Karl, had their attention on him. Karl in his guise as his late secretary, found his current anonymity amusing. It enabled him to observe his surroundings more closely as they were escorted to grandest private dining suite.

The official party numbered six, but there were an equal number of guards bracketing the party. They guards were dressed in suits, to minimise attention, but were still guards to anyone looking closely.

Nicholas and Karl were accompanied by the "Austrian Ambassador" aka Jim Phillips, Prince Joseph, Prince William and Princess Renée. The latter was, for once, dressed befitting a Royal Princess.

Everyone in the party was aware that their conversation was likely to be monitored – either electronically or physically. Their talk was, ostensibly, to bring Karl up to date on matters that arose during his absence and also for the benefit of the Ambassador in cementing good relations.

Renée was trying to look as if she was only there 'under orders', but in fact she was enjoying herself. Her brothers were leaving her alone, and not acting superior, and Karl in his role of secretary was uncharacteristically quiet.

Naturally, Duvall was informed of the important guests, and insisted they have the best possible service. His staff knew he would be coming to oversee them.

When Duvall arrived at the hotel, he went to where the security monitors showed the king's party. This was the first time that Karl had eaten at his restaurant, so Duvall guessed it was the result of the latest anonymous note that he had had Glockner deliver. He had believed that Karl would come to one of his places. The King would want to be sure that Duvall had no intention of mentioning certain secrets.

He hadn't seriously considered that Karl would come alone – but five others and six guards! At least Prince Michael had not come. The former King had done his best to alienate the three cavaliers.

Prince William and Prince Joseph had been delegating for Karl during his absence, under the former King's control no doubt. There was Karl's secretary of course, and that non-entity of an Austrian Ambassador but who was the woman? She was vaguely familiar...

"Michael," Duvall gestured, annoyed that Dupont was keeping well back from him. "Do you recognise the woman?" He pointed to the small screen showing the King's party.

Dupont studied the screen. "I can't really see her clearly."

"No, neither could I. We will go up to the restaurant," Duvall decided.

Michael followed Duvall, not quite sullenly, but certainly not happily. He knew who the woman was, but did not want to tell Duvall.

In the servery of the restaurant, were a number of one-way mirrors. It allowed the headwaiter to direct his staff. Duvall edged the man aside, for he was making sure the King had the best possible service. He pulled Dupont to his side, filing away for later the reaction he had felt to his touch.

"I think I have seen her somewhere," Michael said as if thinking carefully. "Could she have been at the garden party with the blond man?"

"No, not there. The Ambassador is travelling on his own."

Duvall suddenly snapped his fingers. "Renée!" His voice was tinged with excitement.

"Renée?" Michael asked as if trying to imply he did not know who his boss meant. "You don't mean Princess Renée, do you?"

"Yes! Do you remember that Glockner said she was back and being fobbed of with some minor duties?"

He ignored Dupont's reluctant nod, and gestured to one of the waiters. He gave whispered instructions to the man to hover and listen to the conversation at the King's table, and to send the man currently there, back.

Duvall questioned the man who returned.

"They seem to be discussing things that occurred during the King's absence," the man reported, and Duvall waved him back to his duties.

"Well now. Prince Michael must have brought the Royal Rebel to heel at last," Duvall mused. He put an arm around Dupont and gave his shoulder a possessive pat. "When I go in there, I want you with me. I want you to try and find out something about what she has been doing these past few years."

"I don't know..." Michael tried to refuse, but Duvall wasn't going to let him.

"You are a handsome young man, Michael. She is a sheltered, pampered wench. I am sure you can enchant her. She is likely to be livelier than the lovely Jessamine. And you can slip something into her drink."

Michael forced a smile of contemplation on his face and reluctantly accepted the vial of the drug Duvall used to make his cavaliers compliant. It did not occur to him that Duvall had been using the same substance on him.

They continued to observe Karl and his table companions until they were finishing their after dinner coffee.

Duvall entered the private dining room, and went directly to the man his eyes told him was King Karl. He was impeccably polite and formal as he enquired if the service had been excellent.

Nicholas smiled faintly. "It seems, Claude, that you have learnt... much...in the past years. Yes, the service surpassed the best."

Renée heard the faint emphasis on the word 'service' and glanced toward Duvall. He tensed slightly, but maintained his practiced smile. She glanced away and saw that all of her table companions were intent on Duvall. She switched her look to Duvall's companion, but betrayed no sign of recognition.

Dupont was staying back, but dividing his attention between Duvall and herself. It had been eight years since they had been seeing each other and he was the cause of the argument she had had with Karl that had resulted in her exile in Switzerland. However, he and she had also argued back then about his hero worship of Duvall, and his blind obedience to the man. Karl had objected, merely because he was Duvall's ward. She had been angry then, at Michael and at Karl, but perhaps Karl had been right after all.

She heard many things as a doctor, and many of her patients knew Dupont as Duvall's assistant. They called him the bullyboy in a suit, but none had said he was not polite.

Renée met Dupont's eyes, but didn't smile. Karl stopped watching his doppelganger and glared when he realised that Dupont had taken the exchange of glances as an invitation. He had started to rise, but the 'Ambassador' leant over and spoke to him. He sat back.

Dupont moved to stand beside Renée and asked, "Is there anything else I can get for you, my lady?"

Renée waited before answering, but only said, "What can you get me that the waiter can't?"

In a very soft voice, Michael pleaded, "Renée!"

Equally softly, Renée responded, "Go away Michael. I don't want Karl to exile me for another eight years."

Dupont stepped back, uncertain how to proceed. Had Renée just been making a dismissive comment, or had she been implying she wanted illicit substances?

Renée turned her attention back to Duvall. This was the first time she had been close to him. A week ago, she hadn't realised how much the man had affected her family. Not only Karl, but Edward and Julian too. If Derek were to be believed, he had tried to corrupt some of her other brothers too.

Maybe it wasn't surprising. He walked over people for his own ends. He took money from little investors, like her patients, and they all thought the great philanthropist was making money for them. She had heard differently, when some of her patients had wanted to get their money, and found it was 'tied up'. Renée believed that he was using it for himself, to fund his lifestyle.

Derek had told her some things he had found out about Roderick and that information had given her the impetus to go to the hospital and look at Roderick's file again. She had taken certain photos of blood slides and note of other details and quizzed the lab techs with certain 'what if' questions. Their surmises made her thoughtful.

Roderick had looked pale and wasted, and at the time, she had put it down to blood loss. What if he had AIDS, as the techs had proposed? What if he had been gay and contracted the disease in prison? If he was gay back when Karl was young and wild, what of the three inseparable cavaliers? Karl didn't seem to be homosexual. He and Alicia seemed satisfied with each other, and he had fathered children on her. So what about Duvall?

That was the point that had caused her to ask to be included in this dinner. She had told Jim she wanted to study Duvall. He hadn't asked why, but agreed. She hadn't even considered that back before she was sent to Switzerland, but she had been sheltered and naive then. Was Duvall gay? Was Michael? Were those looks he kept giving Duvall, looks of jealousy?

Casually, as if disinterested in the exchange between Duvall and the 'king', Jim stood up and spoke into a break in the conversation. He excused himself and declared he had had a pleasant evening.

William and Joseph rose as well and made it clear that they were ready to leave too. They had taken their cue from Jim, who had received the subtle signal from Nicholas that Duvall had made reference to accepting the invitation. They were leaving to give the two men a chance to talk.

Renée didn't stand immediately, nor did Karl. Jim sensed Renée had reasons for acting as she was, and Karl, as his secretary, was a chaperone for the 'king' and would seem to be a discreet distance away.

"Herr Duvall," Renée said casually, while the conversation with Nicholas was interrupted. "My father wished me to thank you for your consideration towards his two American guests. He hopes you will support the jamboree if it comes here."

Duvall bowed slightly in her direction. "Please tell his Highness that it was my pleasure," he said suavely, and went on smoothly, "Perhaps you would allow my assistant to help you with your coat?"

"Oh! I wasn't going to leave yet!" Renée smiled the gracious smile she had been trained in. "I was just going to ask for more wine."

"Renée..." Nicholas warned in Karl's precise tones.

Dupont leaned over Renée and suggested, "The Lion Bar, downstairs is a livelier place, and I think Duvall and the King have important things to discuss."

"Really?" Renée remarked, leaving her meaning ambiguous. Duvall did not miss the slightly malicious smile she wore on her face as she glanced at the secretary and then the 'king'. She knew Karl had wanted her to keep away from Dupont.

She stood and smiled at Dupont, and hoped that Duvall thought she was being her old rebellious self. He looked smug, as if she was reacting as he intended, and as if he wanted her to go with his assistant. Well, who was conning who here? She wanted to get Michael alone and ask some questions.

Dupont offered her the coat, but Renée waved it away. "It's too warm for it in here and it will hide my dress."

The dress, borrowed from a friend, was designed to attract attention - though it seemed that Michael had not noticed that until now. He slipped his arm under hers. Nicholas gave a stifled sigh and ignored Renée.

Duvall spoke quietly to his assistant. "I will require your assistance later this evening."

Dupont stiffened, and Renée wondered why such an innocuous comment should cause such a reaction. She pretended she hadn't noticed it.

"Surely, Herr Duvall, you don't insist that your assistant is in attendance twenty-four hours a day?" Renée remarked. "I have no intention of going home for hours yet. And since he offered, I intend to monopolise him."

Dupont glanced at Duvall and said, quickly. "Sir, I have not forgotten what you expect me to finish. I will see to it as soon as I have escorted Princess Renée to her place."

Duvall gave an almost imperceptible nod, and it seemed Michael was anxious to leave the room. Renée was paying attention to Dupont's body language and felt him relax once they were out of the room. She snuggled next to him as he escorted her downstairs to the bar.

As she walked, she whispered, "Let's stay here long enough to be seen, and then leave."

Dupont jerked in shock. Renée had been acting cold and distant until then. He thought he knew why – so Duvall did not realise they had known each other before. "Alright," he agreed, cautiously.

The ambient noise in the Lion Bar made talking difficult, but few words were needed. Dupont bought her a wine and they sat at a small table and watched the dancing. Renée was aware of eyes on her, but did not look to see who. When she finished her drink, she drew Dupont up onto the dance floor as a particularly wild dance was in progress.

Michael seemed stiff at first, but soon he recalled how it had been between them years ago and he relaxed into the gyrations. Renée found the moves returning to her too, and was able to dance and be aware of her surroundings. Even the flashes from more than one camera.

Well and good. There would be pictures in the papers in the morning – the Royal Rebel, back in action.

When she felt she had stayed long enough, and wanted to leave, she simply winked at the barman who was a patient of hers, and waited. He sent three drinks waiters to intercept the reporters, while she and Dupont ducked out the back way.

"They will think we are going off for sex," Renée remarked to Dupont as she led him upstairs. She felt an odd reaction from him. Eight years ago, he would have been eager. Perhaps he was gay after all. "Isn't that what Duvall hopes you'll do?"

"Where are we going," Dupont asked, ignoring her question.

"Does it matter?"

"I guess not," Dupont conceded. He stayed silent as he was led back down to the ground floor by the back steps and out to a car. Renée drove him to another hotel.

All she said was, "Since the paparazzi saw me, they won't leave me alone. They will be busy trying to find which room I went to in Duvall's hotel."

Again, she felt a reaction from Dupont, and she was becoming more certain of her ideas about Duvall.


As the door of the hotel room closed behind them, Renée saw that Dupont had gone tense again. She walked around to face him and challenged him, "You are still Duvall's yes-man aren't you, Michael? So what did he want you to do with me?"

Dupont looked away from her. "I..." was all he could force out. Renée moved to see his face and saw the anguish there. "Renée, I ..."

Renée felt her residual anger slip away and her doctor training came to the fore. "Sit down, Michael," she invited in a modified tone, but he obeyed as if it were an order.

He collapsed, more than sat, but wouldn't meet her eyes. He seemed on the verge of breaking down and fiddled to loosen his tie to hide it. Renée studied him, and then sat down on a chair she drew closer.

"Michael? What is Duvall making you do?" she asked him gently, reaching out for his hand. He flinched, reflexively jerking away, but then he took it and held it tightly.

"Why? Why did you leave me?" Dupont blurted. He was looking at her now, wanting her answer.

Renée considered what her doctor's senses were telling her. This was not Duvall's yes-man trying for dirt, but a plea for help.

"I had no choice," Renée said gently. "Karl and I had a fight about my wanting to keep seeing you. I was sent to Switzerland."

"How long have you been back?" he demanded with a bit more force.

"A year or so," Renée told him, but before he could remonstrate with her, she asked, "Does Duvall know we used to know each other?"

"No," Michael told her. "You were the best thing in my life and I didn't want him to spoil it."

The comment gave the adult Renée a great deal of insight. "Why didn't you just leave him?"

"I...can't," Michael collapsed, crying now. "I wanted to. I tried again today – tried to die. I can't even do that. I went back to him like a cur wanting to be whipped."

"Talk to me, Michael," Renée invited. "Tell me everything about you and Duvall."

"I can't..."

"Forget who I am. I am not a pampered naive princess anymore. I am a doctor. I work in the emergency department of the hospital. I have seen and heard things ... I can help you."

It wasn't easy, but Renée persisted. When he had talked himself out, she considered all he had admitted and was glad he had not succeeded in killing himself that day. She was not glad that he had crawled back to Duvall, but she understood even that. It was the only life he knew.

"Do you want to break away from that gay bastard," Renée asked bluntly.

Michael finally met her eyes, as if she had just thrown him a lifeline.

"God's – if I only could!"

"Michael, I want you to talk to some people I know. Will you?"

"Who?"

"That is not important," Renée wasn't going to tell him too much. "It is someone who does not want Duvall to succeed in his plans."

The answer was forced out. "Yes."

Before he could change his mind, Renée stood and went to the phone. She spoke softly, wanting only Jim and Wanda to come, but Wanda suggested Derek, and seemed to know what was happening. She said having him was better – for Michael. She agreed, trusting the American woman that she was beginning to consider a friend.

# Chapter 20

Jim returned to the palace with Prince Michael and Princes William and Joseph, once Nicholas and Karl had begun their discussions with Duvall. Karl's guards had remained with him. Renée had gone off with Duvall's assistant, with every sign of pleasure.

The tiny microphones planted on both Nicholas and Karl were picking up the conversation and Karl's instructions to Nicholas.

Grant said softly, "Duvall is putting on the pressure. I think he believes he has Karl in an impossible position. Nicholas is handling it well."

"Are you recording it?" Prince Michael demanded. Grant nodded, but Jim told him. "We can listen to it all when they finish. Grant, put it on speaker."

It was unpleasant to listen to, and Jim observed the tension in the former monarch.

"I hope your plan works," Prince Michael whispered harshly. "The reputation of my family has been unblemished for generations. I do not want people hearing lies about us, even if you disgrace Duvall, some people will still believe the lies."

Jim stayed silent, running his plans through his head.

Prince Stephen took the initiative and went to fetch his brother, Derek. They both returned quickly and Prince Michael gave his Interpol officer son, a brief rundown of Duvall's talk with Karl.

Derek sent Stephen to find out if Frau Davis was ready. He had intended to be gone to Duvall's club well before then, but he had been delayed by some other official business.

Wanda was just finishing her "make up" when Stephen wheeled himself in. She had already dressed in dark close fitting clothes.

"A few minutes more," Wanda told Stephen, and she quickly stowed items in pockets of her outfit.

As she was finishing, the phone in the suite rang. Stephen rolled his chair so he could answer it.

"For you. It is Renée."

Wanda took the phone and only said, "Hello." Renée spoke quickly.

"I have Michael Dupont with me. He's Duvall's assistant. He wants to tell some things. Can you bring Jim here? We are in the room next to the Ambassador's suite. 217."

"I will tell Jim, and I will bring Derek too," Wanda told her.

"I didn't want it official..." Renée said, sounding reluctant.

"Better this way," Wanda advised. "Better for Michael."

"Perhaps then, at least Derek won't be like Karl or Father," Renée said, sounding angry.

"We won't be long," Wanda promised. She hung up the phone, and gave Stephen a fast summation.

"Renée used to date him," Stephen revealed. "Karl told her to keep away from him, and she wouldn't. He had her packed off to Switzerland. She hasn't mentioned him since she got back. But that was eight years ago."

"As things stand, it was probably a wise move. Otherwise, Duvall may have learnt what she was doing and found a way to discredit her," Wanda said thoughtfully. "I had better tell Derek. I think we need to go there before we go to the club. He might tell us some useful things."

Derek agreed, but he insisted that Stephen have Karl paged and get him to leave Duvall and go to the hotel.


Renée was standing calmly behind a couch where an obviously nervous young man sat. When the door opened, Michael swung around with terror on his face.

Renée rested her left hand on his shoulder. "Hush, it's okay."

They were in a room of one of the Capitol's finest hotels - the same hotel where the American, Jim, had been staying before moving into the palace. In fact, this room was the one directly next to the room where the "Austrian Ambassador" was staying.

Michael swallowed hard as he recognised some of those entering.

"Sister," Nicholas greeted coolly. "What game is this now?"

"Karl," Renée looked at Nicholas and smiled faintly, fuelled by the chance to ignore her brother. "I think you should listen to what

Michael has to tell you."

Nicholas did an excellent imitation of Karl's superior smile and directed it at Renée. He was silent for a moment as if considering, but was actually listening to some terse remarks from Karl about the man with Renée, through a tiny earpiece. "Very well, we will listen."

"Michael, you know Karl and his secretary. The others are Herr Osterman, the Ambassador from Austria, my brother Derek and my aide, Frau Davis," Renée introduced. She was not going to say anything about the fact that Karl was disguised as his secretary. The newcomers all took seats or stood about the room. Renée saw Frau Davis, Wanda, studying Dupont, but Michael was not aware of her.

One advantage of that switch was that Nicholas would listen, where Karl might not.

After several false starts, Michael licked his lips, swallowed again and began to speak.

"Your Majesty, I am Michael Dupont."

"I know who you are," Nicholas echoed Karl's comment. "You work for Claude Duvall."

"Yes. I...am his assistant. I...have been doing things for him that ..." Michael stopped, not wanting to admit to so many people the illegal things.

Renée advised him, "Tell them what Duvall has planned for tomorrow."

"He has people, reporters, primed to challenge you about scandals in the Parliament and to accuse you of deliberately allowing such things. He has others who are going to insist that the royal family has no further place in the ruling of Weisboden. The men who were arrested this afternoon, he has planted evidence for the police to find. The police officers he controls. He is going to smear as many of the royal family as he can. He plans to be Prime Minister. The remaining cabinet will insist you name him interim Prime Minister."

Michael was so intent on watching the fake King, that he did not see the glance between Jim and the real Karl.

Derek moved next to Nicholas. "Tell us all you know."

Michael glanced around the room as if wanting to flee.

Karl, in his guise as his secretary, muttered, "We know someone has been agitating. If you really intend to help, do so. Unless you want to be executed for treason."

Renée glared at her brother.

Wanda sent a thought to Jim, "He wants to, but he is petrified. Duvall has a really tight hold on him."

The 'Ambassador' spoke quietly. "As I am here as an unbiased witness, may I suggest you let the young man speak without implying your dislike of him. It cannot be easy for him."

Nicholas followed Jim's lead. "Renée, get that assistant of yours to take notes."

Renée turned, spotted Wanda as she was moving to obey, and gestured her forward and then wondered briefly why she looked different.

Wanda did not want Dupont to get too good a look at her yet. She had almost finished her preparations for the raid on Duvall's club when Renée had rung. She had grabbed pen and paper before they had left.

Wanda wrote down the answers Dupont gave to the questions being fired at him from Nicholas and Derek. She was memorising them at the same time that her mind was aware of other thoughts going through Dupont's mind and of the grip he had on Renée's hand. It seemed that Renée was his lifeline. What Duvall would do to him if he found out that he was talking of Duvall's plans was clear in his mind. Last time he had disobeyed, he had been brutally thrashed. He feared that happening again. Yet something had pushed him to the point of "enough". Dupont had reached the point where obeying Duvall was no longer tolerable, where the nausea he felt at having to obey was stronger than his fear of punishment.

That feeling resonated in Wanda. She had felt that same resolution... once.

Wanda caught Nicholas's eye when Dupont wasn't looking. She mimed removing her gloves and momentarily dropped her current personification. He looked at her as if to say, "Is that wise?" Wanda did not glance away; she nodded, "Yes".

Nicholas stood up as if to prowl around the terrified Dupont. He moved so that Dupont had to look past Wanda to watch him. He had kept up his questions until that point and stopped as if considering what he had learnt so far.

Wanda rested her pen on the table she was using, and casually removed the cotton gloves she was wearing. The movement attracted Dupont's attention, as she intended. When she stood and moved towards him, he watched her warily.

"I, too, have a question," Wanda spoke quietly, unthreateningly. "Why did Duvall have my father killed?"

She had Dupont's full attention. "Your father?"

"Pierre Roderick," Wanda told him. "With his dying breath he condemned Duvall."

"My father...he died twenty years ago. He was killed....Duvall told me ..." Dupont looked trapped. "Roderick was killed by His majesty."

Renée saw what Wanda was intending. "Your father? Was Roderick your father?"

Dupont nodded, and Renée moved around to look at him. "Michael, I didn't know! But Roderick didn't die twenty years ago..."

"Renée!" Karl, in his guise as secretary spoke warningly. Nicholas overruled the warning.

"Yes," Nicholas confirmed. "I have it on excellent authority that Pierre Roderick died only a year ago."

"No! You must be mistaken..." Dupont insisted.

"I treated him, Michael," Renée told him. "His wounds were deep and infected."

"But then where was he all this time?" Michael asked.

Derek spoke up. "He was in a French prison, convicted of murder. He was released a year ago; his sentence was shortened by five years."

Wanda became the object of Dupont's scrutiny. He paled to ashen. "You are the woman who was in his club two nights ago...but you were dead!" His eyes went to her wrists, and then to her face.

Wanda shrugged. "If you say so. Are you the oldest of Roderick's bastards?"

"I am his eldest child, and the only legitimised child," Michael said with a touch of arrogance.

"So how did you hook up with Duvall?" Wanda asked.

"My father had arranged for him to be my guardian if anything happened to him."

"And his money?" Wanda asked casually.

"He had none," Dupont snapped. "You are not the first to want to share it."

"If I was you," Wanda said thoughtfully, "I would ask to see the document that gave him the authority to take Roderick's money."

It was an idea that Dupont had never considered.

"If we might get back to the matter in hand," Derek suggested. "Apart from the two safes in his office, where else might Duvall hide things?"

Michael's mind was wrenched back to other matters. He had trouble forcing out, "His bedroom."

Wanda suddenly knew what Duvall was doing to control Dupont.

"There is no safe there," Wanda stated definitely.

"I...I have to get back," Michael suddenly insisted. He tried to stand, but Renée held him down.

"I don't think so," Derek began to speak, but Wanda sensed that Dupont's fear was rising. He was recalling what Duvall would do to him.

"If I don't get back, soon, he will want to know why. I...I was meant to talk to Renée and find out what she had been doing for the past years...he gave me something to put in your drink..." he looked at Renée, and dropped his eyes. "He couldn't find anything to discredit you. He... will send someone to get me."

Wanda spoke up and stated, "I think you should let him go back. You do not want Duvall to be spooked."

Jim added his own advice, backing Wanda. "I agree."

Neither Derek nor Karl liked the idea.

Jim looked at Nicholas, but was watching Karl from the side of his eye. "Duvall believes he has you where he wants you, and we want him to be confident of that. We want him to believe that nothing will go wrong."

Karl muttered something and Nicholas uttered it. "Father trusts your advice, so we will let him go – for now."

"Your majesty, I think we should leave now," Jim advised.

Derek nodded, and watched his brother and the two others leave.

"Frau Davis?" Derek queried.

"May I speak to Michael for a moment?" Wanda asked. Derek shrugged. "We need to get going, or Duvall will return before we are finished."

Wanda grinned nastily. "Oh, I think he's going to be quite busy at the hotel for some time yet."

"What...?" Derek asked.

Wanda waved that aside. "Don't ask!" she advised. Shannon, looking nothing like the countess, and Max, would be causing many annoying problems.

Michael was standing up, and looking for his coat. Wanda went to him and gently took his arm.

Only Renée heard what she said to him. "You have made the right choice, Michael, and I commend your courage. I know that you are aware that talking of this meeting will not be good for you."

He nodded, flushed. Wanda wasn't finished. She continued to speak softly to Dupont, meeting his eyes, but her voice was too soft to be heard by anyone else. She patted his shoulder, and spoke a bit louder.

"You do not need to mention meeting all those here now. You have done everything Duvall told you to do." Wanda went on

Michael nodded again.

"What will you tell Duvall about Renée?" Wanda asked.

"Nothing, I won't tell him anything," Michael promised, but Wanda shook her head.

"You need to tell him something," Wanda advised. "He will want to know about Renée."

"Well," Renée considered. "It would be the truth to say that Karl and I had a loud and physical disagreement about my choice of friends, and my determination to slum it. He had me packed off to a finishing school in Switzerland and I had intended to never come back."

"But you are here!" Michael argued.

"True," Renée agreed. "You can tell him that my father gave me an ultimatum and has me doing some PR work but I wouldn't say what I was doing before I came back. He might begin to think I was emulating my brothers in some way."

"Why would you want that?" Michael asked.

Wanda silenced him. "Michael, we thank you for your timely warning. Let us worry about tomorrow. And if Duvall notices your abstraction and asks what is wrong – tell him that the wench would not go to bed with you." Wanda patted his shoulder again. "It would be a good idea if you stayed here for at least another hour."

Michael nodded mutely. Wanda glanced at Derek and they left to go to Duvall's club.


Wanda had changed her appearance for the foray with Prince Derek and his Interpol team. This was to hide her identity, even though this time her entering was sanctioned by Interpol. Derek had a warrant. However, he was intending to keep the execution of the warrant low key. He wanted evidence against Duvall, but he also knew what Jim intended, and that was for the people of Weisboden to learn what Duvall was really like.

Grant had reported when Duvall left the club after his Cavalier's toast. At that time, Derek had the building under covert observation. He knew that Duvall's elite – including Prince Julian and Prince Edward – were still inside. Each of them would be followed when they left the club.

One of Derek's men went to the front entrance and asked to be admitted. He was told, bluntly, that if he was not a member, he could not be admitted and, he could not be made a member without the approval of Claude Duvall. They turned him away, but the man didn't leave. He continued to loiter in sight of the entrance and maintained the attention of Duvall's security.

Derek gave the order to move in. Now it was Wanda's turn to lead. She led Derek and three other men up to the wall at the rear, undetected.

"David has detached the security cameras on this side," Wanda said softly as she reached her hand through an opening to reach the lock securing it. For the time being, Wanda had only some false skin over the dressings on her wrists, so she had movement in her fingers. She needed that to manipulate a short piece of wire into the lock to open it.

It took her longer than usual, but it was still open in less than a minute. She removed the lock and slid a bolt. The gate opened, and the group slipped in quickly and checked around the trucks to be sure they were alone. Wanda already knew they were, and she went directly to the smaller gate that led into the little yard when the kegs were stacked. It was not locked, and she opened it a tiny bit and looked. The kitchen was dark, but the scullery light was on.

She had no need to explain where they were – that had been done in advance, with the warning of things they might encounter. At the closed door of the kitchen, Wanda sensed David on the other side. She knocked quietly and the door began to open.

Derek had a weapon in his hand, but Wanda whispered, "Its David." He put it away, and the team slipped into the darkened room. David relocked the door behind them.

Wanda had advised Derek that David could take two of his men and get them into the casino. Derek directed two of the men to follow, and they obeyed. They knew to expect the door behind the bar and the steps down. Once there, they removed their dark overcoats to reveal evening dress.

From Wanda's description, David knew where to go. He found the secret door to the casino, opened it, and the two men slipped in. He did not ask what they intended, and assumed they were capable of handling themselves. He took their coats and returned upstairs to position himself to watch the front entrance.

Wanda led the other two men to the ground floor stairs. The bottom section of the staircase was well lit and visible from the security office. Wanda stopped in the shadow of the lift well and gestured climbing up, to reach the stairs half way up.

She mentally berated herself for showing off, as she felt the pain in her wrists. Derek grinned faintly and accepted the challenge. The other man followed. From there she led the way to Duvall's office without encountering any people.

She paused outside the door, not sensing any danger. Moments later, she had the door unlocked, and stepped aside for Derek and his man to enter first. She went in after them and kept a watch at the door.

The two Interpol agents wasted no time in beginning a thorough and careful search. Thanks to Dupont's information, they knew where to look for what they wanted. A small pile of film boxes and paper files grew on the corner of Duvall's desk. When they had searched everywhere else, Derek touched Wanda gently and gestured to the safes.

Wanda grinned and felt for her tool kit. Derek watched her work, and was impressed. He had accepted the assurance that Wanda could open the safes, but he had reserved some doubt. He soon had none. The door of the first safe opened.

"I think I need to keep an eye on you," Derek murmured as he moved her aside to look in the first safe.

Wanda grinned, and went to work on the second one. This was the one Duvall had put his latest acquisition in.

Derek gestured for her to close the first safe, before looking in the second. He took out several items, and Wanda sensed Derek's satisfaction. The items they removed went into pockets of their jackets.

They used a dim torch to check that the office did not look to have been disturbed. Just as they were moving to leave, Wanda stopped them.

"Someone is coming," she whispered. "Two."

Derek gestured for her to hide, and he and his partner stood to either side of the door. It opened abruptly, and a figure charged in. He was followed by another man, who reached for the first and pulled him back.

"Duvall is not here!"

"I have to see him! Surely you can call him."

Wanda recognised the second voice, and so it seemed did Derek. He gestured to his partner and acted. Each went for a different man, and in moments had them disabled, hand cuffed, and unable to call out. Wanda checked the passage outside and whispered, "Clear."

Dragging the prisoners with them, the group returned to the stairs. Derek spoke into a microphone and the man outside returned to the front door and distracted the security men, long enough for the group to slip down stairs and out of sight.

David joined them again at the kitchen and placed a wrapped parcel into Wanda's hands. He was going to stay to observe the activity when Duvall returned. She sent to his mind a whispered, "Be careful," and took the other men outside.

They returned to their van without being challenged. Derek sent his team back to their headquarters with the prisoners, and went, with Wanda in tow, to check on the men ready to follow Duvall's elite.

By morning, all those in the Elite, would be under arrest, or waiting questioning. No warning would reach the club, for all the lines into and out of there were going through Grant's board.

Derek finally returned to his car, a dark Mercedes amongst other expensive cars, and they waited, adding to the watchers on the club. After a period of silence, Derek spoke, "You're good. How did you know the men were there?"

Wanda told him, "I am not allowed to tell you that – and I assume whoever you checked up with about me didn't mention such things."

"No," Derek agreed. "So can you tell me how you got to be so good at opening locks and safes?"

Wanda chuckled softly. "Those at the state department discovered that I had a natural talent for it."

Derek's mind betrayed his assumption that they had trained her after she was recruited.

"Did you get what you wanted?" Wanda asked to distract him.

"Yes, I have enough," Derek confirmed. Then after a pause, he asked, "Are you sure that we can trust Dupont? I didn't like letting him go."

"I know," Wanda told him. "But...yes. He will not mention our plans to Duvall. He would prefer not to have to return at all. I believe though, that I am correct in saying that Duvall would be spooked if he did not."

Derek tapped his fingers on the steering wheel. "I am going to have to arrest him."

"Is there some rule in Weisboden, or international law, about questioning people before reading their rights? I think there would be a case for not being able to use what he told you against him."

"Do you plan on being his advocate?" Derek challenged softly. "He has voluntarily admitted to being an accessory to many criminal acts."

"I know, but at the moment he feels like he does not deserve any consideration. He hates himself. He believes he deserves the harshest of punishments, but I would argue with you about whether he wanted to do those things, or personally got any benefit from them. He is basically a decent man, but he cannot go against Duvall."

"But he did," Derek pointed out.

"It took every bit of courage to do it," Wanda insisted. "And it wasn't easy. If Duvall had not had him go after Renée, I doubt if he would have reached the point he did."

"You sound like you understand him," Derek commented.

"I do," Wanda told him, without elaborating.

Derek seemed to sense what she did not say. "What motivated you?"

"I met David," was her simple answer.

"I see," Derek confirmed. "I see indeed." He mused over the earlier question session with Dupont, until his attention was caught by the movement of a group of men.


"We will need to continue this discussion at another time," Derek directed.

He was getting out of the car, and Wanda looked to see what he had spotted. He was striding purposefully towards a group of three men. They were passing out of the light from a street lamp, but Wanda's one glimpse had been enough for her to recognise three wanted international crooks. She instantly understood one of Duvall's aims.

Before she ventured from the car to back Derek up, she saw that the two of his men that had gone downstairs were approaching the group from behind. She stayed put, glad to be relieved of the need to act. She had done enough tonight – her wrists were throbbing. Renée and David would be annoyed with her.

With a minimum of fuss, three arrests were made, and the men were taken to a plain dark van.

Derek returned to his car.

"A good haul," Wanda commented. "First Johannes, now three crooks. All of whom will think they can get off easily."

"So, you recognised them all," Derek asked her.

"Yes," Wanda agreed. "Have the new extradition treaties been formalised?"

"You – know too much," Derek warned with a faint smile. "Do I drop you back at the palace?"

"Unless you need me further?" Wanda queried.

"Not at the moment," Derek confirmed. "But I hope we can work together in the future."

"That would be fun," Wanda agreed.

"Will you be at the press conference?" Derek asked.

"Not noticeably," Wanda said. "But once Jim's plan has gone into action – I have no doubts that things will go as planned."

# Chapter 21

Renée arrived at the palace and went to Jim's suite after first checking on her brother. Shannon recognised her at let her in. When the door was shut, she reported to Jim.

"Karl will be right for tomorrow," was her first comment. "Michael has gone to tell Duvall all is set for the conference and I have spread the word to my friends. They know where to go to get their passes." She glanced at Derek. "How did the raid go?"

Derek told her the highlights, including his high impression of his new assistant. He saw Renée frown, and look at Wanda, but he went on.

Renée nodded, thinking through the plan that she had half formulated. She had been too busy during the day to consider it further.

Jim spoke up, "David will be back soon, and will take over the monitoring of the club. Grant will have the equipment in place in the ballroom before the media are let in. Max will help him with that. Shannon, what has Duvall planned for you?"

"I'll be meeting him early. He has invited me to the press conference, and promised to introduce me to the King. I won't let him slip away," Shannon informed Jim.

"Nicholas and Karl know what to do, and what to expect," Jim finished. "We all need to get some sleep."


Renée strode over and took Wanda's arm.

"Let me have a look at your wrists," she said firmly.

Prince Derek looked concerned. "What is up?"

"Nothing," Wanda claimed, but Renée gave a sound of exasperation, and continued to escort Wanda back to her sleeping room.

She pushed Wanda into a chair and fetched her bag. "You are no better than my brother!" she said in disgust.

"That's why I knew how to handle him!" Wanda said with deceptive meekness.

With care, Renée removed the false skin and revealed the dressings below. They were completely red. "How can I make you stop doing too much?"

A voice from the door said drolly, "Have a rhinoceros sit on her."

Renée turned her glare on David. "You are her husband! Can't you tell her?"

"I am her partner, not her controller," David specified. "And I did warn you that she had an unacceptable idea of functional."

Wanda made a rude noise.

"However," David went on, "She does know what she can and can't do safely. It is just that other people don't see things the same way."

Renée sighed. She said nothing as she carefully swabbed the operation sites.

"Well, you haven't broken any stitches, and they look to be healing already. You were lucky."

Wanda decided to stay meek. She was not going to make fun of Renée's genuine concern. "I do what is needed."

"What are you doing tomorrow?" Renée asked as she redressed the operation sites.

"I will be handing out passes for your friends," Wanda said. "I am not going to be at the press conference. Too much media attention will be there."

"I had hoped to have another talk," Derek suggested, putting his head in the door. "About your insights about Dupont."

Renée gave him a sharp look. Wanda tensed for a moment, and Renée sensed it.

"Later," Wanda whispered to her. To Derek, she said, "As soon as Renée is finished. Was the stuff I gave you from David analysed?"

He nodded. "It was as you suggested - the same as what Duvall gave Dupont to use on Renée. I have spoken to our forensic doctors and there is a drug that can partly counter the effects. I will be talking to all of the Elite before morning, but I am still reluctant to let them loose before the press conference. How can I be sure they will not run off or still obey Duvall?"

Wanda glanced at David, and Renée had the oddest idea that she and he were talking.

"Michael didn't use it on me," Renée assured Derek as David left the room.

When David returned, he had Jim with him. He repeated Derek's question and it seemed to be a question with a different meaning for Jim for he turned his attention to Wanda. "You should be resting!"

"My hands have to rest," Wanda disagreed. "I will be fine with a short sleep. Duvall is expecting his Elite to be there to nominate him and add their support to his claim."

"I am aware of that," Jim said. "But even if they support him we have the means to negate their efforts."

"By shaming them," Wanda pointed out. "They are as much victims as Dupont."

"Very well," Jim decided. He turned to Prince Derek. "Wanda has certain talents. They are classified, but I think she can assist you in determining the mindset of those Elite."

"Indeed," Derek studied Wanda anew.

Wanda sat back in Derek's car as he drove them to the Interpol team's headquarters. "The politicians that were named in the afternoon papers...have they been picked up?" she asked, wondering if they came under Derek's jurisdiction.

"That isn't my affair," Derek told her. "I am here covertly."

"You are here to arrest Duvall, and we are out to discredit him. Since Dupont admitted to placing evidence for the reporters to find, I would assume on Duvall's orders, shouldn't we try to have them publically exonerated?" Wanda proposed.

"I can't override the local police," Derek told her. He concentrated on steering, as he listened to her comments.

"Not even if Duvall owns some of the high ranking police too? We met them when we were taken from the airport," Wanda told him.

"Were any of them amongst the Elite?" Derek wanted to know.

"David didn't have time to tell me."

"So, what are you thinking?" Derek asked her.

"Me? Only if they know the men were set up and abetted it, or if they were acting in good faith, not realising they were influenced by Duvall."

"I will keep that in mind," Derek assured her. "If they are working with Duvall, it might be hard to get them to admit it."

"If you ask the questions, I will see what I think," Wanda proposed.

"I can't use intuition as proof," Derek warned her.

"If you want evidence," Wanda turned to him. "That will take more time. All I was intending for now was to listen to the elite as you question them and try to tell if they were coerced by or cooperating with Duvall. I wouldn't trust the latter, and I think the former should have a chance to redeem their self-esteem."

"What if there is a chance to find evidence for or against these men?" Derek probed. "What if you ask questions that occur to you?"

"I would rather not. I am not an official Interpol agent," Wanda admitted. "Though if you had a gadget like Nicholas and your brother are using...?"

"That is possible," Derek agreed. "And your instinct is correct. It would be better if I did the questioning. You seem to have an appreciation of legal matters. Would that be from trying to circumvent them?"

Wanda chuckled at the understatement. "Think what you will. It might be that I understand the criminal mind and how they would prefer to find a loop hole to slip through."

"Are you talking of Duvall and Dupont here?"

"Duvall, mostly," Wanda said, becoming serious. "Michael is more of a victim and I intend to help him."

"I still think I will need to bring him in – are you going to stop me?"

"No, you need what he can tell you – just keep him well away from Duvall."

"Why," Derek asked as he parked the car.

"Later, Sir, it's complicated," Wanda hedged.

"There are a lot of things I would like to know about you," Derek warned. "I am waiting to see you..."

His phone rang. He had a Bluetooth gadget to answer it. Wanda wasn't consciously listening, but she heard faintly, the report that all the elite were now in custody.

"Ready to work?" Derek asked her.

Wanda nodded.

At the temporary Interpol headquarters, Derek opted to talk to his brothers first, since he knew them personally. He also indicated that he would speak to them without any of his colleagues present. Wanda sensed that he was trying to spare his family further adverse attention. Perhaps he was expecting them to be willing informants, not reluctant ones.

On the way to the first interviews, Derek introduced Wanda to several of his colleagues as a consultant and a medical aide. He had directed them, earlier, to obtain everything that would be needed for taking blood samples and injecting the anti-control drug to neutralise the effect of what Duvall had given them.

She had all this equipment on a trolley when she entered the small room where the two younger princes were waiting.

They glanced at her, and then ignored her - which was exactly what she wanted them to do.

"Why are we here, Derek?" Edward demanded. "Are we under arrest?"

"Helping with enquiries," Derek countered. "Did you drink Duvall's wine at that treasonous cavalier's toast?"

"Yes, Duvall usually has top grade wine. How do you know about that anyway?"

Derek didn't enlighten him. Instead, he asked, "What did Duvall claim that nonsense meant?"

Edward answered readily. "That we were to dedicate ourselves to the betterment of Weisboden and its king."

Julian interrupted. "The arrogant sod thinks he's better than Karl and that Karl can't rule properly without his help."

Derek asked, "Did you have the wine, Julian?"

"No, sod him. He set me up. I dumped his expensive plonk on the plant. Why do you ask?"

"It was drugged," Derek told him, and went on to state bluntly what effect the drug usually had. Julian swore under his breath.

"You are wrong, bro," Edward insisted blandly. "If it was doped, it was to open our minds to make us more intelligent. I always won at cards after his toast."

Derek saw the incongruity and stated, "Edward, you said you owe him 100,000 Euros."

"Oh, that? He said not to worry about it."

Wanda listened and sensed a great deal from the questions Derek asked and the answers he was given.

Julian was angry at how Duvall had manipulated him into doing illegal things. He spoke frankly, and paced the room. He didn't need to be prompted.

Edward, still affected by the drug saw nothing wrong with Duvall's logic as it seemed that Duvall was skilled at speaking with double meanings.

Finally, Derek gestured Wanda over. Edward paid no attention to her as she took a blood sample from Julian. He paid attention when Wanda faced him with a freshly prepared tray of equipment.

"Hey! What is this?" Edward demanded, alarmed. He began to rise and protest further.

Derek pushed him back down into the chair. "It is in your best interests to let my assistant take a blood sample from you," Derek told him. "Right now, I don't think you know what you are saying. I think in this state you may have done things that you don't remember, and those things might reflect poorly on our family. If there is that drug in your system, you may not be charged with treason."

Edward glared at his brother. "You are an arrogant bastard, Derek. What gives you the right...?" He flinched as Wanda inserted the needle, and watched in fascination as his blood filled the tube.

He protested again after Wanda had taped a swab over the injection site and filled a syringe with liquid from a vial.

Derek stood over him. "Edward, this medication will counter the effect of the drug in the wine."

"I don't want it!" Edward insisted.

Wanda paused, at a gesture from Derek.

"Do you remember the question Father asked you this afternoon?" Derek asked Edward.

"Of course," Edward retorted.

"Tell me then, if Karl has to name an interim PM, who would you recommend?" Derek asked.

Edward sensed this was a test, but his answer was to him, perfectly logical and absolutely his own idea. "Claude Duvall. He is a successful business man, has good people skills, and he knows the problems of the poor, and has a lot of good ideas."

"Would you support him if Karl presents another candidate?"

"I can't think of a better candidate," Edward told his brother. "And you can't convince me to change my mind."

Derek nodded to Wanda and she set about preparing Edward's arm for the injection. He jerked his arm away.

"Edward, you have two choices. Allow my assistant to do her work and administer this medication, in which case you will be allowed to leave later, or refuse and remain in Interpol custody pending trial for treason."

Wanda sensed, in that moment, that Edward had the stirrings of alarm. It was not from what she was doing, but that he might in fact be being manipulated by Duvall. He recalled what his father had said, but the words had until then seemed like an idle comment. While his mind tried to grasp the earlier meaning, Wanda finished injecting the drug and taped a swab over the site.

"Ten minutes," Wanda told Derek. He nodded to indicate that he understood.

The counter drug had been injected into a vein, so it would work quite fast.

Julian was still prowling the room, thinking unpleasant thoughts. "Will you be keeping me here?" he demanded.

"For a while," Derek told him calmly.

"I need to make a phone call!"

"Why?" Derek asked.

"To Estelle," Julian said, uncomfortably. "She will be worried."

"Where is she," Derek asked, not unsympathetic.

"At her father's place," Julian scowled. "I need to talk to her – before tomorrow."

Derek considered. "I will have her brought here"

"Her father will insist on coming too. He will think I am going to be arrested."

From where she had retreated, Wanda suggested, "Let him."

Julian snarled at her. "He wants me charged with rape."

"Did you?" Wanda asked mildly.

"No! She's my wife."

"Does he know?" Wanda queried.

"No, he'd have it annulled." Julian modified his tone.

Wanda smiled with a hint of malice. "Let him think what he likes if it gets him to bring her here. She is an adult, is she not? So she can be 'questioned' without him...mmm?"

Julian began to relax now he began to understand her innuendo.

Wanda went on, "Is her father a friend of Duvall?"

Julian nodded. "Do you think Duvall put her father up to it?"

Wanda shrugged. "You should talk to her. Tomorrow at that press conference, Duvall intends to denigrate as many of the royals as he can. If your wife comes with you to support you – it will be a powerful statement. Perhaps her father will see Duvall's true nature, and yours."

Julian considered her words and stood straighter. There was determination in his stance.


Even before ten minutes, Wanda was aware of the change in Edward. It took Derek a minute or two longer. Edward looked around the room as if seeing it for the first time. He took in the official ID on his brother's pocket and paled. His mind was clear now, not muzzy.

"What was that stuff you gave me, Derek? I feel like I was half asleep before."

"Half asleep is probably a good description. Certainly you were in a suggestive mood," Derek confirmed. He started to repeat the questions he had asked before, and this time Edward answered without reservations.

"So, Duvall said he would halve the amount you owed him if you support him as Interim Prime Minister, and in removing your family from all aspects of politics?" Derek summarised.

"And extended the time needed to repay him," Edward added. "He'd been putting on the pressure, so I was relieved to agree."

Derek nodded. "Did you follow my advice?"

"Yes, though I don't know if it will be done by morning. The bank system closes down over night."

"I will allow you to call the bank," Derek decided. "I may be able to convince them to make an exception."

Edward didn't admit his gratitude. He was shaken by his sense of standing on the edge of an abyss.


"I would like you both to wait here," Derek directed. "Please don't try to leave. I may need your help with the other elite cavaliers. Julian, I will let you know when Estelle arrives."


For the other interviews, Derek had a second agent with him. Wanda stayed in the background, except when taking initial blood samples and later when administering the counter drug.

In each case, the interview was recorded, and the same questions were asked. Just before the medication was administered, each man was asked to pick King Karl out of a selection of six photos. One of the other photos was Duvall, one Dupont, one was Prime Minister Rasmussen, one the deputy Bock, and two were just faces.

This had been an idea of Wanda's. She had proposed that under the influence of the drug, they might have been conditioned to associate a different face with the title of 'king' and so it proved. Each man, when asked to point to the picture of the king, had pointed to Duvall.

This was indicated on the video recording by Derek having the man pick up the photo and show it to the camera.

When the drug effect had been negated by the administered medication, the 'pick the picture' request was repeated, and then the questions. This time, they picked Karl, and the answers to the questions were different. All the time, through both sessions of questions, the men believed they were telling the truth. It was not until they listened to the recording of their initial answers did these men realize how they had been cleverly manipulated.

Their initial anger at being detained for questioning turned to concern for themselves and anger at Duvall. They knew, now their minds were clear, what they truly believed, and what Duvall had wanted them to believe and wanted them to do.

It was well into the early morning before they were finished. Wanda was exhausted, but staying awake on determination alone. Derek gave her coffee in his office before asking for her evaluation.

She impressed him with her insights, but in the most part, he agreed. He queried her about the two men on whom they disagreed.

"Hessler, the police minister is fully Duvall's ally. I believe he would warn Duvall of what is happening if he could do so. His anger at being drugged didn't feel sincere. I think he knew of the drug and chose to have it – for situations like this. You will have trouble with him, but I think he knows where much of the manufactured evidence is concealed. Possibly in the judicial HQ."

"Was there anything else about him?" Derek asked her.

"Well, he didn't betray it, but he recognised me. When the 'police' took us from the airport for questioning, he was one of the questioners. He now thinks I am an Interpol agent."

"What about Gruber, the foreign minister?" Derek probed. "He works closely with Karl."

"I sensed resentment from him. I think because all the real foreign diplomacy is done by Karl, or your family, and he is little more than a mouthpiece for what Karl has negotiated. I think he knows that Karl was negotiating that extradition treaty. It makes me sure that the timing of this anarchy is related – especially if you consider those three criminals you apprehended earlier."

"And you feel the rest can be trusted?" Derek asked her, intent on her answer.

"I do," Wanda said soberly. "Are you keeping them here?"

"Yes. They can rest here and go to the press conference from here, but only if they have written and signed a statement."

Wanda wasn't finished. "Most of them will require counselling. They are decent men, tricked into compromising themselves. Some will feel obliged to resign."

"It's my job to get facts. I will brief Karl later. He is still the highest court in the country. He will have to deal with it. He has managed to convince Bock to hold off presenting his resignation, but has advised that he stay away from the press conference."

Wanda yawned, and tried to hide it.

"I will have someone drive you back," Derek offered.

"Yeah, that's a plan," Wanda agreed.


Wanda was surprised when Prince Joseph opened the door to admit her. She knew why Johannes was not there, even though he would have had to be off duty sometimes. She was not too tired to be curious, so after thanking Joseph and assuring him she did not need an escort to the suite Jim was using, she moved to a discreet corner and waited to see who it was that was arriving in the car that had followed hers.

The arrival was a woman, and Joseph greeted her and gave her a hug. Wanda deduced that the family had been ordered home to show a united front. She approved.


The suite was darkened and quiet when Wanda slipped into it. David was awake and knew when she arrived. He stood, stretched, and came to give her a hug before shooing her to bed.

"Be careful going in. Renée is sleeping on a spare bed in there," David whispered.

"Thanks. Oh, and tell Jim that the elite will not back Duvall," she remembered to mention. "Two won't be there – the police minister and the foreign minister."


Without undressing, Wanda pulled blankets over herself and was soon asleep. However, she only slept for two hours before finding herself awake – and unable to return to sleep. After a while, she became aware that Renée was also awake, and she rolled to face that direction.

"I hope I did not wake you," Renée apologised. "How did it go?"

"Well," Wanda summarised. "Two of them won't be there today. The rest are angry with Duvall.

"That is something anyway," Renée sighed.

Wanda sensed something was worrying Renée, and suggested, "But if Duvall doesn't get his way he will hit out at your family?"

"You really do read minds, don't you?" Renée challenged.

"It can seem that way, but this time it is just putting things together. I think Duvall intended to discredit you all anyway."

"That's what I think too," Renée sighed again. "Derek and I discussed things yesterday. I think, between us, we know all the little disgraces that father hushed up. We can counter some with solid evidence but ...all of my brothers and sisters, except Stephen, have been idiots in their time. Or had scurrilous things written about them." She grinned wryly in the darkness. Wanda sensed it rather than saw it. "Some reporters don't care what they write. Some of the stuff is pure fiction – take a photo out of context and propose a scandal. Even I didn't escape it."

"That's the way of the world," Wanda agreed.

"It is, but I can't help thinking that no matter what father says, no one will want to believe the truth. We can't claim Duvall was behind it all. As for Karl, I can't get around the fact that he thought he had killed someone and said nothing."

"Put that way, it sounds bad," Wanda agreed. "But it could also put Duvall in a spot - though if I were him I would not claim to have hidden the body."

Renée studied her. "What are you thinking?"

"First – let us pretend Karl went to the police. There was no body – so no proof of a crime. If there had been, and Duvall removed it, that would make him an accessory. And you can prove when Roderick died."

"What about all his wild carousing?" Renée murmured.

"Were there pictures in the papers? Public complaints?" Wanda asked.

"Some photos, Derek said."

"Where were they taken? In public or when Karl and his friends were relaxing in private?"

"Hmmm," Renée murmured, thinking. "That's a point."

"Most people would agree that what people do in private, so long as no one is getting hurt, should stay private." Wanda suggested. "And this was twenty years ago. Karl has grown up since then, and who doesn't do silly things when they are young? Have there been any more recent scandals about him?"

"No, he's turned into an arrogant prude," Renée said tactlessly. "I hope you don't repeat that."

"Last I checked you were human too," Wanda assured her. "However, as royalty, you and your family will always be in the public eye, and like anyone well known, famous or powerful is fodder for gossip. If the truth is too dull, people twist it, and if people are envious, they will want to pull those people down. Reporters will sometimes prefer a sensational slant on a story, or simply imagine one."

Renée didn't disagree, but her concern wasn't for herself. "Father shouldn't have to deal with it."

"No," Wanda agreed. "He is such a dignified person and understands the responsibilities of his position. How did he handle the incidents when they occurred?"

Renée thought back to what Derek had told her. "The things that happened were dealt with appropriately and he made no public comment."

"Even when the media played it up?" Wanda asked.

"Yes, I believe so," Renée told her.

"Jim knows of a lot of the incidents, but we don't know if they intend to throw some new accusations at your family. He has found things out to help as well. Has he spoken to you?"

"He mentioned some things," Renée confirmed. "Or rather he mentioned them to father and Karl when I was around. But we can't disprove all the old scandals."

"Jim's plan is to use what we have to cast doubt on anything new. Even if we can't prove Duvall is behind everything, we will negate his schemes," Wanda told her.

"Surely he is not behind everything," Renée objected.

"I won't say he set everything up, but he could use what your siblings did, or put them into situations where they would act in a certain way," Wanda proposed. "The incident with Karl was twenty years ago – he has been plotting at least that long. So, Jim has arranged for select reporters to be present. So if we can cast doubt on some of the old news, and make these reporters think that they were conned into making fools of themselves...and then get them amused by how we reveal it ....imply a scandal about Duvall...get them sniffing around him...give hints to where they might find proof that media reports were wrong because..."

"Are you sure that it will work? I can't imagine father doing that."

"Not Prince Michael –you."

"Why me? I'm the least important member of the family."

"Renée, I thought you had proved otherwise to your father."

"Him, perhaps, but..."

"But nothing. Think of all your patients, and all the people who you are friends with you down in the poorer districts...I think you under rate yourself."

"I still don't agree."

Wanda chuckled faintly. "Please yourself, but being under rated by others can be used to your advantage."

"So you think I should do this, because of that?"

"Why not? Duvall doesn't know much about your recent life, that's why he had Michael out to chat you up. He will be working on your old royal rebel image."

Renée made a disparaging noise.

"And how wrong that is!" Wanda pointed out. "Also, you are female and he doesn't expect them to be a threat. Am I right in saying that the adverse comments about your sisters are less blatant?"

"Yes," Renée had to agree.

"So, when the scandals are thrown at you, and your father maintains his dignified facade, and you get up instead – Duvall won't be expecting trouble. And when it is over, Prince Michael's calm manner will be a statement of unblemished trust in his family."

"People will still believe the lies," Renée warned.

"Many will choose to, but the thinking ones may change their minds and really, no family is perfect all the time. Many have their problem children; they will empathise with Prince Michael."

"Maybe or not, but I see what you are getting at. I am used to people talking about us...I will do it, just to see Duvall get discredited."

"Amen," Wanda agreed.

Renée thought for a while and laughed faintly. "Where did you learn to manipulate people?"

"Oh...it's a survival skill," Wanda said dismissively. She wasn't going to say it was to survive against a criminal mastermind.

"Let me guess...you were the wild child of your family," Renée challenged

"Oh, yes," Wanda agreed readily. "My past exploits would put all of your brothers together into the league of saints."

"Hmm, fallible human beings, not career criminals," Renée suggested. "The same goes for the politician victims."

"Oh, and Duvall won't be expecting your band of loyalists..." Wanda suggested.

"I don't exactly know what they can do," Renée admitted.

"Why did you spread the word to come to the press conference?"

"I didn't want the entire crowd to be anti-royalist. They know Duvall is not a saint, and even though Father was always remote, they know he has always had the welfare of the people in mind."

"So, when dire things are implied, they won't blindly believe, but be sceptical – huh? So who taught you manipulation?"

Renée laughed again, "I am glad you didn't leave."

"Duvall should not have stopped me," Wanda said wickedly.

Renée rolled back into a sleeping position, and murmured, "I wish I had known you eight years ago."

"That would have been a right royal scandal," Wanda said softly, but she sensed Renée had returned to sleep.

# Chapter 22

Wanda woke early and went with David to where Renée's loyalists were gathering. The people who had helped Wanda before, and the waiter from Duvall's club, vouched for them to the others.

Once the press passes were distributed, Wanda and David briefed the attendees. These people would not start fights or react to provocation, and where possible would cast doubt on any hecklers and support the aims of the king.

Then David returned to the palace, changed into a guard uniform and took a place where he could inspect the passes of the tech crews coming in.

Wanda returned and took over the monitoring of the bugs in Duvall's club and on his person. Her return freed Max to help Grant and Jim setting up equipment in the ballroom. Jim was now looking like himself and would be standing amongst the international journalists.

Renée passed through the monitoring room, heard that her loyalists had been briefed, admitted that she and the rest of her siblings had to attend Prince Michael.


The paraphernalia of the news media began sprouting in the ballroom as soon as the doors had been opened. By eight thirty, when the public were allowed to enter, even the last minute adjustments had been finished.

Government ministers had seats in rows of chairs near the front, the journalists had a section to one side, and the select members of the public, were allowed to stand behind these groups.

As people came in the door, they had to show their invitations or passes. These were scanned and the information on them compared with the id carried by the people. If the information did not match, the person was refused entry and asked to leave. David, in charge of the equipment, was pleased that the proportion of potential hecklers was on par with the number of loyalists.

Promptly at nine o'clock, the palace media liaison moved to the podium on the stage and announced the imminent arrival of his majesty, King Karl. He requested that those people with seats to be seated.

At the back of the stage was a row of chairs. At the introduction, these were vacant. Nicholas, in the guise of King Karl, arrived from behind the stage, and climbed up to the podium. He was followed by Prince Michael, and a man most people recognised as Karl's personal secretary.

The King was greeted with the music of the national anthem, and all eyes were on him while the music played. During this, a number of people entered through side doors and positioned themselves at intervals around the room.

As the anthem finished, Karl, looking like his secretary, walked down from the stage and over to the nearest of the late arrivals. This was an Interpol agent, though some of the others were his siblings.

He listened as Nicholas Black gave the speech they had prepared, reporting on the purpose and outcome of the talks he had been involved in. From his vantage point, he studied the crowd and having warning of potential hecklers, sought for them. He identified a likely group and edged in towards them. He listened to their candid comments about what Nicholas was saying and began to realise how sheltered he had been from the thoughts of his commoner subjects. He had heard some of these comments from Stephen, but had ignored them – even though his father had advised him to listen.

Karl returned to the dais when Nicholas spoke the 'timing phrase'. Once back on the stage, he passed his father and collected a satchel of papers. He went to stand beside Nicholas, with the papers spread out on a table for easy reference. They were ready for Nicholas to refer to, or for Karl to read from and sub-vocalise answers to give Nicholas through his earpiece. The real King could not fault the performance of the American. His accent was flawless, and he had memorised long sections of the speeches and there was no trace of nervousness – something that Karl himself, had never fully mastered.

The audience was attentive during these speeches, but were now beginning to grow restless. Nicholas had finished giving the outcomes of the talks, and details of concessions and agreements that had been reached. Before he could introduce the analysts from the international economic group, the first of the hecklers called out.

"Your Majesty? Where did you get your advice from? Heinrik Flammel?"

Flammel was the Member of Parliament accused of financial swindling.

The media liaison spoke into a second microphone. "May we have your name and media affiliation, Sir?"

"I am a concerned citizen. What you said sounds good, but if you trusted the word of a swindler – how good is it?"

Nicholas stood unfazed. "If you would allow me to introduce the experts from..."

The heckler cut him off with a second accusation about another parliamentarian. Questions were now being yelled out from other parts of the room.

Both the existing parliament and the royal family came under verbal attack – all being accused of corruption, collusion and incompetence.

The hecklers caused the noise level to increase to a deafening roar. No one could hear if it was all acrimony or if some was disbelief. Though it all, Nicholas stood waiting for the noise to quieten, and seemingly unworried.

Prince Michael stood up to move to Nicholas's side. He was preparing himself to speak out to end the accusations and counter them when Renée walked purposefully to him.

"Father, let me deal with this," she said firmly.

Karl rose and hissed at her. "What can you do? They won't listen to you!"

Nicholas turned his head and spoke to Karl. "We have a plan."

Prince Michael studied his daughter and seemed aware of her confident determination. "Let her do this, Karl."

Being short, Renée wasn't tall enough to be visible at the podium. Grant had allowed for this and had a step for her to stand on beside Nicholas.

Her presence at the microphone went unnoticed until Grant caused a shrill instant of feedback.

All eyes went to the podium and gradually the babble quietened. In that short period of time, Renée's eyes scanned the room. She saw Duvall, looking pleased, standing next to the Countess with her bodyguard hovering behind.

Jim was amongst the reporters, drawing their attention to her. Her loyalists were doing the same amongst the hecklers. Her unexpected presence caused enough curiosity to halt the momentum of the crowd. They were not prepared for her. A murmur of identification spread through the crowd.

"I see I have been recognised," Renée said casually. "And I am pleased that courtesy is still a trait of the people of Weisboden. I hope that will continue and you will allow me to mediate this impromptu discussion, since I, personally cannot add anything constructive to the arguments. I am aware that nothing can be achieved when so many people are yelling at once."

Silence continued for a moment, allowing Renée to continue, quickly. "If I understand what you have been stating, it seems that many of you feel that the government of Weisboden is corrupt and so is the King, who is still the highest authority in this country."

The hecklers loudly called out their agreement. Renée raised both hands and the voices quietened. She was not going to ask what they wanted to happen, but did ask, "Is there one of you who is prepared to state the grounds for your accusation against your monarch?"

Most of media group were now watching her intently. She saw Jim lean towards one of the previously vocal men and whisper something. He too, turned his attention to her as if expecting a sensation.

People called out claims in quick succession.

"He's gay. He's a murderer. He only pleases himself. He is not interested in the common people only the wealthy...."

Renée nodded at each speaker, and when she again raised her hands for silence, she got it.

"I expect you each have evidence to support these claims? Hearsay is not proof in this country."

"Too right princess! We've got pictures and film and witnesses," one man claimed.

"Then, I believe that evidence should be produced so an impartial investigation can be begun," Renée suggested.

Her voice was drowned out by calls for Karl to answer the accusations for himself Karl might have moved had not Prince Michael held his arm firmly.

Once again, Renée gestured for silence. "As mediator for this discussion, I will answer for His majesty. And you are welcome to think less of him than before if it suits you."

Nicholas kept silent, letting Renée continue.

"Now, I volunteered to speak because I am more used to dealing with the dregs of society than the rest of my family are – or so it has been implied in the press. I am not saying that anyone here fits into that category, but there are many people in this world that think if you throw enough mud, some of it will stick."

There were murmurings of, "It doesn't have to stick. It is as plain as daylight."

Renée ignored the provocative comments.

"I know that there are people in the audience today who think that the monarchy here are the biggest parasites on the economy and we all should be ousted and made to work for a living..."

A chorus of jeers gave agreement to her statement. Again, Renée gestured for silence, and got it.

"I am all for working for a living. I work darn hard for mine and as a member of the royal family I know how hard my father and siblings work for the cause of the advancement of this country."

More jeers erupted, and Renée let it continue for a moment.

"Where's your proof, Princess?"

"Yeah, where is it?"

Renée gestured, and spoke on, "If you are capable of listening?" Her calm tone quietened the babble. "You have just heard the results of talks Karl had with the leaders of several major world powers. If you will listen further, you will hear the evaluations of the independent analysts – explaining how the decisions reached will benefit this country. If you have questions, you may ask the analysts. Moreover – just for the record, Karl spent three weeks of his vacation time tied up in those talks. Three weeks of the first vacation he has taken in the three years since he ascended the throne. How many of you would tolerate having to work on your holiday?"

Renée's loyalists drowned out the hecklers and demanded to hear the analysts. They quietened at her gesture. "And after the official business of this conference is over, I will answer your challenges."


Renée stepped down and allowed the experts in economics, banking and finance take over the microphones. She felt Karl grip her elbow.

"I hope you know what you are doing! You are making me a laughing stock!" Karl hissed in her ear. Nicholas was carefully seating himself on one of the chairs, acting with the calm confidence that Karl was currently incapable of.

"I haven't started yet," Renée told him. "But at least, they are listening to the analysts. And Duvall doesn't seem happy."

Diverted, Karl studied his one-time friend. "He wants me to dissolve the parliament. His hecklers will insist...have you a counter for that?"

"Let's see how long he can maintain that charming facade," Renée murmured to her brother. "If he can't, he'll prove himself unworthy."

The official business of the press conference continued, with Jim asking the probing questions that ensured the analyst's conclusions were fully understood. When there were no more questions for them, the men stepped down and the hecklers began again. They called for Karl, but Renée returned.

Some of the journalists called up to her, reminding her of her promise.

"I haven't forgotten what I said," Renée assured them. "And you have just proved that you do not care about the good King Karl has done for this country – just in juicy scandals about the royal family! Okay – you said there were photos and film..."

"Yeah, I have seen film of Karl in a drunken orgy." He went on to give lurid details of what the film contained.

Renée did not blush. "I see you have visited the judicial archives," she commented, as if unsurprised. "I have watched that tape. It isn't very clear, and it is hard to identify the participants since it is over twenty years old. I counter challenge you, who claim that is proof, to find an honest doctor who does not diagnose that everyone on that film was drugged during that episode. I also challenge you to find an honest man who can state that Karl started that business. The matter was investigated at the time and the matter was settled."

"Hushed up, you mean!" someone jeered.

"The record of the investigation is available," Renée said calmly. "It can be released to be reinvestigated by a neutral body – such as Interpol – if that is the wish of the general public."

The hecklers demanded it.

"Very well – that is noted," Renée said calmly. "And in turn, I challenge you to find the place where the film was taken."

"What has that got to do with it?"

"Simple. As a result of the initial investigation, a well-known nightclub was closed down. The same venue was burnt down fifteen years ago. It was a club run by the father of a well-known philanthropist of today. It was said then, that the owner was shamed by having such things happen in his club. So why bring the matter up now?"

That question was ignored. Instead, someone called out, "The king is a murderer!"

The loyalists booed that idea. Renée shushed them.

"Ah...so you think my brother should be arrested for murder?" Renée proposed. She glanced at Nicholas who was standing as if unworried. Behind him, but out of view of the people, Karl was scowling.

"Again...where is your proof? Who did he kill and when?" Renée challenged.

They claimed statements of eyewitnesses, including one having seen him remove the body.

"Very well," Renée considered. "At this point it is only conjecture. I would like those witnesses that you claim to exist to come forward with notarised statements. I will present them to Interpol as well. Since none of this has been presented to judicial authorities before...who was the man that was murdered?"

"He murdered his lover, Pierre Roderick," one of the reporters called out.

"Your name, Sir? And media affiliation?" Renée asked politely.

"Les Owens, World News," the man readily admitted.

"I have heard of you, Sir. I am sure you checked carefully before you made such a claim. However, when you learnt of his matter, why did you not go to the police? You might be considered an accessory."

Owens turned pale, but stood his ground. "I have a sworn statement from a witness. He did not trust the police here to be impartial. I will not reveal my source, here."

"Perhaps, then, you will tell us what you know of the death of Pierre Roderick," Renée invited. She hid a smile. The man did not know how well he was playing her game.

"Roderick and Prince Karl fought a duel, twenty years ago. Roderick died...murdered."

"You will have to give the name of the witness, if the matter is to be investigated. Just recall that there are severe penalties for giving false statements to the police. I give this warning because I know, and I can prove, that Pierre Roderick did not die twenty years ago."

The hecklers wanted proof.

"The investigative reporters here can easily check what I say. Pierre Roderick died last year from wounds received in a sword fight and from the effects of an unidentified poison. He came into the emergency department of the Free Hospital."

The hecklers roared their disbelief.

Renée spoke into the microphone and Grant increased the volume. "I said...it is easy to check. Proof — not creative lies." She looked at Owens. He was scribbling in a notebook. Good, she thought. He is probably not a plant of Duvall's. Probably he was duped too.

"Mr Owens?" Renée attracted the man's attention. Owens looked up. "I believe you to be a dedicated journalist. I saw you making notes about the film mentioned — the drunken orgy one. If you take up the suggestion to have a doctor study the film, perhaps you might get an opinion on another one."

Owens looked up. Behind Renée, another film was now showing on the previously blank screen behind the podium. The other press people pushed forward to try for a better view. They would not be able to identify people from that distance, just the fancy costumes.

Renée looked to where Duvall was, and saw that his body was rigid, and he was glaring at someone. She looked in that direction and saw Michael, looking ashen and standing a few feet away from Derek.

Renée waited for the film to finish. The actions of the people were clear. Two men were fighting, in the cavalier costume and one was bleeding from multiple wounds on face and body. The face of the victor was almost identifiable in one shot and that is where the film stopped, and stayed on for a moment before blanking out.

"You may have more success finding that place," Renée offered. "It is a more recent film."

With inner glee, Renée saw the Countess holding Duvall firmly, and talking to him. The bodyguard was almost close enough to breathe on Duvall. "And, no, Karl was not on that film. Since becoming King, he cannot travel anywhere without a retinue of reporters. So...what else do you wish to accuse my brother of? Being Gay? Well, I have not heard Queen Alicia complain about his expertise, and Crown Prince Albert, Prince Robert and Princess Adrianna are proof of his virility."

The hecklers seemed to have nothing more to say. Some seemed to look towards Duvall.

Renée took the opportunity to chide the audience. "So what if Karl had a reputation of being wild as a very young man. That was a long time ago. All the supposedly wild parties he threw are little more than hearsay. It is no crime if he chose to relax amongst friends, in an ultra-private club. Either way, he is no longer that young man, and even if he did things in his youth that were regrettable, who hasn't? The important thing is to learn from all experiences. So, are there claims against Karl that are more recent than twenty years ago?"

The mutterings were subdued, the hecklers frustrated and her loyalists were grinning.

Renée looked at the media group, and with a faint smile, said to them, "Now. Ladies and Gentlemen, what have you to say about the rest of us parasites?"

She looked around and seemed to spot someone. "Ah, yes, William.

Let's hear what you have heard about him?"

Heads turned to see where Renée had looked. Prince William was lounging against the wall, grinning. Renée herself was looking expectantly at the reporters.

"He once put a fellow student in hospital from a fight," a man spoke up.

"Your name, Sir?" Renée requested.

"Tom Major, Truth," the man supplied.

"Thank you. Has anyone else anything to add? Anyone else have an accusation against Prince William?"

No one spoke.

"Hmm. I am going to start disobeying one of my father's strictest rules about discussing family business," Renée murmured into the microphone. She had every ones attention. "It wasn't once, but twice that William achieved that dubious honour. Both incidents were almost twenty years ago. The first time was when he was defending his brother against bullies. More on that, later. The second time...well, the incident was investigated, and appropriate action was taken. All details were recorded in the school files. Why don't you go and find out the details? That way, you might believe the truth." A small man with an olive complexion walked up onto the stage and stood next to Renée. "Your highness, may I speak?"

He spoke quietly, but the microphones picked up his request. Renée smiled and stepped aside.

"I would like to save some trouble from you," the man began. "I am Andrew Gianetti. I am secretary to Prince William for many years. I was cause of second incident. I was son of diplomat, and enrolled at school for period of my father's posting. I was small, a stranger and had no breeding and so the butt of many jokes and much bullying. Prince William caught his friends at this game and became my protector until I left the school. He and I, an untitled nobody, have been friends since then."

Gianetti nodded and turned to walk off the stage.

"And now for Joseph," Renée smiled sweetly, glancing to where her third eldest brother was removing his tinted glasses. "Why don't you come up here?"

Joseph smiled an equally gracious smile and moved to ascend the stage. He took a small case from his father and laid it on the table next to Renée. He spoke into the microphone.

"What's my crime, Ladies and Gentlemen?" he asked innocently, but he was looking directly at Tom Major.

The crowd was silent, waiting for the answer.

"You were expelled from two schools." Major sensed what Renée was doing and was ruffled, feeling he was being made a fool of.

"Ah, yes," Joseph said as if recalling a memory. "That's right. After William left school, I had to stick up for myself. Being expelled from school was embarrassing enough, but listening to the royal lecture on unseemly conduct that I received at home was worse. My father did allow me to explain my actions. That first school, still full of my bullying classmates, learnt that I did not need my brother's protection. The second school to which I was sent was one where I could choose to pursue a subject I particularly wanted to do. Still, there were those who felt my interest in such a subject was, let us say, effeminate. I proved I wasn't. And I was rather angry at the time."

Renée took over the microphone as Joseph turned to open his case. The audience could not see what he was doing for he turned his back to them. "I would like everyone to listen. Please."

A hauntingly beautiful tone began to be audible. The flute melody increased in volume as Prince Joseph turned around towards the audience. His eyes were closed as if he were lost in the melody.

Everyone in the ballroom was silent until the music finished. After a few seconds of silence, Joseph opened his eyes, bowed and turned to pack his flute away.

Renée resumed her position. "What you won't know is that Joseph composed that piece, as well as others, and will be recording them soon. Proceeds will go to one of the Royal charities."

The audience murmured in appreciation, and the hecklers seemed to be at a loss. Renée waved for silence. "Who am I up to?" Renée mused aloud.

"Kristina," someone prompted.

"Yes, thank you," Renée smiled and added, "There are so many of us aren't there?" Her loyalists chuckled in amusement. "Has anyone any allegations about Princess Kristina?"

No one spoke up.

"That is good, because Kristina is the most circumspect person I know. And to tell the truth, when she was born, I don't think father knew what to do with a girl."

Renée glanced at her father and saw his eyes twinkle at her. He wasn't smiling, but the hands on his cane were relaxed.

"He had three sons already, and they were to be trained in statecraft – but a girl? Well, she was well educated, and groomed to make a suitable marriage. She has always been everything a young noble woman ought to be, and that is in spite of losing her mother at a young age and having to do without one in those important formative years."

The intent listening of the audience encouraged Renée to continue. "Well, in spite of everything, Kristina learnt statecraft too. For those of you who are visitors here, Kristina is married to our Ambassador to the United Nations. Anyone of you with connections over there will realise that she is highly thought of on her own merits. To this, I want to add a comment of my own. I lost my mother at an even younger age, and Kristina was the only mother I ever really knew. I want it to be a matter of public record, how much I value her for that."

Renée was looking directly at a woman standing at the rear of the room, only now unwrapping the scarf that had concealed most of her face. She made a hand gesture of acknowledgement to her youngest sister.

Not far away, the Countess was whispering things to Duvall, and still keeping him from leaving.

A woman next to Tom Major called out, "Is Princess Sophia still in that mental institution?"

Renée queried her name.

"Sheena – Global Information Network."

"She most definitely is," Renée said cheerfully. "They let her out though, so she could be here today."

The audience was expecting more fun to be made of the gossip columnists and they were not disappointed.

"I suppose you found, or remember the headlines? Princess in Mental Asylum? Did you read the article or just assume the content? Yes, my sister was there, and dragged home for a Royal Please Explain. And yes, she went right back, but as a trainee nurse, not just a volunteer helper. I'd ask her to step up here to tell you what she is doing these days, but it is a bit awkward with the crutches. Ask her later – or ring the Mount Telfer Sanatorium and ask for Matron Mont Pelier."

Renée gestured behind her to a stunning woman seated beside Prince Michael.

Prince Derek knew he was next; he gave her a quick grin from his position near Michael. He was positioned between Michael and Duvall, where he could watch the older man. She noticed the unobtrusive presence of Herr Davis just behind them.

There were things she was not going to mention about the youngest of her stepbrothers.

"The worst that I have heard about Prince Derek is that he is some kind of jet-setting debonair crook," Renée had a definite laugh in her voice. "Personally, I am not sure that he is not a con artist. But at least, the Interpol agent there hasn't put handcuffs on him yet."

This comment was deliberate, and Renée glanced at Duvall. He looked like he wanted to flee, and she guessed that the countess was reminding him of his hopes and the need for remaining dignified. Duvall had not yet been directly challenged, but he must be feeling worried.

"If anyone has proof against him – now is your chance to speak up," Renée went on cheerfully. "No one? Good. Next then – Fast Freddie."

Prince Frederick had been given that name by the press on the motor racing circuit.

"Fast cars, fast money, fast women, fast living," Renée quoted the popular comment.

"Everyone seems to blame him for the fatal accident six years ago," Sheena said quickly.

"Miss Sheena," Renée addressed the woman politely. "I am quite aware that the best gossip is from segments of information taken out of context. Yes, that unfortunate event made world headlines, and yes, it was impossible to 'hush up'. And yes, Frederick was high on something. However, I think you should make a point to gain access to the official investigation report. You will find, that a rival of my brother voluntarily admitted that he had spiked his water, just before the race. In addition, many people chose to be character witnesses and all stated that Frederick never drinks alcohol or uses drugs. Medical evidence supports this as drug tests are routinely taken before and after major events. No doubt, the initial headlines about a Prince killing someone were more sensational than the fact that someone made sure he was not in full control of his actions. I doubt that the investigation report had the same size headlines."

Renée knew that her brother still had physical and emotional scars from the accident. "You might like to ask him directly, what he is doing these days," she suggested, pointing to a tall man standing against the wall, just down from the steps to the stage. "You don't have to be quite so fast to catch him these days."

There was a murmur of amusement that Renée allowed as she scanned the room for her next sibling. "I know Mary is here somewhere," Renée advised the audience. "I learnt something interesting about her yesterday. She has spent the last five years studying for her PhD in Education. She will be receiving her degree next week. Her doctoral dissertation was on education methods for children with special needs. She will be working with the United Nations after that."

A woman standing at the back grinned at Renée.

Renée was going to mention Edward next, but held off as she saw him approaching the stage with a look of determination. "I believe Prince Edward has something he wishes to say."

Edward replaced Renée at the microphone. He took a breath and began. "I have had a very difficult time since yesterday, beginning with being read the Royal Riot Act over my gambling debts, and some subsequent unpleasant realisations. I seem to be the current incumbent for the title of Problem Prince." He paused, took another deep breath, and looked directly at Duvall. "I have liquefied all my assets and sent a cheque to he who runs the ultra-private club where I gamble. I have also had myself declared bankrupt and asked for no help from my family to help cover my debts. Duvall, our agreement is concluded. I will not be the one to tell you all my family's secrets anymore."

Edward turned abruptly and went to stand near Prince Michael. Almost as soon as he had gone, Julian bounced onto the stage. Renée knew his 'confidence' was an act.

"I am the Royal Delinquent at the moment," Julian admitted, forcing a smile. "I'm the man with a different lady every week and the one who kisses and runs all the time. The handicap I have is that being Royal magnifies everything out of all proportion. Edward and I have been frequenting the new Cavalier club ever since Claude Duvall re-established it. We kidded ourselves that we were an important part of Duvall's elite – cavaliers pledging to support to king and country. I discovered yesterday, exactly how we had been used. Edward, and I and eight men with impeccable records of public service. I was sickened by what we had done there under the influence of some mind-distorting drug – that was given to us during the thrice-damned cavalier's toast. I am not permitted to say anymore because the club is currently being investigated by Interpol. But that film clip Renée showed earlier is just a sample of what they expect to find there."

There was a disturbance at the rear of the room. Duvall had broken free of the Countess, but was being restrained by her bodyguard while Prince Derek and the man with him were moving towards them.

On the stage, Julian's smile was almost malicious. Then his attention was taken by a woman who had walked up onto the stage. He put out an arm and drew her next to him.

"While I have everyone's attention, I have an announcement to make. Duvall tried to use my weaknesses against me, by throwing lovely and seductive women my way. Well, he succeeded in an unexpected way. I would like to introduce my wife, Estelle. We have been married for four months and we are expecting a baby later this year."

The audience applauded, and the loyalists added whistles and cheers.

Renée felt herself grinning as Julian and Estelle stepped back towards Prince Michael. Julian had not been sure if Estelle would forgive him for the trouble he was in and she didn't think her own father had known of the baby – for he was smiling in genuine pleasure.

"Talk about being upstaged! However, this little exposition is not over yet. The Royal Rebel and the Royal Cripple still stand to be accused. Does anyone wish to challenge Stephen? Don't let that chair fool you. You don't need workable legs to be brilliant."

Renée waited. "No takers? Good. Now me. What do you all think the Royal Rebel has been up to since getting myself sent to Switzerland?"

"What have you been doing?" Sheena dared to ask.

"Keeping my doings discreet, it seems," Renée parried. "I'm surprised that you didn't ask what unspeakable thing I did to get exiled. It wasn't much, just associating with unsuitable people and being seen in unsuitable places."

Renée looked down at a group of local journalists. "I don't expect the media representatives from other countries to have been interested in the least important member of a large family, but the local press always like to know what we are doing. So, what do you know about me?"

Most heads were being shaken in amusement. One summarised, "Nothing much since you left to go to school in Switzerland."

One man was standing mutely, unsure if he should speak. Renée nodded at him and asked, "Louis, would you care to tell your fellows what you do know about me. And I don't mean that rubbish about the six houses I own to maintain my six paid gigolos that you asked about the first time we met."

Louis stood up, but did not ascend the stage. "Sometime after we met, I was in a car accident. I had suffered a heart attack. I was coming to take my little girl to the hospital – she was having a bad asthma attack. She, Princess Renée, came and helped us. Drove us to the hospital after helping Lilli. I almost died in the car. She stopped and did CPR on me, and then drove on. I was too sick to recognise her then. When I got to the hospital, the light was better and I was feeling better, I recognised her. She stayed with me at the hospital. I hadn't thought she would want to see me after our last meeting, but I thanked her and asked her when she was going to let a doctor take over. She told me that a doctor had been treating him all along. She was on her way to work at the hospital when she stopped to help me. Princess Renée is a fully qualified doctor and she has chosen to work with the poorer people, and I know from personal experience that she often forgets to charge those who are too poor to pay. My little Lilli didn't have asthma as I thought, but a worse problem. That is how I learnt that the houses I had been told of were for the parents of very sick children who had to come a long way for their children and needed a place to stay."

"Thank you, Louis," Renée said with compassion. She glanced at her family and said, "Slumming it is only a crime in some circles."

She turned back and announced, "I am authorised to issue a mini-referendum. Do you, the people of Weisboden, want to see the end of the monarchy?"

It really wasn't an unbiased audience. Her loyalists began a chant and it grew in volume. If the hecklers tried to object, they were overwhelmed by, "Karl! Karl! Long live the king!"

The hecklers didn't join in; they were uncomfortable and began to sidle out of the crowd.


Up on the stage, something strange was happening. The King was pulling at his face, and so was his secretary. The latter became the King and the former, a stranger.

Karl stood up unsteadily, and walked forward. He still looked very pale. Renée gestured for silence and left the microphone.

"I am truly humbled by the loyalty of the true people of Weisboden," Karl said with sincerity. "I never doubted that the attempts to destabilise our country was the work of a minority. You may wonder why it was that I partook of this deception." He held up the peeled off false face.

"It was necessary to prove who the organisers of the attempts were. I was threatened as well, and after I alone survived a plane crash, caused by sabotage, my father convinced me to take a protected role. It was not an easy role to play. I did not like being helpless and injured. He also, went against his strictest rule and brought in an outside consultant to investigate the threats to our country. I recognise his wisdom and I am thankful that he is still willing to advise me."

"Are the MP's in the papers involved?" A journalist called out the question.

"All recent events will be investigated by Interpol, at my request. Knowing what I do now about events at an exclusive Weisboden nightclub, I am prepared to provide amnesty for all the men who have had their previously unblemished reputations ruined. As I said, all events will be investigated and all evidence will be thoroughly scrutinised. In this, all journalists involved in these undercover investigative reports will be questioned. All the people who attended that elite club have been questioned and will undergo counselling. Those who were members of the Government will not be asked to resign unless or until unequivocal proof against them is presented to me. On a positive note, Prime Minister Rasmussen is recovering from his indisposition and will be returning to lead the parliament."

Karl turned his attention to Duvall, who was struggling in the grip of Derek and another man. They were forcing him forward and the reporters were trying for photographs. The members of his 'elite' were turning their faces from him.

"It was the intention of the crown to step aside from the everyday ruling of Weisboden, and turn this country into a full democracy. A referendum on that subject was to be announced shortly. Yet there is one standing before me who wished to turn this country into a dictatorship and a haven for international criminals. I have heard from his own lips of his intentions and how he planned to blackmail me into allowing it." Karl announced.

Claude Duvall was no longer the smiling philanthropist. If anything, he was ashen faced in the grip of Derek and the other Interpol officer.

"Claude Duvall, you are hereby to be taken into custody on the following charges - murder, attempted murder, trafficking in illegal substances, manipulating others against their will, extortion, fraud and acts of treason threatening the stability of the realm. I have requested that Interpol oversee the investigation to ensure it is unbiased."

"You cannot call this farce unbiased," Duvall snarled. "All this today – you set me up! I'll have my lawyers sue the whole lot of you parasites for defamation."

Derek said, unemotionally, "We did not set people to make false allegations about prominent people. We spoke truth that can be proved to disprove the lies that were spread."

Duvall spotted Renée and spat in her direction.

Karl saw the gesture that Renée ignored. Her attention was on Michael Dupont, who was being led towards the door at the side of the stage. Duvall saw him too and spoke loudly. "Michael, tell them I am innocent!"

Dupont stopped, turned, and merely said, "No." He turned away again and let the police again lead him away, hands cuffed behind him. He wasn't trying to get free and was, strangely, at peace.

"Traitor!" Duvall spat at his assistant. "I will have you ruined! I'll..."

"Enough, Duvall!" Karl spoke loudly. "You are entitled to a fair trial."

"Fair! With you as the highest authority in Weisboden..." Duvall began. "You are a liar and a murderer and..."

Karl ignored the slander and went on to say, above the denouncing of Duvall, "Under the laws of this country you are entitled to a fair trial. As you indicate, I cannot be considered impartial in this case. Therefore, I have made arrangements for your trial to take place in France, and for you to be tried there under the laws of Weisboden."

Duvall spluttered again, "I have friends who will see you dead!"

Karl waited until Derek reminded Duvall that uttering such threats in front of witnesses was a bad idea.

"You can't deport me from here!" Duvall tried. "There is no law that says I cannot be tried here."

"You want a fair trial, Duvall, you have just ensured that you will not have one here," Derek said calmly.

"As to your statement, Duvall, I can deport you from here. I have successfully negotiated mutual extradition treaties with many of the major world powers," Karl stated. "As there is an outstanding murder warrant for you in France, you will be tried for that after the other charges. And the criminals that you invited here have been apprehended and deported already."

Duvall began to struggle like a demented creature, but no one, still remaining in the ballroom had any sympathy for him.

Prince Michael finally stood up and walked to the microphone.

"Those of you who are members of the press should speak to Prince Stephen before you leave. We have prepared an official press release, and a notarised statement of which matters are not to be discussed. These relate to the discussing of open court cases."

After that statement, Prince Michael, King Karl, and the rest of the royals on the stage departed through a rear entrance. Renée watched Duvall being led away, and glanced around for Jim and his people. None of them were in sight. Her brothers and sisters, who had been down around the room, moved towards her and swept her along after their father.

Frederick summarised their feelings. "You did great Renée. That was just what the doctor ordered."

Kristina gave her a hug. "I think that obnoxious man underestimated the unity of our family when we are threatened. As far as that went, I doubt that I could have stood there and had those hostile reporters eating out of my hand. However did you think of it?"

"Father's consultants worked out the plan," Renée admitted. "I just had some more personal reasons to take Duvall on."

"I'd like to meet those consultants," Mary said. "Will they still be in the palace with father?"

"I think so," Renée said thoughtfully. "Derek has seconded Wanda Davis to Interpol. She helped him get evidence about what Duvall was doing. Duvall tried to kill her, but ... well, she outsmarted him."

"They are all very clever," Joseph said with approval.

When they assembled in the palace, as requested by Prince Michael, there was no sign of the Americans. During the press conference, once he had set up the equipment and Renée had begun her part, Grant had returned to the club of Duvall. He had authorisation from the Interpol agents to permit him to enter. With no one observing him, he removed certain monitoring devices. He brought them back to the palace. He returned to the ballroom and waited for the conference to end.

As soon as Duvall was taken into custody, Shannon and Max slipped away. Jim followed them unobtrusively. David stayed near Michael until Dupont was safely away from the irate Duvall and helped Grant disassemble their gear before they both joined Jim and the others at the truck. During that time, Wanda was packing up all the teams' equipment and personal items still in the palace, and taking the cases out to the hired truck.

They all drove back to the hotel where they had stayed before. All but Wanda would be returning to the States on a chartered flight in the afternoon.

Shortly before they were to leave the hotel, a knock on the door caused them all to become alert.

"Prince Michael," Wanda reassured them. "And others."

Jim opened the door and stood back. "Your Majesty," he greeted with deference as Karl entered first.

He was accompanied by Prince Michael, Derek and Renée.

Wanda drew David back and into an unobtrusive position.

"Afraid he is going to call you to task for disrespect?" David murmured in her ear.

"He can try," Wanda murmured back as Jim was introducing Shannon and Max to the King and Prince Michael. Renée spotted Wanda and moved towards her.

"I heard Derek has requested your services," Renée told Wanda. "I have an apartment in town if you would like to stay there."

Wanda nodded, still with David hugging her.

Jim was now asking, "And to what do we owe this unexpected honour?"

Karl began speaking, and he gave a glance to those with him that included Renée, "Those whose advice I have come to trust, insisted that I should thank you all before you slipped away. I note that I was barely in time."

Jim smiled wryly. It was quite obvious with the cases packed and waiting.

"Our task here was done and it was our privilege to help his majesty. Princess Renée did an excellent job on your behalf."

Karl looked at that moment as he must have looked before his ascension to power. "For which she claims was due to the advice of your people. I have already given her my thanks both for that and for helping me recover. She took the opportunity to advise me that my behaviour towards certain others was less than acceptable and this time I had better not try to exile her to Switzerland for saying so."

Wanda was keeping a straight face, but her mind was full of mirth. David sensed it and whispered a warning.

"So I am here, to thank you all for your unselfish service to both the citizens of Weisboden and to myself. I am told that you prefer to remain unobtrusive, so I will not insist on formal recognition. I do understand why. I hope that you will accept tokens of the gratitude of Weisboden."

Prince Michael slipped two flat boxes from a pocket in his jacket. From the first he took five small medallions which he explained bore the heraldic arms of Weisboden and were only presented to those who performed great services to the crown. These he passed to Karl to present to Jim, Nicholas, Grant, Shannon and Max.

Then Karl turned his attention to Wanda and David. They both straightened, and David dropped his hands to his sides. Prince Michael passed the second box to Karl.

The King took from it, two more medallions, slightly larger than the others, and attached to ribbons. He met Wanda's eyes for a long moment and then David's.

"These are Weisboden Medals of Honour," Karl explained. "For service to the crown, over and above the expectations of duty. Thanks to both of you, I am alive today. I hereby present you with this medal..."

"David Martin," Wanda supplied abruptly, sensing that Karl realised that the names they had been using were not their real ones.

"David Martin," Karl continued smoothly as he pinned the medallion on. David bowed slightly.

"And," Karl prompted, taking the second medal.

This time David answered, "Wanda Martin."

"To you, Wanda Martin, I especially thank. For my life and for the selfless service you gave to the crown of Weisboden. You almost gave your life for a country not your own. I apologise for my earlier comments to you. You are a welcome guest in my palace at any time."

Wanda sensed the new humility within Karl and acknowledged it as he pinned her medal on. "Your majesty, I am greatly honoured. Thank you."

Karl nodded slightly to Wanda and seemed to regain his air of regal command. He turned back to Jim. "I will not hold up your departure any further."

He did not notice David return to hugging Wanda, and giving her a parting kiss. Prince Michael noticed in a glance and looked discreetly away. Renée smiled, as did Derek. The latter looked down to give them tacit privacy. No one heard the parting whispers.

"Give Davy a hug for me. Tell him I will be home soon," Wanda told David.

"And you keep your hands off the king's silverware," David teased. "And what was so funny before?"

Straight-faced, Wanda whispered. "It seems that even the king is not immune to having the royal riot act directed at him. I am glad Prince Michael is not my father."

The King and Prince Michael departed the room, and Jim coughed politely. Wanda and David separated. Wanda took the hint. David had to leave and she had work to do.

Prince Derek offered, "I will have your things brought to the palace."

"Ah..." Wanda glanced at Renée.

"Later," she suggested. "Tie up the loose ends first."

"I will visit before I go," Wanda promised.

Renée nodded. "Derek, can you drop me at the hospital on your way?"

"Sure," he agreed. He was less formal now that his father and brother were no longer around.

Wanda was relieved that she wasn't travelling with Karl. Even on a private errand, his car attracted attention. Prince Derek drove a car of such common make that no one gave it a second glance.

# Epilogue

"You said you would talk about helping Michael," Renée reminded Wanda as they drove from the palace to Renée's apartment in the Capitol. Wanda had been staying at the palace for the past week. "Derek said you understood him."

"I do," Wanda agreed. "And I had a moment to speak to your father and King Karl about him."

Renée, didn't ask what she had spoken about but commented instead, "Derek has taken over the police ministry until Karl appoints a replacement. I suppose, he had to arrest Michael...."

Wanda sensed anger and disappointment in Renée's tone, but did not pry into her thoughts.

"Michael knows he did many things that were not legal, and I think that he wishes to atone for them. He will be in remand for a time and is prepared to help the police investigate Duvall. If they proceed with any of the charges currently against him, he will be tried in Weisboden. As you heard Duvall will not."

"I heard that, and I like the logic Karl used."

"Duvall created a mess," Wanda pointed out. "It must be seen as if justice is being done. The members of parliament that were victimised are not going to be charged and will be receiving counselling. However, for a time, it will seem like they might be."

"You mean until Duvall's trial is over?" Renée deduced.

"Yes. He will be tried on the newer charges first – up to and including treason," Wanda revealed. "Then they will try him on that twenty year old murder. I think you will find that once the extent of his manipulation of people and events is known – clearing of the elite will follow."

"Michael is not exactly one of the elite," Renée said with concern.

"He is a separate case," Wanda agreed. "However, he was as much a victim as the others. I hadn't forgotten that I wanted to talk to you about him, but I would rather talk at your place."

"Fair enough," Renée agreed. "Is David still here?"

"No, he returned with Jim to the US. He went home to the farm we have. Jim usually doesn't have us working together these days."

They lapsed into silence until they reached Renée's place.

Renée showed Wanda to her spare bedroom, which had a bed already made up and a set of bedside drawers and a small wardrobe that matched it.

"When you have cleaned up, join me for coffee," Renée invited.

Wanda returned quickly and waited for Renée to finish setting out coffee and little cakes and seat herself before beginning to speak.

"Are you aware that in this country, those found guilty of treason are imprisoned for life and have all their personal and business assets made crown assets?" Wanda commented.

"I think so," Renée considered. "But I don't think there has been a case of treason for a long time though. What is the point you are making?"

"I believe that Michael has a good chance of being awarded those assets on the grounds that Duvall was using Roderick's capital to make his fortune. That much of Duvall's assets were rightfully Roderick's and Michael was his acknowledged heir."

"Michael might not want it," Renée suggested.

Wanda shrugged. "I just want to suggest, that if Michael does benefit from the decision, and if he might still feel the need to atone...a lot of people, sick children, and so forth might be helped."

Wanda knew Renée saw the possibilities. She said no more on that.

"I was allowed to be present when Michael was questioned," Wanda began. "Later, I was allowed a semi-private session. Derek sat in on it and I think he was profoundly shocked. And that is saying something when I am sure he has been around some pretty horrid scenes before."

Renée was immediately concerned. "How did you deal with it? Are you all right?"

"I am," Wanda assured her. "I had a very good idea of things before I started, and I have had some training in dealing with mental traumas. Let me speak, and try not to interrupt. I will try to cover everything."

Renée nodded, and sat back.

"The first thing I want you to realise is that if Michael had not come under Duvall's influence at such a young age – he would have become a fine, upstanding and intelligent man. He would be the sort of man that even Karl would not object to as a brother-in-law."

"Who said anything about marriage?" Renée asked.

"No one, but I used that as a guide to rate Michael's essential self." Wanda had sensed things between Renée and Michael, but she was not going to admit that.

"I have had to piece together bits of information to understand what Michael has been through," Wanda went on. "Duvall discovered that Michael was Roderick's child when he was about nine years old. His mother had died, and years before, Duvall had been named as his guardian. I would feel sure in saying that Duvall had no previous inkling of Michael's existence, since Roderick was as gay as Duvall and the two were lovers. Roderick had legitimised Michael, but long since broken away from the mother. Anyway, at the time when Roderick was supposed to have died, Duvall and he had previously argued. It was possibly due to the fact that Roderick did have female partners in addition to Duvall. Karl had a fair idea about those two, but never made an issue of it. He has thought back to that time and believes now that Duvall incited the argument he had with Roderick, and the duel. I think Duvall hoped Karl would kill Roderick, to remove his unfaithful lover and so he could have a hold over Karl."

Renée nodded as if agreeing.

"Derek did some checking into Roderick's whereabouts between then and when he returned here. He was in a French prison, charged with a murder. His accomplice was never caught and Roderick refused to name him. The accomplice was believed to be Duvall, but since this country had no extradition treaties, he couldn't be touched. Roderick was released five years early after finally agreeing to name his accomplice. He had a diary in which he wrote about many things. It seems that Duvall had thought he was dead when he took him away from the club. He found out otherwise when Roderick roused in the car. Maybe he had second thoughts, maybe not, but Duvall proposed a scheme, whereby Roderick stayed out of Weisboden. He took Roderick to France, to recover and live, until Karl ascended the throne. Then they were going to blackmail him to gain power in this country."

"They were mad," Renée said flatly.

Wanda shrugged. "Somehow, Roderick gave Duvall control of his personal wealth, with the promise of having it returned with interest when Roderick returned. He probably had a will naming Duvall as beneficiary. I doubt if Duvall ever intended to give it back. When they somehow killed the man in France – Roderick took the rap and Duvall returned to set up the scheme to overthrow Karl."

"So Duvall killed Roderick?" Renée stated.

"Did you doubt it?" Wanda challenged.

"Can they prove it?"

Wanda nodded. "Derek believes so."

"Go on," Renée urged.

"Anyway, Duvall ended up with Roderick's legitimate child. He was in a delicate situation. He controlled Roderick's money on the understanding that Roderick had no heirs of his own. That wasn't true. So, he could not allow Michael to realise this, and decided to control the child."

Wanda paused to order the things that she needed to say next.

Renée was leaning forward, intent on missing nothing.

"Michael was not even ten years old, but he looked like Roderick had at that age. Duvall...there is no polite way to say this... he mentally, physically, emotionally and sexually abused him. Over the years, he tightened his control using techniques involving pain/ pleasure, sex/hypnosis and drug/suggestion until Michael could not break away or disobey him. So he served Duvall's purposes, whether he wanted to or not. As time went on, his essential self became sickened by what he had to do for Duvall, for having to be sexually active for Duvall and with others as Duvall directed. On the day he came to you, he had tried to kill himself, or at least leave and run away. He couldn't. He came back, expecting Duvall to punish him and wanting it for trying to disobey."

"My God!" Renée swore. "He told me some of this but ..."

"No, he was too ashamed at what he had become to tell you all of it," Wanda told her. "He told me, that you had given him a taste of 'normal' and if he hadn't had that he would have known only what Duvall made of him."

Renée sat back and digested what she had been told. She did not doubt the truth of it. Then she looked at Wanda and asked, "How can you be so calm? Did you expect...?"

Wanda shook her head, "I...felt some of this when I was with him. As Derek told you, I understand his mental pain. I am not a priest or a psychiatrist, but I have spoken of things to Michael, and I have made him understand that none of this was of his making, or his fault."

Renée studied her American friend, "Something like that happened to you?"

Wanda nodded. "Essentially that is so, but there are differences. For a long time, I didn't care that I was being controlled. I was doing multi-thousand dollar crimes for a man, craving his commendation. Michael never wanted to do many of the things Duvall wanted of him, but he could not disobey. I knew what I was doing was wrong and didn't care. Michael did."

"How did you break free?" Renée asked.

Wanda had a vivid memory of the moment. "Like Michael, I reached the point of 'enough'."

"What made you decide that?" Renée prompted.

With a deep breath, Wanda said, "I met David."

"And?"

"And the bastard I worked for tried to kill him. So, yes, I know how Michael feels now. Breaking free is not easy. I thought it was, I was working behind his back to get evidence against him, and I tricked him...but at his trial, I saw his look and I wanted to crawl to him and be whipped for betraying him."

Renée reached out a hand to her friend, but Wanda did not need it. "You are over that?"

"Yes," was the simple affirmation. "I had Jim and I had David to help me. Jim convinced the man and his lawyers that I was very ill and later that I was dead. That is why I do not wish to be in the public eye."

"I understand," Renée told her. "So, how can I best help Michael?"

"I can tell you how I was conditioned, and maybe you can work from that," Wanda said.

Renée listened as a doctor, while Wanda told her how Harrison Franklin had trained and conditioned her. When Renée had questions, Wanda answered without trying to shade the truth. She made suggestions for Renée to consider.

After a long period of consideration, Renée asked, "And does this still haunt you?"

"Not anymore. My mind is rid of his commands. I survived and I grew strong. In addition to that, I had help from a very intuitive man. There is a lot more to my life story that I cannot discuss, but the upshot is – I don't look back. I use the skills I learnt back then for worthwhile purposes. And I have a son now and he is the future."

That turned the conversation away from Michael, as Wanda had hoped. Renée could help Michael, with patience, with her love and trust.

"I didn't know that you had a son. You must miss him, and he must miss you while you have been here."

"Yes, but I had important work here, and Davy adores his baby sitter. David went back to him. I won't be needed for more than another day or two. Derek doesn't think there will be much more to find at Duvall's places."

"If I had a child, I wouldn't go half way around the world for days on end...and do dangerous things. You could have died here."

"I didn't," Wanda stated, implying that she wouldn't die. "We were only meant to be here for two days, and like I said, Jim doesn't usually have us working together any more. But that being said, what Jim does is important to world peace, and I like being a part of that - while I can."

"I somehow can't see you wanting to stop," Renée decided.

"I don't, but Jim won't let me do things soon," Wanda said.

"Why is that?"

"I'm pregnant again. He grounded me last time I was pregnant."

"Well, at least you listen to someone! How far along are you?"

"Three weeks," Wanda said.

"How can you possibly be sure that soon?" Renée asked. "Have you been tested?"

"No, but I know I am. I am aware of her."

Renée stopped before voicing her scepticism. "I'd like to..."

"Run some tests?" Wanda finished. "Why not?"

"And change those bandages again," Renée continued, hiding her amazement at Wanda finishing her earlier thought.

Wanda shrugged. "You're the doctor."

Renée fetched her case before Wanda had a chance to consider changing her mind. She set about her work and was satisfied that Wanda's wrist wounds were healing well. After replacing the bandages, she gave Wanda a plastic vial and requested a urine sample.

Wanda complied with good humour – she knew Renée doubted she could know she was pregnant that early. She grinned broadly when the test confirmed her statement.

"You are going to ring Jim, right now and tell him," Renée ordered her.

"I may not be able to reach him right away," Wanda said, not wishing to rush and tell him. She wanted to tell David first. "All right, all right," Wanda agreed when Renée kept glaring at her.

Her call to Jim went to his answering machine, and her call to David rang out. And even though there were many innocent reasons for this, an atavistic shiver ran down her spine.


Just before turning in for the night, Jim's return call came through. From the first greeting, he was all business.

"Have you finished there?"

"As good as," Wanda reported.

"Good. Tell Derek you are required at home. I have booked you on a flight from there to Hawaii. I want you to join me there."

"What is this about?" Wanda asked, but Jim said nothing. "When?" she said instead.

"The flight is at ten, pick up your ticket at the airport."

Jim disconnected abruptly and Wanda replaced the receiver.

"You didn't tell him," Renée accused.

Wanda forced a smile. "He has booked me on a flight back to the states tomorrow. I will have to let Derek know. Jim will be meeting me, so I will tell him in person – more fun that way. I want to ask him if he will be godfather to this one too."

Renée decided she was satisfied, and they both decided to turn in.

Wanda lay awake, sorting out the impressions she had from Jim's call. He hadn't allowed her to ask questions, but if it were about a mission, he usually did not say anything on the phone. His tone had been business like, but Wanda could not help calling it distracted. Obviously then, he had a mission and needed her, or he would not have insisted on her meeting him without going home first.

Perhaps David was on his way there too and that was why she couldn't reach him.

Perhaps....

THE END

NOVELS

### WANDA: FROM BAD TO WORSE

If she was going to die young, like her mother, Gwen Willard was determined to die rich and she had very few years to do it. Her first step was to leave home. She met Hooch, who taught her some exciting and illegal skills. She was the Draco's lucky mascot until she came to the attention of the police. Then her uncanny knack for predicting trouble, warned her to flee to the city and change her name.

Life wasn't easy. She was 15, had little money and no regular job, but her new skills came in handy. Then she crossed the path of an evil and unscrupulous man and she didn't want him to have his way.

### WANDA: CHOOSING CRIME

Wanda was free. She was never going back to jail. But she was homeless, almost penniless and Harrison Franklin had a long and vengeful memory.

Jim Phillips had a long memory too, and Wanda had saved his life. Could he save her from Franklin?

### WANDA: RISKING LIFE TO LIVE

The euphoria of successful heists were what kept Wanda Dean alive. At 23, she was crime boss Harrison Franklin's top agent – well paid for absolute obedience. That's all that mattered. Until she met Mike Johnston and her boss ordered him killed. For that, the Franklins were going to pay. In Risking Life to Live, justice conflicts with loyalty and the penalty for betrayal is death.

### WANDA: A NEW LIFE - HIDDEN SECRETS

Even before beginning as a covert agent for the US Government, Wanda is abducted by a foreign operative. After being rescued, there are signs that she had been subjected to hypnosis. With an important government gathering imminent, her handler must ensure she is not a security risk.

Can Wanda's psychic extra senses help her recognize and resist the implanted commands and clear her for secret work?

### WANDA: A NEW LIFE - FIRST MISSION

On her first covert mission for the US Government, Wanda calls on the skills that made her a skilled thief to convince a revolutionary general that she's an ideal recruit. When her team mates' covers are blown, it is up to her to ensure that two missing scientists and confidential Government documents are not smuggled out of the US.

## WANDA: FULL CIRCLE

Three generations after the alien Kumatan left Earth, their own world is suffering from alien invaders. In desperate hope, one returns to Earth seeking help - little knowing they had left one of their own behind.

Wanda, a child of the third generation, answers the call.

## ERIN: THE FORCING OF WISDOM

For years, Erin has used the intricacies of cyberspace to banish unwanted emotions. Others call what she does hacking, and her manipulations criminal, but now her skill was exceptional - in, out, traceless. She was wrong. Someone betrayed her.

Travis has dangerous plans. He needs an electronics expert – one he can coerce through fear. Erin was perfect.

With the inescapable threat of prison looming, Erin accepts his offer of sanctuary. When she realises his intentions, she is in too deep. But the terrifying of innocents is unforgivable. She cannot walk away. She is an empath and shares their distress. She has to help them, even if it means prison, and insanity…

## ERIN: THE CALL

(including ELISABETH AND TANYA: BLOOD CALLS TO BLOOD.

Elisabeth's sister, Wanda, had been missing for half a year. Multiple authorities had found no trace of her, or her two colleagues. Yet she knew her sister was still alive and had answered a call for help from an alien who had once lived on Earth.

Elisabeth, along with her newly found cousin Tanya, have started to sense things from her missing sister. Enough to know that she is in dire trouble, but not enough to help her.

While looking for traces of the aliens, Elisabeth makes some unexpected discoveries about her family. Yet even with the help of a second newly discovered cousin, she fears she is not strong enough to help her sister and the others to return.

## ERIN: THE CALL

Convicted cyber-criminal, Erin Mason, is startled into awareness in an unfamiliar place, with no memory of escaping and only vague memories of getting there. Voices in her head were urging her to go west, and they were getting more urgent.

After a chance meeting with covert agent, Jim Phillips, when she helped save his mission, he realised that she might be the key to another, more personal quest – to find three missing state department agents.

All he must do is keep Erin safe, and hide her from an intense police search, until he can introduce her to cousins she was unaware of.

However her uncontrolled psychic gifts conflict with a logical mind that prefers the ordered intricacies of computers and electronics. She only wants to shut out the voices and the madness she sees looming.

Can Phillips convince her to help him, before the forces of the law find her?

## KORVU: THE BEGINNING
### The prequel to The Wild One

Jai Ansuni was the first female Atapi sorcerer for thousands of years, but she dare not reveal it. However, when tribal sorcerer, Stacion Ansuni escalates the enmity between Atapi and Kumatan to an ominous level. Jai and her womb mate, Con, try to mitigate his atrocities but can two young Atapi, not even a score of years old, win against the powerful sorcerer?

## THE WILD ONE

Sixteen year old Jai Cassidy thought she was finally free of her family until she is discovered by her other relatives…the ones that aren't human. Jai uses her natural perversity and cunning to escape their control, but catapults herself into the middle of a deadly feud between two alien races.

## ATAPI SORCERESS
### The sequel to The Wild One

Jai Cassidy is beginning her mission of reversing the decline of the non-humanoid Atapi. As a sorceress and an Atapi-Human hybrid, she is vehemently disliked by the male Atapi sorcerers and the humanoid rulers of Korvu. Her task is complicated by the treachery of a group of alien engineers, who are inciting insurrection and harsh reprisals.

## THE TYMOREAN TRUST BOOK 1 - POWER RISING

The Tymorean Trust - When peace rules Tymorea - Peace reigns in the universe.

Chosen to be the Advocates of the mystical and incorporeal Guardians of Peace, twins Tymos and Kryslie must first learn to control and use the power rising in them - or it will destroy them.

On Tymorea, only the ruling Triumvirate Governors are powerful enough to guide the strong-willed alien-bred twins until they have mastered their power.

THE TYMOREAN TRUST BOOK 2 - GREAT ONES
The peace of the Guardian Planet, Tymorea, is in deadly peril. War there will create ripples of unrest and destruction throughout the settled universe.
Tymos and Kryslie, still adolescents, have barely mastered their power and Llaimos is still less than a year old, but they are the three chosen to be Advocates of the mystical Guardians of Peace, to safeguard the Tymorean Trust.

THE TYMOREAN TRUST BOOK 3 - RETURN TO EARTH
Even before the war on Tymorea, the Elders foresaw that Great Ones Tymos and Kryslie would have an imperative mission on Earth.
But as the Tymoreans prepare to build an Earthbase to support them, they discover that specifications for two vital protective shields are missing.
Now, nearly a century later, Tymos and Kryslie must find his work and build the generator before the base is found.

THE TYMOREAN TRUST BOOK 4 - EARTH MISSION
Just before their graduation from the prestigious WSRA Washington University, Tymos and Kryslie Ward deliberately disappear.
The Great Ones have foreseen the capture and death of the new Tymorean missionaries and discovered that the leader of the Eastern Imperium plans to undermine the United World Nations.
Tymos and Kryslie must protect their kin and prevent a potentially devastating world war.

THE TYMOREAN TRUST BOOK 5 – ALIEN CONTACT
Tymos and Kryslie Ward, hide their Tymorean intelligence and abilities while working as low ranked technicians at the WSRA's lunar base. When an alien ship arrives at Lunar One, pursued by a powerful enemy who will stop at nothing to get what he wants, only the two Tymorean Great Ones have the knowledge and abilities to overcome him, but to do so they must risk their sanity, and their souls.

THE TYMOREAN TRUST BOOK 6 – INVASION
Great Ones Tymos and Kryslie go to rescue the crew of Earth's first deep space mission – and discover that Ciriot space pirates have discovered Earth's location. When the Ciriot invade in force, the Great Ones reveal themselves so that Earth can gain vital help. However, Kryslie becomes the victim of Ciriot, who want to control her mind and make her betray the people of Earth.

## TRICKS

Tom and Jo Dwyer had a reputation for playing tricks – and getting detention. They didn't seem to care about that, so long as they made their class laugh. That was until someone began to turn their tricks against them, and it was no longer funny.